Changeling Press. LLC

ChangelingPress.com

The Wild Hunt
Paranormal Women's Fiction
Stephanie Burke

The Wild Hunt
Paranormal Women's Fiction
Stephanie Burke

ISBN: 9781605218786

Publisher:
Changeling Press LLC
315 N. Centre St.
Martinsburg, WV 25404
ChangelingPress.com

Printed in the U.S.A.

Editor: Treva Harte
Cover Artist: Bryan Keller

The individual stories in this anthology have been previously released in E-Book format.

Table of Contents

The Stag (Wild Hunt 1)
Paranormal Women's Fiction
Stephanie Burke

Thomas Bright never would have dropped his glamour if he'd known he'd be going into heat. The one night he decides to cut loose at the decadent BDSM club *The Wild Hunt* just happens to be the one night he meets his mate.

Now The Stag, Kern, is on the prowl -- but he wants more than a one night stand with his perfect Faunus. If he can only convince his little mate to take a chance on him, and still protect his not-so-innocent lover from those who would do him ill for the magic contained in his body...

Chapter One

"Oh my stars, that is big dick energy!" Marshal Gray squealed, jumping in place while he tugged on Thomas's scarf. "Just look at them all!"

"Yeah?" Thomas Bright blinked at the spectacle around them, half of his mind wondering just what he'd gotten himself into by accepting Marshal's invite to be his plus one at *The Wild Hunt*. But the other half, the louder half, was screaming in curiosity and excitement.

He was surrounded by people dressed in all manner of beautiful and exotic costumes, some of them nothing more than glitter and body paint. This was so far removed from his sheltered life and his work in his ivory tower at Johns Hopkins University that he really didn't know how to react.

He was not going to stare in open-mouthed awe at the serious depravity cheerfully going on around him at the famous BDSM club. He was not going to become some slack-jawed yokel because there were some people legit having major foreplay right in the middle of the dance floor... but of course, he was. And he was not going to turn around and slap the shit out of the guy who kept tugging at his tail. It was real, damn it, not some kind of an exotic new butt plug.

Not that anyone would notice here, which was the reason he allowed himself to take a vacation from being so human in his everyday life and instead let his true colors shine through just a little. It wasn't often that he could let go of the glamor he'd cultivated in childhood and just be himself, no matter how mythological and insane that could be. So he was happily sporting a tiny pair of brown leather chaps that sleekly outlined his muscular legs. He was wearing a pair of tiny black leather briefs that he had altered to let his short fluffy tail have freedom of movement while looking like a part of his costume briefs... though in retrospect it did kind of look like a fluffy butt plug. His chest was bare and not that bad looking for an academic who spent most of his time teaching classes, digging through dusty old tomes, and translating them from archaic Latin into modern Latin just to drive his classes crazy when they were assigned to translate them into English. Around his neck, wrapped twice, was a long, soft woolen scarf his mother had knitted for him to keep him warm once he left the near-tropical island climes of Greece. He let his tiny curled horns show, and they peeked teasingly out of the mass of short, wild golden-brown curls that covered his head. His hair always made him look a little younger than he actually was but like tonight, when he let his glamour drop, they sparkled with bright gold highlights that made him look rather magical.

Though now he was kind of regretting not reining it in a little as another set of hands tugged at his fluffy white little faun's tail.

"Stop it," he hissed, turning to slap away still another hand and glare at the woman who was grinning down at him. "It's not a toy."

"No, it's not." She bent down to breathe in his ear, damn his shortness. "That is some major hardware you're packing, little boy. I wonder what the other end looks like? How much do you have stuffed up that pretty hole of yours? I bet you keep yourself all hot and slick for your master at all times..."

Before he could even fathom what to say to that, Marshal was tugging him away from the crazed woman and guiding him closer toward the stage.

Marshal was dressed as a winged red devil and was putting his horns to good use by lowering his head and pricking people to get them out of their way as they moved to the front of the glittering throng just as the music abruptly cut off.

"Good evening, denizens of *The Wild Hunt*," a deep, smooth feminine voice announced as the club stilled. "If I may direct your attention to the front of the stage, I would like to introduce your hosts for the evening. May I present to you, The Stag..." A spotlight flashed on the high, elevated platform shrouded by sheer black lace that cast intriguing shadows against the blood-red walls behind the people gathered there. The spotlight danced over what appeared to be three figures clustered around a large fainting couch before it settled on a large, muscular figure with the most amazing set of antlers attached to his head. As the stage lights brightened a little, the figure... The Stag... crossed arms over the most exquisite chest that Thomas had ever seen. He could admit it. He drooled a little just looking at what he could see of the man and knew from the spike in arousal from the scents of the bodies around him that he wasn't the only one.

"The Wolf," the voice continued, but Thomas could only tear his eyes away from The Stag long enough to take in the shadowed features of a woman with a set of very realistic wolf ears perched on her head, with a gorgeous animatronic tail that waved as she crawled over the fainting couch to lounge at the side of another figure who was beautifully reclined upon the massive thing but still cast in shadows. After noting that there was indeed a wolf being introduced, his eyes went back to the masculine form, still mostly in shadows, with the magnificent rack of horns that he suddenly recognized.

Thomas peered down at his ticket and the black logo embossed on the gold card. There, above the bold black lettering was indeed the set of horns in profile, the very set of horns he was staring at when the announcer spoke again.

"The Bear."

And yes, that man highlighted by the spots was indeed a huge bear of a man. Taller and broader than The Stag, The Bear, was near the bottom of the couch with crossed arms as well, and his muscles just popped.

"Mercy," Marshal whimpered, tugging at Thomas's scarf again. "The things he could do to me."

"Like break you in half," Thomas whispered, his eyes going back to The Stag. It was like he couldn't tear his gaze away.

"And the beautiful, the charismatic, the dangerous owner of this fine establishment, ladies, gentlemen, those undecided, in between, or neutral, may I present to you... Master of The Hunt!"

The spotlights disappeared as the stage lights went up fully and everyone got their first real look at their hosts for the evening.

The Master of the Hunt was shrouded in black silk robes that hid his or her frame. Seriously, this was a case of true androgyny and Thomas would bet what little magic he possessed that it was exactly how the Master wanted it. Their face was covered in a lacy black veil that hid their face entirely. Their hair was a dark, wavy fall that was not contained and allowed to fluff up wild and free, almost as if it had a mind of its own.

The Wolf was now lying at The Master's hip, her lightly tanned skin a startling contrast to the solid black of the fainting couch and the silk that surrounded The Master. Her light gray wolf's ears twitched as the painted black fingers of The Master gently stroked over them, and her matching tail thumped once in happiness. Her hair was a blending of perfect blondes that flowed over her shoulder and around a toned body wrapped in bangles and chains of sparkling silver. She glanced over the crowd with disdain and stretched her long, tight frame before settling at The Master's side, contentment pouring off of her in waves that Thomas could almost feel.

The Bear was a massive presence at the foot of the lounger, his long, startlingly red hair nearly the color of freshly spilled blood trailing over his massive chest. He was impressively large, with a black leather harness that cut across a bare chest dotted with a liberal dusting of red hair and matching freckles. The smile that spread across his face was deadly, exposing some serious fang-type dentures and painted black gums that were sexy and scary at the same time. He had a rounded set of fuzzy black ears on the sides of his head, their attachments lost in the thick wavy hair he sported. He shifted, and his muscles on his arms just seemed to explode with his motion, the tattoos that covered his lower arms only adding to the look of overall strength that he exuded like fine cologne.

Thomas tore his eyes away from that beautiful man to stare at his best friend as Marshal again whined as if someone was hurting him before he tugged at his scarf once more.

As Thomas's eyes shifted back to the stage and to The Stag, he suddenly understood the affliction of arousal that was affecting his best friend, because he found himself tugging on his own scarf and whimpering as his eyes beheld The Stag fully.

The man was walking sex, and it should be

illegal for him to parade about the general public with all of his… his Stagness showing.

He was tall, though not as tall as The Bear. A little over six feet, maybe. He was muscular but didn't have the sheer dimensions and mass of the red-haired friend who stood beside him. His skin was a deep dark brown, the color of freshly turned earth or rich chocolate diamonds that showed no flaws under the bright lights. His hair was a mass of ropy locks that flowed neatly down his back and over his magnificent bare chest. He was wearing a pair of low-slung leather pants that exposed every ripple of the eight-pack he called a stomach, and his eyes… from this distance they appeared to be solid black.

Thomas would have to remember to congratulate whoever did their makeup because all four were amazingly sexy and mysterious with quite a bit of danger sprinkled on top for that overall exotic and erotic look. He would have to remember to write a letter or give them a call later because his eyes were busy eating up The Stag like his last name was Dahmer and it had been some time since his last meal.

"Oh my stars," Marshal whispered, tugging at Thomas's arm this time as he tried to get his attention. "The Stag is looking at you."

Thomas couldn't answer because he was too busy eye-fucking that perfect specimen of a man. Of course he noticed that The Stag was looking at him, almost as intently as he had been staring the man down. He would've had to be dead not to notice those perfect eyes and that perfect face and that perfect body turning in his direction. Oh sweet Fauna, he was smiling and exposing a set of double-fanged teeth that made Thomas want to tilt his head to the side and beg for a dominating bite.

He felt his tail flick in excitement as he watched those dark eyes focus in on him and only him. He preened a little, as was his nature, moving from one booted foot to the other, dancing in place as his excitement grew.

The Stag's eyes widened a little then he grinned wider, leaning forward and licking his beautiful, full lips.

Thomas felt his body shiver as those eyes danced over him, and he didn't even notice when the music started again and the host of humanity that surrounded him began to heave and move to the deep bass rhythm that came pouring from the speakers.

His instincts were suddenly on high alert and his cock was growing and tenting out the front of his briefs. He felt his pupils dilate as he sniffed in the direction of The Stag, but there was so much arousal surrounding him that he could only catch a faint whiff of that mesmerizing man on the stage. What he could smell turned his knees to water, and if it wasn't for Marshal holding onto his arm, he would have tipped right over and fallen on his face before the most beautiful man he had ever beheld.

Then something he never felt seemed to take possession of his body. He found himself reaching down and removing Marshal's hands from his arm. And while The Stag looked on, he licked his own lips in return, a smile pulling open his lips to expose his own dainty set of fangs. When The Stag's eyes seemed to flash in appreciation and desire, it was like suddenly there was a tangible cord holding their gazes trapped together. Then he felt the front of his briefs dampen with his growing heat and his asshole grow wet with the slick he was suddenly producing, then he leaned forward and mouthed two words that had The Stag leaping from the stage and heading in his direction.

With a wicked laugh, his tail flashing wildly, Thomas gave in to the urgings of his instincts and pulled away from his friend. He threw himself into the crowd, getting lost in their vibrant movements, covering his scent with their arousal, teasing and turning, becoming the most delicious prey for the mighty Stag to hunt.

The words he'd mouthed, "Fuck Me," were still on his lips as he threw himself into the mass of hungry humanity that surrounded him, because, like any good prey, he would lead his hunter on a mighty chase before he allowed himself to be caught.

Chapter Two

Kern was too far gone in lust to even realize he had migrated to the edge of the stage. His eyes were on the tiny slip of a… man? No, there was something decidedly magical about the shining little star that drew him in.

"I'm going --"

"Hunting." The Master chuckled, waving him off as The Bear took up his position near the high arm of the fainting couch, keeping a cautious eye on the revelers who were partying like the world was about to come to an end.

There was always danger about, but here like this, near the core of *The Wild Hunt*, almost nothing could touch his charge. So with a smile at his fellow Huntsmen, he darted to the edge of the stage and slipped into the shadows like the master hunter he was.

It didn't take long for him to catch the scent of his prey nor to see the telltale shining brown curls that topped the little tease's head. There was a cute set of horns attached to the top and for a moment he wondered if this creature was just a human with some really good theatrical costuming connections.

His own set of massive stag's horns, all fifty points of them, had been mistaken for costume props by the humans they had on staff. He laughed and joked with them as they asked how the massive things were attached to his head and he had waved away their question, telling them that a magician never revealed their secrets.

If he had told all of his secrets they would have probably passed out at the sight of his glowing red eyes, his triple set of fangs, and the wide velvety tail he kept hidden from view. Though all of his attributes could be explained away by a good theatrical make-up artist, he knew that if someone looked close enough they would be able to tell that no adhesive held the horns in place and no strings were able to make his tail flick in agitation in such a realistic manner.

The point was to stay hidden in plain sight so they could continue with their good works, but there was something about the small man that made his magic rise.

So now Kern was on the prowl, tracking his prey by the enticing scent and the fleeting glimpses of his little, red-scarfed tease with the curly hair as the small body darted in between dancers and trailed through the several rooms that they held open for public viewing during this masquerade.

He almost had him in the hall of chains, a room painted mostly gray, where several small, circular stages were surrounded by hot and horny people eager for a show. A few submissives stood or knelt chained at the behest of their dominants, some being paddled, some being spanked with various impact instruments and bare hands, others gagged and crying so sweetly that it made Kern pause for a moment to stare. The overwhelming smell of arousal filled the air and a look at the DM showed the dungeon master's unconcerned face and meant that everyone was playing safe. So he moved on.

He picked up the alluring scent again and his little minx darted into a room where three masters were giving classes on shibari. The two women and one man were not explaining what they were doing -- that was for a different time and a class that you had to sign up for -- but they were putting on a great show, wrapping what seemed to be miles of cording around their willing, living sculptures. One woman was already suspended in midair, her arms snugly wrapped behind her, one leg bound to her chest while the other hung in a perfectly straight line, her position accenting her strength and the artistry of the man binding her.

Kern quickly passed through that room and down the hallway, following the aroma that was growing more delicious each time he found it. He grinned when he realized that the most perfect face, with its cute little cleft chin, had the most amazing set of golden-brown eyes... and they were peering at him through a crowd of people.

The hunt was engaged.

He took off after the smaller figure, getting a tinge of something magical in their scent now that he was closer. It intrigued him. In all of his years in the human world, no one had moved him like this. It was this strange instant connection that developed without even saying a word. His cock was hard in his pants, his breathing elevated; he was even beginning to sweat a little as he moved through the press of hot, sweaty bodies and wild movements that were more in place in an orgy than in this mainly human club.

He ignored the comments about his costume that were being bandied about; he didn't feel the touches as people groped his ass, patted his back, and tried to cop a feel of his bloated cock, restrained behind leather. Nothing existed but those golden-brown eyes and those tiny curling horns.

He caught another glimpse from the fleeing tease, the flicker of a white, flagging tail, and bared his teeth, a low growl rolling up from his throat. His little treasure was now moving down a less crowded hall, away from the hands that groped at him, daring a look over his shoulder. Kern almost swallowed his tongue when the little beast licked his lips before darting into a room that would spell his doom.

This was the private domain of the Huntsmen, and no one was allowed back without permission. Seeing the great stag hounding him so closely, the security guards stepped back and even were good enough to close the door behind him, trapping the two of them into this dark, quiet place.

"I caught you, little treasure," he called out as he entered the room, peering into shadows to see where his little one had hidden. "What do you offer me to release you?"

"What do you offer me to keep me?" came the quick reply, and Kern felt his heartbeat triple as the soft words flowed like a soothing balm through his ears.

"Well, first off, you're in my house, little one. I only accept the most impressive of tributes, like that cute little ass of yours."

There was a purr of amusement that further relaxed some of the growing tension within him.

"And secondly, I caught you, little star. I'm the one to set up the terms of your release."

"Release." He giggled. "I think I like that."

"Honey," Kern heard a growl in his voice that he made no effort to hide. "You made me an offer when I was up on that stage. I need to know right now if you meant it. Because if you didn't and this is just fun and games to you, I'm going to open that door and you will never see my face again."

"And if I meant it?"

"Then I'm going to need your consent, your eager consent, little star."

"Little star?"

"You shine brightly, little one. So how about you step out of the shadows and show me how brightly?"

He saw from the dim light of the recessed lighting a flash of pale skin and then using preternatural speed, the pretty one was there before him in the blinking of an eye.

His little one gasped and took a step back. Kern reached into the shadows where he had hidden himself and pulled him out into the light.

"Fuck," Kern breathed, inhaling the rich scent of a creature he had not had the pleasure of beholding in more than a few hundred years. "Faunus."

Kern found himself pressing his little treasure against the nearest wall, protecting him against its flat surface, lifting his hand to protect that precious face.

"Y -- yes," he stammered as Kern pressed the front of his body against his strong back and that perfect rounded body, feeling his tail flagging against his clothed erection.

"Do you want this?" He bent down to nip at one pointed ear, reveling in the sound of the choked-off bleat his little star almost managed to hold back.

"What are you?" his little horned one breathed, sounding nervous even as he pushed his ass back, grinding against his cock.

"Does it matter, little one?" Kern replied, licking away the pain of his sharp nip before lowering his head further to nibble at the back of his neck.

"No," his horned one... no, his little star... moaned, his small one's hands scratching at the wall as if for purchase. He could feel him tremble in his arms.

"Do you want this?" Kern asked again, angling his head so that his massive rack of horns would not slam into the wall. Honestly, he should just glamour them away, but something about this little Faunus had his magic feeling wild and untamable. He could fight the powers that existed within him or he could exercise control and restraint with his little star.

"Yes," the Faunus whimpered, turning his head to the side, an unnatural twist by human standards, but there were no humans in the room.

"You know I'm going to fuck you, little one?"

"I'd be pissed if you didn't," he growled, his one visible eye daring The Stag not to measure up to the excitement of the chase.

"Call me Kern." He chuckled, low, dark, and nasty before his hands went to the flagging little tail and gave it a tug.

His Faunus whimpered, his legs going weak for a moment before he gathered his wits and strengthened his stance. "Call me a slut and I'll go down on you," was the quiet response that almost knocked Kern off of his feet.

"Oh, you pretty little slut. That did it for you? You want to be called nasty little names? That gets you all hot and bothered?"

"You have no idea." The Faunus struggled to turn around, and Kern let him.

He was beautiful. There was no other word to describe this delicate-looking creature who stood up defiantly before him. His eyes were sparkling like jewels, his chest was rising rapidly with his deep breaths and sniffs, his body… oh yeah, he was a well-built little thing. And he wanted The Stag. His scent made that clear.

"You… are not human?" It was like he already knew the answer to that question but just wanted confirmation. "You smell like fire and earth and air." He sniffed again, his cute little nose working overtime.

"I am not, you little slut." The words were torn

from his throat and he watched, pleased, as his Faunus' pupils dilated in hunger. The rich smell of him, almost a heat smell, made Kern lean in closer, grip the scarf that was falling from around the other one's neck, and pull him closer.

With a whimper, his little star dropped to his knees, his hands going to the buttons that held the straining leather of Kern's pants closed. He was a mess, hands getting in the way of his nose as he buried his face in Kern's groin, snuffing hard.

"Spice. You smell so spicy."

"I bet I taste better than I smell." Kern chuckled as his star stared up at him in open-mouthed wonder before he got those buttons undone and The Stag 's heavy cock fell out of his pants and directly onto his star's face.

Instead of backing up or looking offended, his little one looked rather gleeful and he wrapped both hands around the shaft and began to pet his cock gently.

"There is so much of you…"

"You know, you can't talk if your mouth is filled, you little slut. How about you fill it?"

Then Kern found himself locking his own knees as his Faunus lightly, almost tentatively, licked at the head of his cock before the greedy little thing was swallowing him whole, right down to the root.

"Fuck!" he gritted out, his hands digging through the soft curls on his head as his Faunus began to bob his head, squirming as if he were experiencing the pleasure of the act himself.

Then when those little hands gripped his ass, Kern found himself helpless to do anything but fuck into that perfect little throat as his little Faunus silently urged.

"So good, so fucking good, little star," he moaned, combing his fingers through his star's hair until they reached out and danced around the base of his little one's horn. That drew a long, protracted whine from his little one's throat that vibrated around Kern's cock in the most delicious of ways.

Kern tugged a little on his horns and gritted his teeth as the Faunus began to suck even harder, one hand leaving off kneading the cheeks of his ass to tug his pants down further to cup his balls.

Shit, Kern thought, as he felt fire shoot up his spine and his muscles grew taut. This little fucker was going to suck his brain clear out of his body through his cock. The wet, slurping sounds of his sucking were loud and uncaring as his little one pulled on him and drew his scent in with wide, quivering nostrils.

"You are going to make me blow my load, little one," he cautioned and almost groaned. From where he was standing over the Faunus, he could see down his back to where that little white tail was flagging like crazy. He really was getting off on this. The scent of his magic was growing stronger, almost as if his little one was pulling energy from him, not that he would have minded. For a blow job like that, Kern discovered he would willingly give up a lot of things, including his sanity.

Finally, when he felt his balls began to churn, he gripped his little one's horns and pulled him upward. His little star let go of Kern's cock with a whine and a popping sound before he glared at Kern.

"I was not done."

"You are done for the moment if you want to get fucked."

That shut him up and an overjoyed look danced across the Faunus's face.

"Eager," Kern breathed as he reached down to unwind the scarf from his little star's neck. Then fast as a blink, he spun the little one around and had his hands trussed up with his own scarf before the Faunus could complain.

"What do I call you?" he demanded, spinning him around again and easily hefting the smaller male in his arms. "Mr. Tumnus? Are you popping in from Narnia? Is there a White Queen chasing you?"

"Do it and die." The Faunus glared up at him. Kern chuckled because it was cute and it drew away some of the urgency he was feeling to just bend his little one over and shoot a load all over his back. "I am Bright."

"Okay, Bright," Kern began as he carried his prey across the room toward a black leather padded table.

This room was set up for the occasional times one of the Huntsmen brought someone back for a little play while they were working. Granted, this room was probably going to be in use after he was done with this little hookup, but for now, it was clean and private and had some of the best toys all prepped and waiting to be used... like the leather-topped spanking desk that was specially made for role play.

"I'm going to bend you over this desk, eat your little ass until it's dripping, and then fuck you through it. You okay with that?"

"More than," was the immediate reply and he found himself having to hold onto Bright a little tighter as his little star squirmed in delight at the idea. "You are so big... I bet you'll split me open."

"See?" Kern breathed, struggling to maintain his composure. His cock was growing painfully hard and his body was taken with fine tremors. His instincts were screaming at him to bend the little smart-mouth over and just slam into him, but he knew that his little Bright had to be prepared first. He didn't want to hurt him, and from the way his heart and magic was responding, he might want to do this again and again with the little Faunus... over a protracted period of time... maybe even years.

But for now, he placed Bright down on his little star's shaky feet and began to tear at his clothes. It took almost nothing to shred the tiny little briefs he was wearing and expose that beautiful, plump little ass. Those rounded cheeks quivered as his fluffy little goat's tail flagged upwards, exposing the soft white fur underneath it.

"So pretty," Kern praised, not knowing if he was talking about the tail or the ass. Either way, he was going to play with them both.

Kern dropped to his knees, mindful of his sharp horns, and tugged the little tail. Bright whimpered, dancing from foot to foot as he attempted to spread his legs. The leather chaps he was wearing outlined everything Kern wanted to consume so why bother waiting?

With Thomas' tail held up high and proud, presenting, Kern gripped his cheeks and spread his little Bright open. His tiny little pink hole was almost shy looking and so small. With a groan he leaned forward and gave him a good sniff, bringing in the scents of magic and soap and the underlying scent of his flesh. Still, he tossed some quick cleaning magic at him before he ran his tongue up and over that tiny little hole.

"Fuck!" Bright let out a loud bleat as his whole body shook. Kern leaned further in, lapping around his hole, teasing the tight muscles as his little star begged for more.

Not one to deny a lover, Kern sucked and nibbled at the tight ring before slipping his tongue inside.

Fuck, his Bright was tight and wet, his inner muscles feeling like silk as they clenched around Kern's tongue. He fucked him a little harder, a little faster until Bright was begging and pleading, his arms straining against the scarf that held them in place over the small of his back.

He was delicious, his little Faunus, and Kern felt the urge to celebrate as he tasted the slick his little one was starting to let down.

"So good, baby," he purred, and Bright began to stomp, begging for more.

"Please, Kern," he pleaded. "I feel so empty."

With a snarl, Kern rose to his feet, spun his little star around, and easily hefted him onto the table. One tug of the scarf set his hands free and the little one immediately started pawing at him, tugging Kern over his body as he lay back on the padded desk.

When Kern resisted, he whined before laying back and spreading his legs wide, pulling his feet up on the table so that his wet hole and his pretty cock were exposed to The Stag's hungry view.

Fuck, he was beautiful. His cock was straight and dark pink with an angry looking head that leaked clear fluid over the tight muscles of his stomach. His balls were small and tight, tucked neatly up against the base of his cock. His puckered hole was shadowed but exposed by the spread of his thighs. His Faunus looked up at him and a pitiful wail rolled from his throat.

Kern's eyes traveled up to his face where he saw a desperate hunger in his beautiful eyes, in the lips still swollen and red from sucking Kern's cock, and the deep flush of his cheeks that trailed down his neck and halfway down his stomach.

His Faunus was beautiful.

Growling, he cleared the two steps that separated them and gripped his thighs hard, spreading them even wider and making a place for himself between them.

"Please, Kern." Bright was shuddering in need, tears filling those big, luminous eyes. "I need it. I need you."

That's all it took. Kern stroked his cock twice, whispering words that magically coated him with lube, before pressing the head against his little lover's asshole.

Bright, for his part, was tugging at his back, his nails tearing the skin as he pulled him close enough to wrap strong legs around his waist.

Conscious of his horns, Kern placed his hands on either side of Bright and leaned over him, scenting at his neck again, licking at the salty sweat that began to bead up on his skin.

"Now, now, now," Bright was chanting as his spicy smell grew as sweet as honey while Kern positioned himself.

He eased inside his lover's tight silken heat in one long slow stroke. Bright let out a wail as he was filled, and trembled in Kern's hold. Fuck, Bright was perfect with his anal muscles trembling around Kern's cock as his hole seemed to suck him in.

More and more, he mused, amazed that his little star could take all of him, and he didn't stop pushing until he was seated fully inside his lover. Bright's legs trembled as they held Kern close, his hands going right to his horns.

Kern reared up, pulled out about halfway before

slamming back inside his lover's hot, welcoming body. "Yes," he breathed out, burying his face in Bright's neck as shudders flowed over his body.

Being inside his Faunus was like sliding home. It was like Bright's body was made just for him. He slid out further before working his way back in, closing his eyes as he ground and circled his hips, seeking the spot that would make his lover --

"Kern!" Bright screamed as Kern hit that spot that made his lover clench tightly around his cock.

"Right there," Kern promised, dragging himself out only to slam back in deep, working the head of his cock against Bright's prostate with each slide of his hips.

Soon he built up a rhythm that had Bright crying and had his own toes curling in his boots. He felt his magic rise up within him, felt his own tail pop into existence as he loomed over Bright, fucking him good and hard.

The faster he moved, the more perfect his Faunus felt underneath him. He opened his eyes and looked down to see his lover's curls bouncing each time he bottomed out, saw that almost too pretty flushed face, saw that those eyes were open but lost in pleasure as he gave himself over to the lust that was running over him.

"Yes, yes, yes..." His little star was panting, whining as he tugged at Kern's larger body. "I'm gonna come," he suddenly shouted and Kern began to move faster, slamming into the smaller body as his Faunus reared up and sunk his teeth into his chest, directly over his heart.

"Bright!" Kern called out as he felt his lover convulse around his cock, felt his release break over him as Bright's teeth sank deep into his skin, tearing flesh and drawing blood.

But Kern could not complain as the flash of pain added to the ecstasy that was swamping his body. He roared out his pleasure as he stood straight up, holding his lover in his arms, and he began to slam his hips upwards, fucking into him hard until he felt his own climax rip through him.

It tore from his body, flooding Bright's passage as fire erupted into his mind. His body shook uncontrollably as he gave in to his need to rut like an animal, pounding relentlessly into the smaller body he held tightly in his arms until he was almost dizzy with the feeling running through him.

His magic reached out for his Faunus, his instincts screaming *mate* as he fucked him through the last of his orgasm.

Then spent, he spun around, collapsing back on the table, holding his Faunus tightly to his chest.

"Fuck, yes," he moaned as his mind started to function again.

Kern opened his eyes to see Bright, a sweaty, wrecked mess panting on his chest, licking his lips free of blood while his fingers teased at his horns.

Damn, his mate was looking perfect, debauched, and... *mate?*

Kern blinked as he stared down at the huge, seeping bite mark on his chest and really, he wanted to curse and rail at the fates that had allowed this to happen, but his instincts were clamoring for him to return the bite. He held back by force of will even as his magic reached out for the Faunus on his chest.

"That has never felt so good," Bright was whispering as he snuggled in closer. Automatically, Kern's arms went around Bright's body, holding him in place as he shifted around. "What are you? These horns are real. I know real horns when I feel them."

"Cernunnos," Kern found himself speaking through the shock that wanted to vie with the lassitude taking over his body. "I am called Cernunnos."

At hearing that, his little Faunus squeaked and lifted his head, staring at him in disbelief. "Um... Celtic... god?"

"You've heard of me?" Kern asked, pleased at least to hear that acknowledgment. "Not too many people know who I am."

"I teach Mythology at Johns Hopkins," he shyly informed him.

"You are not shocked that you just fucked a god?"

"I'm a Faunus," he returned almost primly. "Um... I know about magical beings, all sorts of magical beings... and which ones don't exist. I'm from Greece so..."

"So one gets used to seeing magical creatures parading around in the faces of men."

"I wouldn't call this parading," Bright teased, tugging at his horn and making Kern shudder in pleasure as his cock started to fill with blood once more inside that delicious little body. "Oh..."

"Yeah, oh," Kern groaned and his little mate moaned as his cock shifted within him.

"Well, I guess it would be rude of me not to tell you my name."

"I would appreciate that." Kern grinned. His little Faunus was unshakable it seemed.

"Thomas Bright and I don't usually do this."

"Giving mind-blowing head?"

"Fucking complete strangers but I think I may be... um..." he swiped a little more, wiggling down on Kern's cock.

"Are going into heat, my mate. I think our magics are pushing you into heat." Kern reached out and gripped his tail, giving it a tug that pulled a whimper from his little star's mouth.

"See how your body reacts to mine? Feel how your pretty little tail is lifting up and pushing to the side for me? I love seeing that tail flagging. See how your perfect little hole is wet and loose for me? It's winking for me, baby. Your body is making itself ready for me to claim it."

"No, only with a true candidate for my... did you say mate?"

"Yes, I did," Kern informed him.

"Um, there has to be a bond for that."

Kern pointed to the rapidly healing bite mark on his chest and smirked as his little star blushed.

"But I didn't... we can't --" But then he moaned as Kern shifted to make himself a bit more comfortable. "Oh, creators."

"We need to go someplace to talk about this incomplete bond."

"It's incomplete?"

"I need to return the bite, little star. Until then it's more of a half-bond."

"Fuck me again first?" he urged and Kern bit back a moan as his Faunus began to gently rock, riding him as best as he could while he was being held in place.

"You are going to be sore."

"Don't care."

"We have to talk about this --"

"Later."

"Thomas Bright!"

"I burn." Thomas looked up at him with huge, glittering eyes and Kern was lost.

Kern fucked him twice more on the padded desk before he got Bright's address out of him. With a quick and rough drawing of a trailing circle, the god of fertility, travelers, commerce, and animals transferred them from the back room of *The Wild Hunt* to Thomas's living room... where he fucked the Faunus twice more before the sun began to rise.

"I'll be back tonight," Kern promised a drowsy Thomas before he pulled himself away from his little star who lay sprawled out and sleepy in his bed. "We have to talk about this bonding, little one."

"Tonight," Thomas promised. "We'll talk tonight."

Satisfied that all was good, Kern activated the traveling circle once again and transported himself back home. He was exhausted but also elated.

Somewhere around his third orgasm, he realized that having a mate wasn't so bad. While using his Faunus's shower, he realized that his instincts and his magic agreed with him. It wasn't all about sex, he knew, but it was about potential.

After all these years, finally, there was a possibility that he had found his true mate.

He had never felt happier. After centuries, the forgotten god would no longer be alone.

Chapter Three

"Oh, someone is walking funny," Caille teased Kern as he stumbled into the living area above *The Wild Hunt*. The wolf goddess was grinning as she lounged across the couch in their communal living area. She was wearing his favorite hoodie and a pair of fleece sleep pants that were covered in rainbows and unicorns. Her bare feet kicked lazily as she lay on her front on the massive sectional that dominated the well-lit room, her head peeking over the arm as she tried and failed to hide her amusement.

Each of The Master's bodyguards had suites on this floor, complete with small, personalized kitchens, but they almost all universally agreed to take their meals together whenever they could. To that end they also spent a lot of time in their communal living area watching television, playing games, and just enjoying the fellowship of the only people in the country who knew what it was like to exist as nearly forgotten deities.

"Don't you have anything better to do than to clock my comings and goings, wolf? I know you haven't gotten laid in years but that's no reason to try and live vicariously through me."

"And I wouldn't have to live vicariously if you sat your ass down and told me what kept you away all weekend. Was the sex that good? Can the poor little bit of sweetmeat you followed home still walk? You were salivating after the poor boy, hunting him down like a bloodhound, and now you come in looking like" -- Caille motioned with one hand over his body as he stood in the doorway --"that."

"Like what?"

"Like twelve miles of bad road." The remark

came from the kitchen where a tall, muscular redhead stood in front of the open refrigerator, wearing a T-shirt that strained his frame and a pair of running shorts that had seen better days, a smirk upon his handsome freckled face. "Like you were ridden hard and put away wet. Like you broke your dick and --"

"Okay, enough of that, Arcas." Kern rolled his eyes at his friends... no, at his family... as he stepped into the room and collapsed on the couch next to Caille.

"At least he showered." Caille giggled. "So he may look like twelve miles of bad road but he doesn't smell like a whorehouse."

"A little respect, please, for my poor, battered body." Kern grinned at his brother and sister before running a tired hand over his face. "I'm not as young as I once was."

"You are a fucking fertility god," Caille pointed out as Arcas joined them on the couch, sitting near Caille's head, a bottle of water in hand. She flipped over onto her back and popped her feet on Kern's lap. "One little human shouldn't be enough to put you down like that. You eat humans for breakfast."

"First of all" -- Kern rolled his eyes at his sister as he absently began to rub her feet --"Just no. Human flesh is probably the nastiest thing in existence." Arcas nodded and Caille hummed in agreement. "And secondly, Thomas Bright isn't human."

"Get out." Caille sat up, pulling her feet from Kern's hands as she faced her brother. "You found a non-human on freak night? What are the odds?"

"About a million to one." Arcas sipped from his bottle before turning his curious blue gaze onto his brother. "And you found him here? What is he?"

"A Faunus."

"Really? For real?" Caille bounced excitedly on her knees. "You found an actual Faunus outside of Greece? You lucky bastard."

"He was pretty cute from what I saw..." Arcas's voice trailed off as he closed his eyes, lost in memory for a moment. "So that little flagging tail was real?"

"Very real." Kern grinned. "He looks like the Barberini Faun up close."

"All curly hair and sultry looks?" Caille hooted in delight. "Did he spread out for you over his bed, legs all parted to give you a good look at his everything?"

"If his dick is as small as the Barberini Faun's, then I hope he's a very eager bottom. That's not much to play with."

"First off, ancient Roman genitalia was always small because the assholes thought that real cocks and balls were ungainly and inelegant. True proportions were rarely shown unless it was all about the fertility. And secondly, my mate is a very eager and greedy bottom... but I'd let him get a leg over if that's what he wanted. I would do just about anything for him."

"Wait, mate?" Arcas sat up, abandoning his bottle of water to slide closer to Kern and Caille. "You found a mate?"

"And he's so cute and innocent." Kern sighed, thinking about the huge, golden-brown eyes of his mate.

"Not so innocent from the looks he was giving you." Caille snorted. "Or was that some other Faunus wrapped in black leather begging a certain horned fertility god to fuck him?"

"You know how mate magic can get." Kern waved her comment away as he relaxed back into the sofa. "But he is so cute and sweet and get this, he's a professor of Mythology at Johns Hopkins humanities department. Isn't that so precious?"

"Sounds like cheating to me," Arcas teased.

"No, more like using what you have to make life work for you," Caille corrected the redhead. "Kind of like how you gingers steal souls until you can become a real boy."

Arcas stared at Caille for a moment before he snorted. "Fuck you, wolf," he decided on saying after a moment. "I don't need their souls; I just have to bathe in their virgin blood."

"Then you'll never be a real boy with the rate of virgins around here," Caille teased back and Kern just sat and grinned, the thought of his mate joining in the teasing with his family doing more to relax him than any sex marathon on offer. Okay, maybe not doing more to relax him, but it was still a picture worth contemplating.

"So when do we get to meet this wunderkind?" Arcas asked. "I'm very curious about any person who can grab your attention and keep it, let alone be good enough to be your mate."

A small kernel of warmth in the center of his chest expanded as Kern easily read the desire to protect him emanating from the huge bear god. It was the love of his thrown-together family that had sustained him for years while he existed feeling like only half of a whole.

"Thomas, you said?" Caille added, a genuine smile spreading across her lips. "You know, the longer it takes for you to get him over here the longer the name Thomas the Faunus is going to stick, right?"

"Thomas would hate that." Kern chuckled. "I may have to steal that one."

"Feel free." Caille nodded. "I can come up with

more."

"And I intend to introduce him around as soon as possible. He is a working man, you know. He just can't up and abandon his duties to sate your curiosity." He nodded to his brother and sister before he stood. "And before that happens, you know I have to inform The Master."

"They will be thrilled." Caille giggled at the thought before tossing herself flat on her back on the couch, without a by-your-leave, dropping her feet in Arcas' lap. "You know The Master hates for us to feel deprived of anything, and they always think that in order to be a truly happy deity one must have all of their mental, physical, and emotional needs fulfilled."

"You know that means The Master will be pushing for you two to get off your asses and find your own mates after this, don't you? And then they will want grandchildren."

Both Caille and Arcas shot him evil looks as, laughing, Kern made his way out of the communal living area and down the hall that led toward their private suites.

He would have another shower and put on more appropriate clothing than his walk of shame leather pants and tight T-shirt before he went to talk to Manx.

This was one of the best days of his life, he decided, and he began to whistle as he moved into his rooms. After this, it would take a good old-fashioned sword and shield war, complete with death and dismemberment, to bring him down.

* * *

"I fucked a god, and I liked it..." Thomas sang softly to himself as he limped his way into his office. "He tasted just like chocolate thin mints --"

"There you are!" Marshal's worried voice made

Thomas jump as his best friend sprang up from behind his desk like a jack-in-the-box. "Where were you? I was so worried. You ditch me in a BDSM club to go harrying after some dude with antlers and then you turn off your phone for the entire weekend. I was about to call the National Guard or the FBI to get them to track you down. Are you okay? You're walking funny…"

Marshal's voice trailed off as he examined his friend from the top of his curly hair to the bottom of his sensible leather brogues. "You didn't."

"Oh, yes I did." Thomas couldn't help the wicked smile that spread across his lips. It was times like this that he thought his little curling horns most apropos. "Again and again… all weekend long."

"You dog," Marshal breathed before moving around Thomas's desk to embrace his friend. "I can't believe it."

"Believe it, my friend." Thomas chuckled. "Though I can hardly believe it myself."

"You scored the second sexiest man in the room."

"Second?"

"Sorry, but you know I have a thing for redheads."

That made Thomas laugh outright at his friend before he gave him a hug in return before moving away.

"So do tell. And I mean all the nasty little dirty bits because your friend looked fit as fuck."

"Oh, he is," Thomas confirmed.

"And hung like a horse."

"That too." Thomas took a very tentative seat and ignored his friend's snickers at his movements. "And fucks like a bull."

"Lucky you." Marshal looked impressed. "He was just the perfect thing for you to climb out of your little shell and start living life. You know I worry about you trapped here in your private world."

"I am not trapped," Thomas protested as he reached into his messenger bag and pulled out his computer tablet. "And I didn't bother to turn off my phone. I just didn't answer it. I was too busy--"

"Too busy to even call your best friend and let him know that you weren't kidnapped by an Ed Gein wannabe?"

"You know I can protect myself, Marshal." Thomas examined his friend's face and saw some real fear there. It made a wave of guilt wash away some of his giddiness. "I am sorry I didn't answer or text you to let you know I was safe and I'll never do it again. Promise. But remember I am a fully grown Faunus and I can get out any time I want, and besides which, there is also something very... interesting about my dear stag."

"He's secretly a power bottom no matter how toppy he looks?"

"He's magical."

"Get the fuck out," Marshal breathed.

"Really, my dear little kitty cat. We are not the only two magical things haunting this city."

"So, what is he?" Marshal demanded. "Spill your guts, Bright. Your closest friend and brother from another mother needs to know."

"He's not from your pantheon, that's for sure."

"There aren't that many deer running around Northern Africa, Bright. We would get antelope or gazelle... that is assuming the horns are real."

"Very real and very sexy looming over you," Thomas admitted, a blush brightening up his cheeks.

"And his eyes… they turn red when he comes."

"And his cock?"

"Marshal Gray," Thomas exclaimed as the glared at his friend. "I refuse to talk about my mate like that."

"Mate?" Marshal's voice rose three octaves as did his eyebrows as he stared at his best friend. "No one said anything about mates. Thomas --"

"Look, it's a thing, okay? I don't know how it is with Bastet's descendants but for us Faunus, we all tend to have mates. It's not like we'll die if we don't find them or even if we find them and it doesn't work out, but it does tend to make us fertile."

"So now you can knock some girl up --"

"No, not quite." Thomas felt a flush of embarrassment that he hadn't felt the likes of since his parents sat him down and explained the birds and the bees… Faunus style.

"You don't mean --"

"Yes." Thomas dropped his head to his desk, all pretense of working pushed aside now that Marshal was getting all up in his business. "Yes, you are thinking correctly. I can now become… pregnant."

"Because you found your mate."

"Because I found my mate and I went into a mini heat and I just spent more than forty-eight hours sexing him up properly." Thomas sighed as he rolled his head to the side to stare at his friend. "I don't know what to do."

"What's the problem? You found your mate. You are compatible with the sex thing. You may have to wear a condom if you don't want to be an unwed mother and a blight on our academic community --"

"Marshal!"

"What? You are worrying over nothing, Bright."

"But he is literally a god."

"So were our ancestors."

"But he is one. He once went by Cernunnos, Marshal. You know who that is, right?"

"The fertility god who talks to animals, gives safe passage to travelers, was killer at business, and for some reason is the god of bi-directionality or something like that. He once was a big deal but other than that, not too much is known about him."

"So then you know my dilemma, Marshal. The man is a god, and a powerful one at that. And he wants me for a mate? I don't know."

"What? A minor god not enough for you?" When Thomas only glared, Marshal went on. "My mother just wanted me to marry a doctor... or marry me off to a doctor... she has healer on the brain. I think my staying history -- or non-staying history -- made her a little leery of my life choices, but I still stand by my decision to date that up-and-coming rock star. I'll never get to trash a hotel room again but I did learn to play more than two chords on the guitar."

"Marshal, can you be serious here?"

"I am being serious, Bright. Look, you have someone who has to be one of the most sexed up men around. Do you know why that's a good thing? He's seen it all, done it all, and is probably looking for a relationship. You never have to worry about something exotic grabbing his attention because he's been there, done that, and got the T-shirt."

"That's true." Thomas sat up straighter as he stared at his friend.

"Not to mention the fact that you don't have to hide what you are. You can be your cute little Faunus self and play your pan flutes or dance around naked or whatever you goat-horned little fuckers get up to when no one is listening."

Thomas glared hard at Marshal, but the man was making a few points.

"So why are you scared, Bright? You don't have to take him for a mate because biology says so. Nobody's going to die if it doesn't work out, and today there is no stigma attached to being a single father. Hell, if you are preggers, all you have to do is go on a learning sabbatical and come back with a curly haired kid that will have all the female and some of the male staff begging to be an auntie or a sitter. He's hot, you're cute, and together your kid would win the genetic lottery, give or take a few sets of horns and, after all, what's glamour between family? And besides, if this guy --"

"Kern."

"If Kern is who you say he is then even if you aren't together he'd be a decent father and provider. What have you got to lose?"

"My dignity? My autonomy? My privacy?"

"Your loneliness?"

Damn, Marshal had a point.

"Look, I'm not saying go off and marry the guy and run off to wherever the fuck he comes from, lay down some magical vows, and live life according to Celtic myth, but it doesn't cost you anything to try."

"I might develop feelings, Marshal. It would be so easy to do with him."

"Then you catch some feelings. A broken heart isn't fatal but you can be crushed under the weight of what-ifs if you give up before you try."

"I kind of... well, I bit him." Thomas felt another blush heat up his face as he stared at his friend. "Hard."

"Well, you started out in a BDSM club, Bright. Those things tend to happen if the sex is really good anyway."

"Yeah, but according to him, I kind of already started the mating process."

He blinked as Marshal just stared at him... and stared at him some more.

"What?"

"I didn't know, okay? I didn't even mean to. But he was fucking me --"

"With his enormous schlong --"

"With his enormous schlong, Marshal. Geez, yes. Kern has a big dick, a really big dick --"

"He's a fertility god. I knew that."

"And while I was being split open like his name was Vlad the Impaler, I kind of lost control and I bit him over his heart."

"And that is how you start the mating process?"

"That is how we started the mating process."

"So... you kind of put a ring on him and didn't bother to get one for yourself, is that what you are telling me?"

"It wasn't like that, Marshal!"

"So you marked him as yours but you are walking... limping... around free and clear?"

Thomas glared at Marshal for a moment before he sighed and dropped his forehead back down on his desk. "That's what I'm telling you."

"So what the hell is your problem, Bright? From where I'm sitting, he's got the shit end of this thing with you dithering about your fear on the other side."

"I just don't know what to do."

"You better know what to do soon, my friend." Marshal stood up and made for the door. "Because from where I'm sitting, you are the one holding all the power here and you're afraid?"

"I think there is something he's not telling me,

Marshal."

"There is probably a whole lot he's not telling you, with you heat-fucking him all weekend. I don't think that leaves much time for conversation."

"Marshal --"

"Unless you call screaming his name and begging for more conversation."

"Gray!"

"I'm just saying don't be unfair to the guy. I mean, you have an ancient god after your indecisive ass and you're being given the option to try for a relationship. Maybe you need to cast aside your fears and really think about what you are doing."

"You've given me a lot to think about," Thomas admitted as Marshal opened his office door to move down the hall to his own office.

"Hey, I come from healer stock, Thomas. It's something that my kind excel at. So think about it but don't take too much time to come to a decision. You're feeling confused and he doesn't have a magical claim on you. Can you imagine how he's feeling?"

Chapter Four

"I have a mate!" Kern danced into The Master's penthouse, singing loudly as he proclaimed his news. "I have a mate. I have a mate. I finally have a mate."

"And do you have manners as well?" Manx, The Master, asked as they sat at a low table, flipping through some papers they had piled before them. There was a cooling mug of tea at their side and as almost always happened when in their place of residence, Manx's face was uncovered.

"No." Kern snickered as he dropped down beside Manx on the couch they were occupying and watched as his friend and leader went through receipts and membership information from their masquerade night. "I existed in a time before they were needed."

"You are not much older than I," Manx offered, peering through long, sooty black eyelashes as they stared at Kern.

Their eyes were an undefinable swirl of faceted colors while their hair was a deep, undefinable shade of black. Their face was certainly beautiful but also rather foxlike with its pointed chin and wide-set eyes, and was decidedly neither male nor female. Manx, as always, was dressed in solid black from their relaxed looking long black tunic to their lightly textured cotton pants. Their bare feet were curled underneath their thighs as they sat on a very comfortable leather couch.

"But still young enough to celebrate the fact that I've found my mate."

"After all these years?" Manx focused their full attention on Kern as The Stag settled himself on the couch.

"After all these years," he confirmed, his smile wide and contagious as Manx grinned in pleasure.

They leaned forward and sniffed at him, only to pull back confused. "It doesn't scent completion."

"My little Faunus may have started the process, and did it unwittingly at that, but I am giving him time to come to a decision about completing the bond."

"Well, aren't you selfless, my Stag." Manx spoke with concern in their voice.

"Well, it's a long, sordid story that begins when my mate saw me and fell into heat and is stalled now where my mate accidentally bit me and started the process."

"And he didn't know what he was doing?"

"He hadn't a clue, which is cute and disturbing at the same time."

"A Faunus," Manx mused. "It's been a long time since I even heard of a Faunus living outside of Greece, let alone one away from their clan."

"My Faunus is a professor of mythology. He's independent and living away from his family and clan."

"Odd."

"And what's odder is that his people never explained mating to him. He didn't even know that he could become pregnant through sex with me because he is a true mate. Something that his people forgot to inform him of before he made his way into the human world."

"That is strange." Manx's gaze traveled over Kern, and The Stag had to offer a smile, pleased with his master's consideration and concern.

"I know, but I explained it all to him, and when he appeared confused, I told him I'd give him some time."

Kern looked around as the Master's hounds slunk into the room. Dark as night and made of nightmares and dark wishes, three of the huge shadow hounds moved silently into the room and perched at Kern's feet. As if sensing their master's mood, the three hounds stared at Kern, whining lightly as they stared from him to Manx.

"Even though an uneven bond leaves you at a disadvantage?"

"He's… skittish." Kern decided on the word.

"But not skittish enough to call you to hunt in the middle of a crowded masquerade?"

"Well, once the heat died back he was amazed that someone knew about him and didn't care. He was even more shocked to learn who I am, though I am surprised that he even knew anything about old Celtic beliefs. Because he teaches mythology or is a mythological creature himself, he wasn't too shocked to know that I was once heralded as a god. If anything, he seemed to be more in shock that I wanted him."

"Lacking confidence?"

"More like fearful."

"And he showed up to what amounted to a rather large orgy?"

"He had a friend."

"And is his friend magical as well?"

"I don't know," Kern admitted. "I don't know much about him but the basics. But I plan on changing that tonight. I am meeting up with my mate again. I promised him dinner."

"Then maybe you should tell him of the danger he is in with a half-bond, my Stag. You don't do him justice by keeping such things from him."

"I plan to rectify that tonight, Master, and then make time to bring him here for you to meet."

"Yes." Manx purred softly, reaching out a hand, and instantly one of the hounds came to nestle under his palm. "I should like to meet this Faunus, Kern, this skittish Faunus."

"I don't think he'll be so skittish when he learns the facts and what's at stake."

"For you both I hope that is true."

"Believe it. First of all, once he discovered the horns didn't pull off, he never panicked, not even once. And secondly when I told him I could taste the flavor of creature he was by his scent he was more intrigued than anything. He was fearless in his heat, a greedy, demanding bottom, and he seemed eager when I told him I would return this night. I think things will be okay."

"I do hope so."

"Now what has gotten your pretty little face all twisted up like it was when I first walked in?"

"Balancing these books," Manx grumbled, their nose wrinkling as they stared down at the numbers for a moment, before a calculating expression crossed their face. "But you are good at commerce, are you not, my Stag?"

"Relatively so." Kern snorted at Manx's words. "And before you pop some veins in your brain, just give it to me. I'll have this fixed in no time."

"Wonderful." Manx grinned as they leaned back into the couch, still petting their shadow hound. "That is what I pay you for."

"You pay me to guard your body when we are public and to gather together your little packages from time to time. That's it."

"But I wouldn't be a good master if I didn't utilize all of my familiar's skills. I wouldn't want you to feel like you are not contributing to our success. After all, a good work ethic is essential for rearing baby magical beings."

"You don't even know if he's knocked up or not."

"You are a fertility god. Of course, he's pregnant… or will be very soon."

"Manx!"

"Well, it's not like I didn't hear his screams of passion from where you were nailing him in my private chamber, of all places."

"Not like you ever use it." Kern snorted at Manx before flipping through the pages of figures. "It's about time it got some utilization."

"And thank you for reminding me of my celibate state."

"You could always call The Morrigan."

"And I could always use your antlers as coat hangers."

"It would be too much trouble to hunt down another bodyguard." Kern waved away the threat. "Besides, if you listen to how I do it you may want to try and do it again yourself before, you know, the sun goes super nova or the polar ice caps melt."

"You are such a smart-ass," Manx grumbled, shooting Kern an amused look. "I wonder why I put up with you."

"Because you love me, and I am such a smart-ass because I learned it from watching you."

"Ass." Manx laughed outright.

"You know you love me." Kern smiled, pleased to be lightening the mood for one of the people who loved him like family. "I'm adorable."

"And you may be a daddy."

"And I might just have the perfect mate."

"Remains to be seen." Manx's laughter eased off and they settled further back into the couch with a small sigh. "But I believe things will turn out wonderfully for you, Kern. You deserve it."

"I do, don't I?" Kern agreed, and for a moment he thought of golden-brown eyes, that fluffy white tail, and the small horns that graced the top of his mate's head. "I think this time, I will get what I truly deserve."

* * *

That night Thomas did his level best to hide his nerves and actually consider all that was being offered to him.

Of course, his day was made a bit more difficult by the well laid limp that he couldn't hide. It had his students once more guessing about Mr. Bright and how he suddenly gained a love life, was sporting some kind of injury, or had some kind of embarrassing procedure done that he just didn't want to talk about.

"Is it hemorrhoids?" one of his more sarcastic students inquired as Thomas gingerly took a seat behind his desk instead of talking while pacing in front of his podium. "You can get them from sitting on the cold hard library floor, Mr. B."

Thomas loved his students, he really did. Every year there was an influx of students signing up for his mythology course thinking that it would be an easy grade or, for some strange reason that he wasn't aware of, they thought he was hot. Mixed in were a bunch of students dedicated to anthropology and linguistics, as well as archeology -- and of all things -- geology, who were in it to learn. By the end of his first week of classes, most students who weren't there to learn found themselves dropping his classes when they saw the workload and the attention to detail he demanded from them to get a passing grade, let alone excel in his classes. His syllabus usually separated the wheat from the chaff, but it was generally his first lecture that sent the rest of the unwanted students packing. What was left was a core of intense individuals who thrived under his teaching and hungered to know more.

Which was why it was such a surprise for him to learn that his students were gossiping about his personal life.

"Hemorrhoids?" he asked, flushing a little as he thought of actually why he was having a hard time sitting.

"Yeah. We've seen you sitting on the cold floor of the library before, Professor B," his favorite student Theresa offered. "It's not healthy and you are not as young as you used to be."

Thomas rolled his eyes at that one and rose to his feet. "I do not have hemorrhoids, Theresa, but thank you for inquiring after my health."

"Then you got laid," Bruce, another one of his favorite students, added. "I know what that feels like."

Bruce was on the lacrosse team, a polyglot like himself, and was studying to be a diplomat with a major in political science with an emphasis on European conflicts. That was the last thing he expected to come from his very straight-laced student's mouth.

"Bruce --"

"So, who's loving you, Prof?" Theresa added. "Because as hot as you are, generally you don't have them knocking down your door. We never see you out and about on the town, and even when the admins throw those parties that we are all forced to attend, you never bring a date outside of Professor Gray."

"And as Professor Gray is your best friend and his conquests are leaving him flowers and begging for him to return their affections when he tosses them aside, it's safe to assume that you aren't boffing him." Bruce grinned like a well-fed sphinx as he leaned forward in his chair, as if expecting Thomas to answer.

"As we are currently discussing the political ramifications of Aeneas and his doomed love affair with Dido --"

"And how they got busy for a year before he realized that she just wanted him to gain control over the Trojans. And speaking of Trojans, did you use protection, Professor B?" Bruce asked, all grins and butter-wouldn't-melt-in-his-mouth smiles. "If you were getting up to the things that Dido and Aeneas were supposedly doing…"

"This is about the mythology of Rome, people," he snapped, though his censure wasn't as effective since he was sitting behind his desk. "Not my love life."

"So you do have a love life?" Theresa looked fascinated, as did the rest of the twenty-two students that made up his senior class.

"That's not what I said."

"It's what you implied." Bruce clapped his hands in glee. "Now is it a man or a woman?"

"Or a man and a woman," Theresa added and then he lost them as the whole class began to speculate.

It was a man and Professor Bright was a power bottom… way too close to the truth but since he was already blushing, no one really took notice of it.

It was a woman and she was into spanking. It was a woman who loved pegging him. It was a woman who directed a man to peg him. It was an orgy, Greek style, as he was from Greece. It was that hot new assistant football coach who kept eyeballing Professor B when he was in the cafeteria.

It was really too much.

Thomas stood up, ready to tear down some students on the subject of staff privacy and human decency when his alarm rang and his classes were done for the day.

"Read up on the Trojans and the Aeneads because after this conversation it is going to be on next week's final," he called out as his students exited en masse, still contemplating his sex life.

His evening was not made any better by Marshal's smirking looks as they left their department and headed to their cars… or the curious looks given to him by the other professors in his department.

It was almost a relief to make his way into his end row house that evening and kick his shoes from his feet. His messenger bag was tossed aside and his keys hung on their neat hook by the door before he noticed a delicious smell emanating from his kitchen.

All growing thoughts of a hot, soothing bath were tossed to the curbside as Kern exited his kitchen wearing the tightest jeans known to mankind and a T-shirt that strained the confines of propriety as well as the broad expanse of his chest. His stag was grinning at him, bare-footed and wearing an apron that declared *Hunters Do It With Their Meat* tied around his waist.

He was the sexiest thing that Thomas had seen in awhile.

"Almost ready to eat?" Kern asked, and without even thinking about it, Thomas began to pull his clothing from his body.

"Yeah, I am so ready to be fed --"

Kern yelped as his lover threw himself at him. He barely managed to catch his little star before the Faunus was tearing at his apron, pulling it up and out of the way.

"We were supposed to talk. Be talking…" Kern tried to engage his brain, he really did but it was a losing battle. "You could be pregnant --"

"Feed me your cock."

"The bond --"

"Wants you to feed me your cock."

Thomas's hands were winning the war of the clothing and it was all Kern could do to remember to turn off the stove before carrying his lover to his bedroom. Sex in the kitchen was so unsanitary and uncomfortable... especially when there was a nice bed a few feet away.

By the time he made it to the bedroom, his star had tossed his apron to the side, pulled his shirt over his head, and was working on the jeans he was wearing. Kern tossed him onto the bed and within seconds had his little mate as naked as the day he was born.

"So beautiful." Thomas was panting, his eyes traveling over Kern's body as he scooted back on the bed and made grabby hands at him.

"That's my line."

"I only speak the truth," Thomas insisted as he spread his legs and waited.

"Aren't you sore?" Kern felt compelled to ask as he peeled out of his jeans and climbed into bed beside his mate.

"Just a little."

"Wanna fuck me instead?"

Kern watched as his lover's eyes brightened as he contemplated the question. "You would let me --"

"I would feel blessed if you did."

"Thank you for offering." Something in Thomas's body language changed, the lust turned down a bit and was replaced with a look he was too scared to define. "But maybe later? Can we just go slow?"

"We can do slow," Kern promised, reaching for a bottle of lube he placed on the bedside table when he let himself in via magical circle to his lover's home.

Magical lube was all well and good, but there were a few things that humanity had gotten right. Long-lasting lube was one of those things. As he watched, Thomas flipped over onto his belly and climbed to his knees, wagging his pretty little ass at Kern.

"I like it like this," he informed him archly, looking back over his shoulder at Kern, heat building in his eyes.

"I can do this, little star." Kern felt his cock harden at the sight of his lover in a sweet submissive position. His hair was tousled and he smelled like frustration and harried youth, but underneath that was his mate, the perfect sweet and spicy aroma that made up the scent pile of the one he could see spending his life with.

The sight of his mate, thighs spread on the bed, his petite pink balls swinging as he swayed, his swollen hole still a bit red and puffy from their earlier activities... he was perfection.

"You look so strong and sure." Thomas was speaking again, his voice low and deep. "And I know that there are several things we have to discuss, but I'm a coward and I don't want to face them now. Right now, I only want to feel good, Kern. And you make me feel so good..."

Kern felt his heart explode. His baby was perfect and he needed him. He rapidly slicked up his cock and moved up behind Thomas.

"There are so many things I want to do to you," he spoke softly, running his hands down his star's back, feeling his soft, supple skin give under his hands.

Thomas let out a low moan at the feeling, arching into his touch as he turned and dropped his forehead into the pillows. "We have time," he promised and Kern nodded in agreement.

"We do. And when we next climb into this bed, I'm going to take you apart slowly. I'm going to undress you." Kern pressed several teasing kisses to his nape. "I'm going to spread you out and lick every inch of your body. I'm going suck on these little pink nipples until the air caressing them will make you cry. I'm going to tease this delicious cock of yours. It's so pretty, baby. All sweet and perfect, hot and hard in my hand..." He began to stroke his lover, watch the way his body writhed under his caresses as he pushed back into his touch.

"I'm going to get you hard, baby, and when you think you can't take more, I'm going to sit on this pretty little cock and fuck myself until you scream."

"Kern--"

"And then when you fill me up with your load, I'm going to climb off, spread your legs, and fuck you through this mattress."

"Fuck, Kern!"

"I'm going to spank this round little bubble butt until it's all red and warm for me and I'm going to slide my dick so deep inside of you, you'll taste me, my little star."

"Yes, please," Thomas whimpered, reaching back and spreading his cheeks apart, exposing his hole to his lover.

Kern bent down and ran his tongue over his opening, teasing him just a little, relishing the taste of his natural slick before he pulled back. "Now, baby?" he asked and Thomas began to babble an answer.

"*Shhh*," Kern soothed him. "I got you."

And then he was pressing his slicked up cock into his lover's body, closing his eyes and groaning with relief as Thomas opened up and eagerly accepted his penetration.

"So perfect, my mate," Kern praised, and Thomas melted around him.

The pace he set was sweet and gentle, just the thing his baby's sore hole could take. He didn't want to fuck him long or hard, he didn't want to give him true pain, but he needed Thomas to know how he felt.

"Never have I ever met someone like you before, my mate. You are so sweet and wicked at the same time. You don't stand for bullshit and you go after what you want, yet you seem so untouched and unbothered by this world. How can someone as perfect as you exist?"

He began to pump Thomas faster in his hand while he increased the speed of his thrust, the tight clench of his lover's body making him close his eyes in bliss. So wet and warm and giving...

"I love fucking you, having you this way. I love feeling your skin heat up beneath my hands, feeling your magic thrum under your skin... I've waited hundreds of years, Thomas, and never have I ever been blessed like this before. You... I think that you will complete me."

Kern reached down and pulled his lover up, sitting back on his heels and settled Thomas deep onto his cock, this new position sliding him further than he had ever been inside him. Thomas's hands went up and around his neck, holding on as they slowly rocked into each other.

"So perfect." His mate purred in response and Kern felt his whole body shudder in delight. This was what he wanted. This was what he could have for the rest of his life if only he could convince his lover to take a chance with him. "Mine."

"Yours," his little star agreed, though Kern knew within in his heart that forever had yet to be determined.

"Yes, mine."

He began to fuck him a little harder, just a little faster while he gripped his lover's cock in his hand and began to jack him off hard.

Thomas bucked in his grasp, crying out as his rhythm broke, and then Thomas was moaning like he was still in heat, before Kern posed him face down into the bed and tightened his grip on his lover's cock, letting him fuck into his hand as he wailed in pleasure.

It only took a few more strokes for his little star to break, his inner muscles clenching around Kern's cock while he sprayed his hot seed across Kern's hand. And after that, a few strokes later, Kern joined him in ecstasy, pressing himself as deep as he could go and letting his climax take him.

"Fucking perfect," he praised, stroking his lover until they both calmed.

* * *

"You know, we are never going to learn about each other if we keep doing this," Kern whispered, pressing soft kisses to Thomas's slack mouth.

"I know, but I can't help myself," Thomas groaned, turning into his lover's embrace to snuggle into the larger man's chest. "I finally started listening to my instincts and they just want more of you."

"Well, maybe I can understand that because all my instincts are screaming at me to bite you, to complete this bond, but it has to be your idea, Thomas."

"I know, I know," Thomas grumbled then felt a blush burn his cheeks as Kern lifted him as if he weighed nothing, and repositioned him.

There was dinner to be eaten and conversations they needed to have, but all of that went away as Thomas's aching body gave in to his craving for sleep with his almost-mate beside him.

"You need to eat."

"I need to sleep," he countered, cracking open one bleary eye while making grabby hands at Kern before the Stag relented and crawled into bed beside him.

"This is not healthy for you, my mate. You may be carrying my child and my instincts are screaming at me to provide for you."

"Does dick count?" Thomas teased. "Because you just served me up a healthy serving --"

"Be serious, Thomas. There are things you have to know about me and about the magical community that will surely notice you because of me."

"Can we be serious tomorrow?" Thomas could barely keep his eyes open. "I can barely function and I have early classes..." He yawned and snuggled into the heat that emanated from Kern's body, wanting nothing more than to crawl into the man and never let him leave.

"When does your day end?"

"One," Thomas spoke around another yawn. "Finals, and everyone is getting ready for them."

"Then I will pick you up at school for a late lunch. That sound okay?"

"Sounds fine," Thomas mumbled, already falling asleep.

Tomorrow was good. Tomorrow was great. They would discuss this thing between them tomorrow. For now, he would close his eyes and try to picture a future with this man doing this very thing for the eternity Kern would demand that they stay together.

So far, he was not seeing a downside at all. In fact, if this was his future, it was looking mighty fine indeed.

Chapter Five

Well, he was limping worse than before but it was so totally worth it. The smug look on Marshal's face was even more gratifying until his best friend started asking some very uncomfortable questions on the way into his office.

"So did you talk to him?"

"Well," he hedged.

"What?" Marshal demanded as they stopped at Thomas's door. "You think you can just fuck away all of your problems?"

"We didn't get a chance to really talk --"

"'Cause you were too busy trying to get his dick in your ass?"

"Marshal!"

"I'm on to you, Bright," Marshal hissed as Thomas opened his door and stepped inside, his best friend on his heels. "You have got to stop this, whatever this is you are doing, and just talk to the man."

"Whatever I'm doing?" Thomas asked as he very carefully sat behind his desk and pulled out his tablet to get ready for his stupid seven a.m. class. Why would he even schedule a class this early?

"You are running again."

"I can barely walk, Marshal --"

"This is just another way for you to run from the issues you are too scared to face." Marshal plopped into the seat in front of Thomas's desk and glared for all that he was worth. "You are using sex as an escape and you know it."

"I wanted to talk to him." Thomas gave up the pretense of going over his notes. He could teach this class in his sleep actually. He looked up at his friend. "I

really did. But I walked in and he was in my kitchen --
"

"You gave him a key? Because that screams commitment."

"No, I didn't. He was just there."

"So he magicked himself inside..." Marshal mused. "Well, he is the god of travelers so --"

"Anyway," Thomas interrupted before Marshal could get going again. The Egyptologist was hard put to stay on task if something interested him, and it looked like Kern's past exploits had drawn his friend's interest big time. "He cooked for me and I just kind of melted. I mean he was standing there, barefoot, wearing the most insane apron and..."

"All thoughts of conversation fled at the sight of the mighty stag being domestic."

"He's coming for lunch today," Thomas informed Marshal, and ignored the sudden light of interest that grew in his friend's dark gaze. "And I promise to talk to him."

"So you came to a decision?"

"Not yet. I just need to know more about him, about what he wants... I just... I don't know, Marshal. This whole thing terrifies me."

"Not the god part, I am assuming, 'cause you keep fucking him."

"No, not the god part." Thomas rolled his eyes at his friend before huffing lightly and settling back in his chair. "That doesn't bother me. I've met minor gods before, back at home."

"So it's the relationship thing, the mating thing. What's got you so frightened, Thomas?"

Marshal was looking so earnest, his long, wavy black hair pulled back in what he called a professional man bun. His golden eyes glittered with concern and he leaned in closer to him, his gaze intent as all that intelligence and knowledge was centered directly on him. It was kind of unnerving in a way, but it was also comforting to know that this friend cared so much about him. Maybe it was time to really tell his most trusted friend what had happened to him.

"It's one of the reasons I left my clan." Thomas sighed, crossing his arms as he tried not to get lost in his memories. "It wasn't just because I wanted to expand my horizons. It was because… it was just better for me to be away."

"What happened to you, Faunus?" Marshal's eyes narrowed as he stared at him and Thomas felt his unease grow. What if his friend felt differently about him after the telling?

Well, he decided with a sad sigh, there was no hope for it now. He had to tell his friend what happened.

"I was a fool. I was a fool that almost brought ruin to our clan."

"One lone Faunus is incapable of destroying a society that is ancient and well-established, Thomas. Nothing you could have done would have brought ruin to your people."

"Well, for one, I was fucking a married king."

"Say what?"

It was almost amusing, the sudden twist on Marshal's face as he digested his words. His expression went from disbelief to confusion to disbelief and then indignation. Maybe he was going to lose his best friend after all.

"I was in a years' long relationship with a mated man, Marshal, and he was a king of a neighboring clan."

"So." Marshal leaned back a bit. "Now that

you've gotten the shock value out of that statement, tell me the whole story, the real story."

Thomas huffed and wished that he had stopped for coffee on the way in. Instead he reached into the mini-fridge he kept beside his desk and pulled out a bottle of orange juice, offering one to Marshal who reached out to accept it.

It gave him some time to organize his thoughts as he twisted open the bottle and took his first sweet, tangy sip. But then he knew he had stalled long enough and that Marshal wouldn't let up until the curious cat had gathered all of the facts.

"When I was younger, I met an older man who knew of my interest in the human world."

"World traveler, then?"

"He owned the company that contracted to sell our goods to the human world. In recent years, artisan products have become big sellers and my clan was very traditional. I mean I never even saw a computer until I was about ten and then I had never seen a television until I was fifteen."

"That is very traditional, my friend, almost to an insane degree."

"Truly." Thomas nodded. "You have no idea. I learned to shear sheep and process their wool by hand before I even learned to operate a cell phone. I learned to press olives for oil and to create dyes from flowers petals before I even learned that there was a way off our small island. I learned to make wine according to the temperature and the season before I knew what a car was. We were very isolated and the king of our clan kept us that way."

"So what changed?"

"Aleksy." Thomas sighed the name that he thought he would never speak again. "Aleksy Adamos.

When I was roughly nineteen and thought myself a man, I was tasked by my king to handle a negotiation from Adamos about some of the newer products my clan had created as new selling points. My Ariti clan had been made very prosperous in recent years by the sales of our artisan and one hundred percent natural products. My mother alone was bringing in thousands per month with the sales of her scarves and shawls... and the orders for her custom work are still growing and considered museum pieces. Between my studies of languages and of our histories in Greece, I learned to work the loom under her. In fact, it was my idea to start crafting woolen and silken jewelry, incorporating semi-precious stones into patterns of soft necklaces, bracelets, and ornamental hair ties. Since it was my idea and my work that was drawing some attention, it was up to me to present a business plan to Adamos for future sales. He was the one who came up with the idea of marketing to humans and was our direct link to the outside world."

"Your clan rested on the whims of one man?"

"Well, when you put it like that, yes. Aleksy Adamos is a genius when it comes to the business world. With only taking fifteen percent of our overall sales, he managed to help our clan amass hundreds of thousands of dollars and keep ourselves in materials we needed to maintain our businesses and to live rather comfortably."

"Yeah, a traditional clan would not need much."

"We were happy. I was happy, and when I met with Adamos I had a plan. Of course, looking back it was elementary, but it was something that had promise. Adamos said he saw that promise and set about teaching me about the world of man."

"That must have been fascinating for someone

who had been as isolated as you."

"You have no idea." Thomas leaned back in his chair, a smile pulling at his lips. Even though it all went bad, that time in his life had been so exciting, so liberating, so educational... "He gave me books and introduced me to the modern world. Under his tutelage I learned so many languages and the history of the world. He taught me that my little slice of the planet was not all that there was. He expanded my world."

"You trusted him."

"With my everything." Thomas took a deep breath and then another fortifying sip of his juice, just trying to push back the happy memories. It didn't do well to dwell on them knowing where he would end up. "I trusted him and I asked him to share my first adult heat. I was twenty-three at the time and he was attentive and eager... he said he wanted me for a mate and I whole heartedly agreed with him. Why not? He was a direct descendent of Pan, he was worldly, he treated me like I was delicate and special... he said he loved me."

"And you shared a heat."

"And afterwards he said he didn't mark me because he wanted me to be able to give full consent when it was done. I was so proud. He said I had to keep it a secret because of our age differences, but he promised as soon as I got older and a little more education under my belt he would tell my parents and then move me off of the island to his home in Crete."

"And it didn't strike you as strange that he wouldn't just, I don't know, go and ask your parents for your hand?"

"What did I know about the real world? My mind was lost in books. I got my first degree through long distance learning not long after he met me. My mind was in the books or knitting jewelry or on him. I was always in a rush to learn more, do more... I was defending my first PhD when something seemed a bit off to me. Someone mentioned about a huge party at Adamos's house and he said that there was something important he wanted to tell me the day before. I was lost in academia and really didn't pay attention but when one of our buyers mentioned the party, I thought that's what he wanted to tell me about."

After a protracted silence, Marshal asked, "What happened?"

"I got dressed up and I went to present our newest product, one that I had come up with on my own. Knitted metal jewelry. I taught myself to knit thin gold wire, and I added all kinds of protecting and precious stones. I basically made a set of mating bands and went to present them to him during the party, something to publicly let everyone know how we felt about each other and what the future held for us. All of the clan kings would be there and my father thought it a bit odd that I suddenly wanted to go to one of these meetings when I always made some excuse to avoid it, but I assumed he thought I was just taking more of an interest in the business side of things."

"Disaster happened?"

"On a scale that rocked the foundations of our little world."

"What happened?"

"I made it there, dressed in the best that I had to offer, wearing my mother's more famous scarf patterns and carrying the bands in a gold box. As the host, Adamos entered soon after the party started. When he saw me come down the receiving line, he looked a little nervous, but I thought that was just because I was pushing the mating issue a little. He still shook my hand and gave me the most confusing look, but I just went with it, stupid little me, with a smile on my face."

"Someone figured it out?"

"Oh, he made an announcement about my new jewelry line and how it was going to be successful. He called me up to speak about it because my knitted jewelry was on everyone's to buy list. In fact, several women were wearing my pieces at this party."

"And you kissed him?"

"Worse. I stood up and held up the box and everyone leaned forward to see what the new product was all about because of course, they expected me to announce something new and big. So I pulled out the mating bands and the reaction was instantaneous. People loved them. They were so beautiful and sparkly... And I turned after explaining how I came up with the idea and gave all the credit to my lover and future mate, Aleksy. It was then the screaming started."

"Good gods." Marshal paled on his behalf and Thomas let out a sad chuckle.

"Something like that. I announced that I was getting mated to the man of my dreams, that he had promised me during my last heat and then his heavily pregnant wife started yelling and crying. I don't know who looked more surprised; me, him, or her."

"For fuck's sake." Marshal took a huge swig of his juice. "For fuck's sake, Bright."

"I know." Thomas laughed bitterly. "His parents were screaming, my parents were threatening to kill him and to go to war over it, his wife was doing her best to beat his face in, and I was left standing there with bonding bracelets and a look of confusion on my face. It was her parents who shielded me when he turned his wrath on my head. His wife's father stood up and demanded why he had defiled such an innocent young man. That made everyone quiet down and it brought attention back to me."

"I just bet it did."

"It was nasty, Marshal. I was standing there and then I started crying. It all came out, how he was kind and sweet, how he loved me and shared my first heat and promised to mate me when he felt I was older and more mature. I told them how he helped me with the human world and getting my degrees and was always there when I had questions or issues. I kind of broke down when I told them how he said we would start our own family and that I was the love of his life. I think by that point his wife and I were both in each other's arms bawling like babies, Marshal. I just let the whole thing out, told everything. And then someone asked why didn't I know he was mated, that it was the event of the year, two years prior. And the response was I was on my island learning to knit jewelry and taking classes and I just didn't know. His wife got me out of the room, her parents shielded our retreat, my parents were trying to do their level best to murder him. It was bad."

"At least they all got the full story."

"And overnight I became the poor little dim-witted fool who didn't know anything about the world and had gotten taken advantage of. His wife got me back home, stayed the night with me where upon she told me he was an abuser and a user but she was not going to give him up. He was worth millions and she was going to do her best to make him pay for his indiscretions against the both of us. But she also added that I couldn't be there, that I couldn't be on the whole island of Greece."

"She had that much power?"

"In our corner of the preternatural world, yes, she did. She was a descendent of Zeus. I had to leave, or our business that kept the people of my clan stable and comfortable on our island would disappear and we would all be homeless beggars before the year was up."

"Ouch."

"Yes, so I was summarily pitied and laughed at while my belongings were packed. Me and my broken heart were shipped over here to a position that she had gotten for me. I had successfully defended my dissertation and earned my PhD, so for her it was just a matter of dropping my portfolio on the right desk. She gave me a lot of startup money, bought and openly wore the mating bands I had created, forcing him to wear his as well, and saw me off to America with a smile. Her money made it easy for me to get on the list for my citizenship and she still sends me postcards and baby pictures."

"That is too cruel and you know it."

"I think she is genuinely trying to be nice, to make up for what she forced me to leave behind. I haven't been back to Greece since and though I mourn the loss of my family and friends, my innocence, I can't go back. It's just too painful."

"You still love him?"

"Nope. My love for him died the moment I learned about his wife, but my trust... I don't trust easy."

"You ignored me for weeks before you realized I wasn't trying to get into your pants and just wanted a good friend I could trust my magical nature to."

"And you are the very best friend that I ever could have, Marshal, but this has kind of made me relationship shy, especially with magical creatures, and most assuredly when mating is brought up."

"But your god isn't mated, Bright. And what's with that last name? It's not your family name?"

"My father requested that I change it in order to stop the embarrassing rumors that were going to harm our family business."

"Fuck him."

"My reaction, actually. And then I got my name changed."

"And your god? Like he said, he's not mated, he is eager for you, and you would be the only one."

"Until maybe something better came along."

"You sell yourself too short."

"I am scared out of my mind, Marshal. I don't want to lose everything again."

"You won't. It's not the same. You are not that scared little boy. You are a grown man and you know nothing you did would ever force me from your side. Is this why you never date?"

"I can't even trust myself to know when something is wrong in a relationship, Marshal. How can I just trust someone else?"

"Maybe it's just time for you to really grow up." Marshal stood, still holding his half-finished bottle of juice. "Maybe it's time you start trusting yourself. You can't get a decent relationship working if you constantly question your own judgment."

"So what do I do?"

"Stop fucking him and ask him some questions. And then, you know, maybe learn about him so your opinions are based on fact. And then decide if you are brave enough to take that leap.

"Marshal…"

"And it's time to get to class. You are having

lunch with him, right?"

"Yeah."

"Would it make you more comfortable if I tagged along, just for a little bit? Just until you get your bearings with him."

"I -- I think I would like that." Thomas offered his friend a relieved smile. He was not going to lose Marshal as a friend because of his past stupidity.

"And for the record" -- Marshal paused before exiting the room --"It was not your fault. And if anyone says that it was, they are full of shit. You just trusted the wrong man, Bright. Maybe you should stop beating yourself up for the stupidity of others. And you need to tell the wife to stop that shit. It just keeps the past alive."

"But --"

"She's probably miserable with her millions of dollars and her perfect kids, and her cheating ass liar of a husband. Misery loves company and I think it's time you realize that you've found better company to pal around with. Later, Bright."

Thomas felt... he didn't know what to feel and he really didn't have time to puzzle it out. Looking at his clock he realized he had ten minutes to get across to the Humanities building to start his classes, and walking was a bit of a chore.

Cushions, he thought to himself as he scrambled out of the room. *Next time bring cushions.*

Chapter Six

It was during the last moments of his last class of the day that an unnatural silence filled his lecture hall.

Thomas looked up from his lectern to notice that not one eye was on him. That could only mean one thing. Kern had arrived.

As his voice trailed off, the sound of the stag's footsteps seemed to ring out even in the not-so-empty lecture hall. Dressed in an obviously bespoke suit of uncompromising black, paired with a crisp, black linen shirt, Kern looked handsome, powerful, and rich as Rockefeller. His hair was pulled back into a tight tail and trailed down his spine while his eyes glittered with hunger as they zeroed in on him.

Thomas felt his breath catch as he realized that all that masculine beauty was there just for him. He found himself struggling to hold onto his glamor as his tail wanted to flag and he wanted to lower his head in subservience. But he swiftly pushed those thoughts aside knowing that this was not the time nor the place for supernatural shenanigans, not with so many humans watching… thought he did have more trouble hiding his sudden and nearly painful erection. *Thank goodness for lecterns*, he thought as he cleaned his throat to bring his class's attention back to him.

Although, by the time he forced his brain cells into functioning, Kern had climbed up the three stairs that led onto the small stage where he and his disguising lectern stood.

Before he could speak, Kern placed a large picnic hamper on the floor at his feet, took two large steps forward, and suddenly Thomas was surrounded by the strength and the spicy scent of his stag… who was lowering his head and…

Gods, what a kiss. Kern pulled his head back and slammed his mouth onto his, parting his lips with his beautifully fluid stag's tongue and tasting the inside of his mouth.

Thomas gripped Kern by the shoulders, holding on tight as the force of the kiss bowed him backward when his lover's arm pulled him close. One of Kern's thighs slid between his, pressing unerringly up against his erection, and he nearly lifted him off of his feet as he stood up to his full height.

Thomas was hard pressed not to wrap his legs around Kern's waist and demand he take him for a ride, but he managed to control himself as the white noise ringing in his ears became recognizable as the cheers and claps from his students.

"Way to go, Prof Bright!" someone shouted, and more whistles and catcalls followed that statement along with a few people declaring how hot his boyfriend was, and of course Theresa calling out that she understood why Thomas was having problems walking.

By the time Kern broke off the kiss, Thomas could only hang on to the man and try not to faceplant right in the middle of the floor.

Then he was saved by the bell as his alarm went off, signaling the end of class for the day, not that anyone was going anywhere. Instead of leaving, his students gathered around, doing their best to get a good look at the man in their favorite teacher's life.

"Where did you meet?"

"I didn't know you could pull such a hot man, Mr. B --"

"I didn't know Prof Bright was gay?"

And more disturbingly, "Can I be your third?"

Thomas found himself saved from having to

answer any awkward questions by Marshal's arrival.

"All right, you heathens," his best friend in the world called out as he entered the hall and shooed his students away. "This will not be on the exam, but I am sure that I can convince Professor Bright to assign you some archaic Latin love ballads and odes to kissing to translate into ancient Egyptian before English if you all want to stick around…"

And the hall cleared out fast.

"And now that that's done --" Marshal laughed "-- lunch?"

"Hmm, cat," Kern rumbled in his deep voice as he finally released Thomas from his hold, though he didn't let him get far. "I smell sand and incense… Descendent of Bastet?"

"Oh, he's good." Marshal nodded to Kern, though he was speaking to Thomas.

"I have met your kind before, little healer. Your kind are almost always healers of some sort."

"And you are a Celtic god," Marshal pointed out. "Thought I have to admit, you look stunning with or without the horns."

"I thank you, friend of my mate." He looked down at Thomas and he felt his heart jump at the hungry look in his lover's eyes. "By your comment, I am to assume you are joining us for our meal?"

"If that won't be an imposition."

"Never." Kern spoke softly as he bent down to place a kiss on Thomas's forehead.

"You know, that kiss was probably filmed and will be all over the Internet before we leave the building," Thomas felt compelled to point out.

"Good." Kern nodded. "Then they will know that you're taken and that you're mine. Are you aware that several of your students find you sexually arousing?"

"Comes with the territory," Thomas admitted with a silly grin. "Not that I would touch any of them or even look twice at a student of mine." He shuddered at the thought.

"Like those unschooled youngsters would hold your attention at all," Kern agreed. "And will that be an issue for you?"

"An issue?"

"The kiss."

"Oh, no," Thomas admitted. "I have tenure. I'd have to be caught screwing you in front of students in the middle of the day for me to get into any real trouble. You will probably spark a lot of curiosity with the admins as well as the rest of my students though."

"That is good." Kern pressed another small kiss to Thomas's forehead, burying his nose in his curls for a moment before releasing him completely. "I don't want to get you into any trouble."

"Unless you've already gotten him into trouble," Marshal added, eyeballing the hamper with some curiosity. "As in knocked up and in the family way."

"That would be a blessing," Kern admitted, then shot Thomas a look. "But only if my mate so desires. It is his body, and though I would wish him to continue carrying my child, if he wanted to terminate any pregnancy, I would still stand by his side."

"Quite open-minded for a fertility deity." Marshal cast Thomas a telling look and Thomas, in turn, felt his heart melt a little more when it came to this fascinating creature who wanted him.

"That is... I didn't expect that," Thomas admitted, looking up at Kern, finding more and more to like about him.

"Well, for one thing, it is your body, my mate,"

Kern spoke with authority. "And secondly, as much as I want to have a say in your decision, ultimately the decision has to lie with you. Only you know your mental, physical, and emotional condition. The decision has to be yours. To do otherwise would mean that I would steal your body autonomy from you. I want a mate, a partner, an equal, not a slave forced into something that they will resent for the rest of our lives."

"Good answer." Marshal's words broke the tension as Thomas continued to stand there and stare at his mate with open-mouthed awe. "So... food?"

"Yes." Kern visibly took a reluctant step away from Thomas and moved to heft the basket. "I have brought us a proverbial feast due to The Master's interference."

"The Master?"

"I shall explain presently, but first we must find a place to dine."

* * *

They found a place at a nearby park that was fairly empty and within walking distance of the university.

"So, you felt the need for company for our major talk?"

Kern was getting straight to the point. He wanted his mate to want him equally and he understood that there could be no lies or half-truths between them.

"Everyone needs a little back up," Thomas replied, looking sheepish as he settled himself on the large blanket that Kern had produced from the basket after kicking off his shoes. "It makes us prey animals feel more secure."

"Right." Kern snorted, amused by the wit and

daring of his little mate. "Like anyone would consider you prey. You hunted me until I caught you and then you tagged me, my little shining star. There is nothing weak about you."

"Except his decision-making skills and his serious imposter syndrome," Thomas's friend Marshal chimed in. "What?" he added as he kicked off his shoes and eagerly dove into the basket, ignoring the heated look his friend was giving him. "You know I'm telling the truth here, Bright."

"Is he now?" Kern smirked at the blush that flowed down his little mate's cheeks and neck. He knew how far down that pretty flush of red went and it made him growl a little under his breath... which made Thomas blush all the harder. "You don't feel you have the right to be with me, my star?"

"It's not that," his mate decided after dithering over a moment on what to say. "It's... there is so much we don't know about each other. We need to know things before we make an informed decision about how to proceed further."

"Then what is it you need to know about me?" Kern asked, tilting his head to the side as he observed his pretty little mate. The man could already be pregnant with his child and that warmed parts of him he thought were long dead. Before all of this happened, before the rushed heat and the wild sex and of course, the partial bond they now shared because of the bite his little star had bestowed upon him, he thought he would never have this happiness again. He thought about the torque, the ancient symbol of his power he had brought out especially for his mate. If he was not going to bite him and complete the bond this day, he could at least offer him this personal protection. And Thomas was right, there were a lot of things he needed to know, he needed to be protected from.

"Well, how old are you, for one? I haven't a clue and I only know your true name because I study ancient mythologies."

"That is not my true name," Kern informed him as he reached past the cat friend and dug into the basket, producing several closed containers of food. He began to lay them out on the blanket while Thomas was startled for a second by actions that weren't very Alpha-like, before digging into the basket to remove plates and forks, setting them up a place to eat. Kern was glad the picnic hamper he brought came with a setting for four people. They wouldn't have any trouble accommodating his friend when it came to the small feast he had brought with him. "In fact, no one but me knows my true name. The Celts named me what they would based on what they thought I could and did do for them. But my true name, my name of power, I only share that with my mate, my family, and my master."

"You have a master?" Thomas appeared curious and not angered by his answer. That was a good thing.

"Don't we all have a master or a leader of some sort? You've seen mine and I will explain that later. Hopefully you will be patient while I explain some truths about myself."

At his mate's nod, Kern continued. "As for my age, I am not sure exactly how old I am. I stopped counting centuries ago but I have seen civilizations grow from their infancy into great nations and then crumble, only to be lost to the hands of time. I know languages that no one has ever heard spoken and more that humans have forgotten entirely. I am ancient as the land itself, my mate, and I have experienced almost everything that human and preternatural beings can experience in their lifetimes. Suffice it to say I am old enough to know what I want, and I want you."

That blush came back and Kern found himself charmed all over again by the perceived innocence of his mate.

"That's…" His little star trailed off as he stared up at Kern, his wide brown eyes shining with some unnamed devotion Kern was too scared to contemplate.

"That was a beautiful answer," Marshal interjected as the silence between the two of them grew. "And that means that I am going to research the hell out of you until I uncover more of what you aren't saying."

And that made Kern laugh. He threw back his head and laughed like he hadn't in a long time. His mate's little cat was very amusing.

"You said family?" His star finally asked another question after Kern started opening up food containers and exposing tender cuts of deli meats and cheeses, cool and savory salads, several containers of fruit, and a container of small cakes drizzled with a decadent chocolate frosting. Say what you would about Manx, but they sure knew how to pack a picnic lunch.

"You've seen them, my star. The Wolf and The Bear."

"Of course." Thomas paused in filling his plate to stare wide eyed at Kern. "They have to be magical too in order for you to parade around in your real form like that. Are they gods as well?"

"That is up for them to tell you or not," Kern informed him in a very serious tone. "It is not my place to speak of such things."

"And your master?"

"Oh yes, The Master of the Hunt. They can't wait to meet you."

"You want me to meet them?"

"Of course. They are my family. They will be your family if and when you decide to complete the bond."

"If?" Thomas looked truly puzzled. He shared a look with the cat before he focused those cautious eyes back to him. "You are not going to force the issue?"

"I want a mate, not a slave. I believe I told you this before." Kern stared at his mate until he nodded in agreement.

"I believe you."

"Good. Now what else do you want to know?"

"Any past or current relationships I have to worry about?"

"I understand the need for that question as you see where I am currently employed, but no. I once had a relationship with each, The Bear and the Wolf, but those associations have long since passed though the love and respect remain. I am not going to lie. I have never been a monk, but the moment I laid eyes upon you, I terminated any budding encounters that I had planned for the future."

"So no side pieces?" The cat asked as he eagerly tore into his food. "No bunny-boiling women or men going to knock on my brother's door?"

"None." Kern snickered. "Bunny boiling?"

"*Fatal Attraction* is a classic and should be viewed as a cautionary tale by all people in serious relationships." The cat eyed him for a moment before offering a smile to his little star.

"I believe I have missed that cinematic lesson but I assure you there is nothing fatal about my attraction to your brother. And now I have a question of my own."

"Okay." Thomas nodded, finally starting to eat a sandwich he had concocted. That act of providing alone eased some of the pressure Kern's instincts were pushing in him to provide for his mate. "Ask away."

"Have you ever had a relationship of a sexual nature with the cat?"

They both choked on their bites of food, Kern was pleased to see, in shocked horror.

"Oh, gods no." Thomas's gaze snapped to his friend's before they whipped back to Kern's. "He's a slut."

"Hey!" the cat protested. "I am not a slut. I just enjoy all the delights that the creators designed my body to feel. And if I care to share those delights with a few consenting adults, it's nobody's business but ours. And I never thought to sleep with you, Bright. I want my lovers letting their kink flags fly high and you, my dear, are a shrinking violet."

"I am not." Kern's mate's eyes narrowed as he glared at the cat. "I am perfectly fine with my kinks."

"If your kinks include sitting on cold library floors reading dusty arcane texts that people have long since forgotten and never really cared about in the first place. There's a reason your kids thought that you had hemorrhoids instead of a lover when you limped in to work Monday."

"Fuck you, Gray," his star seethed, the blush returning with a vengeance.

"Not even on your best day," the cat teased back. "You are so vanilla I could probably pull wafers out of your ass."

"Yeah, you two have never fucked." Kern interrupted the academic smack-down he could feel building, as amusing as it was.

"We could have," his star seethed at him. "We would look good together."

"You would," Kern agreed. "Look good together, I mean, but ultimately you would bore each other to tears. You need a firm hand, my star. You get off on being spanked and I have the feeling that your cat would get off on doing the spanking."

"Damn straight." The cat nodded before tearing into his sandwich again. "I know what I like and what I like falls into the lemon category... or chocolate. My brother from another mother can't give me that... But I think your friend the Bear can."

"Arcas?" Kern snickered. "You like Arcas? You haven't even met him."

"I have a thing for redheads," the cat declared, digging into the basket again to retrieve a bottle of water. "And from the look of him, carpet and drapes match perfectly."

That tore a laugh out of Kern and he automatically elevated the cat in his mind as someone who needed protection. If something went down, he would have his little star's family protected.

And speaking of protection... "In the belief of true transparency we have going on here, I have to tell you that The Master wants to see you. There are things that we can't speak of in public and you need to be truly informed of what you are getting into."

"Full disclosure." The cat was staring pointedly at his little star. "A guy could get behind that."

"Do you have classes planned for the rest of the day?"

"Just one," Thomas admitted, looking down at his empty plate in what looked like surprise before he started creating another sandwich. "Why?"

"I would like to get you over to *The Wild Hunt*

before the day is done. There is a lot I have to tell you."

"Is this dangerous?...'Cause this smacks of danger." The cat was staring at him in suspicion.

"You may come along as well, little cat. There are things you both need to know. The magical world is not as safe as you may think it to be. And a relationship with me is a bit more complicated than you would have with any other man."

"I served my time," the cat informed them both, polishing off the water and eyeballing the cakes with interest. "I am free after this and for the next day as well. I have been planning a sabbatical for a while now and trying to convince this stubborn goat to go with me. My classes are limited until after the finals next week and then I am good to go for the summer."

"I'm done," his star admitted as well. "I am just doing recaps for my grad students. The exams will be administered next week and I have yet to determine if I want to spend my summer off sweating in Africa or working on some old manuscripts that are on loan from The Walters Art Gallery. They have a new exhibition this fall about ancient Greece and I want my name attached to it."

"So after we finish consuming this fine meal, we can go? I want you both in the know as soon as possible, for the things in my life are sure to affect you both."

"Wow, that is very adult and trustworthy, wouldn't you say, Bright?" the cat teased, and his little star rolled his eyes at his friend.

"That is very admirable," his star agreed. "And there are some things I need to tell you as well."

"About your reluctance to complete our bond?" Kern asked and grinned as his mate started a little bit. "I knew you were not a virginal innocent when I took you, my little star. I know that you have had experiences before me and that common sense would tell anyone that those experiences shaped you into the man that you are today. Even your reluctance about completing our bond tells me a lot. So if you feel the need to let me know why you are skittish today, then it would be my pleasure to listen and then prove to you why I would be a superior mate."

There was silence except for small talk during the rest of their meal and then when all the food was consumed and the detritus of their lunch packed away, they made their way to *The Wild Hunt*, the cat and his star in one car following closely behind his truck.

It was a small but important caravan, and though he suspected, Kern didn't know for sure that the set of eyes he felt on them were real or just part of his imagination.

Chapter Seven

The Wild Hunt certainly looked different in the bright daylight than it did in the sultry dark evenings.

For one, the place was larger than Thomas figured. Really, the whole building was a converted warehouse that stood about four stories high. It was housed in a nondescript stone building that blended in with its counterparts on the block, though it took up most of one.

Instead of going in through the front, Kern led them to a private parking lot that sank beneath the building, then up to an elevator that shot them directly to the top floor.

"I called my family from the truck," Kern spoke softly as the elevator stopped and the huge metal doors slid open. "They are all here for us and they can't wait to meet you."

Thomas tried to force a smile though the butterflies in his stomach and the nerves that were making him regret the huge lunch they had consumed. "Really?"

"Oh, yeah," Kern confirmed. "They're excited to meet the man that finally caught my heart."

"Your heart?" Thomas found himself asking as Marshal was peering around the open area that led into a living area, curious as the cat that his stag named him.

"Of course, his heart." The rich soft voice that answered him belonged to no other than the person that had been introduced as The Master.

They were tall, nearly as tall as Kern, so that put them around six feet. Their hair was long, dark and flowing, hanging to the center of their back in inky black locks of silk streaked with diamonds. Their eyes were some undefinable shade that he would just refer to as brilliant and dark. Their skin was pale and velvety looking, firm and ageless. And their face... it was neither male nor female but a perfect blending of the two. They smiled and Thomas felt his knees almost buckle at the wave of energy that seemed to roll from them.

At their smile, a low whine filled the room and several shadows detached themselves from the leather furniture and reformed in the shape of some very large hounds that swirled around their feet.

Marshal took a cautious step back and Thomas felt his heart rate triple. Who and what was he dealing with here?

"You do know that my Stag could have come to me at any time and gotten the half-bonding bite you placed upon his chest nullified if he so wished?"

"No," Thomas breathed, his gaze going over to Kern, who managed to look all beautiful, masculine, and kind of sheepish at this revelation.

"Well, he feels a lot for you, Thomas Bright. And when one of my Huntsmen decides to give his heart over, it is a big deal. Won't you please come inside? And bring your curious friend too."

Thomas entered the area with Kern at his side and his brother at his back and nearly turned and went back into the elevator when he saw who was waiting for them, seated pretty as you please on the couch.

"Introductions, of course." Kern placed a hand at the small of his back and ushered him further into the room. "The beautiful lady is my sister Caille, known to most only as The Wolf."

The Wolf was a beautiful woman with long, wavy, dark blonde hair, the kind you knew would look brighter in the sunlight. Her eyes were amber and her skin deeply tanned. She had an ageless smile but those full lips pulled into a more amused smile when she noticed him giving her the once over.

"You are lovely." Caille spoke with a deep, compelling voice as she returned the scrutiny. "No wonder Kern is so taken with you." Then she tilted her head to the side as she examined Marshal. "And you brought a little kitty cat for us to play with. How sweet."

Thomas could hear Marshal humph from behind him before his friend moved to stand beside him and give Caille a hard glare. "Smells like wet dog all of a sudden."

That brought about delighted laughter from The Wolf as well as the others in the room and Thomas felt himself relaxing a bit.

"The ginger is Arcas, known as The Bear."

"So very delighted to meet you," Marshal spoke after a moment of silence and Thomas could see why Marshal was so enthralled by the man.

His hair was a bright red with golden facets underneath the rich color. His eyes were a bright clear teal and his face was dotted with small freckles that looked like kisses from tiny fairies. His body, however, was a thing of beauty. In a small tank top and causal sweatpants, he cast a very muscular and well-developed masculine figure in casual dress.

"Hello, kitty-kitty-kitty," Arcas purred at Marshal and the man preened. "You gonna come out and play with us?

"Oh, I came out a long time ago, fuzzy-wuzzy. And if it's an invite to play, I have to be sure to give you a copy of my contract so you won't be shocked when I turn you into my bearskin rug."

"And," Kern cut in as a delighted glow filled

Arcas' eyes, "This is the one of whom I have spoken, our Master of the Hunt, Manx."

"I can see why you slept with them all." Thomas felt the words slip out of his mouth and then felt that hateful blush redden his face.

"You told him?" Caille giggled, crawling across the couch, her short hooded sweat jacket riding up and her tiny pair of shorts exposing a sleekly muscled set of legs. She leaned up on the arm of the chair and shot them all a grin. "Oh, it has to be true love."

"And to be fair," The Master added, "I've never slept with any of them. They are not my style. I would ask that you all take a seat. My love life is part of the reason I wanted to speak with you. And please, call me Manx. These three go with The Master just to make me irritated enough to spank their naughty asses, though that's never going to happen either."

And if that didn't send a shift of fright up Thomas's spine, nothing else would, but he gamely moved deeper into the living room and took a seat on a couch across from where the trio were now seated.

Once settled with Marshal at his left and Kern at his right, Thomas found himself leaning into the warmth and comfort of his mate, glad that his stag was there for him.

"Thank you, Manx," he spoke politely as he was taught. "What does…why…I am confused."

"Then let me explain." Manx offered him a smile. "The magical world is not a safe, happy place for our kind. There are beings out there that want to do us harm."

"I've never seen any danger here." Thomas had to be honest with a being that possessed such immense power. The energy coming off of Manx eclipsed even the strange surges he felt from Kern, and he was considered a minor god.

"Then I have been doing my job, as most of this city is under my protection. You, though, you were a shock. Not so much your Egyptian friend here. Marshal Gray has been on our radar for some time now. It is how he got a ticket to our masque. We wanted to see what he was and to offer him some protection because he obviously didn't know the dangers of running around undeclared."

"Like luggage?" Marshal asked, as always his mouth running before his mind had a chance to catch up.

"Danger?" Thomas asked. "And you were aware of him, but not me?"

"It's not like you play around the city." Kern laughed. "And as for your little cat, oh yeah, he gets around. He's safe and consensual and very sane, but still, he plays around and people have taken notice."

"Great," Marshal sighed, crossing his arms over his chest. "Voyeurs."

"Not like we were actually looking for you, kitty-kitty-kitty," Arcas chimed in, his voice taking on a gruff edge. "But some of the people you were playing with are under our protection and therefore under the scrutiny of those who would do us ill."

"Danger?" Thomas repeated as it looked like his friend was going to start a flirting session with The Bear right then and there. "There are dangers that I'm not aware of?"

"It is why I urged Kern to bring you in to talk with us," Manx, still looking amused, explained. "He expressed a desire to be open and honest with you and I find myself agreeing. After all, you are not a casual hook up he wants to keep around for a while. You could shape up to be the love of his life and that in itself is unique and special."

Thomas found his eyes going to those of his mate's and want settled deep in his chest. His mate really was being truthful and honest. That was something that could make him love the beautiful beast of a man.

"But the danger here is very real," Kern spoke after reaching out to grip his hand in his much larger one. "And I wanted you both to understand what you have walked into."

"So tell me." Thomas turn this gaze from Kern's back to Manx's. "You are starting to scare me a little."

"It is partially my fault so I shall explain," Manx began, settling back in their seat directly across from them, Arcas sitting upright at their right side while Caille curled up into a ball on their left. "Many years ago, I was considered a master hunter, a god in my own right, whose job was to hunt down the evil in this world and devour it. Gods, humans, fae alike, I would hunt them for their misdeeds. Pantheons held no meaning to me -- the lines of god and goddess worship get blurred after eons anyway and time doesn't matter to one such as I. Once I am on the hunt, I can use any means available at my disposal to get my targets eliminated."

"You are that powerful?" Thomas asked, a little bit awed.

"I was selected by elder gods to police those who would follow in their footsteps, so yeah, I had to be more powerful than the average god."

"Manx of the Moddey Dhoo..." Thomas breathed. "But you are supposed to be a special black dog haunting the Isle of Man..."

"And St. Padraig was Irish and actually drove snakes from Ireland," Manx scoffed. "I would say, as I am sure you know, that histories see what it wants to see and tosses out things that make them uncomfortable. It is true that there was a spectral hound that haunted the Isle of Man, but only because Charles, the Earl of Derby and the king of Man at the time, employed idiots for his security. Someone was playing with the old gods and I sent one of my minions to retrieve the totem they were playing with. What followed was the most stupid game of "Dare the Spectral Doggie" I have ever seen. Maybe being stationed out there with only the sounds of waves and men complaining was enough to drive his soldiers mad, but some of them duplicated the totem and I had to keep sending my minions out to retrieve it. Finally the bastard who was making the things -- out of clay no less -- was cornered and the drunk idiot ran himself into the sea rather than give up the necklace his gram gave him. Idiot. That started the rumors of ghostly dogs haunting people on that island and killing the unwary for generations, and the damn tale stuck."

"That is... actually, that does make more sense than a ghost dog haunting the place for a while only to disappear after a soldier got sick after challenging it."

"There is almost always a logical explanation behind most myths, Thomas the Faunus, as I am sure you are aware."

"Stupid rhyming name." Thomas glared at his mate, who had the audacity to look a little sheepish at the nickname he was sure would hang around his head for all of eternity.

"It's cute." Kern snickered then winced when one of Thomas's sharp elbows hit him in the side.

"But what is not so cute is the tale I am about to tell you." At Manx's dark tone, all amusement fled.

"I was once tasked by the people of the Tuatha

Dé Danann, the people who are the direct descendants of the goddess Danu. It is said that her son was a powerful leader, and the goddess Morrigan herself protected these people in Ireland by creating great waves of fog that shielded them from view and provided cover for their armies to attack their enemies while staying safe from detection. It is said that her son had that power to control the water as well, but often with these kind of magical inheritances, the control was diluted over time as the people began to fade and then to interbreed with the humans around them. Eventually even the direct descendants could not control the weather. This is where Dagda the Fifteenth came into play. He discovered a way to leach the power from those who contained even the smallest bit of magical energy and claim it for himself. But in order to do this, he caused the death of those he captured. I was tasked by my lover, The Morrigan herself, to find him and kill him, which I did. Unbeknownst to me, when I caused his existence to cease to be, he had passed his teachings on to others who were not present at his side; his collectors if you will. Long after he was gone, they continued his work, capturing and torturing magical beings for their power. But this time it was not for something as mundane as bringing back some forgotten magical control. No, they want to resurrect him."

"Is that possible?" Thomas asked, his mind going over every myth of resurrection he could remember.

"I doubt it, but that hasn't stopped the generations of killing." Manx sighed sadly. "I have hunted them all down but for a few dozen different groups of cultists that exist here."

"Here? As in this city?"

"As in America," Manx corrected. "For a country

that holds fast to its Christian beliefs, there are a lot of those who believe differently, even within the churches and temples that exist here. These people find it easy to hide and disguise their doctrines as religious beliefs when in actuality they are actively seeking out the magical populace, grabbing those with the weakest or little to no defensive magic, and killing them by draining their magical energies. Magical beings cannot exist without their magic to sustain them, so people like you, Faunus, and your cute little descendent of Bastet are in real danger."

"But… but how?"

"Please allow me to continue," Manx spoke gently to Thomas, and he was very grateful for that. On a scale of one to ten his fear level had just jumped to eleven and he really didn't know what to think. Had being with Kern put him in some very real danger?

"The goddess Morrigan herself charged me with wiping out Dagda and his ilk, which I did. She believes that I should be responsible for taking out his cult, which I had no idea about but suddenly was part of the deal we made when she decided it should be. We almost came to blows over it, but going to outright war over the issue would no doubt bring about the knowledge of our existence to every human who walks the earth. I don't want that. I know humans. The sheer number of them and their creative weapons would destroy all of us magical creatures no matter how powerful we may be. The Morrigan doesn't know humanity like I know humanity and would prefer just to attack and kill the cult members, thereby bringing about the knowledge of our existence, yada yada yada…" Manx waved one hand as they rolled their eyes at their disclosures.

"To make a long story short, she managed to

contact the cult and create a truce of sorts. I am to gather any and all magical creatures under my protection and mark them as such. These creatures are not to be hunted or harmed by the Cult of Dagda and she won't kill them, but they found a loophole. Any magical creature unaware or who just happens to be caught without protection is fair game."

"That's just wrong!" Thomas exclaimed, leaning forward and almost yelling at Manx. "That doesn't make sense."

"The Morrigan is a goddess who has not had dealings with human beings in over three centuries. The last time she had direct contact with humanity, they fell over backward giving her what she wanted, no questions asked. People have come a long way since then and she doesn't understand them."

"And you told her that?" Thomas asked, almost sliding off of the couch as he got closer to Manx.

"I did," Manx huffed.

"And it got them kicked out of her bed," Caille chimed in and Manx groaned, covering his face with his hands.

"A lover's tiff? I could die because of a lover's tiff?"

"No," Kern corrected gently. "You could die because you are connected to me and I am a known agent of The Master of the Hunt who rarely has more than one dealing with actual human beings."

"What?"

"How do you think they know who to go after? They have a tight and hidden spy network, Thomas. They follow all of our steps, and as I am a known player in this game, the cultists often follow me and try to snatch up people I try to bring in to safety."

"Explain." Thomas turned to face The Stag, his

eyes going hard as a huge lump settled in his chest.

"We are *The Wild Hunt*: The Stag, The Wolf, and The Bear," he explained. "Manx found us each at a point in our lives where we needed to be -- well, needed. I was the first, a nearly forgotten god who wanted to do right by humanity, who had the knowledge and power to move amongst them without drawing attention to myself. I eagerly claimed the role as a Hunter, and as such I move to collect those who know about the cults, who are too afraid to exist on their own in human lands, and who seek out Manx's protection. I cannot tell you why Arcas and Caille joined up, although I can tell you that we act as bodyguards to The Master and we retrieve and protect those who cannot protect themselves."

"Bodyguard? But..." Thomas looked from person to person, mentally evaluating the magical punch they each possessed -- and it was immense, though nothing as powerful as what came from The Master of the Hunt.

"My power is strained," Manx explained. "Every time I offer protection to a magical being, a little more of my magic goes into their protection and not my own. Therefore, my Wild Hunt protects me when I am drained. They keep the others from trying to kill me because only the magical beings that roam free are under protection for the truce. There are no provisions to protect me or my agents. If they take me out of the equation, the truce disappears, and the cult is free to hunt anyone that they please."

"And so Kern, because they know who you are and who you follow... they know about me now."

"Yes," Kern agreed. "The attention that I give you, the adoration and time that I give you, it will be noted sooner or later."

"And that can get me killed."

"That is why I brought you here, Thomas."

"To force a mating? To force my hand to get what you want."

"Nothing like that," Kern said, but Thomas was frightened and panicked words were flowing from his mouth.

"So, I mate you or die? Is that it?"

"No." Kern turned to face him but Thomas was suddenly filled with fear and anger and it all had a target in his want-to-be mate. "You have choices, Thomas. That is why I brought you here."

"To mate or to be marked until at a later date when you decide to force the mating bite?"

"That's not what he said, Bright," Marshal tried to interject but Thomas was too far lost in panic to think clearly.

"Mate or to be marked... or get murdered. Those are my choices as far as I see it." He rose to his feet and pulled away from Kern. "You set me up."

The room stilled and Thomas was so far gone he could barely breathe, let alone move. His eyes were wide and terrified, staring at Kern, who was looking at him in obvious horror.

"That's not what this is, Thomas. You know that."

"Do I?" Thomas snapped, his heart racing as he looked for a way out. "I know that either way, you get what you want."

"Thomas --"

"Okay, enough of that," Marshal interjected, rising to his feet to grab Thomas by the arm. "I think it best I take him home until what you all said sinks in. He is... I don't know what this kind of shock is called but he has his reasons for it."

"I don't want him to think --" Kern also rose to his feet but Manx moved to intercept him, holding him back. "Thomas!"

"It's okay, Kern." Marshal offered him a smile while he moved them toward the elevators. "Thomas just needs to process. Tomorrow. Come to class tomorrow and bring us back then. Goodness knows I want to talk to you all more. I didn't know I was putting myself on a magical murder menu and I want off of it. My kind are lovers, not fighters, so I see the need for this defense. Bright will too, but he needs a hard reset of his brain and then he will be able to hold a conversation like an adult and not a panicked child."

And Thomas had nothing to say to that because he was already beginning to regret his outburst. He was still fearful-- that was all a lot to take in, but he was calming a little as his friend spoke for him.

He just... he had lost everything once. He didn't want to go through that again, and he couldn't imagine where he would run now that he was a magical creature on the radar of an evil cultist. It was a plot out of a Hollywood movie. And what if he was pregnant... his child would be in the same, if not more danger. He needed to think.

He got one last look at The Stag as he stood there surround by those who called themselves his family, and the look of devastation on his face was heartbreaking. And then as if he was skipping time, he was climbing out of his car and being dragged into his house by Marshal.

"I fucked up," he spoke softly and Marshal, directing him into the bedroom, snorted.

"You think, Einstein?" his friend and brother snapped, but then he sighed deeply and led him to his bed. "It was a lot to take in and you panicked. I understand why you did but you never got the chance to explain to Kern why you are so skittish, as he put it."

"I… I think I messed it up before I even got into a relationship," he sighed. "But I didn't know what to think. Murder and cults, Marshal? I mean, what the hell?"

"I know." Marshal dropped onto his bed beside him and kicked off his shoes.

Thomas looked down and saw that his brother had removed his shoes at some point so he pulled his legs into the bed and rolled to his side. Marshal climbed in behind him.

"I could end up dead."

"I know, and being friends with me could have put you on their cultist hit list."

"What?"

"You remember what they said? That some of my affairs had caught the attention of the magical community? Sooner or later they would have come after you for being associated with me."

Thomas blinked at that then groaned loudly. "I am a fool, aren't I?"

"You panicked." Marshal spooned Thomas and stuck his nose in his friend's curly brown hair. "It happens."

"What if I blew my chance, Marshal? What if I let my fears control me to the point where I will never have anything good in life?"

"He understands."

"He looked so lost, Marshal. I don't… I did that."

"And he will be in your classroom tomorrow, waiting for you to calm down and explain things to him."

"I hurt him."

"Yes, you did, but a man doesn't bring home a man, introduce him as his mate to his entire family, only to give up after one misunderstanding. At least your little spat is nothing like Manx and The Morrigan. Who ever heard of such stupidity... and I bet Manx is still being loyal to that goddess. That is just... wild."

"You think he'll come tomorrow?"

"I know he will. That man gave his heart to you, Bright, after you took a chunk of it for your own. He could have had the half-bond dissolved, you heard that, and he didn't. He wants you. A simple argument is not going to change that. Now take a nap. Afterwards we'll order in some dinner and then I'll sleep over. I am not too keen on either of us going around without protection after what I learned tonight. And tomorrow you two will straighten out your disagreement and all will be well."

"You think so?"

"I know so." Marshal snorted. "You are talking to someone who has extensive experience with love and relationships. You'll be back to sexing instead of talking, and walking with a limp in no time."

He hoped so. Thomas laid his head down and prayed with all of his might that his best friend was right, that Kern would be waiting for him in his classroom tomorrow, and that everything would be all right.

Chapter Eight

And bright and early the next day, Kern was *not* sitting in the back of his classroom like Thomas had hoped. Instead, a stern looking Arcas was there in all of his red-haired glory, making his students pay more attention to The Bear than to the ancient Roman myths he was outlining in his review.

Finally after the last student had fled, casting strange looks at the silent man in the back of his classroom, Arcas moved to the front of the lecture hall, an anxious Marshal barreling into the room as he moved.

"So, the buzz is that you have a red-haired boyfriend and you have dumped the tall black one... or that it's a threesome with some very impressive looking men. That's why you were walking funny earlier in the week."

"Don't they have anything better to do?" Thomas whimpered, before turning his attention to Arcas. "Where is he?"

"Do you care?" was the response.

"Of course I do," Thomas grumbled. "I was... I was in a bad headspace."

"And he was up and pacing most of the night. He has exhausted himself with pain and worry and that was even before he was called out to retrieve someone."

"Wait... he's out protecting someone?"

"Are you angry that he is not here?"

"No, I am concerned because you said he was exhausted."

"You're cute," Marshal interjected. "But not cute enough to get away with being an ass to my friend. Behave yourself."

"So you can defend one you call your brother yet I cannot defend one I call my own?"

"Didn't say that --" Marshal began, but Thomas stepped in between both of them and raised a hand.

"Time out. I was wrong and I want to apologize. I panicked for reasons that I have to offer only to Kern and if he forgives me, we'll go on from there."

The Bear looked at him curiously before he offered," You really mean that? You will give him a chance?"

"I have a bad past," Thomas explained. "It's no excuse for what I did, but it is a reason. I have to apologize to Kern and then hope I haven't screwed everything up. I really want to get to know the man better and...and I have to say that I'm not opposed to being his mate in full."

After that, it took almost no time for Thomas to gather his things from his office, and together all three men exited the building. Thomas had informed them that he was going to go back to *The Wild Hunt* and wait for his mate. They had a lot to discuss and he still owed the others an apology for his behavior.

Arcas, he informed them, was sent to see to their protection by Kern himself. He didn't want his mate alone and vulnerable with no protection at all.

Thomas felt even more like a heel after that discussion. He just wanted to get to his stag and explain about his past lover and how the whole ordeal left him very skittish, to use Kern's word for him.

"And not just for the safety it offers?"

"No." Thomas decided that he owed his mate's brother at least some explanation. "I can go back home if I want safety... There are people I can contact, powerful people who will help me. It's not for protection that I want him. I think... I think I have finally grown up and that I want to continue my maturity with someone who is, well, he's wonderful. I want to spend my time with someone wonderful like Kern. I never before knew what I had to lose with him until I jeopardized it all."

They were almost to the car they would all be taking back to *The Wild Hunt* when the first inkling that something was wrong hit Thomas.

He paused on his way to the car park and looked over his shoulder. He swore he could feel something staring between his shoulder blades, and he didn't like that feeling.

"Do you feel --"

"*Shhh.*" Arcas hushed him, pulling him behind his bulk as he went on the defensive. Marshal pressed close to his side. If he had fur, Marshal's scruff would be standing on end, so anxious did he look.

The attack came out of nowhere. Several people swarmed them in the afternoon sun, unconcerned with people passing by or any casual observers of the attack.

They came at them hard and fast, all wearing pendants that glowed while they swarmed Arcas, trying their best to separate them from the larger man.

"Fuck!" Thomas screamed, kicking out at one man who tried to get a grip on his arm, pulling him further away from his people.

Marshal was hissing, his hands striking out to slam into one man's nose while he spun around to gouge his fingers in another man's eyes.

Arcas was throwing powerful punches that sent his attackers sliding on their backs over asphalt and into parked cars, setting off alarms as they flew. There were at least four people lying at his feet and what looked to be seven or eight more coming for him.

Thomas kicked another man in the nuts, biting

back an evil smile as the man screamed in pain before swinging his messenger bag back into the face of another, feeling satisfied as he heard the crunch of bone that probably signaled that he had broken a nose. Good. The bastard deserved it. He moved closer to Marshal and Arcas when something slammed into his head, knocking him to his knees before he fell face forward into the dirt as darkness claimed him.

* * *

"Run!" Arcas commanded Marshal as he spun around to see Thomas go down.

"Fuck!" Marshal bellowed as he raced after the two men who were dragging an unconscious Thomas into a van that had screeched to a halt beside them. He tried to follow but another man got in his way, and by the time he knocked the brute off of him, Thomas was gone.

But the men with the strange pendants remained and they were loaded for bear… literally. Half a dozen more men had arrived and with them they brought glowing rods that made him feel nauseated just being near them. He tried to move in to help Arcas, but the man bellowed for him to get back.

"Get to The Hunt!" he shouted as the men piled on and his bear was lost to view.

Deciding that the man who had been dealing with these cultists, and it had to be cultists, knew what he was doing, Marshal raced toward Thomas's car, grateful that he had a set of keys to the damn thing.

He looked back once to see two men breaking off from Arcas's attack to follow him, but were stopped as, with a roar, the redhead threw himself at them, knocking them to the ground before the pile up of men covered Arcas once more.

"Shit, shit, shit…" Marshal cursed as he climbed

into his friend's car and peeled rubber out of the car park, racing for The Hunt.

He didn't know why there weren't a string of cops following him as he raced through the city streets, finally screeching into the underground parking lot at the club, ignoring the mechanical arm that tried to keep him out, ramming through the thing like he was the main character in an action flick, ignoring the alarms that were blaring in his wake.

He slammed the car into park and raced for the elevator, slamming the intercom button as he danced from foot to foot, trying not to cry.

"Marshal?" a voice called out and then security was surrounding him, shouting questions and demanding answers.

"They took him!" he screamed, holding back tears but barely. "They took him. They took Thomas!"

When hands grabbed him, he tried to fight back. A fist traveling towards his temple was the last thing he saw before darkness took him.

* * *

"You sure are anxious to get back," the man in the body-covering cloak teased him as Kern stepped into the circle he had drawn on the basement floor after he completed the last rune in white chalk.

"I have my reasons." Kern offered the man a smile before he gestured for him to enter the traveling ring with him.

"And do they have to do with the smell of a half-bond wafting from your person?" the man asked.

"You have no idea." Kern laughed a little. "I gave my little star some news yesterday and he didn't take it well. So today I am eager to get back and talk it out with him."

"And complete your bond?"

"As soon as you are taken to The Master and offered a place of safety, yes." Kern thought of his little Faunus and the look of devastation on his face, and knew that his past was not as easy and comfortable as Kern had assumed.

"The path of true love never ran smooth," the man spoke again as he stepped into the ring. "It's the reason why I am still seeking my one and true. I hope things work out for you, man."

"Thank you." Kern mustered up a smile for him. "Me too. He is so special and unique. I think if he turned me away I would pine for him for the rest of my days."

"Then fight for him," his traveler urged him. "And if I can help in any way, you just let me know. I understand my request pulled you from something important, but you are the only person that I could trust not to be leading me into a trap."

"And you are an old friend, Bran," Kern assured him. "And a trusted ally. Getting you to safety is important too, and I have my brothers looking after my mate. But I want to make it clear that when we get back to The Hunt, I'm going to abandon you and go after my Faunus. I need him more than I need air, so you will have to do introductions without me."

"Understood." Bran threw back his head and laughed, the hood of his cloak falling back to expose the various tattoos covering his person from his exposed neck and hands to the tops of his bare feet. "You have more important things to do than to hang around with old friends."

"You'll get along just fine." Kern laughed. "And when I introduce you to my little star, you will understand my haste and rudeness. He is so vulnerable and strong at the same time. He is a contradiction, a mixture of old world and new, with the most bright and sparking mind. I think I love him, Bran, and that is saying something."

"Well, I can't wait to meet this paragon, my friend. I am sure he is so special."

"That he is." Kern clapped his hands to activate his traveling circle and relaxed as the runes glowed as they should. "When you finally meet him, you'll understand what true greatness is, what power there is in gentleness, and my friend, you will understand why I would move heaven and earth to hold onto his love. I would do anything for my little star. Anything."

And Kern learned how those words would be tested the moment he stepped out of the circle with his new rescue and into the chaos that suddenly enveloped all who dwelled within *The Wild Hunt.*

The Wolf (Wild Hunt 2)
Paranormal Women's Fiction
Stephanie Burke

Caille knows the hearts of men, and she has been ripping them from their chests for centuries. Now, as a member of *The Wild Hunt*, she wants nothing more than to rip apart the men who dared steal one brother's mate and kidnap her other Hunt brother. Nothing and no one will stand in her way... even the curiously attractive new partner The Master of the Hunt has given her.

Bran the Blessed had been in a cave for what seemed like an eternity, growing back his body and learning about the new world with the aid of his companion crows. He relied on no one except his friend, Kern, who brought him out of his solitude and offered to introduce him to the new world. Problems arise when his friend's mate has been kidnapped by murderous cultists, leaving Kern unable to function. There is no way Bran, the once-powerful King of Wales could not assist with this hunt as a new Huntsman... and then there was Caille.

Instantly intrigued with each other, the two Huntsmen become pawns in a dangerous game where the elite go to satiate their darkest desires and where the cultists themselves hope to gain more power and influence. Vowing to protect this budding relationship, Bran will do anything he can to protect his new family, even if it means he became one of those who play with wolves.

Chapter One

"Kern. You -- your mate has been taken."

The words seem to slam into Kern with the weight of a ten-ton semi. As soon as the words left Manx's lips the world seemed to cease to exist for the Stag.

Bran watched as his friend turned ashen with the news, his head lowered as an anguished whine tore from his throat. Bran, The Raven, then watched as his friend's head snapped up while his eyes blazed bright fiery red.

"They took my mate?" The words roared from his throat as his fists clenched. All the veneer of humanity slid from his person like a duck heading to water. His hair snapped with an electricity and life all its own; the dark skin of his forehead split, and in an explosion of blood, his massive, fifty-point horns exploded from his forehead. The smell of animal musk and dry dust and vegetation filled the air, as did the sound of his pants ripping off his body as thick thighs swelled further, bursting free of the material that held them bound. Bran watched in horrified shock as Kern's human limbs transformed into thick, fur covered appendages of a stag.

"My mate! My little star!" he raged as his fingers curled into claws, and as he reared up to his full height, his horns, still dripping with blood and tissue, touched the ceiling. Several red-orange markings circled his eyes as his power pulsed and Bran was reminded, Raven that he may be, his friend Kern was a god.

"Calm --" Manx stepped forward, their arms outstretched in a soothing manner that Kern ignored as his gaze went from face to face in the room.

The cat-smelling one named Marshal was curled into a miserable ball on Manx's leather couch, his eyes wide and fearful. The really pretty wolf-blood was biting at her full lips, her blonde hair in disarray as if she had been running her fingers through it for quite some time. And Manx, dressed as they usually were in immaculate black, looked to be holding back anger of their own.

"No… calm…" Kern struggled to speak through a sudden and dangerous looking mouth full of fangs. Then he began to speak in a language so old that even Bran couldn't take his meaning. The sometimes hissing, sometimes guttural words were dark and nasty as they invoked fear even in Bran, someone who had faced death by decapitation, and were sounds that no human throat could replicate.

Kern's eyes tracked wildly across the room for a moment before he took a step toward the chalk portaging circle that still faintly glowed with the magic that Kern had invoked to get them to *The Wild Hunt*.

"No." Manx boldly stepped in front of the behemoth that The Stag had become, unafraid and their voice ringing with authority. "You will not go tearing through this city hunting for him. That would destroy all the work we have done to keep ourselves hidden from humanity."

Kern spit out a few more strings of sound masquerading as ancient words before he tried to push past Manx, but the master of *The Wild Hunt* was not having it. They snapped their fingers and an eerie red glow surrounded Kern.

He spun around, fresh anger and betrayal dancing across his face before he collapsed into a gigantic heap of flesh, fur, and horns on the ground.

"Fuck," Manx spat out, standing in the middle of

the room, looking up at the heavens as their fists clenched in rage at their side. They stayed standing there for a moment before they began to visibly calm. One by one, their major muscle groups began to loosen, starting from their bare feet and traveling upwards until a placid look came over their face. Then more gently, "Fuck."

Gracefully spinning toward their fallen subordinate, Manx squatted and easily lifted what had to be the tremendous amount of weight of The Stag before they easily began to carry him down a darkened hallway, after shooting them all a look that said not to move even as no words passed through their lips.

"So, I am Bran." The Raven spoke in the uncomfortable silence that fell as Manx exited the room, carrying Kern like he was an injured child. "I agreed to become the newest member of the Hunt."

"Bran," the Wolf muttered, her eyes flaring gold for a moment before they settled into a rich amber color. They were beautiful.

"That I am." He offered her a nod before turning to stare at the battered looking man on the couch. "And I am at your service."

Tearing his eyes away from the man who smelled distinctively of cat and sand, he faced the wolf again, noting that she had moved a bit closer while he observed the other man.

She was beautiful. Her hair was a wild swirl of blondes, golds, and silvers leading him to believe that she would be a silver-white wolf. Her skin was tanned and her eyes were that searing amber that resembled heated steel on a blacksmith's anvil before he pounded out the shape of a sword.

Using a weapon to describe her was good because she moved like a warrior, each step of her bare foot precise as she moved closer to him.

"You come at a rough time, Bran," she said after cocking her head to the side and staring at him, apparently evaluating him as a magical creature and a man. "We may not give you time to grow acquainted with our little family before we have a serious problem to deal with."

"From what I gathered, someone attacked and has stolen the mate that Kern is so in love with. Who is that much of an idiot?"

"The Cult of Dagna the Fifteenth." The Wolf spat the name like it was poison.

"They are still around?" Bran asked, his own head cocked to the side as his gaze traveled from person to person in the room.

"And they have grown in power," she admitted before taking a seat next to the cat.

"After all these years?"

"It's humanity," the Wolf snarled. "They have lost faith and therefore seek to replace true belief with whatever false god promises to give them more of what they want."

"The faster the better." Bran sighed, shaking his head as he thought of human societies and how they developed. "I could not foresee any of this happening when I let my head be placed on a pike to protect the land that I loved."

"Your head on a pike?" The Cat seemed to pull himself out of his doldrums to sit up and stare at him. "They put your head on a pike?"

"Uh." Bran chuckled softly, holding back an embarrassed caw that wanted to escape from his throat.

"You are Bran the Blessed?"

"You know of me?" Bran let out a small grin as

he moved closer to the Cat.

"Thomas... My... Thomas was an expert in ancient mythologies and he once told me of Bran the Blessed who rode to save his sister from an abusive Irish king."

"Something like that," he agreed. "But I wasn't a giant, I didn't lay my body down so that my men could cross over it to get to the castle where Branwen and my nephew were being kept, and I sure as hell didn't let those bastards build me a house so that they could stack a hundred enemy soldiers inside hidden in flour sacks. I have no idea how history gets this stuff twisted."

"So you didn't --" The Cat began again and Bran, after rolling his eyes at the ludicrous lies being told on his behalf, began to explain.

"Branwen was married to an Irish bastard of a minor king named Matholwch. That is true enough. And our half-brother Efnisien fab Euroswydd did take exception to not being able to play big brother and make Matholwch jump through hoops to take her hand, so he got drunk and acted the ass and killed some of the Irish bastard's horses. I made amends and made Efnisien apologize and that was that. But bad blood will always out and after Branwen gave birth to my nephew, her lord began to harm her at the behest of his advisors. I think they wanted a way to placate their hurt little feelings because I didn't bow and scrape to them over something as minor as an insult when the marriage between Branwen and that bastard would have united two kingdoms. I think they wanted to rule it all and my nephew Gwern was in their way. At least if they started a war and the two of us kings murdered each other they could turn my nephew into a puppet and rule through him."

"That seems... very human." The Cat nodded. "And that is the meat and bones of the tale, though in Thomas' explanation it gets wilder."

"That is one way of looking at it. Long story short --"

Bran ignored the Wolf's call of "too late," and continued with his explanation.

"My sister got word to me that she was being abused, forced to work like a scullery maid, having servants lay their hands upon her, being separated from her son..."

As he spoke, Bran's accent became something more decidedly Welsh in his diction and pronunciation. The whites of his eyes dimmed into an ominous gray and his voice dropped a few octaves in tone.

"They were waiting for us. The advisors to that idiot king knew that we were coming and fired on us as we approached the coast. The whole bridge thing? I captained my own ship and I ordered the other captains to follow my lead as we positioned our vessels in such a way that our army could cross over them to reach land. It was effective because they did not expect such cunning from a Welsh king."

"So you never said, 'The man who would lead his people must first become a bridge'?"

"Oh, I said it." Bran's gaze zeroed in on the Cat's. "And I meant it with every breath of my being. And me owning a magical cauldron that held power over life and death." His chuckle was nasty. "Why in the hell would I give something like that away? Power over life and death? So much bullshit."

"So." The Cat seemed to get more comfortable with his presence, even moving a bit further away from the Wolf and closer to him. "That didn't happen?"

"No, what happened was that I brought my idiot half-brother along with me to put the fear of the elder gods into that Irish bastard. And the day was won. But that drunken idiot Efnisien knocked little Gwern into a barn fire that was set to celebrate our victory and I wound up having to call on the elder gods for protection as the death of an innocent stripped away all the favor the gods handed to me. In a bid to save my lands, I offered myself up, but I wasn't an innocent, so my life didn't equate. Therefore I offered up the promise of pain and torment as a sacrifice and my soul, as dented and stained as it was, was accepted. My head was lopped from my body and I was kept alive so I could feel all the agony of a true death without actually dying. My head was placed upon a pike and what was left of my soul was used to keep invaders away from my lands so long as people remembered me and my sacrifice."

"That is not the story I was told, the one that the world knows." Bran relaxed as he saw the curiosity in the Cat beat out over his worry and fear.

"Well, this is the true story. I was placed so that I could watch the land shift and sway with the passage of time. People worshipped me, my sacrifice, and the elder gods until I developed into a minor god of my own. Having your head placed on a pike on top of White Tower for centuries... overlooking your lands with nothing but the ravens for company, watching as your people change and forget about you, watching how the invaders eventually took over and my people were bred out or integrated until you discover that your sacrifices were pointless. Yeah, I think that is what the elder gods wanted me to learn."

"But you have a body --"

"I grew one. They saw fit to eventually bury my body though my raven friends marked my own sacrifice by staying where my head had once been piked. I took in their wisdom and offered my protection to them as the need for me decreased. I became their god and I protected them and in return they willed me to have the life that I once sacrificed for a nation who forgot about me -- except for trite children's stories to make them behave at night. *King Bran is watching so you better behave.*" He shook his head, as if disgusted with the whole idea. "Anyway, over the generations, I changed and regrew a body to match the head. The Ravens kept me abreast of what was going on in the world and kept me hidden until I felt the need to become useful once more."

"And Kern is your friend?" the Wolf asked and Bran felt his interest pique at the sound of soothing tones. "If you were hidden --"

"Kern is the god of travelers." Bran gave her a small smile. "He stumbled upon me, naked in a cave and speaking to my ravens. He was loath to leave me there alone so he brought me clothing and information about this new world, and told me when I was ready to strike out across this new frontier he would come and get me. After listening to his stories, I knew that when I was ready to become part of something bigger I would pledge my loyalty to The Manx."

"And he went to get you and his mate disappeared." The Wolf didn't hold back any punches when she added, "How can you help us now?"

"In any way I can," he answered honestly, because he was sure that only honesty would work with this particular creature.

"That's good." The rich tones of the Manx caught them all off guard because everyone in the room jumped when their voice seemed to come out of nowhere.

Bran blinked because he was positioned on his seat in such a way that he could observe that hall that the Manx disappeared down with his friend, and he sure as hell hadn't seen them walk in.

"Because?" he asked, rising to his feet. In the face of such power, an outsider just didn't sit in disrespect.

"Because I don't have time to dance around on ceremony here. Kern is in a state that I have never seen in my centuries of knowing him. It took my strongest magics to quell the hunger in him that will lead him to murder anyone and everyone until the return of his mate."

"Can he…" Bran mentally stumbled a bit, his mind tripping over the idea that his friend, the gentle giant that had taught him new languages and brought him what he considered the most important news of this modern century, could go around murdering people.

"He can control animals and travel, amongst other things, Bran the Blessed. His instincts drive him to protect his mate and that is all he can see now. So yes, I can see him calling upon his animal subjects and having them run amuck in this city, destroying all in his path to achieve what he wants."

"So if he started killing off cult members, they will bring his mate back?" Bran asked, hopefully, and then deflated as the Manx shot him a dark look.

"One cannot slaughter humans in this day and age, Bran the Blessed. Though there are no protections for humanity in the contract I am forced to operate within the confines of, the attack and death of so many humans would bring their authorities down upon our heads."

"But we can kill the cultists?"

"To the last one because of this breach." Manx's grin was, if anything, more terrifying than the sight of Kern losing control.

"Even though it's not a complete bond?" the Wolf asked, excitement making her rise to her feet.

"A partial mark is still a mark," Manx assured her and then turned once more to Bran. "And now, if you will accept my mastership over you, I can put you to work. What say you, Bran the Blessed? Do you come under my will and serve me as you would your elder god, forsaking all others but me?"

Bran looked at the creature that stood before him, radiating such menace and power. Could he find himself giving everything he worked so hard to achieve over the centuries over to one such as him?

Then he thought of the way the Manx stopped and controlled his friend. There was enough power in the creature to destroy Kern, this he knew and felt. Yet the Manx had incapacitated him, stopping his rightful vengeance in a way that did him no harm and was now actively trying to find a missing mate that wasn't even fully bonded to one of his subordinates. Could he follow such a creature?

He looked to the Wolf and saw no fear in her eyes or in her actions as she casually walked over to the dark-haired creature and wrapped an arm around their waist, snuggling into them for a moment before pulling away and observing Bran, looking like a pale twin to her master in the way they both observed him.

Even the cat, who was not magically marked as belonging to the Hunt at all, was looking to the Manx with no fear and a lot of hope in his eyes.

What kind of powerful being had such control over people while not exerting any force upon them at all? It could be that they were the kind of creature who saw the world the way he once did, as a place that was dangerous to those he cared for so he had better give all to protect them.

That was a kind of being he could follow.

"I will serve you." Bran nodded his head and dropped to one knee. "I will follow where you follow, your enemies will be my enemies, I will fight at your side or at your behest, carrying you banner with pride and dignity. This I swear."

"Good enough. Raise your head." The Manx of the Moddey Dhoo nodded to him, and Bran felt a flash of heat as it felt like something imprinted itself inside of his skull before he felt a wash of energy rush over him.

He blinked several times as his vision beheld gold, just for a moment, before he looked around the room with new eyes. He could feel the power emanating from the Wolf, suddenly knew how dangerous that petite looking woman was, felt the age and energy within that beautiful body. He could see the spatter of blood from many a human that covered her, hidden from view from all but those who had enough power and intelligence to see. She was not to be trifled with.

He turned to the Cat and could see that, although not marked by the Manx, there was some ancient protections surrounding him. It wouldn't be long before that male pledged his loyalty as well, even though he had no great power about him.

He looked down at his hands and then back to Manx where he could see the gold and black bands of light that connected him to the immense well of untapped power that existed within the creature, the lover of a goddess.

After all of his rapid observations and the sheer might of the benevolent creature that stood before him, there was only one thing left for him to say.

"How may I serve?"

Chapter Two

"I hate people! Fuck!" Thomas threw back his head and screamed his anger to the world in garbled words as he realized he was stuck in someone's idea of a fucking jail cell that felt like it was underground.

There was no sun, minimal light, and it felt like the ass end of someone's cold root cellar. He was still dressed. That was reassuring, but someone had made off with his socks and shoes. When he rolled from the thin mattress someone had tossed to the floor and finally gained his feet, it felt like the stone floor tiles was sucking all the heat from his body.

He was not steady and he hated that feeling; the world was spinning around him. He could barely stand. His vision was soft and hazy and his head... He could think clearly, but that was about as far as it went for lucidity. He tried to speak but his mouth wouldn't work and he had never been so thirsty in his life. He obviously had been drugged because that was the only explanation for how dry his mouth was and how scattered his thoughts were.

With the echoes of his scream echoing in his head, he collapsed back into the bed, his hands going instinctively to his stomach as he curled up into a little ball of misery.

It had to be the cultists, he thought as his hands began to shake. They had gotten to him. He had been warned and his dumb ass had let his fears grab ahold of him for too long.

As his lay there and contemplated his foolishness, the maybe baby in his stomach, the memories of his brother fighting the horde of tattooed men who had snatched him from the campus parking lot... Arcas...

Fuck, Arcas! He rose to his feet as fast as he could and stumbled his way to the thick steel door that led to his prison. Was Arcas still around? Had they killed him? Was he there somewhere?

He remembered a blow to the back of his head, being pulled into a van, his consciousness fading in and out... Arcas still fighting.

Thomas ran his trembling hands over the door, noting that it didn't have a doorknob and was cold to the touch as the damn floor. He had to be underground. He pounded on the door weakly to the beat that was pounding in his head, and the sound of those hits just echoed around him, breaking the uncomfortable silence with the realization that he was essentially alone, underground, and very much taken.

Even in his worst nightmares, he had never contemplated anything like this happening to him. Kern had warned him, but he was too angry, too scared, too busy comparing the man that cared so much for him to the man who had just used him... He had taken too long to pull his head from his ass and this was the result.

He stopped his futile assault on the door as his balance gave out and he slid down the cold steel door until his ass hit the equally cold hard ground. He was trapped and he couldn't get out and they were going to sacrifice him and maybe he was with child and...

The thoughts swirled around his mind, more questions and no answers, until he could no longer keep his tenacious hold on his consciousness and he softly drifted into the comforting darkness once again.

* * *

Caille stared at the interesting man who strode beside her through the police tape and refuse the humans left in the parking lot where the Cat had informed them Thomas's abduction had taken place.

He was dressed in a long, black, sleeved duster that immediately set him apart from all the people still milling around as the sun began to set on another hot summer day. His hair was short and artfully styled so that he maintained a very attractive bed head look that she had seen with some of their more affluent clients. He was sporting a heavy five o'clock shadow that only brought attention to his solid, square jaw and the cute dimple in his chin. His ice-blue eyes were the color of the sea just before a storm hit and were framed by thick dark eyebrows and long lashes that made him look like he should be strutting down a runway instead of stalking around a crime scene in the growing dark of dusk.

He was wearing loose harem pants made of linen, and the dark leather sandals on his feet looked partially Romanesque as their laces climbed up muscular calves and tied just below his knees. He really stood out in a crowd. Caille the Wolf didn't know if that was a good or bad thing.

"Can you pick up anything?" he asked, his voice sounding rough and harsh while still carrying a distinctive Welsh lilt. "I don't really know what I'm looking for."

"Well, Arcas was here." Caille turned her head back to the crime scene and inhaled deeply, pulling in the scents of metal and exhaust, the stench of sweating people, the stale smell of perfume and deodorant, and underneath that, the wild scent of humanity. She moved around the lot, her mouth open taking in small puffs of air as she moved. She stopped suddenly, her head jerking to the left as she caught more of her Hunt Brother's scent.

Automatically, she moved in the direction that

was a bit farther from where the main scuffle had taken place, the small hairs on her arms and the back of her neck standing on end. There was blood.

It was just a few drops but it was enough to garner her attention. Caille moved over to the spots, only about three drops, but it was a scent that didn't really belong on the ground on this filthy parking lot. Her brother was injured.

She knelt down and touched them, feeling the energy and power in those few drops. In order for them to take him down, they had to have something magical and dangerous to those like her.

"Arcas?"

She looked up at the man, Bran, beside her, noting that he was paying close attention to her actions.

"Yes, and the scent trail stops here."

"Could it be that they have him and Kern's mate in the same location?"

"Not if they are smart." Caille rose to her feet, her gaze traveling around the lot before she focused in on the ice-blue gaze of the man named Bran. "We can track Arcas, and if he is being held where they are holding Thomas, we can easily find him."

"You fear he is dead?"

"Not dead," Caille declared, baring her fangs a little at the new guy. "If he were dead, we would all know. The Manx's magic would snap in an indefinable way. You will learn this as their magic adjusts in your body."

"Apologies." He offered her a short bow. "I fear that I'm going to have a steep learning curve when it comes to *The Wild Hunt*."

"You'll learn." She offered him a nod as she moved about the area, still drawing in scents.

"What can you smell now?" Bran asked as he quietly followed her. He moved with the grace and economy of motion like the warrior king he once was.

"Fear. I can smell Thomas' fear and how he fought to get away from his captors. I can smell Marshal --"

"The Cat?"

"Yes. I can smell him, his blood and sweat, how he fought before he was compelled to run away for help."

"I am guessing that your Arcas didn't want him captured?"

"No, then they would have the ability to drain two lives instead of one. Plus, from what Marshal says, Arcas wanted us to know what happened here. So the little Cat did what cats do best. He evaded and escaped back to us. Caused quite a stir too, driving through barriers and demanding attention."

"I can imagine."

Caille turned to stare at him at that point, eyes a bit narrowed. "I doubt that you can. You can try but until you form a deep bond with us, like the bond that Arcas, Kern, and I share, you cannot imagine the horrors that we felt, feeling the distress in our bond, knowing that the mate of one of our own was taken and why. You can't imagine that terror, Bran."

Wisely, the man said nothing though Caille felt that she has ruffled his feathers a bit, so to speak. Well, he did carry the overall wild scent of cold air and petrichor, the scent of freedom and of the ravens who'd made him their god, if his words were to be believed.

"Anyway, unlike in the movies, I can't scent the make and model of the van they used. It smells of hot metal and exhaust, just like a million other vehicles that drive through the streets. The fact that Arcas' scent disappears tells me that they took him as well, but probably did not keep him. They are already in clear breach of the contracted truce, and killing a member of the Hunt would bring the wrath of Manx down upon their heads."

"But not Thomas?"

"He didn't accept the mark of protection, and though he has a partial bond with Kern, it was not completed. If the bond had been completed, the protection would automatically transfer to Thomas as well as any of their offspring that may form of their union."

"So, we can assume that they took Arcas someplace after rendering him unconscious and dumped him."

"Their excuse would be that he interfered in their pick up." Caille snorted. "They fall back on that excuse a lot. They didn't know, they feared for their lives, they didn't understand why they were under attack. They've done it to other collectors that Manx marked to bring in, those who want protection, but this is the first time they attacked one of us."

"And you are a big deal in the magical community?"

"*We* are a big deal," she reminded him, again flashing fang at him, watching as he flushed a little in... she inhaled deeply... pleasure. That made something warm settle in the pit of her stomach despite the fear and anger she was doing her best to keep repressed.

"We." He nodded, offering her a small smile before his head jerked to the side in a very avian manner. "And I think we are being watched."

Caille turned her head in the direction he was

looking, her eyes narrowing as she tried to divine what Bran was talking about.

"Red shirt, khaki shorts, glaring at us from under a baseball cap. Almost suspicious as is the lack of security here now and when the attack took place."

"He's just glaring?" Caille asked. She was ready to rush the little asshole if Bran could give her even the smallest reason to.

"He was in the security booth and not in uniform. He has been tracking our movements since we arrived and you started walking the scene."

"Circumstantial."

"This I know," he offered, then hummed under his breath softly.

Caille didn't know what he had done but the feel of magic pouring off of him was powerful. Out of the corner of her eye, she caught a flash of black that swooped in and perched on a nearby power line.

"I called in a little help. My buddy there will follow the man in red and report back to me where he goes and when. It may not be a lot but I hope it is some small help as we are stymied here for the moment."

"I concede your points." Caille turned to face him fully. "They know who I am and probably are puzzled as to who you are. He may follow us and not lead us anywhere, you know. Probably documenting everything about you at the moment."

"True. But even if he follows us, he has to report back to someone, right?"

"And your little friend can hear anything he reports by phone?"

"He can, plus he has wonderful eyesight which means he can see and remember anything the man texts. Like I said, it's not much as we are flying blind here, but it is a step."

"Okay," Caille agreed. "And we are getting nowhere fast here."

"By the way, did you get a reason for no security being here?"

"From what Manx has gathered from our contacts on the police force, the guard suddenly took ill and had to leave. There was fifteen minutes when the lot wasn't being watched by human eyes and that is when they struck."

"Security cameras?" Bran asked as Caille motioned him to follow her.

"Caught Arcas and his charges moving into the lot and then it all went blank."

"And the witnesses?"

"Those who would speak to the cops?" Caille snorted. "Police are not really considered trustworthy these days and most people just pretend shit like this didn't happen. If it didn't affect them in some way, a lot of people turn and walk away... or record it and put it up on social media and bypass the police altogether."

"And have any such videos popped up?"

"Marshal is looking into that." They exited the parking lot and slowly moved toward the car they arrived in, ignoring the man in red who was quietly shadowing them. Bran had a good eye, she decided, for picking him out. "The poor Cat needed something to do as he was driving himself crazy with guilt for not being able to help his friend."

"They were close? The Cat and Kern's mate?"

"Like brothers," Caille confirmed. "Like the Hunt, family not by blood but by choice."

"And he is fairly magical?"

"Thomas?" she asked and he nodded.

"He is pure magic, a pure Faunis, but you know

the problem with that, right?"

"No real defensive magic. If I remember correctly the Faunis race on the whole are artisans whose only real magic involves disguising themselves and their clan, fertility, and the ability to take on human form."

"And Thomas was from one of the oldest clans, in exile if you will. There is a lot of power in a purebred magical creature, unlike most of their targets whose magic has been watered down by the inclusion of human blood in their bloodlines."

"So more bang for your buck, so to speak." Bran winced a little as Caille and he arrived at the car they came in and Caille disengaged the locks. He would never get used to this modern way of travel. "They get a big boost of magic to do whatever they want for all the hassle of taking a magical creature with partial magic."

"What they do," Caille informed him as she slid behind the wheel , "is sacrifice innocent beings in an effort to bring back a power hungry, idiot descendent of the goddess Danu who started murdering people to draw in their magic so that he could have the power to control the weather."

"And they want to bring him back, why?" Bran asked as he slid into the passenger seat and slammed the door. "And the man in red is taking down the tag number. He's in a car about three cars behind us. My raven is watching."

"Good. Let him tail us." Caille decided right then and there to visit a local bondage shop and see if the little spy would follow. "And I guess his followers wanted the power he promised, so boom, a cult is made. And that desire for power was passed down by the original idiots who worshiped him and then on and then on until we have these cultists who are worshipping a man who wanted to make it foggy or rainy on a whim. I have no idea what they think they are going to get out of following a many-centuries-dead asshole, but here we are. Those fanatics are murdering people to suck out their power to feed into a well that is supposed to bring Dagna the Fifteenth back to life."

"It sounds really stupid when you put it that way," Bran conceded as Caille started the engine and proceeded to lead their spy on a merry little chase.

"They have made a religion out of killing people. And when the bad guy feels that he is right, that he is correcting some horrible injustices and that his actions are righteous --"

"It's damn hard to make them see reason."

"Agreed." Caille smiled as she stopped for a yellow light, making sure that the spy was keeping close. "And these cultists don't seem to have reason or common sense. They just blindly follow, ignoring the blood on their hands and the disasters they leave behind."

"Which makes them extra dangerous."

"And quite easy to fluster as they feel that anything and anyone not for the glory and honor of their false god are heathens. Which means that just about everything we do offends them." Caille knew her smile was growing quite evil and liked that Bran returned her look with a smirk of his own. "So, wanna rustle some feathers?" She giggled.

"Oh this sounds like fun," he replied, his head tilting to the side... very birdlike... and he waited for her to explain.

"I'm in the mood for some shopping. And if he has to follow us and report what we are doing..."

"We can fluster him into making some serious

mistakes. That sounds like a lot of fun."

"Stick with me, my innocent little boy." Caille laughed at his indignant squawk at the word innocent. "I'm going to teach you what *The Wild Hunt* is all about."

"I thought it was about protecting magical creatures."

"Oh, as *The Wild Hunt*, that is our main goal. But *The Wild Hunt* the private social club? That's a whole different animal."

"Really?" He almost seemed most eager as he grinned at her.

"Oh yeah, really. And I think it's time we outfitted you properly."

"A uniform?"

"Leather." She grinned back at him. "I'm thinking lots of leather."

Chapter Three

The shop Caille took him to was unlike anyplace he had entered since he regained a fully functioning body. It looked like an exclusive leather shop and a torture chamber had had torrid sex, and produced The Run and Hide.

He was idly poking at a leather helmet that was shaped like a horse's head when the most interesting person he had ever laid eyes upon walked over to them and grabbed Caille's hands, adding to a fascinating explanation about Pony Play and where that horse's tail on something called a butt plug was supposed to fit. Not that he couldn't figure it out with a name like a butt plug.

"Good evening, gentle folk." The person gave them a bow and Bran watched as silky-looking green and purple hair flowed over their shoulders. When they rose to their full height, Bran could count no fewer than five piercings on their face alone. There was one in each eyebrow, one in their left nostril, and two placed under their bottom lip so that the large metal half circles embedded there made the piercings looked like a goat's beard.

They smiled at them, their solid black eyes taking in the slightly confused look that Bran could feel on his face to the smirk that Caille was wearing on hers and Bran knew that he was in for trouble.

"Good evening... Sir?" Bran questioned softly. So many things had changed in society since he'd his head lopped off that he sometimes felt like he was navigating rough, rock-filled water just to greet someone. Besides, this person was wearing a waist pinching corset of bright green leather than matched their hair. They were wearing thigh-high, high heeled boots in unrivaled black that had to give him an extra five inches of lift from the look of them. There was a strange dress shirt in black under the corset that made their shoulders seem wider than they were but also aided in the hourglass shape they had going on. Covering their bits was one of the tiniest pairs of shorts he had ever beheld on a person. Between the boots and the bottom legs of the shorts was a flash of about an inch or two flash of ink-covered thigh. Their eyebrows were arched and the delicate beauty of their makeup added shadows and highlights until their face looked to be reshaped by the artistry. Their full red lips curved up into a close-lipped smile and two highly arched eyebrows went up as Bran rose upright from his small bow.

"Sir is fine," the slim young man reassured him with a smile that now showed a set of fangs one of his hunting hounds would have envied. Bran examined the pierced salesperson carefully but couldn't detect any signs of magic.

"Thank you." He offered a small smile in return. "I really didn't want to assume and cause friction between us when we've just met."

"Ohh, Caille." The painted man turned to her. "I like this pet. It has manners."

"He," Bran corrected, having the distinct feeling that he was being kindly mocked but not really understanding how.

"I really didn't want to assume," the most interesting young man returned, and Caille broke out into snickers.

"Don't be mean, Fang," Caille lightly chastised once she got her amusement under control. "I brought him here for you to work your magic."

"Really?" the painted man, Fang, asked. "You

got yourself a new playmate. It's been years, Madam, and I wondered if you would ever find a person suitable for your needs."

"Excuse me?" Bran's gaze traveled from Caille to Fang and then back again. "Playmate?"

"No, Fang," she corrected. "Bran here is not my lover."

Right now Bran wanted to add but barely resisted the urge to speak. Caille was someone who was really doing it for him in all the right ways. She was competent at her job, quick on her feet, and from what he could smell, a very mature wolf-shifter. There was the feel of ancient power around her but unlike The Manx's or Kern's magic, it didn't feel like a blunt object to the face if you weren't prepared for it. He had been told he had a similar energy about him so he had made it his duty to hold back any expression of his own magic. He knew that he was ancient, considered a god by many, and he didn't want to crush any magical being who knew of him under the weight of Bran's personal energies.

"Pity," Fang jokingly complained. "From the way he was staring at that butt plug, I had just assumed that he was into some serious pegging from you."

"As fun as that would be" -- Caille giggled darkly --"not this time."

"What is pegging?" Bran's question sent them letting out loud peals of laughter as he interrupted the two.

"I'll explain later, darling," she cooed at him, and Bran felt a blush highlight his cheeks as he realized that he had indeed been eyeballing the butt plug out of curiosity. Then to Fang, she said with a sly grin, "He's the newest Huntsman."

"Really?" Now Fang took a step back and examined him carefully from his sandaled feet to the tips of his short fluffy black hair. "He doesn't give off the feel of a top."

"Because he's not." Caille's voice abruptly turned dark and commanding and Bran assumed time for pleasantries had passed.

"Madam." Fang's amusement disappeared and a subservient expression settled on his face.

"You think that in order to qualify as a Huntsman you have to be a dominant?" she questioned, taking a step closer to Fang. "Because I can assure you that is not the case. In order to be a Huntsman you have to maintain control, self-awareness, and be extreme in every measure when it comes to sexuality. The Raven here more than qualifies on each account." She turned her gaze to Bran who quickly nodded to whatever she was talking about. He knew she would explain when they exited the shop but for now, she wanted him to behave like a good partner and play along.

"No, Madam," Fang was quick to assure her as his gaze traveled over Bran once more. "You are correct and I humbly apologize for my words and any disquiet they have caused."

"Then get him outfitted." She casually turned toward the front of the large dimly lit store as a soft chime let them know that someone had entered the shop. "I want him in black and platinum from head to toe."

"Yes, Madam." Fang's stance relaxed a bit and Bran realized that the man hadn't even fully raised his head to address Caille. He was beginning to understand what she meant by dominance. It was clearly a power play that would leave him below her in status, under anyone deemed more powerful in a sexual nature. That sounded like *The Wild Hunt* from what Kern had explained. Looks like his reputation was going to be the submissive Huntsman. Strangely, he was very much okay with that if Caille would put that dark edge in her voice while they fucked. If… if, he meant to think, if they fucked.

There was something about this place, or maybe it had been because of the amount of time had passed since he had someone warm and wiggling underneath him, that had him fighting to maintain control over his growing erection.

"In that case, may I see what I'm working with?" Fang questioned lightly and Caille got an absolutely deviously evil look on her eyes.

"Why don't you take off your shirt, Bran?" Caille commanded, because no matter how nicely it was put, it was a command. That sent a warm flow of heat through his veins and almost made him forget that they were here for a job. The front door chimed again and this time the person they were waiting for ambled in, looking stuck between appalled and enthralled.

He noted that Caille looked like the cat that had gotten the cream from the pleased expression she was wearing now that their plan seemed to be working out just fine.

Trusting his partner to do her duty, he let his duster fall from his body to pool at his feet as he fully exposed the tunic he was wearing. The black linen garment had been a present from Kern and the silver-blue runes embroidered along the collar and hem were words that declared his greatness and his power. This was carefully pulled off, nearly reverently folded, and draped over one arm.

He turned to Fang and watched as a red flush

filled the other one's face as the young lad licked his lips at what he saw.

Bran knew he was attractive and that his body looked to be fit and strong. There was a light dusting of dark hair on his chest, and his nipples were so red they looked rouged. His musculature was not what he had when he was an active warrior king, but he was still sharply defined and as the kids said now, swole. He watched as Fang's gaze traveled down his body to stare at the waistband of his low-slung pants before they traveled up again to stop at his neck.

Ah, his neck. This was where he had some work done. When his body was finally resurrected, it came with a stark reminder of what he had sacrificed to keep his people safe. There was a thin dark band that encircled his neck that expertly mimicked the marks left when the ax parted his head from his body.

Even though his fellows had complied with his wishes, he would never forget the fear that filled him as his friends... no, as his brothers, had placed his dying body upon the chopping block and let the ax fall.

No, now was not the time for those dark thoughts, he reminded himself. Now was the time to rejoice in the tattoo that disguised the mark left upon his neck. The lines that marked his death had been replaced with the most delicate and beautiful Celtic runes that he had ever beheld. They were intricate and almost ethereal. The line that marked his decapitation had been so delicate, thanks in part to the sharpness of his fellow's blade, that it appeared as if it had been deliberately placed there as part of the design. And the runes themselves, he could feel them pulse with a power of their own. They had been placed there by a very talented Fae tattoo artist that Kern had been able to find. It was painful, but not as painful as getting run through with a sword by your abusive and malevolent in-laws.

Bran shook off his musings as he heard footsteps move closer. The trap had been set and it looked like their curious prey was moving in to take the bait.

"A chest harness," Fang decided, drawing Bran's attention back to the small, quiet man. "Yes, a chest harness that crosses over his chest yet leaves his well-developed pecs exposed. And those nipples..." Fang let his words trail off for a moment before turning his eyes to Caille. "Maybe he should consider getting them pierced?"

"They are stand-out features," Caille mused and Bran almost rolled his eyes at her questioning tone. There was amusement there too but instead of being embarrassed by the whole thing, Bran began to preen, sticking his chest out to emphasize his developed pecs and tossing his hair in a regal manner. This was almost too fun and he got a jolt of arousal at his own actions that went straight to his cock. Caille was looking and she was delighted at what she saw.

"Indeed." Fang nodded once before turning back to Bran. "Raven, you say? So all of his equipment should be raven-black."

"Indeed," Caille agreed before spinning around to the man who had cautiously stepped ever closer to him. "What do you think?" she asked, turning to the man who jumped a little at being suddenly addressed.

Yes, it was the same man who had been stalking them since they left the parking lot where the abduction has taken place. He looked a little shocked at being spoken to directly but he manfully moved closer, his eyes on Bran's chest like it was an object made for worship.

"Me?" he cautiously asked.

"You." Caille smiled at him and the tension in his shoulders relaxed a little. "I need an outside opinion. Do you think a black harness would do him justice? He is so pale that it will stand out a lot and I don't know if that's a good thing or a bad thing. A third opinion would be welcome."

"Uh," the man stuttered before he stepped close enough that even Bran, with his senses just a little higher that a baseline human, could smell his arousal. "I think red or brown would detract from his natural beauty."

"You hear that, Bran?" Caille giggled softly. To him it sounded menacing but Bran understood what their hastily thrown together plan was all about. To their stalker it must have sounded like agreement because he relaxed fully and stepped in front of Bran. "You have natural beauty."

For his part, Bran used the attraction he was feeling for Caille and turned it toward the man in question. He let his gaze roam over this body as if he could see beneath his clothing, letting his eyes linger for a moment on his crotch, before looking up into his eyes.

There was some intelligence there so Bran knew he had to play this perfectly to get close enough to complete his objective.

"So," he purred, preening a bit. "You think I'm beautiful."

"Uh." The man cleared his throat. "Yes, you're beautiful and I think you know it."

Bran permitted a smile to pull at his lips as he allowed his gaze to linger on the man's face, memorizing his features, before he turned back to Caille. "He said I'm beautiful."

"And you know it, you tease." Caille showed her

amusement.

"Black is perfect," the man continued, seemingly unable to take his eyes away from Bran. "And not just plain black. If he were mine I would use the leather that's embossed with a feather print. I heard you call him Raven and I think that would be pretty."

"I just happen to have a chest harness with a feather pattern," Fang contributed to the conversation. "I have a host of animal prints and embossed leather. Mostly because a lot of people in the lifestyle know that our shop caters to *The Wild Hunt* crowd. They like nothing more than to dress to impress, and leather is a good way to grab the attention of those closest to The Hunt."

"Really?" Caille laughed. "Do they really think that The Hunt can see animal print embossing from where we sit high on the stage? From where they sit, in the dim club no less, I bet that they can barely make out faces, let alone what they have stamped into their leather goods."

"Please don't let that get out, Madam." Fang gave her a deliberate flirty wink. "That would probably cut our sales in leather goods in half."

Even Raven had to chuckle a little at that before he turned his full attention to the man. "Feathers, you say?"

"Feathers," the man almost breathlessly repeated. "Yeah, feathers would look really nice even if you can't see them from afar. It would be something that's just for you and the one who tops you."

As he spoke, the man moved even closer, almost closer than what social niceties would allow, or so Bran had been led to believe by those who helped integrate him into these modern times.

"Back off, Romeo," Caille snapped, jerking the

man out of the daze he appeared to be in and making him jump back, a blush staining his cheeks. "I don't care what fantasies your mind is producing about him, but you are standing too close and it's rude."

"Sorry," the man stammered, his blush deepening. "I kind of lost myself for a moment."

"Well, find yourself and never behave so disrespectfully again. You were pushing boundaries that you really don't want to cross."

"I apologize." The man backed away further. "I had no intention of disrespecting you or him."

He turned away and went to stare at some leather chaps on sale nearby, his attention obviously split between Bran and the leather goods as he slipped his cellphone out of his pocket.

The man stayed there as Fang swiftly outfitted him in a bunch of leather straps that constituted the aforementioned harness.

Leather straps were not a foreign concept to Bran. After all, he used a leather baldric to hold his swords in place. But never had he been seen outfitted in leather quite like this. It crisscrossed over his chest, emphasizing the size and strength of his pecs. The leather itself was butter soft and about two inches wide, with some serious brass rings that held the straps in place as it crossed between his pecs. It was also crisscrossed in the back and easily held his body tightly, making him adjust his posture until he was standing tall and proud. It felt rather comfortable, and when he turned to look at himself in the mirror, he decided that he liked what he saw. The darkness of the leather contrasted beautifully with his pale skin, and his red nipples stood out as if put on display. The harness only emphasized the size and shape of his pecs and didn't drop any lower, leaving his tight, six-pack ab muscles on display.

Not too bad for a centuries-old man, he decided as he moved away from Caille and Fang, closer to their target who was still loitering around.

"Hey," he called softly, gaining the man's full attention. He turned to face Bran, dropping his cellphone in his pocket, a surprised look on his face. "What do you think? I think you were right about the feathers." He twisted a little, straining against the harness so his muscles popped out just a bit.

"She called you Raven," their stalker answered, the blush again highlighting his rather plain features. It was no wonder he was called upon to act as a spy. With no outstanding marks and a nondescript face, he could easily blend into a crowd with no one really taking notice of him. He was painfully average in every way that Bran could see.

"You heard that?" Bran smiled at him. "I didn't know that you were close enough to hear our conversation."

"It's not like I was spying or anything," the man hastily defended himself. "I just caught that bit of your conversation."

And as Bran was sure that the man wasn't even in the store when they shared info with Fang, this just proved that the man knew more than he was letting on.

"And you were paying attention because you thought I was beautiful." Bran decided to ease him away from that line of thought. He didn't want their mark getting too suspicious.

"And I was right." The man sighed, relaxing the muscles that he'd tensed up at the beginning of their conversation. "You look fabulous."

"And something you would want in a lover?" he

asked, lettings voice drop into deep tones, letting his Welsh accent grow a bit stronger. "Because I know what I like in a lover."

"What's that?" the stalker breathed, looking like he would scarcely move because if he did this fantasy of his would break under the strain of reality.

"A bold man who sees what he wants and takes it." Bran stepped into the man's personal space and pressed his nearly bare chest, the main focus of his stalker's apparent desires, against his. He held back a smirk as the man's breathing stuttered and a low moan flowed from his lips.

Upping the game, Bran wrapped his arms around the man, pulling him in as he lowered his head and stuck his nose in the man's neck, inhaling deeply.

The action had two-fold results. He caught a good whiff of the man, something he could relay to his guardian ravens, and it took the man so off guard that he didn't even realize that Bran had stuck his hands in his loose pants pockets and lifted his phone.

"What are you doing?" Caille's voice made him jump back and he did his best to look contrite as his stalker began to stammer excuses as to why he was touching something that didn't belong to him.

"Rude and disrespectful," Fang raged, stepping into the fray as Caille pulled Bran to her side by the back of his harness. The phone was easily transferred to her during this exchange as Fang began to berate the stunned-looking stalker. Within moments the man was run out of the store for disrespecting the unwritten rules of their society with his figurative tail between his legs, and Bran was doing his best to look contrite.

"Honestly," Fang warned Bran. "You can't get close to everyone who turns around and says that you're beautiful. That's the perfect way to court disaster that no one can get you out of."

"And with that said," Caille interrupted Fang's budding lecture about proper submissive behavior, "we will take the harness and three more in that exact feather style."

"I recommend a leash as well," Fang grumbled, but quickly got into a conversation with Caille about styles and colors.

This new world was strange but invigorating, Bran decided as he watched Caille and Fang talk about him like he wasn't even there. And from the heated glances that Caille was throwing his way, he knew he was about to possibly be educated more than his little heart could take, let alone his body. But he was a warrior and warriors never ran from the unexpected. Especially, he decided, letting his own gaze roam over The Wolf, when the rewards could prove to be exceptionally worth the risk.

Chapter Four

With phone in hand and leather harnesses ordered, and yes, The Raven would be wearing the one he currently had on out, Caille paid for their purchase, and the two of them made for *The Wild Hunt*, the prized phone in their possession.

It didn't take them long to retreat to their base of operations, and when they entered the set of apartments that Manx claimed as their own, they were both riding high on adrenaline and lust.

The ride there was particularly difficult for Bran. Since he had entered life in the twentieth century he had been struggling to adapt to this strange new world. Thank the goddess for his ravens because without them he would be totally and completely lost.

They had warned him about changes in society and how so many different people occupied the territory called America. There were Black Africans that he had only heard about in stories and in the recollections of his avian friends. Sure, he had seen Africans among the Roman soldiers who were invading the land but they were distinctly Roman and were few and far between. He also took the time to learn of how they came to be in this land and the fight for equality they were still raging. He knew that if it was up to him he would have tried to wage war on his oppressors but understood that sheer numbers and modern weapons would only result in his death, a pointless death because the victor writes the history and those who enslaved would do anything to show themselves in a grand and godly light. To engage would have meant widespread loss of life so they were taking the democratic approach and trying to, for the most part and varying degrees of success, work their problems out with the people they now shared a homeland with. They were an integrated people and he could them fascinating from their varied earthy skin tones to their facial features that seemed exotic and beautiful to him.

And there were the people called Asians, who also made a place for themselves within the Americas. He knew them through rumor and conjecture as the Seres people from the land now called China. They were people he had been told were great traders of silks and other rare and exotic items that only few could afford. Because of their complexions, not as dark as the Greeks or as pale as the Romans themselves, they were considered people from "beneath another sky."

He shuddered as he recalled his sessions on the Native populations in this country and how they were abused and murdered by those who would claim the land as their own. It left him unsettled when he read about the dishonorable tactics the invaders had used to subjugate and control these people and was happy to see that though the attempted genocide was harrowing, the Native population still had a presence and were struggling to get their voices heard. It reminded him of how his Tribe and the Tribes of his nation, young in the eyes of their invaders, had been subjugated, their language twisted, their lands mined for its precious resources that went to fill Roman coffers and then were left abandoned when their precious ores played out. But his people survived and the Natives of this land would continue to survive and strive as well.

Then there were the Hispanic peoples who were just Roman in his eyes but were so much more than he thought he understood. After his death, the Romans invaded the Iberian Peninsula or Hispanic to most Romans that counted, and their people, their culture, and their language was integrated with the Roman's, expanding and recreating languages that he had never heard. It was fascinating and he took the time to learn Spanish and Portuguese, and well as brush up on his Latin and Italian.

He didn't even want to think about the clothing choices most people made. To his eyes it seemed like they were wearing next to nothing or way too much, and through years of observation, it seemed to him there was never a happy medium. Fortunately, his ravens' eyes prevented him from going into full-blown shock when he saw what passed for fashion. Gone were the woolen hose, plaids, chitons, and himations that were comfortable and multi-functional. Today men wore braccae, or breeches, that sometimes disguised the strength of their legs. And their shirts... they had upper garments that didn't fall low enough to cover private parts politely. Women wore tight garments that exposed their whole body lines, and things called brassiere that were nothing like the strophium that women had used to bind their breasts. He didn't know if he was comfortable with that or not but he had to admit the bounce and state of women's breasts in their bras were very attention grabbing. In fact, most of modern clothing was as confusing as it was simple. Confusing as to why a man would not just wear a chiton for easy access for urination and for sexual conquests. A few tugs and you were ready to go no matter the time or place. Now a man had to deal with belts and buckles and the horror show known as zippers to release his manhood. And the women, there was no more lifting up a himation for a willing lusty lass and just plowing away. They had even more layers than the men from what he had observed. Pants and zippers and panties... there was no quick and easy way to gain access to the most treasured of playgrounds.

And the horseless carriages that traveled at dizzying speeds that made the world flash by and sometimes upset his stomach... Radios for what they considered music and television, and... It was one thing to see and hear about the miraculous changes that occurred in the world over the years yet another thing entirely to experience it for himself.

In that way he was grateful to Kern -- Cernunnos -- for finding him and harboring him in a safe place where he could heal and discover the new world he had awakened in. For that and many other kindnesses that the traveling god had bestowed upon him, he would do anything to help repay that debt.

But now riding in the car with Caille, a lot of his plans went straight out the window. The woman skillfully driving her car was confident, beautiful, and so desirable he was glad he was still wearing the harness to remind himself to hold his desires in check.

Only that wasn't working out so well and now he was glad he wore a long tunic over said harness to help hide the erection he had been sporting since he donned the very strips of feather embossed leather that marked him as a thing to be controlled and tamed.

And yes, he wanted Caille to be the one to try and dominate him. After having to have so much control in his life and being responsible for the lives of others, frankly, he was tired of the responsibility. And now he had to find a place in this new world so that he wouldn't be dependent on those he owed so much to... Yeah, a few hours of her having control of him sounded perfect.

He had researched bondage in passing as part of society's sexual advancements and it wasn't too different from the games he played while he was a king, though the sexual props and aids were different.

Once they pulled into the garage, he followed along behind Caille, very conscious of how her bottom looked like a ripe peach and how the restraints he was wearing under his tunic only seemed to make his arousal spiral higher. He felt his cock swell further as she turned and winked at him in the elevator.

"So," she purred as they both stood in the elevator car, staring up at the numbers as they ascended. "Leather really does it for you, huh?"

Wolf, he thought as her eyes gleaned amber for a moment. Then she flashed him a grin, exposing her small, dainty fangs.

"It's really nice leather," he commented, casually dropping his hands to cover his crotch, thankful for the many familiar layers he was wearing. Even if she could smell his desire for her, at least she couldn't see it. It was stupid and strange but that knowledge made him feel a bit more comfortable about the sex situation. Sure, he hadn't been laid in years, but that didn't mean he couldn't put up the illusion of control. Everything in this new society was about illusions anyway. "Almost as nice as the deer hide my tanner would make for me when I was still king."

There. Remind him and herself that he had royal leanings and he was in control.

"Yeah, but I bet it didn't make your nipples hard or your cock swell." Her grin got more seductive, more challenging. "I know you are hiding it behind your many layers but a hard dick is not difficult to miss, especially when you are in my profession."

"Your job is to observe people."

"My job is to hunt people, no matter who they are and in varied sets of circumstances. You can learn so much from body language, and yours says you want me to tie you down and fuck you hard."

Bran almost choked on the statement he wanted to make in response. He looked down and yup, he could see the outline of his hard cock pressing against the front on his harem pants.

"And your body language?" he finally questioned, needing to put his mind in this game, and from the way Caille behaved, this was a game to her.

"My body language?" She turned away from him as the elevator stopped at Manx's floor.

The doors slid open as he began to speak. "Your nipples are hard, your pupils in those beautiful amber eyes are dilated. Your breathing has increased just slightly, your heart is beating a little harder, and I can smell your wetness, woman. It's delicious and the scent of it has been getting stronger since I pulled off my tunic in that shop. It spiked when I put on his harness and now you are shimmering, probably sliding around in your underwear because your body is weeping for my touch."

The smile fell from her face and a low growl rumbled from her throat.

"Body language," he reminded her. "It's what a warrior uses to ensure he doesn't fall in battle."

She huffed in his direction before turning her pert little nose in the air and strolling out of the elevator as if the sweet aroma of her growing arousal at his words didn't fill the elevator.

With a grin, he followed her out of the elevator and into the living quarters of Manx, arriving just in time to hear her question her owner as she handed over the phone.

"Where is Kern?"

"Still sleeping," Manx mumbled, concentration fully on the phone they handed over. "And sleeping is where he will stay until we unravel this mystery a little further. The Cat is watching over him and will alert me if there are any changes in the bond that he can feel or see."

"In that case, we are going to go and rest up." Caille blinked innocently at Manx… and then leered at Bran. "That's the phone from one of the men that were spying on us. We had him so frazzled in Fang's shop that I bet he doesn't even know that he lost it. It has to have some vital info on it because we both observed him speaking on it several times, getting instructions I believe."

Manx murmured in approval and a smile spread across Caille's face. Her scent changed; it wasn't such a deep arousal as she stared at Manx, and Bran relaxed as he realized he wouldn't have to fight such a powerful personage as The Manx for her affection.

It was about then that he realized that he had set a course that would lead him straight to Caille's bed and maybe… well, in the future he would have to see. That was a solid decision that made him leer back at her before he got control of his facial expression, trying to put on the serious mien that was expected. This world, after all, was all about illusions.

"I have a feeling we are going to need the energy later." Caille attempted to sound calm and collected but was fooling no one in the room.

"You are going to fuck." Manx waved their hand absently as they moved across the room to connect the phone to a computer set up on a desk. "You aren't fooling anyone."

Bran blinked at Caille and then at Manx before

he crossed his arms over his chest and glared at everyone in the room. "Really? You know what we are going to do?"

Manx turned back to them, eyes gleaming as they turned their attention away from the phone to smirk at the two of them. "You want to fuck because you are horny as hell, Bran. Caille wants to fuck because she is stressed out over what is happening to her brother and she has always used sex as a release. You both find each other disgustingly attractive in physical and mental terms."

They both inhaled sharply at his words and Manx shook his head in apparent amusement. "Children, I don't know if you understand what I truly am at my root. I can smell the heat scents wafting off of you. You smell like a bunch of horny sailors getting leave and looking to get laid. But your passions are not flowing about indiscriminately. You are fixated on each other and you are wasting time when you could be fucking by trying to show that denial is not just a river in Egypt and interrupting my work."

* * *

"So," Bran drawled as Caille led him to her floor -- apparently each of the Huntsmen got a floor in his building --"You are in heat?"

Caille glared at him, her blue eyes flashing green for a moment before she crossed her arms and glared at him.

"What?" He couldn't help teasing her a little. "Did your master strike a nerve?"

"I am the queen of winter," she growled, pacing around the room as she examined him from head to toe, her ever-changing eyes settling on a rich amber color. "I do not go into heat. And Manx is *our* master now."

"Well, I didn't hear you correcting our master…"

"He wasn't really wrong and you know it, Bran the Blessed," she purred, pausing in front of him. "His wording was just a little off."

"So you admit that you want me."

"About as much as you want me," she countered. "I can smell how much being under my hand turns you on. You crave control, Bran, and you want it from me."

"Do I?" Did he? He kind of did. Caille was beautiful and exciting, and frankly, after all he had seen, after all of the women his crows had observed, he never found many of them sexually exciting. Beautiful and worthy of being worshiped, yes. But a woman this stimulating who set his nerves aflame and sent his body reeling with more than lust? No.

"You know you do." She grinned as she backed up, reaching out to grab his hand and pull him forward. "And if you don't, you better say something now. There is a difference between what your body craves and what your mind wants. If you don't want this, say so."

"Oh, I want this." He found himself smiling back at her, his blood heating as he followed where she led. "I want this more than anything at this moment."

"Fair," she agreed as she pushed open a door and led him to one of the most opulent bedrooms he had ever seen. "I want this too."

The room was done up in a very pale cream color with gold accents, dominated by a huge black iron bed absolutely drowning in fluffy lavender pillows.

She stopped and closed the door with a wink before kicking her shoes off one at a time. Whoever thought that removing footwear could be so sexy?

With his heart racing, Bran leaned to the side and

removed both of his shoes, wiggling his toes in the plush carpet. He wanted to see what would happen next. His cock in his pants was hard and growing painfully harder. He inhaled deeply, drawing in the scents of herbs, sweet flowers, and the heady scent of a woman ripe with need and longing. Yes, he was so loving this.

Her shirt went next. She crossed her arms over her chest and whipped it over her head, her wild blonde hair flying about as she shook her head to pull the golden strands from her face. Her eyes were glowing, and a low growl rolled from her throat.

"Sweet goddess," he groaned as he let his jacket slide from his shoulders and pillow at his bare feet.

"That's right." Caille put her hands over her full breasts, trapped in one of those bras. God, he loved the modern era, loved how even their underclothing accented a woman's shape and form, emphasizing how truly amazing femininity could be. "You need to worship me."

She pointed to the ground at her feet and instantly Bran was on his knees, burying his face in the vee of her thighs, inhaling the rich scent of her wetness as she flowed for him.

"Good boy." Her voice dropped lower as her fingers buried themselves in his hair, pulling him closer.

His hand came up to cup her ass, feeling the firm round flesh beneath his palms as he nipped at her thighs, feeling the muscles flex as she slid her legs apart, just enough so that he could push his face in her crotch.

"Undress me," she ordered and happily he complied, pulling at her pants until they slid down her hips and dropped to her feet. Casually she stepped out of them, kicking them to the side and standing before him in nothing but sheer silken panties.

"You know what to do," she told him, lifting one leg and dropping it over his shoulder as she bent over him. "At least I hope you do. They did eat pussy back in the ancient classical era, right?"

He pulled his head back far enough to stare into her glittering eyes, a wicked smirk on his face. "Do you think civilization would have developed if we didn't?"

"I take that as a challenge." Caille laughed, gripping his shirt and with a rip, rending it in two. Bran damn near purred at that, at the strength she showed as the pieces of his tunic fluttered down to hang around his arms. He released her long enough to shake them off before looking up at her through the curtain of her long wavy hair.

"That was my favorite tunic," he complained while his cock throbbed and dripped with his lust. Damn, power turned him on.

"Was." She gripped the back of the leather harness he still wore and pulling him in, her leg pressing against his back, holding him in place. "Now be a good boy and finish your dinner and I just might get you a new one."

Growling, Bran leaned forward, gripped the thin matrix of her soaking wet panties between his teeth, and ripped them off of her body. Caille tightened her grip on him and Bran willingly pushed his face into her pussy.

Yes, this is what heaven actually was. She was wet and soft, shaved as he had never experienced before. Women of this century seemed to not take stock in body hair, and he loved it. No hairy legs or armpits, or apparently, crotches. He dove in and took his first taste.

Fuck yes. She tasted of power and lust while at the pinnacle of womanhood. He closed his eyes, pressed his nose into her clit, and began to lap at her wet folds.

Caille's voice disappeared into a series of breathy moans and panting sighs as her fingers tangled in his hair and jerked hard. He loved that, the slight pain that came from her pull. He purposefully jerked against it, just to get more of that sharp pain. It felt so good. He groaned his pleasure and felt her shudder harder against him.

He had no idea how long he ate her out, his tongue lapping at her wet slick that flowed from her body like rain. He covered his face in it, lapped it up, and felt his own cock weep harder at her flavor. And when he leaned up to suckle at her clit...

"Yes, baby," she cried out her approval. "Just like that."

So he doubled his efforts, rapidly lapping at her swollen clit before sucking it hard and teasing it with his tongue.

How he loved women! And it seemed like he had the most perfect one right there in his arms.

Bran was so into his feasting that he almost cried when she tightened her grip on him and the first wave of her climax tore through her.

She screamed, letting her passion be heard as she shook and quivered in his grasp. He almost cried out in sorrow as her grip on his harness changed and she shoved him away.

He landed on his ass and looked up at her, shocked. He was really getting into his meal when she pushed him back. He wanted to cry. Hell, his cock was already weeping in his pants. He knew if he stood up, there would be a very large wet spot to show just how much he liked her taste.

"Very nice," she complimented, as she reached up and ripped her bra away. "Now get on your feet. I'm not done with you."

Only a fool would ignore that order. He scrambled to his feet, chest heaving as he swiped one hand across his face, for a moment staring at the slick on his fingers before licking and sucking each and every digit clean.

"Bran the Blessed, Bran the Giant. Let me see what I have to work with," she demanded, pointing to his pants as she leaned back against the door, staring at him with her glowing, hungry eyes. "Off. Get them off now."

"Don't be surprised at what you see," he panted, rubbing at his neck, which was still tingling.

"Come on, big man. Let's see what you got. I thought they called you a giant? You don't seem all that tall to me."

"What they were referring to in all the legends is what's in my pants." He tugged at the tie that held his pants low on his waist and it released quickly. He stepped out of his pants, his heavy cock dragging low and painfully hard as he moved.

"Fuck." Caille inhaled sharply, her eyes going wide for a moment as they stared at his cock. The sight of him fully erect made her aroused scent even stronger. "How…"

"Runs in my family," he bragged.

She moved in close and slapped at his erection with the flat of her hand. He hissed in pain but that was quickly eclipsed by the warm glow of pleasure that followed the blow. Bran felt his knees grow weak and had to lock them to keep from tipping over.

He reached for her, and with a dark chuckle she

flowed into his arms, wrapped her fingers in his harness, and jerked him forward into a kiss. Her mouth devoured him, her tongue forced its way into his mouth and she began to taste him from the inside out.

He moaned, his hands going to her hair, pulling her closer as one of her hands went to his back, clawing at his skin, each scratch sending fire shooting through his body. He shook in her grasp and pressed harder against her, feeling the soft skin of her stomach caress his cock. He began thrusting against her gently, a slow grind that felt so damn good he thought his head was going to explode.

"Remember, I'm the one in control."

"Because I give it up to you."

"That's not all that you are about to give up."

Bran had nothing to say about it because she was telling the truth. He was willingly giving up power to her and he was loving it. He had been in control for such a long time... it felt freeing, actually. He had never felt so free and happy in his life.

He felt the magic within him begin to hum softly and his neck began to tingle even more. But that was quickly ignored as Caille took a step back and posed, her bare breasts bobbing with her movements, their hard pink nipples calling to him.

"You're beautiful," he insisted, reaching out and cupping her flesh in his hands. Damn, she was warm and soft. Modern women were nothing like their ancient counterparts, though he appreciated them both. Frequent bathing and modern grooming habits really did make a difference.

"Am I what you wanted me to be?"

"I want what you are," he promised, for a moment seeing everything that made Caille Beara, the Maiden, the Lady, and the Crone and wanting them all, for together they created the tantalizing creature known now as Caille. "I see you and I want you even more."

"Beautiful raven," she purred, pressing up against him. Bran felt compelled to close his eyes as she ran her fingers through his hair, her nails softly scratching his scalp.

Bran opened his eyes and cooed, yes he cooed for her, willingly exposing himself to her.

Curiously, Caille reached out and touched the glowing marks before she hissed and pulled her fingers back. Bran watched this, watched the glow from his runes shine across her pale skin, the blue lights sending a kaleidoscope of colors dancing across the flesh.

"What --"

"Protective runes," he answered, reaching up to caress the glowing marks.

"So… you get horny and they glow?"

"No." Bran shook his head as the strangest urge to tug on the skin of his neck took him. "It's not supposed to act like that…"

He trailed off, plucking at his skin then wincing as he felt something pull from his neck.

"Oh, now that is cool," Caille praised, giggling a bit as she backed off to watch.

"Did it hurt?" he asked, pulling more and extending her arm upward until a thin glowing line was held in his hand. "Touching this power? It's primary focus is to become a weapon for protection."

"No, actually it tickled. I feel Kern's hand in this…"

"He told me I would never be without a blade in my hand again." Bran tugged more until the line of blue light thickened, and suddenly he was holding a broadsword.

His shock must have shown because Caille moved closer once again and grinned at him. "Yeah, Kern doesn't like us to be defenseless." She held up her hand, and there was a funny twisting of light that made Bran blink, and when his gaze settled upon her hand again, it had shifted to a gigantic paw with razor-sharp claws.

"Wild," Bran breathed, looking from the sword in his hand and back to where Caille was easily handling a partial animal shift. "I can't do that."

"You weren't designed to," Caille responded. "You were a giant and a warrior. You are the only one here who can't shift... unless you are about to sprout feathers..."

"No," Bran shook his head, swinging his sword of light and runic magic a bit. "I sometimes wish I could sprout wings, as you say, and fly with my friends, but seeing through their eyes occasionally is enough."

"So you have no natural weapons at your immediate disposal." Caille nodded. "I understand what he did. He has horns, Arcas can turn into a bear, and I, well..."

"Ravens and wolves," Bran shrugged. "I knew what you were the moment I set eyes on you."

"And we all have natural weapons. We can never be unarmed... unlike a chattering bird brain that I know," she teased and he couldn't help but smile.

"So he ensured that I would always have the means to protect myself," Bran said. "But this... this is wild."

He released the broadsword of light from his hand and it snapped back around his neck, faintly glowing.

"That's the first time you noticed the glow?"

"It's the first time I've been worked up enough to feel my personal magic flow." He closed his eyes and concentrated on pulling the force he felt flowing through his body back and knew he succeeded in holding in his magic when Caille appeared again and ran her fingers over the skin of his neck.

"I like that," Caille purred. "It means if things go south, I don't have to spend time trying to save the new guy."

"I like that you think you have to protect me," he countered, only a little bit sarcastic.

"I don't know a lot about you, Bran the Blessed. I trust you to a certain extent because Kern placed such faith in you."

"You know enough to want to fuck me."

"I know the potential for maximum pleasure is there so why shouldn't I reach out and grab what's offered?"

"*I* offered?"

"From the moment you eyed me like a rare steak at the parking lot. I knew for sure when I got to put his harness on you." She placed a hand on the supple leather that was a constant reminder that he wanted to submit to her. Bran was honest enough to admit that to himself. "Your eyes nearly glowed when I touched it, touched you. You trust me enough for me to get you to where you need to be."

"Maybe more," he admitted. "More than is healthy for me. And some of that trust comes from the trust Kern holds in you and your crazy little family, but I know for sure that you would never abuse me or harm me sexually, Cailleach Beara. That's not the game you play."

"And I love to play games."

"What games do you want to play with me?"

Caille stepped back and examined his bare body, his cock jumping as he felt a spurt of precum roll down his cock. Damn, he was so hard he felt like his skin would burn and even that was a tingling, tight kind of hunger that he craved.

"How do you feel about anal?"

"This ain't my first rodeo, gal," he spoke darkly, his Welsh accent going thicker. "I am a warrior and I have bonded with my brothers in such a manner. But unless you are hiding something where I can't get to it, lass, you don't have the parts to bugger me up the ass."

"But did you like it?" she asked, her eyes glittering as she danced her fingers up and down his chest.

She backed him up until the backs of his knees hit the mattress of that sumptuous looking bed. He sank into silken pillows and plush softness that made him swear he was lying on a cloud. He opened his mouth to respond when she grabbed one of his nipples and gave it a hard pinch. Any words transferred into a yelp as he arched underneath her, nearly unseating her from her perch on his groin.

"Sensitive." She chuckled, bending over to lap at his sore flesh before pulling the poor abused nub into her mouth.

Bran groaned, letting his head fall back amongst the pillows as pleasure rolled through his body. He liked that very much. Her mouth was hot and wet, her tongue like velvet, and the suction was perfect. He could only imagine how wonderful that practiced mouth would feel on his cock.

"I like that." Bran lifted a trembling hand and ran it through her hair. Fuck, look at him, shaking like some untried youth and she'd only just begun.

"You'll like the rest of it more, I promise you." She released his nipple with a pop to tell him. "So, anal play. Did you like it or did you just put up with it?"

"I don't do anything I don't like more than once." He grinned down at her. "And I love to fuck and to be fucked."

"Were you any good at it?"

"Fucking or getting fucked? Because I can promise you, I've had no complaints either way."

"And with this new body?" she questioned. He felt a little shocked at the question, actually. "I know you've had it for a while. So have you taken it out on a test run?"

"No," he admitted. "I hadn't the time or the inclination for such frivolities. I was too busy learning how to function in your society and I am still having issues. If not for my ravens, I would be in dire straits."

"So what you are telling me is that this body is a virgin?"

"Well..." He pondered that for a moment before he nodded in agreement. "I'd be telling you this. I have no idea how this body is going to react. It's nothing like my old one though it is similar in form, if not its function."

"So you have no idea how this body, which is lovely by the way, is going to react."

"Well, I guess it's time for me to find out." He smirked, thrusting his hips up so that his hard cock pressed against the firm warm flesh of her ass. "Though I have to say, some things haven't changed at all."

"I'm going to take your virginity all over again."

"Lass, I haven't been a virgin in a long time."

"This body is all fresh and new... and I'm going to mess it up, Bran. I'm going to pop your cherries, all of them, and you are going to thank me for the privilege."

She leaned up over and to the side of him, pressing her breasts right into his face as she pulled open a drawer from her bedside table. And since they were there...

"Naughty," Caille hummed, as he lifted his head enough to pull one hard pink nipple into his mouth.

She tasted of salt and perfume, he decided as he laved the hard nub of flesh with his tongue. She pressed into the caress and he dropped his arms over her back and sucked like a newborn babe. He rolled his tongue over her nipple, nipping at it a little, feeling his erection jump as she shivered in enjoyment.

He could have stayed there forever, or as long as his control held out, because every moment more he spent with this woman was just pushing him closer and closer to the climax he wanted to hold off on -- until he was buried deep inside of her.

Just as he pulled off and licked his way to her other lonely nipple she moved away... and then he had to resist the urge to cry like that aforementioned newborn babe.

But she was shimmying her way down his body, her soft flesh caressing and bathing him with her essence -- thank you, goddess, for allowing him to exist right now -- and was sliding between his legs. She sat up, which was a crying shame because direct skin contact was such a beautiful thing, but one of her hands gripped his cock, stroking it a little and making things a little bit better. She reached out and pulled something from her bedside table, hefting it in her hands and holding it up for him to observe.

"Have you ever seen a butt plug?"

"Well, don't they think of everything," Bran

mused, staring at the heart-shaped device of black plastic she held, noting the wide flange she held it by at the base. "I am assuming that it will... uh..."

"Slide neatly into this little hole you are about to let me play with?" she asked, arching an eyebrow as he saw the other things in her hand that she pulled from that drawer. How much stuff did she have in there, anyway?

"I am?"

"Oh, you are." She licked those perfect, full lips and her bountiful yet perky breasts bounced as she snapped on a rubber glove.

To be honest, Bran did feel a little bit of... not fear per se, more like anxiety as she popped open a bottle of lube and began to slick up her gloved fingers.

Bran closed his eyes and sent a message out to his birds to quickly send him uses for butt plugs, and what he got in return almost made him come right on the spot.

The visual parade played out in his mind like a movie of women and men, happily bending over and spreading their cheeks while accommodating partners' slid fingers and then those adult toys in varying sizes and shapes, up their assholes.

It was erotic, it was exotic, and it was something that he was more than willing to try with her. He opened his eyes just in time to hold in a scream as she dropped his cock, hefted his balls in one hand and gently began to rub one slick finger around his hole.

"*Cara 'ch chyffwrdd,*" he moaned, the Welsh slipping out. "Caille, I love your touch."

"You are about to love it even more," she promised. "Now relax and let me..."

Bran closed his eyes and inhaled deeply twice, anticipation building. He recalled all the times he allowed himself this pleasure as king; instead of taking, allowing himself to be taken. He remembered the burn and stretch and how it thrilled him so much it was something he didn't allow to happen often or he might lose himself in it.

"Good boy," Caille praised, circling her finger until he got used to the touch and felt himself relax. This was nice. This was beautiful. This was what he wanted.

Then she pressed one finger in.

Bran hissed and he lurched upward, this feeling startlingly new with this fresh body. It wasn't uncomfortable, but it was a bit more intense than he remembered.

"Good, baby," Caille calmed him, one hand going back to his cock and stroking him softly. "Now be a good boy and let mama in."

The combination of stimulation to the sensitive nerves near the opening of his hole and her hand squeezing his shaft just the right way did almost as much to relax him as her words. He threw his head back and pressed down into her thrusting finger.

"Yes," he panted, his heart beating faster as he adjusted to this intimate caress. This was so reminiscent of his time spent alone with Taliesin, his bard, one of the few people he allowed this pleasure with his body. How many times had he pushed Taliesin onto his bed and fucked himself raw on his prick? Goddess, how he longed for those carefree days. But Caille's finger sliding in deeper pushed those memories out of his head.

How he missed this, the raw feeling of being opened and possessed. He closed his eyes and began to grind down on her finger. It was slimmer than his bard's cock, that was for sure, and now that his new body was getting into it, the sensations began to match the ones in his head.

He wanted more. He demanded more.

"Another," he called out, arching his back and riding down on her single finger, spreading his thighs a little wider.

"As you wish," she agreed and Bran hissed as he felt the cool lube and then the slick slide of a second finger pressing in alongside of the first.

"Fuck." He breathed through the pinching finger and cursed when she began to spread them apart, stretching him wider.

He almost lost it when she bent over and drew the head of his cock into her mouth. The slick wet heat felt so good... her tongue pushing back his foreskin and lapping at the sensitive head beneath...

He was losing his mind. He really was. His body was becoming nothing more than a tool for pleasure. Fuck, this was perfect. She was perfect.

"Yes, more." He found himself begging. "Please more."

The third finger made him swear as it almost felt like it was too much. Still, his greedy body wanted more. She began to thrust a little harder, curling her finger and touching --

"There!" he called out as she touched his prostate. "There! Again..." Then he closed his eyes as his toes curled and every muscle in his body tightened. He let his head flop to the side as he tried to stop from coming like an untried boy, but damn, it was so hard. He was being stretched and she knew how to hit that little button of pleasure in his hole. He was wiggling and whining like a hound in heat and her lips locked around his cock made it even harder to maintain.

He made the mistake of opening his eyes and

watching as she hungrily slurped down his prick, sliding him to the back of her throat while her free hand rolled and tugged at his balls.

He was on fire. His back arched as he fucked down on her fingers harder, panting and sweating.

"I'm going to come --"

She swiftly pulled away, allowing his hard cock to drop against his stomach while her fingers slithered free. He whimpered at the loss and then blushed at the totally hungry sounds he was making.

"Not right now, you aren't," Caille corrected, picking up the plug and liberally dribbling it with the lube. "Not before I come again and believe me, Bran, I will come again."

She slid down further on the bed, her long soft hair cradling his thighs and then she leaned forward to lap at the base of his cock before pulling one tender ball into her mouth. Her tongue worried at the loose skin before she sucked hard and Bran screamed as he gripped the base of his cock to prevent himself from spilling right there and then.

"Relax," she admonished him, after letting go of one soft orb before sucking down on the other one, letting her teeth graze him slightly.

Bran whimpered again and did his best to hold still. He was trying so hard to be good for her that he barely noticed the tip of the plug entering his body. But he tensed up when he realized what was happening. The tension began to cut his rush of pleasure.

"Relax, baby," Caille purred, leaving his balls alone to begin licking up his prick. He looked down and watched her very pink tongue lave his skin as she lapped up all the precum that was spilling and leaking down his shaft. "Just a little more..." She pressed harder and Bran called out as the plug slid in deep, the tip settling against his prostate.

"Fuck," he panted, his whole body seizing as the lubed plug pressed inside of his hole. The sweat beaded on his skin as the feel of the stretch, the burn of it, zinged his nerves. Cool fire raced up his spine as she slowly forged a path for the wide bit of latex as it slid further inside him.

The sensation of penetration stole his breath. His heart was pounding and his breathing grew raspy as small whimpers and groans left his parched lips. He closed his eyes to savor this feeling of possession, of his taking, and he wanted more.

It stung, it burned, and it felt so perfect.

"Caille." He gasped her name as the stretch almost became unbearable when the widest part of the plug forced itself inside his body.

He gripped the pillows at his head as his thigh muscles stiffened. Automatically his legs spread wider, making it easier for him to be taken.

"That's right," Caille praised. "So good. So good for me, Bran. Perfect. Just perfect. If you could only see what you look like."

Bran could imagine, with his eyes closed, his head tossed to the side, his legs spread out in a wanton fashion, swearing and rolling on the sheets like a whore in heat...

He bet he looked damn beautiful and hungry.

"Caille --"

"A little more... just a little more, baby. You are doing so well. Just take it. Take it all for me." With that said, she allowed her fangs to show and lightly scraped them along the head of his cock as she gave the plug a little twist.

"Fuck, yes!" Bran roared, his whole body arching, his toes curling as he threw himself headlong into this forgotten pleasure. "Caille!"

"Just like that," she purred as she gripped the end of the glove and pulled it from her hand inside out. "Maintain just for me, just for a little longer."

Bran's hips were dancing in the bed, pressing the plug against his sweet spot before turning his hips upwards as the rounded plug hit all the nerves in his ass just right. This was torture; wild, amazing, sexual torture and he didn't want it to end.

But then she pulled away again and he was really going to scream in frustration this time but instead, his eyes popped open as she straddled his hips, pulled his prick into position, and slid down, hard.

"Caille!" he bellowed as the force of her riding him slammed his hips back on the bed and in turn slammed the tip of the plug right into his sensitive prostate.

He bucked up hard, and laughing, Caille grabbed onto the chest harness and slammed her hips down once more.

Bran was going crazy. He didn't know what felt better, the hot, slick heat encapsulating his cock or the hot, tawdry pleasure of having his ass fucked with the plug each time she slammed down.

His mind was whirling, his vision whiting out as the most beautiful filth poured from her mouth.

"That's it. That's my little bitch. Give it up to me. Take what I give you and give me what I want."

Bran knew he was screaming, incoherently crying out, but it was too much. His spine was burning, the muscles of his stomach were growing tighter, yet his hips were getting looser as he fucked up into her and in return was fucked harder by the plug and her incredible bouncing. Again and again, she rode him, demanding that he give himself over to her, that he give her his all, and he was helpless to do anything less.

Bran tried to hold on, tried to make this act of passion and hunger last. His hands gripped her hips... damn, those hips moved so fluidly in his hands...there were lights behind his eyes and...

"*Cathreni 'm crazy!*" he shouted -- you're driving me crazy! -- and she threw her head back and laughed as she rode him still harder. Her amber eyes were glowing and her fangs were glittering in the light being cast by his runes. She was fierce and exciting... and he was going to come. His hands dug into her flesh, bruising her skin with marks that were not going to last long, as he threw his hips upwards, fucking her harder. If he was going to embarrass himself and blow like a youth, he was going to make it count. He cried out as he slammed upwards, the plug riding him hard as he gave in to the wild pleasure running through him.

Then her hips stuttered. His eyes stayed on her face as she began to growl, then the growl became a howl as she threw back her head as her inner muscles began to grab and milk him. It was too much. He screamed as he felt his balls slam up into the base of his cock and then his cock vibrated as he exploded deep within her.

He whined as she collapsed on top of him, her body stilling as they shivered in each other's arms. He couldn't remember ever feeling such ecstasy in his life. His muscles trembled in exhaustion, his heart raced, he was sweaty and overheated, and he loved it. He wrapped his arms around her body and held her close, pressing kisses to her head, and she moaned in relief as their bodies came to rest.

"Perfection," he breathed. *"Ach' 'n arddun..."* -- You are beautiful -- but her hand pressed against his lips, quieting him.

"Enjoy the moment," she breathed, and he decided that she was right. Here and now, there was nothing else they could do so it would be smart to just lie back and enjoy.

Chapter Five

"If you are done fucking it out…"

Manx's amused voice pulled Bran from the contented sleep he was in and made him wince as he realized the butt plug Caille had used on him was still inserted.

"We good, we good…" Caille mumbled from her spot beside him, her blonde hair covering his chest, the warm weight of her a comfort all in itself.

How long had it been since he woke up beside a warm, soft body that didn't belong to the ravens who had settled around his sleeping form each night? He couldn't recall but he knew that now that he had the sensation again, he really didn't want to let it go.

"Very good." Manx looked a little worried but was trying to hide it stood at the foot of Caille's bed, tapping their foot. "Because I have some information that I think we need to share."

"Kern?" Bran breathed, still worried about his friend.

"He's still asleep and I want him to stay that way… for now," Manx revealed, running fingers through their hair before they turned serious eyes toward them. "I now know where they are holding Arcas."

In an instant, despite the lack of clothing, Caille was on her feet, moving toward Manx, gripping them by their shirt sleeve. "Where? Where is my brother?"

"You are not going to like this." Manx sighed deeply before reaching out and gently placing their hands on top of hers where they gripped the fabric of their shirt sleeve.

"Manx, tell me."

"Apparently, it takes a lot of money to finance a

cult," Manx explained. "And any new sources of revenue are deeply exploited."

"That makes sense." Caille looked scared as her breath began to stutter a bit. "Manx --"

"That phone was a wealth of information and you both did well in lifting it. I have discovered that this cult, as disgusting as it is, engages in dog fighting."

"They... they can do a lot with Arcas, Manx." Caille began to shake and Manx gripped her hands harder even as Bran made his way to his feet, disregarding his own naked state, and wrapped his arms around her shoulders. "Just tell me."

"Right now, they have him drugged. With what, I don't know just yet, but they are trying to force a shift."

"They know what he is?" Caille looked ready to run from the room at that very moment and attempt a rescue all on her own.

"They know, Caille." Manx lifted one well-manicured eyebrow. "It's not like we're hiding from them."

Caille seemed to wilt a little at that before she nodded in agreement. "Hosting some of the largest BDSM parties as covers to bring our people into safety is kind of in your face."

"And they are still finding all kinds of loopholes to keep on with the business of bringing back Dagna the Fifteenth."

"And that means they are going to do something really stupid with dogs and my brother."

"From what is flowing on their Photonote circle, they are going to provide them with entertainment never before seen, a shifting Man-Bear against as many dogs as they can sneak in there."

"That is rather stupid, isn't it?" Bran had to ask because it just didn't add up in his mind. If you want to keep your cult a secret then you did your best not to draw attention to it.

"Unless their goal is to expose us and scare the human population so badly that they come after us with pitchforks and flaming torches." Manx looked more angry than worried but that didn't seem to comfort Caille any.

"They outnumber us." Her voice was wooden as her body froze. "It will be angry mobs and screaming evangelicals, just like The Burning Time all over again."

"It will not come to that, Caille, My Wolf." Manx pulled her from Bran's arms to wrap her protectively within their embrace. "I will never let anything like that happen again."

Closing his eyes, Bran pushed his question out to his ravens and instantly his mind was flooded with images of people, mostly women, all being accused of black magic and witchery. These women were burned at the stake, they were hung, and tortured as fearful humans looking for people to blame for their misfortunes found a scapegoat in them. The images, the scents, the raw emotions, the fear and anguish from the accused, the outright hatred from those doing the accusing… it was enough to send him stumbling back from Manx and Caille until the backs of his legs hit the bed and he found himself forcibly sitting, then yelping and lurching to his feet as his butt plug hit his overly sensitive prostate.

"Yeah, that's got to go," he muttered, blushing red as Manx carefully observed him before turning to Caille.

"You did good breaking him in." He offered her

a smile which she tentatively returned. "But you must remember the care and treatment of your toys. You don't want to scare him away."

"Hey!" Bran protested but winced again as the tip of the plug hit some nerves that sent confusing messages to his brain. Yes, it kind of felt good but then again it felt like it was a little too much. He wound up standing there, wondering if it would be bad etiquette to pull out a butt plug with his host and essentially his boss in the room.

"Don't worry, little wolf," Manx then promised her as Bran's actions caused the mood to lighten in the room. "I have a plan. We have a few hours of daylight left."

"And we still don't know if they actually want to expose us," Bran felt the need to add. "No matter what their private chatter is about, exposing us will expose them, and in this country cults are not taken too lightly."

"Good points." Manx nodded in approval. "Ravens are always known for their keen insight, and I noticed you asked for help from them about some of the things we discussed. May I ask what caused you to seek out answers?"

"The Burning Time." Bran inhaled deeply. "That was... that would not have been allowed under my rulership as King."

"But times have changed since the ancient classical period." Manx bit their bottom lip in concentration.

Bran heard a gasp and turned to face Caille, who was staring at him in awe. "You are old," she finally said.

"Rude." Manx laughed and Bran rolled his eyes at both of them.

"I am well-seasoned," Bran finally defended himself, amused despite the situation brewing.

"You spent most of your time marinating as a single head in a crypt." Manx kept laughing. "How on this planet did you get seasoned?"

"Ravens." Bran chuckled. "They have racial memory. Everything they see, they share, and they took to me as one of their own. So they still continue to share when I don't understand certain things. Kern would visit and fill in some blanks, but my go-to guides in this world are still the ravens. They never miss anything."

"And what one knows, they all know." Manx dropped the amusement and their face turned to one of contemplation as they observed Bran.

"Do they know anything of the cult and their actions?"

After closing his eyes, posing the question to the ravens, he winced as he was hit with a font of colors and emotions -- frustration being a key one. After being lost in that cacophony of sound and parade of feelings, Bran blinked back to the present, processing the font of information the ravens sent him before speaking.

"They know nothing and it frustrates them. There must be a ward of some kind in place, but they can confirm the have seen our stalker return to the store owned by that Fang person, in all probability seeking his lost phone. They followed him to a place near Sykesville before they managed to lose him."

"Sykesville." Manx nodded. "That coincides with the information on the phone, at least." Manx gave them both a grin before hugging Caille hard before pushing her back so that they could meet her eyes. "So I have a plan to bring our Bear home."

"Do tell!"

"How do you feel about infiltration and wreaking some controlled havoc?"

Caille's eyes gleamed and a wicked smile showing her growing fangs crossed her face. The sight of those fangs really did something for him, Bran realized, as his cock lurched in inappropriate interest. He did his best to ignore it. Damn, he was growing very fond of this woman, but it was her words, brimming with loyalty and protectiveness that pushed his attraction to her into something that was growing deeper.

"Point me in the right direction. Those who harmed our family will pay. They will know the wrath of the Huntsmen for I will chew it into their skin and imprint it on their souls."

And fuck, Bran thought as his heart lurched in his chest. He was falling in love.

* * *

"So this is a dog fight..." Marshal Gray let his voice trail off as he followed Caille who was dressed to impress in a tight red gown, and Bran, who was basically shrouded from head to toe in flowing black.

"Try to look excited," Caille advised, taking his arm and grinning at him with her perfectly rouged lips and sparkling blue eyes. "You are looking rather pissed."

"These assholes took my brother and --" he bit off the words. "They took my brother. They all deserve to burn in hell."

"Do you even believe in hell?" Bran asked, moving behind them like the ghost of all assassins past, but he couldn't really care less. His ass was no longer aching from the forgotten plug, his ravens were circling, doing their best to feed him information as he needed it, and he was finally going to do something to help pay back Kern for all that the god had done for him.

"Drown in a cesspool?" Marshal asked tentatively, looking up and back at Bran, his eyes sparkling with intent. There was a hint of danger in those eyes. No one knew what an Egyptian Cat was capable of, and Marshal didn't seem too keen on letting anything really personal about himself slip out. Right now, he was a man with a purpose and that was getting his brother, the Faunus, back safely with his mate so they could complete the bond.

"That's more like it," Bran approved. "Drowning someone in shit and slop seems most appropriate and won't offend someone's religious sensibilities."

"And it's an all-purpose kill," Caille added as they moved up the line of cars and walked slowly toward the ruins of the huge McMansion that was supposed to be hosting this fucking travesty of entertainment. "If it has lungs, then it has to breathe… eventually."

"And a lot more charitable than some of the executions I've witnessed," Bran happily added. "I am at least glad to see that some of the barbarism I was still expecting to be around has changed and humanity has gotten a little more discreet with its hatred and fear."

"Hatred and fear?" Marshal asked as they moved past other couples dressed similarly to them but who moved with a sense of entitlement and excitement.

"You have to have a level of hatred already in your heart for your fears to play upon. That, my friend, is a recipe for revolt and anger when someone gets a little hint of power added to the mix. It's how we justify most wars we start, how husbands who abuse their wives feel that they are the wronged party and have every right to take their anger and frustration out on the one they have control over. It's how kings choose how and when to execute those who stood against them or who redirect the fear and hatred they cultivated to encircle them like a protective barrier toward that king instead of those he wants to suffer. The hatred and fear are still here, mark my words. The difference is that the people who at one point had no choice but to obey, can now read."

"Ah, reading and freely sourced information is the key to bringing most tyrants down," Caille offered as she neatly stepped over several pits in the uneven ground along the driveway that led up to the McMansion.

"Free press is an amazing thing. So is technology that lets people in the midst of going through calamity the ability to record it or even share it live with the world. It's more difficult to disguise our bad behavior, no matter how big and powerful someone is, if their dirty deeds are broadcast for all to see."

"I totally agree." Marshal nodded once at Bran, as other people drew closer when they moved to the side of the McMansion. And on to some really intimidating guards standing beside a massive steel door that looked like it led to an underground cellar.

Bran closed his eyes for a moment, allowing his ravens to feed him information about the place.

The dilapidated mansion near Piney Run State Park was the perfect cover for something like this. It was nearly covered by a canopy of thick leaves from the centuries- old trees that grew wild here. Everyone had been advised to arrive in nondescript vehicles near the park, and some very nice upscale buses picked up the arriving guests and dropped them off at the base of a long drive that led to the mansion. This time of year buses zinging through the town of Sykesville didn't even raise an eyebrow from the locals. There were so many old mansions renovated into wedding venues that if anyone caught sight of the well-dressed people boarding one of the custom buses, they would just write it off as another marriage happening and think nothing of it.

They all fell quiet as they moved closer to the large steel doors and the two huge men who guarded it.

"Showtime," Marshal mumbled as he reached into his pocket and pulled out a very pretty, custom built cellphone, one they conveniently cloned to hold all the vital information needed to attend this party their way, including the digital invitation they had acquired when amassing it through the links in said phone. "Are you sure they won't recognize us?"

"Bran, they have never seen us before. You are barely a blip on their radar, little man." Caille laughed and Marshal nudged her a little with his elbow as they moved closer. "And me, I'm always on a stage or in a back room. Even following me the only real description they have is of a blue-eyed, blonde, very aggressive woman who radiates power."

"That's you, all right," Bran purred. "Beautifully aggressive, and I wouldn't mind you being aggressive with me again."

"Oh, you know I like that." Caille sent a wink back toward Bran before she giggled rather loudly and simpered a bit, holding tighter to Marshal's arm. "And believe me, I have plans for that ass as soon as we see this thing through."

"Guys, really?" Marshal interrupted, pausing to glare at the both of them. "I mean, I am standing right here."

"Then take some notes," Bran teased. "You can always learn some things from ancient gods."

"Please," Marshal scoffed. "You guys are so old you probably fart dust. I seriously doubt that you could teach me anything."

"Oh, you'd be surprised, little man." Caille leaned down to purr in his ear which got her a pout from the Egyptian Cat. "But you would also be surprised to know that one of my powers is the ability to change my appearance and trick the mind of those around me."

"But you look the same to me," Marshal observed. "Still beautiful as hell but also unique in the way that you move and present yourself. Like a playful but dangerous creature that would tear someone's throat out with their teeth, given half the chance."

"That's because I want you to know who I am, little man. But for everyone else here, their perception of events are slightly different. You are seeing me while they are seeing a green-eyed, red-haired bombshell. And for fun, the people in the fighting arena will see a svelte brunette with serious hazel eyes."

"Breeding confusion when it comes time to tell tales after we get Arcas out of here," Bran finished as the line to get inside moved forward and they were almost next to get in. "Even with those who have been touched by magic, like most of the cult, Caille's power covers us all so all they will see is a powerful and bored businessman with his latest sugar baby and a bodyguard who wants to see some action. You can smell the anticipation and excitement. Bloodsports always rile up those who think they hold the power of life, death, and fate at their hands."

They said no more after that because they were being pushed forward. Marshal presented the digital invitation on his cell, which was scanned, and then the huge, menacing guard offered them a smile as they were ushered forward after hearing their instructions.

"You will be known as Mr. and Mrs. Star," the one wielding the scanner informed them. "All bets will be processed via phone entry. As your app is in order, you already know it is a twelve fight night with bets being taking for all events ending fifteen minutes prior to the actual engagement. For our main event, all bets will be taken until fifteen minutes into the bout."

Bran causally nodded to the side of the large mechanical doors where a metal detector was discreetly in place. He also noted that there were several lock boxes that already contained an array of side arms and other dangerous weapons. It was a good thing they opted for "the no guns to draw attention to themselves" option. Who needed guns when you had magic, claws, and fangs?

"You are confident the bout will last more than fifteen minutes?" Marshal asked, playing the part of a bored rich businessman perfectly. "I don't want to place a bet and have you guys pull a Mike Tyson, thirty seconds and then the match is over."

"I assure you, sir" -- the guard smiled benignly as if imparting great wisdom upon them --"You will have more than enough time to place your bets. As you know, for the main event, there is an at least fifteen thousand dollar buy in."

"You must think you are going to get a lot of bids with a buy-in so low," Marshal mused and the man smiled.

"Sir, what you are about to see will be so unprecedented that you will pay to even get the remains of the losing animal, just to have a souvenir of what you are about to witness."

And there are the fanatics, Bran mused to himself as Marshal offered the man a wicked smile before they were urged forward.

As the outside appeared to be a dilapidated ruin, once they stepped inside the large steel doors they all were amazed at the opulence they stepped into.

"This is some James Bond shit..." Marshal trailed off as their feet sank into a rich red and gold runner that hailed the entrance to another world.

The outside might look destitute, but inside it was a far different story. The trio followed the runner down a set of stairs to a wide arena that looked to hold maybe fifty well-heeled people. Waiters circulated with trays of cocktails and the stereotypical champagne while others were distributing canapés to the milling throng.

"Nothing too heavy is being served," Caille murmured, leaning on Marshal's shoulder and looking helpless and meek as she nodded at the passing trays.

"Some may have a weak stomach, and it wouldn't do well to vomit in public and tarnish their reputations." As he spoke, Marshal thumbed through the phone app in question and winced at what he saw. "Ah, fascinating. This site is constantly updating and now it is confirmed that there will be some exciting tiger on panther action. I wish I was making this shit up."

"The fuck?" Caille whispered as she leaned further on Marshal so she could read the app as well, her eyes moving rapidly as she scanned the offerings. "These people are sick bastards. Why do they call it dog fights when so many exotic creatures are being abused? They actually have kangaroo boxing. What the fuck?"

"The more exciting the better," Bran murmured, shaking his head. "Be thankful they haven't dropped any humans in the arena."

As he spoke, they all moved amongst the guests, and finally took a seat near the front of the arena rails. Stadium seating allowed for everyone to see all of the gory action, but they wanted to be established up front just in case they had to actually go into the ring.

Caille and Marshal took their seats while Bran stood menacing behind them, using his height and his silent demeanor to keep the other guests seated nearby from getting too close.

"You know the plan?" Bran asked as Caille wrinkled her nose. "Caille?"

"It stinks of old blood, fear, and…" she trailed off as she inhaled again. "Sexual arousal. There are some sick fucks in here. Some of them are getting off on this."

She didn't sound surprised, just resigned.

Bran closed his eyes and inhaled, pushing his senses as far as he could. The pong he inhaled almost made him want to puke. So much blood and fear. And if he could smell it so clearly, it must be driving Caille mad.

"Can you smell Arcas, Caille?" Marshal's question snapped Bran's concentration, and he mentally decided to get back with the plan.

"No, and I need to get to wherever they are storing these poor creatures to try and find him. I doubt that they would have him rooming anywhere else."

"I can't get a raven in here," Bran informed them, "but I didn't think I would be able to in the first place."

"So," Marshal decided. "We go with Plan A, A

for Arcas."

"And we have to move the timetable up a bit." There was a growl in Caille's voice, and unlike the sexy growl that turned him on when they were going at it hard and heavy, this growl spoke of violence and bloodshed. "I refuse to sit here and let any innocent creature be harmed."

"We may not have a choice," Bran pointed out. "We don't want to blow our cover."

"Fuck our cover," Caille hissed. "I need to get my brother out of this deathtrap."

"That's not part of the plan." Marshal was quick to intercede. "We need to create a distraction and --"

"If that's what you think" -- Caille stood up and slapped the shit out of Marshal before throwing her nose up in the air like an offended southern belle -- "then I'll go where I am appreciated."

She stormed off as the men surrounding him snickered or shot Marshal conspiring looks.

"I was warned to never stick my dick into crazy," Marshal said just loud enough for those around him to here. "But it's too damn entertaining not to."

That drew a round of laughter that was quickly silenced as the sound of the steel doors closing drew all conversation to a halt.

"Ladies and gentlemen," a masculine voice spoke over a very good sound system. "Good evening. I am glad to see so many smiling faces with so many accounts bursting with disposable income."

There was general laughter after that and Bran took a look around to see about maybe a hundred people crammed elegantly into the arena space.

"Our first bout will begin shortly but please remember, no filming, no photography, and for our own safety, we will be using the old fashioned motto, *leave no evidence,* as our sticking point. If you do try to film this and any of our bouts, we will find you and you will not enjoy the consequences of your actions." There was a moment of silence for that to sink in before the voice continued. "If you check your apps, I am sure you will see the exciting line up we have for you staring with our first bout, Baghira the leopard versus our reigning feline champ... La Tigra. Who will win? A beautiful sleek creature designed to rain death from above or the striped queen of the jungle with her fierce claws waiting to disembowel its prey? Bidding will stop fifteen minutes before the bout begins so, ladies and gentlemen, please remember the fifteen thousand dollar starting bids and may lady luck ever be on your side."

"Starts in thirty minutes," Bran whispered to Marshal who nodded, his eyes still in the direction that Caille had hurried off in a huff.

"Great," Marshal muttered. "Our timetable --"

"Not important." Bran spoke as he let his gaze trail around the arena. "I'm trying to get a count on how many guards with guns we have to get through to get out of here."

"I counted seven hiding in the shadows," Marshal informed him, pointing with his eyes, the pupils elongated in a very feline matter before they returned to human standard. "They are fairly visible so I guess they want their company to feel secure as they watch the bloodletting and torture of innocent animals."

"That means that there are probably three times that amount back in the staging area and the offices."

"You think Caille knows?" he asked, switching his gaze to Bran.

"Oh, I think she does." He gave Marshal a wink.

"In fact, I think you had better start betting or you will be the one blowing our cover. Caille is a grown goddess. She knows what she's doing."

Nodding, Marshal began to tinker with the phone, placing a bid of twenty thousand on the panther. "I hope the dummy accounts Manx set up are accurate or we are going to get bounced out of this place so fast..."

"Well, you have to bid." Bran looked around once more. "There are so many cameras... I wonder if Caille's ability to disguise her appearance beats surveillance equipment? I mean even if it doesn't, there is going to be nothing but confusion if they burst in here looking for her."

"And they are not going to do that now." Marshal sat back in his comfortable chair. "At least not until we get the fuck out of here."

"So we have roughly twenty minutes to find Arcas and escape this place after creating a distraction that will keep attention on the arena." Bran nodded as he grinned at the Cat. "Maybe it's time you order me to go and find your sugar baby."

"You just worried that your new lover may be in over her head," Marshal teased, and Bran sent him a wicked grin.

Was he worried? Maybe a bit more than he would have been if they didn't have... whatever this one day and this odd situation placed them in, relationship-wise. Really, Bran wanted more and he didn't want his potential lover to be harmed before they could actually define what their relationship was.

"Maybe?" he offered, trying to not get lost in the possibilities of what could be and keep his head in this dangerous game.

"Go and find the bitch," Marshal snapped loud

enough for those around him to hear. "I'm tired of her tantrums embarrassing me. Maybe it's time I found a new piece to hang off my arm."

"I'll be fine," he added when Bran played the part of reluctant bodyguard. He handed him the cell phone and then snapped, "Go."

Nodding, Bran loped off in the direction that Caille had ventured, trusting her nose and the story they'd set up to safely lead them both in the right direction.

* * *

"Fucking men." Caille sniffled as she walked down a hall, tears running down her cheeks as she discreetly took in the number and placement of hidden security people. There were not as many as she expected, which was a good thing. Less throats she would have to tear out.

Still playing the hurt, pitiful woman, she sniffled loudly, taking in the faint scent of magic mingled in with the scents of fear, arousal, and death that seemed to permeate the place. This was not the first time this type of exhibition had been put on here, but if she had her way, it would be the last.

Sniffling harder, she picked up a faint whiff of the spicy scent of her bear, so she cried a bit harder as she made her way toward that scent.

Well, she couldn't really say that the scent was *her* bear per se, as she no longer was sharing a bed with him and hadn't been for a long time, but he was still her brother and she needed to punish those who had taken him.

Her mind briefly flashed to Bran and what he hinted at when he mentioned that today's punishments were less barbarous than the ones he observed or even ordered, and wondered if he had any ideas that would be so horrific, it would warn the cult members away from them permanently.

Bran... now that was a spicy meatball. He was so responsive in bed, so intelligent and knowledgeable about times in history that she didn't bother to recall, and that kingly noble streak that ran through him was so powerful she was shocked that he wasn't shitting swords and crowns.

She couldn't forget how awesome he was in bed. It was a strange thing to consider, especially now when she was throwing herself headlong into danger to save her brother, but something about The Raven soothed her. She almost instantly trusted him, the kind of trust that had taken years for her to develop with her fellow Huntsmen. She really didn't believe in love at first sight -- look at the mess Kern was in because he'd led with his heart instead of his head -- but there was something growing between the two of them. Something she really wanted to explore. She shook off the memories of how perfectly he had filled her and turned her attention to where the scent was leading her.

There were several guards, she noticed, who made note of her passing, her sensitive ears picking up on the conflicting descriptions they were giving about her as she pushed her ability to cloud the mind.

She stopped when she noticed that there were no more well-dressed people meandering around and the silence of this death trap became almost deafening. There was a guard ahead; not a stationary one, a patrolling one, so she ducked into the first room that she saw.

The man startled a little at her appearance but quickly followed her into what looked like a rarely used office.

"Miss," he called out, pushing the door open to see Caille, a pink-haired party girl illusion she pushed into his mind, sitting on top of a desk and sobbing her eyes out. "Excuse me, Miss. You can't be in here."

Caille sniffed a bit harder, before looking up at him with huge green eyes drowning in tears. "I'm... I'm so-sorry," she sobbed, "I -- I was looking for... for the bathroom..." She broke down in tears, crying harder than before.

She could feel the man's heart harden as he stared at her, cruel brown eyes narrowing in anger.

"It's back up the hallway that you just walked down." He stepped closer and instantly Caille could smell the scent of animal, of blood, and of anger wafting off of him. She sniffed in his direction and there... she caught a stronger whiff of Bran. He had to be in the direction that the man passed.

He stepped toward her, reaching out to grip her arm roughly, jerking her to her feet as she turned to face him fully.

"You will not offer me aid?"

"I told you where the bathrooms were. You can't be down here."

"You have no care for me?" she asked again, pitifully swiping at her face with both hands.

"I only have a care for my job, which you are making more difficult for me at the moment."

"You have no idea how difficult it's about to become." Caille's voice came out dark, crackling, and strong as she jerked away from the man and let her crone visage strike fear into his heart.

He gasped, nearly tripping on his feet to step back from her, his hands going to the rifle strapped to his back as his heart began to race. "What the fuck are you?"

What he saw was hundreds of years of anger, the pain that each animal felt being forced into the arena, the soul-wrenching pain of each death foisted upon those innocent creatures who lived and died in this area.

Her eyes were solid black, her face wrinkled... the flesh tearing away from her skull. Vibrant pink hair had turned into a stringy, gray, greasy mass that hung limply over skeletal shoulders. Her nose was rotting away beneath his horrified gaze as her smile split her lips and thick black puss oozed out.

"Oh, God, what the fuck are you?" he gasped and Caille smiled wider as she felt his fear nearly drive his mind to the breaking point.

"Goddess," she corrected him. "And you didn't feel the need to pray when you led all of those innocent creatures to their doom..."

"Fuck!" he screamed, bringing the rifle up, his finger on the trigger, but a wave of her mind pressed fear so deep inside of him that his heat began to race so fast that it skipped beats. "No." He clutched at his chest as he let the rifle fall and slid down to his knees.

"What you feel is the fear of every animal you led to death." She stepped closer. "Their pain. Their suffering, their hopelessness and despair."

The man's heart froze. His bladder let loose and he slumped lifeless to the ground. His breath rattled in his chest and Caille offered him one final smile.

"So sorry to ruin your day and make your job more difficult, but I guess I'll be seeing you in hell, because your life is a partial ransom for all the lives you have taken. I guess I'll have to get the rest from your cult brothers."

Caille felt all life leave his body. Then quickly shifting back to her normal form, she grabbed him by the ankles and pulled him deeper into the room. Pulling the radio from his ear, she took a moment to listen to the chatter. When alarms were not raised, she wrinkled her nose at the urine smell filling the room and began to strip. She took a moment to crack the door open before she stepped back and began to concentrate.

It took her mere seconds to stand in the chill of the room naked and even a shorter amount of time for her to draw her energies into herself and push.

There was a flash of light, and where once stood a beautiful naked goddess now stood a large pale blonde wolf. The beautiful and disproportionally large animal lifted her nose and took one more sniff before darting out of the room and toward the scent she was tracking.

She gave no further thought to the dead man she left behind. She was on a mission and well, if anyone harmed her brother, the arena would flow red with the blood of the guilty.

The goddess Cailleach Beara swore it into being. So mote it be.

Chapter Six

With her senses becoming even keener in her wolf form, Caille darted down the spiraling halls, sliding in and out of shadows as she stalked her prey.

The smell of her brother Huntsman grew, and her mind dropped all other concerns as she tracked him. Her animal instincts were riding her hard as she turned a corner and ran smack into a trio of men, two guards and one man in a white lab coat.

"Fuck, one must have gotten out," one of the guards gasped as she stumbled back, crouching down, her hind end higher than the front as a low growl rolled from her throat. Both men had smaller caliber guns drawn though they both had rifles strapped to their backs.

"Bait animal?" the man in the lab coat asked as the two guardsmen began to surround her, herding her in the direction she actually wanted to go.

"Too pretty," one of the guardsmen commented. "Probably something special and pretty for the bear fight. Look at how large this fucking dog is."

"Wolf," the man in the lab coat commented. "You can tell by the formation of her muzzle and the way her ears are situated. She is an exceptionally healthy animal."

"If you say so, doc." One guardsman spoke softly, as if not wanting to agitate the large animal in front of him further. "But that don't explain what she's doing out."

"And what do we do with her?" the other asked, circling around her.

Caille looked back at him for a second before putting her full attention on the so-called doc.

"We put her in with the bear-man, of course."

The doctor snorted.

"But he hasn't shifted yet --"

"And being left helpless with an apex predator will probably do more for getting him to shift than all the drugs we pumped into him."

Fuck, Caille thought as she absorbed as much information as she could. Time was running out for her to create a distraction but should she do that when she was finally going to be placed where she needed to be?

"In with the bear-man then." One of the guards laughed nastily.

"You're sick," the guard behind her said to the doc. "He's not shifted yet and that wolf will tear him apart. Look at those fangs!"

"It's not like it's a real man anyway," the doctor callously spoke.

"So why don't we just take them back to the temple and kill him there...draw his life energy someplace safe without all of this show?"

"So that the creature that hunts us can catch a whiff of his energy and come barreling in, accusing us of breaking the contract? It's much safer this way."

"So we are breaking the contract." The guard behind her sounded a bit disgusted with the whole thing.

"Only if we get caught." The other guard laughed as the man called doc stepped back.

"Herd her down the hall and into the bear room. The first bout is due to begin in ten minutes."

After that, Caille allowed the men to herd her down the hall, making an act of snapping and snarling, but moving forward with her tail between her legs.

In no time at all, she was being kicked into the room where a burly naked redhead sat in the corner of the room, bloody scrapes and bruises rising up on his skin.

"Arcas," Caille gasped, her human voice sounding odd even to her own ears, coming from her wolf body. "Arcas, can you hear me?"

Arcas lifted his head and Caille gasped as the red pits of his eyes seemed to catch and hold her own gaze, sending fear sliding down her spine… as did the growl emerging from his throat… growing louder and louder until a full blooded angry bear roar filled the room.

There was no recognition in his eyes. There was no humanity left in his face. He lurched to his feet, his fingers and toes tipped with massive, razor sharp claws as his upper lip rolled back to expose black gums and deadly looking fangs.

Fuck, she was in trouble.

* * *

Time was wasting and Bran really didn't know what to do. He looked down at the phone and noted that he only had five minutes before the betting ended that that meant about twenty minutes before the first fight started. He had no idea where Caille was and had no idea where to start his search for The Bear.

He really had no idea who he was looking for but he knew he could possibly feel the waves of his magic if he transformed or was already transformed. He really had forgotten how useful his ravens were, how much he relied on them, and now that he didn't have them he was feeling the loss.

But he had a role to play and he stuck to it, first walking down the long hall where Caille had disappeared before he abruptly changed direction. Now as he walked, he noted the commiserating looks from other bodyguards who heard the ruckus either directly or through rapidly spreading gossip and the security guards who looked at him with something akin to pity.

Putting a long-suffering look on his face and shrugging at one security officer in the universal symbol of *what else can I do*, he moved on, looking in shadows and alcoves. He could see a few people making out, some security guards avoiding duty, and dust bunnies. He also counted about twenty armed security guards and about fifty cameras set up in strategic places.

As he moved further from the pit of the arena he felt a sudden wash of familiar energy. It had to be Caille, he mused. And she would only shift if she had found her fellow Huntsman... or if she was being attacked. He took a moment to look around but noticed that no one was reacting in any way. There was no rush to protect or no intense chatter on mics, so he moved on.

He looked down at the phone again and cursed under his breath. Betting had officially stopped and now he had fifteen minutes to figure out a way to get them out of there.

Fuck.

He had to trust in Caille and just do what his job was to do in the first place. Bran kept moving back toward the bathrooms.

The doors were mechanical so the security had to open them. Okay, what was a good way to focus that issue... stampede.

Great. How to start that one? His wanderings took him back toward the steel doors and the locked boxes filled with guns.

That point noted, he paced back toward the bathrooms as people started filtering back toward their seats. Time was running out. So he did the only think he could think of. He ducked into an alcove and pulled out the phone. He dialed a number he had been taught by his ravens and put the phone to his ear.

"9-1-1, what is the nature of your emergency?"

"Dog fighting," he hissed. "I'm a reporter for the *Sun* and I got invited to this party but it wasn't a party. They are fighting exotic cats and dogs, and there are guns everywhere and they locked us in. Get me out of here... Shit!" He hissed. "I think they're going to kill me!"

"Sir, where are you?"

"Sykesville... I don't know... in an old mansion... shit! They found me!"

Then he hung up, convinced that he stayed on the line enough for them to trace the call. With a bounce in his step he made his way back to Marshal and whispered, "Exit achieved. And if I played my cards right, we should be getting our escape through outside means."

"Ten minutes left." Marshal began to wring his hands, looking more and more nervous. "What the hell is Caille doing?"

* * *

"Fuck! Arcas!" She ducked a powerful swing that ruffled her fur as she dove out of the way. Thankful she was still in her more nimble wolf form, she ducked around her brother without taking another hit.

Arcas was slowly transforming. The drugs she could smell in his blood or fear was finally getting to him because as she watched her brother was slowly shifting from the beautiful red-haired man he was into a gigantic red-furred monster.

It was strange seeing such a slow change, kind of disturbing really, but the thing that really made her fur stand on end was the blood red pits that had taken over his eyes.

Snarling, he moved faster than any natural bear as he lunged for her again, this time catching her in the side, causing her to yelp loudly, grateful that her thick skin under the fur was hard to tear. That is not to say that there weren't several bleeding spots on her body from where he got in lucky blows, but she was getting tired and he was getting in more lucky shots.

Arcas was just lumbering around the room, swinging at anything that moved, proof that his mind was not firing on all human cylinders. Though the cloying medicinal smell was easing in his scent, the smell was still strong enough to addle her brother.

Caille had a plan. If she could wait until he was fully shifted, she could finally break the fuck out of this room, then they could rush the people and none of the mundanes would ever be telling tales of rampaging humans. But first...

Caille ducked another swing and went on the attack, diving around the swinging arm and snapping at her brother's heels. He roared in anger and took another swipe, but his frustration had the added benefit of forcing him to shift fully.

"About damn time," she hissed, and the sound of her voice seemed to drive his anger further.

"Asshole. Getting yourself caught! Getting kidnapped like an idiot!" As she castigated him, she maneuvered herself in front of the door.

He roared in response to her taunting and lumbered in her direction at full tilt. Sinking low as he lunged, Caille ducked between the bear's legs and slid out of the way.

His form too massive to quickly change directions or even stop, the gargantuan red bear bashed into the cell door, splitting it down the middle with a loud cracking sound as the full weight of his body slammed into it.

The door gave way and Caille, never one to waste an opportunity, leaped on his back before dashing down the hall, laughing to herself. Several startled security guards raced in her direction to investigate the noise.

She dodged around a few long legs as she could hear the radio chatter getting extreme. "The arena doors!" one enterprising guard screamed , and Caille dodged past him, racing ahead along with the screams of fear and panic behind her... and the roars of one irate red bear.

Plus side, she was smelling less and less of the drugs in his scent pile. Downside, he still wasn't in his right mind. He was still raging against her, the soldiers, and the world, and that made him dangerous.

Caille raced headlong around corners, as security threw doors open, allowing for an easy route to the arena. The killing pit was safer than having him go after the not-so-innocent people, less fallout for them in the long run, so she slowed enough for him to catch sight of her before she took off running again.

Her actions proved fruitful because faster than she thought, she was racing into the gigantic arena pit, her paws sinking into the soft sand, the smell of old death and pain filling her snout.

Arcas roared as he raced in after her and then the real screaming began.

"Ladies and gentlemen. There has been a sudden change in our order. All previous bets have been canceled. You now have fifteen minutes to place your bets... Wolf versus bear. Who will come out on top?"

Vaguely, she was aware of someone calling her name but she was given no time to contemplate it. Arcas' bear form had space to move, and that made him even more dangerous. Suddenly, she couldn't think. All she could do was dodge and pray that Bran found a way to distract people so she could transform and get the fuck out of there.

* * *

"Holy shit," Bran breathed as he took in the size of the wolf that rushed into the arena. From the feel of the energy rolling off it, he knew that he was looking at Caille in her shifted form. But he had no time to contemplate how beautiful she was in movement, for fast on her heels was the largest, reddest bear he had ever seen.

"Oh, fuck," Marshal hissed. "Time's up. What the hell are we supposed to do? Where's the exit strategy?"

"On its way?" Bran tried to sound confident, but one of the ravens was sending snippets of a song where someone was screaming "nine-one-one is a joke." Whoever said Ravens didn't have a wonderful sense of humor?

"They better get here now!" Marshal all but shouted as Arcas dropped to all fours and rushed Caille, who barely had time to dodge out of the way. Being in open space gave her more maneuverability but it did the same for The Bear.

People around them were cheering in excitement, the sound of their voices turning into one huge cacophony of sound. The gaping maws of their open mouths reminded him of the endless hunger of the creatures he had fought and killed to keep his lands safe, of the seething demons that haunted his nightmares, of the mindless, screaming horrors that humanity could become on the battlefield when fear and anger drive them senseless.

It was a chilling picture and the only thing that

tore his mind away from the violent worshiping troglodytes that surrounded him was a sharp scream of pain from the throat of a wolf.

"Caille!" he found himself calling out, moving to the railing of the deep pit of the arena as he watched her go tumbling ass over heels into the sand.

She was quickly on her feet again, but this time she was favoring her left side. She was injured and there wasn't anything they could do to help. If they made a move the men with guns would mow them down. If they protested no one would hear them anyway. They were trapped in a situation where all they could do was watch in horror.

"Ladies and gentlemen," the voice called out and suddenly Bran was once again aware of the passage of time. He felt a sharp sting in his palms and looked down to see where he had dug bloody crescents into his palms, he had been squeezing his fists so tight. "The betting is now closed and now to add some excitement... release the hounds!"

"No!" Marshal screamed as The Egyptian Cat began to pace, looking for all the world like he had placed a wrong bet and was afraid of losing his hard earned cash.

"Marshal." Bran stepped close to the shorter man. "Calm down. We don't need to do anything to draw their suspicions until the distraction comes and we can get the fuck out of here. All of us. Together. Trust in Caille."

Yet even as he spoke, Bran felt his own heart lurch in his chest as the steel doors slid open and into the arena rushed a baying pack of dogs, all large breeds, and all salivating like they couldn't wait to get a taste of blood.

At that point, Marshal lost it. Tossing all caution

to the wind, The Egyptian Cat rushed the railing, and in a feat that only a feline could pull off, leaped clear over the railing and landed in a crouch next to the wolf… who staggered to a stop and just stared at him.

There was a moment of silence before someone shouted, "Twenty thousand says that crazy gymnast man bites it first!"

"Fifty thousand on the bear getting the man!"

"I'll see that bet!" someone else screamed, and then it was a free for all.

Bran backed up as several armed security guards moved in his direction and he did the smart thing and ducked amongst the once again screaming, yelling bodies, and made for the front gate.

There was nothing he could do for them now but try and sow more confusion and buy them some more time.

Fuck, he hated when he had to improvise. But as a king, he had been looked upon as a master strategist. Time to put some of that brain power to work.

* * *

"What the fuck, Cat?" Caille hissed as she shook off the pain of that last blow to face The Cat that stood between her and Arcas. Even in his maddened state, The Bear stood back and stared at The Cat, his red head tilted to the side like he was calling his stupid ass crazy for trying such a stunt.

And as for the once baying hounds, they rushed toward Arcas and then almost as one, they froze and backed up as far away from him as he could get.

"I'm here to rescue you?" he asked, a nervous chuckle in his voice before he cursed and leaped out of the way.

Arcas was rushing toward him, but not with the same maddened speed as he was moving in before.

The Bear was slowing down. Caille took a big whiff in his direction and almost jumped at what she smelled. The drugs were now rapidly leaving his system, but there was no time for celebrations. The people were now roaring for human blood, and the sound and smell of their bloodlust was driving Arcas mad once again.

With a roar, he lunged toward Marshal, who leaped up in the air, flying over the bear's head in some parkour acrobatic shit, before landing in a crouch in the sand behind him.

Caille took this opportunity to rush Arcas, snapping at his body and driving him further away from The Cat while they tried to vie for more time.

"Good one," Marshal called out as he coughed, choking on the sand and probably the scent of old blood and death, she decided, before she raced around Arcas, slipping under a huge paw as he swung at her again. "But I don't know how long I can keep this up."

"How are we going to get out of here?" she called, panting as the pain in her side began to get to her. She probably had a cracked rib due to the last blow Arcas delivered and she was not moving as fast as she once was.

"Bran said he had it covered."

"He better hurry," she hissed as Arcas dropped to all fours and rushed her. "Shit!"

She could not dodge out of the way in time. She went down in a rush of sand and sound as The Bear slammed into her.

She blinked once as Arcas hovered over her, hesitating for a moment before he jerked, yelping in pain as Marshal landed on his back, his teeth transforming into a cute set of fangs before he sank them into The Bear's rounded ear.

It did the trick. Arcas was no longer interested in her and was now rising up on his hind legs, roaring and shaking, trying to knock the clinging cat off of his back. But Marshal had grown claws and had sunk them in deep, holding on for dear life.

Caille gained her feet and limped out of the way, glad for once that their supernatural nature kept most normal animals in fear of their presence, for the dogs were staying put. The people, on the other hand, were on their feet, cheering and stomping, screaming for more blood as those in the pit fought for their lives.

A sudden uptick in screaming had her turning her attention back to the Cat and The Bear, and she howled at what she saw. Arcas has somehow unseated Marshal and had sunk his fangs into the forearm he used to shield his throat.

Marshal threw back his head and yowled like a scalded cat, and in that very instant, Arcas froze. He pulled his teeth back and lifted his huge furry head, the whites of his eyes returning as he stared Marshal's face.

He could be coming back to himself or ready to tear his throat out, there was no clear way for Caille to know. So, she swiftly gathered her energy, ready to leap between Arcas and Marshal when the sounds of gunfire caused a whole new cacophony to fill the arena, the sound of terrified men and women running for their lives.

* * *

"Evade, evade, evade," Bran chanted to himself, and he ducked down to disguise his height and made his way toward the sealed steel doors.

Security was still mobilizing, people with earpieces racing to and fro while the waitstaff seemed to disappear into some of those doors he was reluctant to open.

Marshal's actions, unexpected and dangerous as they were, did have the right amount of shock and awe to buy them some time. While security was trying to figure out who let the bear out, where the wolf had come from, and how in the hell a pampered millionaire with more money than common sense survived a leap into a pit that was nearly fifteen feet deep.

Never one for wasting his chances, Bran ran out. There had to be a way to get them open, and from the sounds of the roaring crowds, his diversion wasn't going to arrive fast enough to make the cult members open the doors themselves. Hell, he wondered even if the peacekeepers even had the power to open those doors on their own. So it looked like he was going to have to give them a little help and provide more of a distraction to get them out of this jam.

He was near the doors when the same burly security guard he met on the way in stopped him. "Sir, please return to the arena."

"I wish I could --" Bran began as the man pulled his sidearm from its hip holster.

"Sir, I am not asking, I am telling."

So Bran rolled his eyes and held his hands, palms up, as he backed away.

"Well," he mused, "I tried to warn you."

The guard relaxed his grip on his weapon and that's when Bran struck. Pulling his own powers forward, he felt his neck runes began to glow as he reached up and touched them. With a jerk, he pulled the glowing symbols from around his neck, making the guard curse and take a step back as the flowing blue energy took the solid shape of a sword. Then with a speed that was still unmatched since his days on the battlefield, Bran the Blessed sprang into action, swinging his glowing broadsword upward with a two handed slash, cutting the guard's arm from his body.

His screams were drowned out by the roars of the bloodthirsty crowd as the man went down hard, holding his bleeding stump in his hand.

The other security guard, hearing his partner scream in pain, rushed toward them and then froze as he saw Bran bringing up his sword to strike at him.

"Fucking light saber..." the man hissed before Bran was rushing him, causing the man to back up and trip over his fallen partner before, in a move befitting a trained swordsman, Bran stuck fast and hard, aiming for his neck, not even flinching when he felt his sword of energy pass though skin, tendon, and bone. The second guard's head went flying, and when the first opened his mouth to scream again, Bran slammed the tip of his blade through his head.

Blood immediately poured forth and flooded ground, flowing down the stairs in a macabre red river as Bran neatly sidestepped it and released his hold on the glowing broadsword. It snapped back around his neck with a slap and the man made his way to the gun boxes, using his godlike strength to rip one open.

Inside he found a small caliber handgun and hefted it into his hand. As he had no idea how to work modern weapons, he closed his eyes and called on his ravens. Instantly his mind was flooded with operations of this particular hand gun model, a Desert Eagle semi-automatic. Within seconds he knew how to work the damn thing but had an idea that his shot would be for shit until he had some practice. Chambering a round in, he spun around just as someone gasped in shock.

Bran spun around and then grinned at who he saw. Why, if it wasn't his stalker.

With one hand he reached out and jerked the

man to him, passing the barrel of the gun under his chin.

"I know I'm probably a pretty shitty shot right now," he purred into the whimpering man's ear. "But I have a feeling that at this close range I can't miss. So how about we do something like open up that pretty little steel door for me?"

"They'll kill me if I do," he gasped, both hands held up in front of him.

"And I'll kill you if you don't."

That decided the matter. The man pointed to a hidden panel in the wall and after leaving him there with a threat of "no funny stuff," Bran watched as he hit a few buttons and the doors began to slide open.

"Good boy," he praised and then lifted the gun into the air and started firing off rounds.

First there was a stunned silence and then there was a wall of humanity that began to rush the doors. Bran stepped out of the way, dragging his hostage with him as he flexed his energy and cloaked them both in the shadows.

Just as the well-dressed barbarians began to rush the exit, there came the loud sound of sirens and enhanced voices coming from police speakers ordering everyone to stop.

"Now," Bran said to the man, "you have to make a few choices. I can let you go and you can try your luck with the police, with your cult friends, or you can come with me. Now what do you want to do?"

"You will kill me..." the man whimpered and Bran laughed low and nasty.

"Maybe I will and maybe I won't. But if I let you go your cult friends will be burying you within the hour. With the cops, depending on if your cult has any cop friends, you may last a day or so... or you could end yourself while rotting in jail. If you willingly go with me, you may just make it out of his bullshit alive. Tick tock. Time's passing. What's your decision?"

* * *

There were gunshots, and screams, and then the mass exodus of the so-called crowd of humanity that had just been betting on their lives. Caille looked over at Arcas and sagged in relief. The smell of drugs was mostly gone in his scent pile and he was slowly shifting back to his human form.

Marshal was frowning, staring down at his arm in confusion, and the dogs were still being very smart animals, smarter than the humans at least, and were staying back, very far away from them.

Looking around and not seeing anyone left surrounding the arena, Caille took a chance and shifted back to her human form, cursing as the more delicate human shape suddenly felt the full brunt of her aches and pains.

"Fuck you, Arcas," she shouted. "How did you let yourself get taken? You're smarter than that!"

"Caille?" his hoarse voice mumbled before he collapsed into the sand. It was then that Caille noticed that she had done some real damage to him as well. She sighed, then winced as the growing pain in her side made breathing difficult. Yeah, she was looking at some fractured ribs, and as the sound of sirens reached her sensitive ears, she realized that she could not heal them without everything seeming suspicious.

She was frowning at Marshal, trying to figure out how to get out of this one when Bran's voice reached her.

"Listen," he hissed, and she looked up to see him peering down into the pit at them. "I have to run. I am disguising me and our mutual friend so here is the story. Marshal, you are the reporter that made the 911 call and then dropped the phone running for your life. Caille, you were looking for your brother when you got snatched up too. You'll have to come up with a reason why. I have to get out of here as your constables... uh, your police are here. Do you understand?"

Caille nodded, then winced before scowling at the collapsed Arcas. By the time she looked back up, Bran was gone.

"I just love a man who understands I can stand on my own two feet," she muttered before taking a look around them. They were closest to the door. Neat. The dogs were still cowering... harder to explain, but still good. They could do this.

Moments later as the police arrived, they saw a shaky looking man wrapping a jacket around a naked woman's trembling, bruised and bloody body while an equally bruised and naked man was collapsed on the sand.

"Get them out of there!" someone called and when the cowering dogs didn't move, the door to their arena was slid open and several officers moved in to hustle them away from the cowering dogs.

"You scared them away." Caille rubbed her eyes and began to sob. "Thank goodness you showed up. They were going to kill us."

"Thank you." Marshal was getting into his own acting job as he looked back over at a dazed Arcas who was being helped out by two skittish officers. "I didn't think you were going to make it in time. I made the call and then they caught me. They threw me in here with them then turned a pack of wild dogs on us," he hissed, holding up his arm still dripping blood from Arcas' bite.

"You the reporter?" one of them asked and Marshal nodded.

"Yes, but please get us out of here. I think that's the man that was reported kidnapped and I don't think he's doing too good. They were drugging him and then there was the woman... Oh man, I don't know what they did to her but she needs to go to a hospital --"

"We will see to it, sir," an officer promised as he called for a medical transport and informed them that they would have three victims.

As they moved out into the early dusk, Caille bit back a smile as she watched those rich assholes who were so self-important that they would pay to watch another living being be torn apart alive try to explain their way out of trouble while what looked to be several news crews circled, waiting for their chance to rip into some privileged flesh.

Soon Caille found herself sitting on a gurney, wrapped in a thermal blanket beside Marshal as they loaded Arcas into another ambulance. She caught his eye long enough for him to nod at her. He'd heard the plan and understood. Everything was going to be okay.

"I love it when a plan --"

"Stop!" Caille glared at Marshal until the Cat fell back into his terrified reporter in over his head role. "Just stop. I want to go home, get a shower, and check on Arcas."

"And Bran," Marshal pointed out. "You know, the man who trusted you to do what needed to be done with no interference from him?"

"And to get laid," she added as a small smile pulled at her lips. Bran had trusted her to see to matters on her end and he hadn't hopped in being all caveman about helping her and totally ruining their operation. She liked that, she liked that a lot. "Isn't he sweet?"

"If you say so," Marshal mumbled. "But you know we lost our chance at getting any worthwhile information out of the place. The cops are going to take it all."

"The objective was to rescue Arcas. Objective met. Achievement unlocked. And now we can go home."

"But the cult still has Thomas..."

"And now Bran has secured us a hostage who just happens to be a font of information from what we recovered in his phone."

"Do tell?"

But she never got to tell because then the paramedics were returning for them and Caille had to go back to being a shocked and traumatized woman and Marshal had to go back to being an injured victim of a cruel joke played by fate, and an invite to a nosy reporter.

But things were looking up. Soon they would find Kern's mate, end the cult, and everything could go back to normal.

Victory was so close she could almost taste it.

Chapter Seven

After everything had been said and done, it had been so incredibly easy to fool the police, which made for a relatively easy doctor's visit. The hard part had been making sure everyone kept their story straight. That's where having superhuman hearing really came in handy.

All Caille had to do was to mumble out the story she elaborated on during the uncomfortable ambulance drive to the nearest hospital emergency room and they were all set. The boys had heard her words and she could listen in. Arcas described picking up his brother's boyfriend Thomas from the university where he worked because he had felt uncomfortable about some homophobic taunts he had received after he came out to his classes. Thomas' best friend Marshal had tagged along to keep Thomas company and didn't feel that they were in any danger until they were set upon by some strange men dressed in matching uniforms and tossed into a van, with Marshal escaping to call the police and report the kidnapping.

That much was easily corroborated with a few phone calls to Baltimore's police department but after that, it got a little tricky. Yes, Marshal was a freelance reporter, that was actually true, as he had written several op-ads about culture in Baltimore, sometimes doing more in-depth pieces about certain neighborhoods and the help that they needed to thrive. It was easy enough for him to tell them that he had received the invite on-line and had shown up out of curiosity, hoping that a small party would get his mind off his missing best friend. Once there he was locked in the room and threatened by crazy men with guns. They wanted to know what he saw and he could honestly say that he didn't see anything. They left him alone in a room long enough for him to place the desperate phone call before they came back, discovered his phone, and broke it into pieces in front of his face. He was then knocked around until the same jackasses who'd attacked his best friend then tossed him into an arena surrounded by screaming men and women to be set upon by dogs.

Of course he recognized Arcas, the redhead who had been taken with Thomas, but he didn't know anything about the blonde woman who was tossed naked into the sand-filled pit with them.

Caille, sobbing uncontrollably, choked out a story about going back to the place where her brother, the red-haired Arcas had been taken, along with her boyfriend. She had only wanted to see if the police had missed anything, if someone watching had seen anything, but her search was fruitless. Then once she had dropped her boyfriend off at his home, she went out to pick up some ice cream and other comfort foods when someone snatched her off of the street. No, she didn't get a good look at their faces 'cause someone rapped her on the head and she passed out. She woke up naked and cold and when pounding on the door delivered no help, she collapsed into a mass of useless tears. She didn't know how long she sat there sobbing but finally some men came out and dragged her into the arena where she saw her brother being attacked by dogs... as the many bites on his body could attest. She was about to just give up and die when Marshal had been thrust into the arena with them and he heroically went after the dogs, giving her time to try and drag her drugged up brother to safety. She thought they were done for until she heard sirens and shooting and the dogs backed away and the good people of the police department's SWAT team came in and rescued her from a gooey, painful death. Gag.

Arcas had the easiest story to tell of them all. He was fighting in the parking lot to protect Thomas. He was dragged into a van. He was clocked in the head and shot full of drugs. He remembered little else as everything was a haze. His story was made all the more believable by the frightening amounts of ketamine in his bloodstream. The doctors told him he was fortunate to remember as much as he did.

After a combined two hundred and sixty-four stitches, they were kept overnight for observation while the police investigation continued.

And what did the police find? Not much. It seems they caught some people dressed in waiter's outfits chucking hard drives, phones, and papers into a huge fireplace in the kitchen as fast as their arms could move. The computer hard drives went into the fire first, and it appeared that no one was really talking.

They were beginning to think it was new and dangerous gang of some kind. Maybe they had a problem with gay people as quite a few gangs did and Thomas wound up on their radar. Maybe drugs were involved because they found a hefty stash in the building along with cages filled with exotic animals. Hell, maybe it was an insane form of fight club where the rich who couldn't get their jollies off of abusing the people they deemed beneath them anymore and moved on to bloodier faire. There were questions building up with no clear answers.

So after taking their statements, the trio were allowed to make some phone calls which led to a tearful boyfriend, Bran in his best acting job to date, rushing in to check on his girlfriend.

He was also conveniently driving a minivan that

had room enough to fit them all.

The trio was handed bags of antibiotics and painkillers, promised police protection... which they turned down, and gave assurances of not leaving town for anything.

Caille dozed in the front seat while Bran drove them home. Her falling asleep she chalked up to self-defense. The Raven couldn't drive for shit and she had no problem telling him so.

"My ravens taught me and Manx gave me a quick lesson before I came here," he pointed out. "Give me time and I'll improve. I just need practice."

"Not brave enough to get in any vehicle with you again," Caille muttered before closing her eyes. When next she opened them, she was in her bedroom, naked and tucked under her covers. Beside her lay the warm, large mass of the man she had chosen to grace her bed.

"Well, hello there," Bran purred, snuggling her closer, and she grinned as he began to press gentle kisses on face before taking her lips in a pretty decent good morning kiss. "How are you feeling?"

"Fine, but the stitches pinch. I am pain-free and healing, but I have to slow it down because I'm sure I'm going to have to talk to the police again, and whole and hale wouldn't fit after the stories we told. Also, I am so hungry I could eat a horse."

"No horses, but I am sure I can come up with some bacon. After you answer a few questions for me."

Caille pulled back to she could look into his face. The runes on his neck were faintly glowing like they were when he got all worked up and pretty with sex, and her at her curious look, he began to explain.

"Manx is in with our stalker --"

"You really found him there? That incompetent boob?"

"I guess good help really is hard to find." He laughed. "Or so the ravens tell me. And now the ravens are telling me that there is one angry little cultist in the basement singing like a canary."

"Manx has a way about them."

"Indeed." Bran nodded. "They are very insightful. And your brother is acting strange."

"Kern?"

"No. Manx is not allowing him to wake up until they have some solid information to feed him because that stag is going to blow. Your brother Arcas is much recovered and for some reason is avoiding Marshal like the plague. Marshal himself noticed but is back to sitting with Kern and waiting for some solid intel from Manx."

"Arcas bit him. He is probably feeling upset about harming one so much more powerless than himself. Give him a few days and he will get over it."

"So to sum up, our stalker --"

"Your stalker," she corrected.

"We found him together," he teased. "We have to share custody."

"You know too much popular culture for someone who has been locked in a crypt for thousands of years."

"Ravens," he reminded her. "They have this awesome racial memory and they impart all of their wisdom unto me. I only need to be reminded of some things I've never encountered before I can recall them perfectly."

"Convenient."

"And frustrating. I asked for information on operating a gun and now I have years of American gun rights legislation running through my head."

"Yeah, that can be distracting," Caille admitted,

pressing a kiss to his lips. "But you did so well."

"I was scared out of my mind, Caille. I didn't know what was going on and there was the damn door that needed controls to open, as me tearing it from his moorings would have drawn too much attention."

"But you found a way."

"Yes, I used my runes as a weapon, decapitated a guard, slayed another, tore open a gun box and threaten to blow the head off of our stalker before shouting to you all what was going on and escorting that idiot back here where I was sure Manx was going to probably torture him to death."

"And how do you feel about that?"

"After looking at all your wounds, strangely satisfied. It's not like I'm going to lose sleep over the matter. I am more worried about Kern and his mate."

"And that," Caille began, again pressing soft kisses to his full soft lips and his chin, just a bit prickly with a five-o'clock shadow. "Brings me to my next question."

"Ask away."

"You didn't jump into the pit with me..." Her voice trailed off as she tried to organize her thoughts. She was still sleepy and kind of in in awe at the man who was now in her bed.

Really, he was learning and growing so fast and he trusted her. He was beautiful and he trusted her. He was a perfect lay, the perfect submissive -- and he trusted her. She wasn't fool enough to think one bout in her bed led to that but she had to know why.

"You are a capable woman." He nodded and waited for more.

"That's it?" Caille finally asked him. "You let me do my job because you find me capable?"

"I find you beautiful and strong. I find you

absolutely astounding as you have the power to do almost anything you want, yet you locked yourself in with Manx to protect humanity."

"Manx is more powerful than I --"

"They are more powerful than all of us combined, yet you still put your faith in them. And you are part of an amazingly caring family who would sacrifice almost anything for each other."

"I wouldn't go that far --" She stopped as he placed a finger against her lips, halting her speech.

"Take the compliment, Cailleach Beara. I recognize your strengths and I see the beauty in you."

"You wouldn't say that if you saw what I showed to a guard who had me trapped in a room --"

"You are beautiful. I know the legends and you are still beautiful. Your soul glows, woman. You are so strong and capable, you're frighteningly competent, and I knew you know how to handle yourself. You have done so on many occasions in our brief acquaintance and I know in my heart that that once you say you will accomplish something, you will accomplish it."

"Even though you haven't known me for that long?"

"Kern has told me so many stories of your greatness, oh, and how you are the mischievous heart of this family... I saw the greatness when you left to help even the innocent animals in that pit. You couldn't stand by and watch any innocent be harmed. I trust you, Cailleach Beara. I trust you to know your own strengths and weaknesses. I trust you to know when you are over your head and when to ask for help. And, most of all, woman, I am beginning to trust you with my heart as much as I already trust you with my body."

"Bran..." she breathed, her eyes wide at his heartfelt words. Caille could always read the truth in a person's heart, one of the reasons she didn't take on a lot of long-term lovers. It was hard to trust someone when you could read all the nasty little thoughts in their heads especially when they were directed at you.

Some men didn't like her confidence, her strength, or the knowledge of her own greatness. Some felt intimidated and others felt lesser in her company. But not Bran. From the moment she first touched him... well, he just felt right.

And now the honesty of his words rang out true and clear, the meaning ringing in her heart like a bell.

"You want more than just sex with me."

"I wouldn't turn down a roll with you now, woman." He chuckled as she snorted at him. "But I want more. I don't know where this thing between us is going or if it can even progress more than it has now, but I want to find out. I know that it's not fair of me to spring this on you when your family is struggling so but --"

He never got further than that. Caille threw her arms around Bran's neck and pulled those pretty, full lips grinning with pretty words down to hers.

Clothes seemed to disappear as they moved together. Hands were flying over bare skin as they celebrated the joy of actually being alive.

"Oh fuck, I didn't think that I was going to make it," Caille muttered in between kisses, and Bran understood as he returned each and every one, trading face kisses for face kisses until he gripped a handful of her hair and jerked her head back, exposing her neck. She smelled of hospital and sand and panicked frenzy, but underneath that he could smell pure Caille. He ran his nose down her neck and she whimpered, her hand clutching at his shoulders to ground herself in the here and now.

"I knew you were going to make it," he responded, littering her neck with kisses and bites. "I just thought that I was going to let you all down."

"You would never," she responded, digging her nails in his skin, leaving scratches that wouldn't linger long but for while they lasted, the happy sting of them would drive his passions higher.

"Never say never," he responded, but then pulled her head down to stare into her beautiful eyes. "But that Cat though... that leap... I didn't think he had it in him."

"He was trying to protect me." Caille giggled. "Isn't that too precious?" She snickered a little more as she pushed her forehead into his neck, inhaling his scent. "I don't have the heart to tell him that I didn't really need the help, but he looks so confident being the hero."

"I think him jumping in that pit had more to do with him protecting Arcas from you."

"You saw that?"

"Oh, I saw that." Bran shook his head a little before pulling at Caille's hair again to get at those luscious lips. "I bet he wishes he was doing what we are about to do right now."

"And what are we about to do?"

Caille hissed in pleasure as Bran began kissing down her neck to her beautiful breasts. He laved at her nipples, sucking first the right and then the left into his mouth, nipping, licking as he pulled and toyed with the tender flesh.

Caille enjoyed this. Her moans and sighs grew in intensity as she wrapped her legs high around his waist. Already he could scent the perfume of her lust and his mouth began to water.

He nipped and sucked down her stomach, past her cute little navel and straight down to her pussy, pushing her legs wide to make a place for himself between her thighs.

"Yes, boy. You know what I like," she called out in approval and Bran used his thumbs to gently tease at her clit while he dropped his head to lap at the slick running freely from her pussy.

She smelled spicy and of flowers, and she tasted of salted honey and heat. He could die happy with his face buried between her thighs. He began to run circles around her swollen clit, making his lover squeal in pleasure before he nudged her sharply with his nose. She must have liked that because her legs lifted so that her heels rested on his shoulders, fully exposing her to his hungry gaze.

Bran was grinding softly into the silken comforter that covered the bed, seeking some friction for his painfully hard prick. His heart was racing and his breathing was labored as each whiff of her made him want to breathe her in deeper and faster. He vibrated his tongue as he slid it inside of her, reveling in the feeling of her muscles contracting around his tongue.

Caille was singing out, crying her pleasure, and the sound traced from his ears straight to his cock. The sounds she was making were almost as delicious as her body. He tilted his head to the side to sink in deeper before he began to rapidly flick her clit. His thumb at her clit pressed down hard and he could feel her muscles tense as her first climax ripped through her.

He tongued and lapped at her inner walls as they contracted, drawing out her climax until her screams eased and her body fell lax in his grasp.

He pulled his tongue free to lick at her swollen, red labia before he began to shower her clit with kisses and love. He was drenched, his face dripping with her slick and he loved it.

"More," she called, her hand in his hair tugging him upwards and, never one to make a lady wait, he slid up her body to slam his mouth onto hers.

Caille eagerly lapped her own slick from his face, kissing and biting at his lips as her legs went around his waist. She was wasting no time in getting what she wanted.

Bran gripped her hips, shifting her higher, and he used one hand to stroke his cock a few times before repositioning himself at her sopping wet opening.

"Fuck me now," Caille demanded as he teased the both of them by running the head of his prick over her slick, welcoming pussy. She was so hot and tight and wet and…

"Now, damn it!" Caille growled, and Bran felt the sting of her nails as they slid down his back and found a home deep within the meat of his ass.

"Fuck, Caille --"

"Give me what I want! Fuck me now!"

Okay, the time for teasing was over. Bran positioned himself and slammed deep inside her with one powerful thrust.

"Bran!" Caille screamed his name and Bran felt his heart and his cock swell even larger. Yes, he could see himself enjoying this every day for the rest of his life. Immediately Caille began bucking and grinding underneath him, fucking herself on his hard cock, and Bran bit his bottom lip and tried to hold on as the tight muscles of her pussy slid up and down his hard length. This was joy of heaven and the torture of hell all rolled into one.

He felt his toes curl and his muscles strain and he pulled back and slammed into her as hard as he could.

Caille screamed her pleasure demanding more as the bed began to shift, the headboard pounding against the wall. He hoped the black iron left a dent in the wall, proof that he was banging the woman of his dreams while she was cursing, hungry for more.

So he pushed in her, his muscles straining and sweat covering them both as their cries almost drowned out the sound of their wet bodies slamming together. He was fucking her hard, ramming into her heat, swearing in Welsh and in English at how good it felt.

And Caille, she was tearing at his ass, her heels pressing into his thighs, holding him in the perfect position. He knew it was the right spot because after shifting his hips and adjusting his thrusts, she squealed and threw her head back, her eyes closing as she began to pant. He rode that spot, making sure that when he pulled out he swirled his hips to stimulate her pussy, and when he slammed back inside, his shaft ran against her swollen clit.

Bran knew how to fuck and he was using every trick he could remember to bring his lover pleasure.

Time seemed to stand still as they tore and growled at each other, until Caille threw back her head one final time, calling his name as her pussy went wild around his cock. She was coming and coming hard.

"Fuck," he cursed into her neck as the sound and feel of her climax pushed him over the edge.

His cock jumped and spasmed deep within her heat, bathing her in his seed as he tried to regain some muscle control.

He managed to pull himself out and roll to the side as his muscles finally gave way. Caille rolled to his prone body, snuggling in as the release from the tension that dogged them from the moment they sneaked into the animal fights.

"You are going to be the death of me," he groaned, wrapping an arm around her waist as the other toyed with her hair. "Death by sex. But what a way to go."

"You won't die," Caille teased. "They cut off your head and you're still here. But little deaths from now on... only little deaths."

Bran murmured in agreement but was too tired to really comment.

He was laying, content, with a people who he just knew, would become family, and finally, he was ready to dive into this new world. It wasn't perfect, these modern times, but they were not as bad as he expected them to be. And how could they be? He was running with his ravens and he had a wolf at his side.

This new life was going to be... interesting.

* * *

In a small basement room, Thomas Gray pressed his palms to his flat stomach, sure that what he felt there now was a spark of life.

He closed his eyes and let his tears run, feeling sorry for himself and cursing himself for being an idiot. He had overreacted to his mate's words and his own fears. He had run from the very thing that would have offered him protection and safety. And when he tried to go to his mate, to make things between them right, he had been taken. How he missed his mate.

"Kern," he breathed softly to himself as he stared up through the sliver of a ground level basement window at the nearly full moon that hung in the velvety black sky like an orb. "Please... please come and get us soon."

The Bear (Wild Hunt 3)
Paranormal Women's Fiction
Stephanie Burke

After observing the mistakes made by his fellow Huntsmen, Arcas, the Bear, refuses to follow their example. He immediately claims his mate, a descendant of the cat goddess Bastet. Their pairing will be powerful and his mate is courageous, wise, and sexy as hell. Too bad they have to bring down the remnants of a murderous cult and stop a demonic disaster from being let loose on the world.

Marshal's no fool. From the moment they met, he has been drawn to the red haired Bear. He didn't think world ending events would ensue to make their developing relationship a bit more difficult to navigate. But now The Hunt was on the move and nothing would stop them from achieving their goals: rescue Kern's mate and save the world.

Chapter One

"Fuck." Arcas paced in his room, fighting the urge to heal the many bites, bumps, and bruises he'd received as he kept trying to purge the insidious drugs from his system. That those bites and bruises had come from one he considered his sister just made him... What *was* he feeling? Angst? Frustration? Anger? Well, yes, there was anger. A whole lot of anger, but there were more underlying emotions he refused to process.

He was angry. That he was sure of. In fact, one could say he was way beyond incensed and approaching furious at a rapid pace and there was nothing he could do to stem the tide of righteous anger that filled him to overflowing.

He remembered each one. He remembered their faces, their nasty little comments, how they treated him as a beast, something less than human... less than the animals they had gathered for this modern-day travesty of a gladiator sport. They had treated him like he was an object. Brave in the face of the drugs they had constantly injected into his veins and blew in his face. He remembered them, each and every one of them from the time he opened his eyes in that piece of shit van after they dosed him the first time to the time when they applied electric cattle prods to his back in an effort to make him shift... because there was no way he would ever forget that no matter how hard he tried.

So now he paced as he tried to process what it felt like to be knocked completely off the food chain. They didn't even want to steal his life energy, they just wanted him dead as if he didn't matter, as if he didn't live and breathe and think. They just wanted him dead, almost as an afterthought. And what was worse, they'd made him attack his sister.

He remembered her wolf form screaming at him as he lunged at her, unable to stop the cursed animal within him from acting on instinct and trying to obliterate any threat that would do him more harm. He was grateful he was incapacitated enough not to clearly think or he surely would have done more harm to his sister than he had actually managed. He shuddered as he remembered the feel of not being in control of his own body, of being a visitor in his own mind, screaming in futility, as the world turned into madness around him.

And he remembered his taste...

It was the taste of *him*, of his blood that gave Arcas the final push to take control of his own body and its actions once more. By then, it had almost been too late. He had been moving in for the kill. Caille, no matter how powerful she was, would not have been able to fight off the power of a god who was still being actively worshiped every time someone looked into the night sky. He would have snuffed her back to her component parts. It would have taken her centuries to re-form and it would have all been his fault.

So, yeah, add guilt to the pile of emotions threatening to drive him insane now, thank you. Guilt for not being fast enough, for not being strong enough, for not being wise enough... just for not being enough. Because of him Kern's mate had been taken to parts unknown. When he opened his eyes in that rocking van, Thomas hadn't been there. He could add nothing to the hunt for Kern's mate, but he did remember each and every face that had hovered over him, had lorded over him, had spit in his face and applied their boots to his body. He remembered each and every one, and they would pay.

And there was him... How could he ever be

good enough for Marshal? He himself was weak and useless… and… and… his blood.

Gods above, Arcas had never tasted anything as sweet… Marshal tasted of sunshine, of desert sands and of lotus petals. He had tasted of his forever and that was such a travesty it almost brought tears to Arcas' eyes because he had almost killed the man.

Caille, a goddess in her own right, would have survived. But The Cat… he was not being worshipped, had never been worshiped because Arcas could taste that in his blood. He was immortal but not invulnerable. If he hadn't acted when he had, Arcas would have been responsible for the destruction of his own mate.

That was something Arcas could not abide. So he paced in his room, withheld the healing he could have so easily done to his human form, and he did his best to stick to the story The Raven and The Wolf, along with help from his mate, had constructed. It was laughably easy how eager the police were to accept their convoluted tale. The story had all the hallmarks of a movie of the week. There were rich assholes to blame, an insane group of homophobic cultists who had access to poor, abused animals, and there were guns and drugs, lots of drugs. Hell, in this world where people cared more about animals than their own brethren, it was so easy to play the sympathy card. To add to the human interest angle, there was an obvious blended family, a person of color, and the sexual orientation of the one still missing man. The right reporter could earn themselves a Pulitzer with that story. Exotic animals were just the icing on a journalistic cake that was going to be served up on all media platforms, and with today's sentiment about eating the rich… well, companies and stocks were going to be dropping like flies after a judicious application of bug killer.

Yet now, here he was, pacing ineffectually in his room, feeling his blood pressure rise as he sought to find some outlet for his wrath.

Yes, wrath was the perfect word for the emotions he was now feeling. Wrath and rage were coursing through his body, heating his blood, and making him want to explode.

But it was an impotent wrath for the moment for there was no clear target to aim his ire at, no one single person to blame... but himself.

And fuck, he had never been so angry in his long, never-ending life.

A knock at the door drew him away from his mounting self-anger, and as he spun around, a snarl on his lips, ready to tell whatever well-meaning sycophant disturbing his solitude to fuck off, he froze as a familiar scent suddenly filled the room.

It was -- it was The Cat... his mate... and he smelled concerned. Torn between wanting to hide his face in shame and run away or try and beg for the man's forgiveness, Arcas' higher brain functions froze and he stood there, in the middle of his room, a whimper on his lips and an appeal in his eyes, vulnerable as he had never been before.

In the face of his new emotion, this shame, flooding his brain, Arcas, the Little Dipper, The Great Bear, the once greatest hunter in all of Acadia, froze like a deer in headlights.

Chapter Two

"Hello?" Marshal had tapped on the door he knew led to his friend's... No, Arcas wasn't a friend. He wasn't sure what Arcas was, but he knew he cared about the red haired man more than he probably should for someone he knew next to nothing about.

And it had nothing to do with Arcus throwing himself headlong into danger to save them or how hot he was although, let's face it, the boy was smoking hot. Marshal couldn't put a name to why he felt so drawn to the man. From the moment he met him he wanted to be all up in his space, something he was amazed no one called him on. When he had seen the tall redhead struggling in his bear form in that damn pit... he had to do something. No, more like he had been compelled to do something. So he had thrown caution to the wind and taken a leap of faith, hoping everything was going to be okay and his intuition hadn't failed him.

He did think his intuition was kind of wonky when it insisted he shove his arm into the mouth of a fucking full-grown red grizzly bear but he had done it without really thinking.

Acting without thinking... that was one of the reasons he was on the bad guys' collection list. And unlike his crazy brother Thomas, he didn't have any real connection to the protection a partnership with a member of The Hunt offered.

Oh, sure, Manx had accepted him and he was now under the protection of a superior creature, but it wasn't the same feeling of belonging he noticed circling around Caille and Bran.

Now those two were amazing to be around. They just slipped into partnership like a duck to water. It looked effortless, though Marshal was adult and wise enough to know what appeared on the surface often wasn't what was going on underneath... keeping to the example of the duck. But now the two of them were locked up on Caille's floor, probably doing unspeakable things to each other, and he was knocking on the door of The Bear that almost ate him.

That thought was perfect for a kinky sex novel, but now was not the time to be letting his mind drift into a gutter. He wanted... no, he *needed* to check on Arcas and once again his instincts were telling him this was the correct thing to do.

"Hello? Arcas?" He knocked again before trying the doorknob. If The Bear was sleeping then he would beat a hasty retreat, but if he was awake... well, maybe they could hold a conversation about what the hell was going on. In addition to easing the push he was feeling toward the redhead, it was better than sitting by and watching tears roll down the unconscious Kern's face.

That was heartbreaking even in a comatose state, Kern was aware his mate had been taken and was probably imagining all kinds of things happening to Thomas. And the fact the two had a partial bond probably made everything worse. Kern could probably feel Thomas' despair and was unable to do anything to ease it.

This whole situation was a clusterfuck of immense proportions, and although they were moving as fast as they could to rectify this whole mess of problems, it probably wasn't happening fast enough for the two star-crossed... no. They were not star-crossed. Marshal would not jinx their efforts by thinking like that. They were confused? No, that wasn't the right term either. Idiots. They were idiots in love. That seemed to fit.

Before he could stand there and come up with

some new and fantastical terms for the two major catalysts for this situation, the doorknob twisted under his hand and the door swung open. Marshal felt his breath catch as Arcas, bruised and angry looking, stood in the doorway, glaring down at him. Why did the man have to be so tall?

"What?"

Marshal wrinkled his nose as the question was spat at him, tilting his head to the side as he examined Arcas.

His blood-red hair, with its orange highlights, was free and hanging in lank ringlets around his face and shoulders. He was wearing a tank-top, presumably for maximum effect to show off his stitches and bandages for anyone not in the know who was snooping around. He was barefoot, and damn if his toenails weren't painted black. That was kind of cute… well, kind of hot, Marshal's brain interpreted, as he felt his cock plump up a bit and take notice. It wasn't a full chub, but it was getting pretty close.

Arcas' legs were encased in the designer lingerie for men known as loose sweatpants, and his bulge moved and shifted under the soft material.

The man was trying to kill him.

Arcas also had a sprinkling of freckles over his face, arms, and body. His extremely pale skin made them stand out all the more and Marshal found himself wanting to play connect the dots with them… preferably naked in a hot bubble bath so he could see that pale skin flush red with heat. Now that was an image in his mind that moved his cock from interested perk to full chub in the time it took for Arcas to cross his arms.

"Yes." Marshal cleared his throat. "Well, I wanted to come in and check on you."

"I'm fine." Man, even his voice, low and gravelly, was doing things to his insides.

"And if you ain't the grandaddy of all liars," Marshal teased. "*I'm fine* is the lie we use when we feel like shit and don't want to talk about it."

"Great." Arcas nodded. "Then I don't want to talk about it."

He moved to shut the door in Marshal's face but The Cat stuck his foot in the doorway, thankful Arcas stopped and didn't injury his foot. Broken bones were a bitch to heal and he was already having a hard enough time controlling his body's natural need to heal what had been injured in the pit.

"Do you feel the pull?"

His shouted question made Arcas stare at him with narrowed eyes before he looked heavenward as if for some answers, then stepped aside and retreated deeper into his room, leaving the door open and the option to follow up to Marshal.

The Cat wasn't an idiot. Of course he opened the door wider and slipped in before closing it behind him.

"About that pull..."

"We are mates." Arcas turned to face a bank of windows that ran the length of one wall in his bedroom, giving Marshal his back.

Arcas said nothing more, and Marshal took this as a cue to move deeper into the room, his eyes on his... Mate.

"So." He moved closer, almost close enough to touch, but still keeping some distance between them. "Mates. Is that what this feeling is? This pull..."

"Mates," Arcas confirmed. "I knew it from the moment your blood touched my..." His voice trailed off as he turned his head to the side to stare at Marshal. "Not that I deserve it."

"Is this a guilt trip?" His mate crossed his arms over his chest defensively and huffed at the question. "Because I didn't pack for one and I'm not really up for travel through the ridiculousness of your current mental mindscape."

That got him an arched eyebrow, and Marshal took that as a win. He moved closer.

"Are you going to blame yourself for what happened to you while under the influence? Because let me tell you, that is some specious reasoning you got going there. That's like saying you should have been able to pull a Superman and save everyone just because the sun was shining. Here's a hint, Bear Boy... this is not a comic book, impervious heroes don't exist, and blaming yourself for something that is out of your control is how mental institutions and pharmaceutical companies make their loot."

That made Arcas chuckle, and his shoulders relaxed as he turned to fully face Marshal. "So feeling guilty is just plain stupid?"

"Just plain."

"So you are saying I deserve you as a mate?"

"Just so." Marshal nodded his head with confidence.

"So..." The Bear trailed off. "Is this some kind of divine reward or punishment?"

"Fuck you." The words just slipped out but Arcas' laughter made him not even try to justify his reasoning.

"Okay."

That killed the laughter. And what nearly made him swallow his tongue was how casually his mate began to undress.

Marshal had seen his Bear shirtless. He had noticed the tall, thick redhead before but Marshal had always been engaged with his plaything for the night so he'd done his best to ignore the beautiful man's presence.

But now he had his full, undivided attention, and Marshal hadn't felt that giddy since he first discovered what sex was.

His mate was pale -- which was typical for general redheads of course -- but Arcas' skin was like a pearl. It was creamy with tints of pink and soft blue in its tone. And covering all that skin in thin swirls was the most lovely, silky looking chest hair. Oh, holy goddess, his Bear was a bear.

Marshal bit back a moan by stuffing the heel of his hand in his mouth, but the pressure of the lust that just hit him had to come out somehow. He was just glad there was no one there to judge him… the world's number one bossy bottom was struck dumb by the sight of his mate's chest. It was embarrassing… kind of… but not as embarrassing as the sudden tent that popped in his pants. Yeah, and there was a damp spot to show where he was so excited he was leaking precum like a faucet.

He looked back up at Arcas' eyes, watched the gleam of knowing awareness at what he was doing to him, and wanted to sass him a bit. Oh, how he wanted to sass, but his sarcasm had dried up for the moment while his brain kind of… short-circuited. And when Arcas ran his hands down his pants to frame the bulge of his cock -- and what a mighty fine bulge it was -- Marshal just decided to give up how turned on he was.

"You play dirty," he stammered, coolness melting under the heated gaze of his mate as he stumbled forward… hands out.

"I play to win," Arcas corrected, thick long fingers toying with his zipper. If it were true what they said about the thickness of a man's thumbs, then he was going to have to find a shit ton of lube before that monster got anywhere near his ass.

By then though, Marshal couldn't care less. He had reached his nirvana, his Shangri-La, his new nesting place, the soft fur on his mate's chest. It was so soft Marshal just wanted to bury his face in it. And since this visual foreplay was going to lead to sex anyway, why should he deny himself?

"You smell so good. A little like a hospital still, but so damn tasty." He knew his words were muffled by Arcas' chest hair, and that made him so grateful for the fur. He didn't want to give his mate any new ammunition or blackmail to hold against him.

"You find hospital smell tasty?"

"No, I find spice and man sexy. Better than the Old Spice worn by my first bearded older man. He showed me really how to really appreciate beards. Yes, that was a joke, and a warning -- I'm going to be sitting on your face later. You should know discovering I could have multiple orgasms at his hands is some powerful scent association, let me tell you."

"You can tell me more later." Arcas outright laughed at him. "After you do more than just bury your face in my chest hair."

At his words, Marshal leaned over and pulled one soft pink nipple into his mouth. *Ha! Showed you*, he thought as Arcas hissed at the suction. And if he hissed at the nipple suckle, what would he do when teeth were applied?

"Marshal."

Marshal noted his soon-to-be lover jumped and pulled hair when he bit at his nipple. So he did it again. Marshal was crazy about hair pulling.

He pulled off his mate's nipple and offered him a

mischievous smile... just before he latched onto his other nipple and pinched the wet one.

He felt Arcas shift, then there was a rip as cool air hit his back. So, double nipple stimulation got his clothing ripped off. He gave a moment's mourning for his JoS. A. Bank custom dress shirt as the ripped material fluttered down his arms like the white flag of surrender sliding down. It really was a nice shirt... but not as nice as having Arcas' hands claw at his back.

So... his mate was very sensitive. He placed that knowledge into a mental vault he was building for all the things he was learning about his mate, and decided he was a very lucky man. His mate wanted him, plain, ordinary, best sidekick in the world, him.

Sure, he was magical in some ways, but other than that he was baseline human. He healed a bit faster, had better reflexes than most men his age, but that wasn't extraordinary. He couldn't shapeshift outside of growing a five o'clock shadow, and like his catlike ancestor, it was hard to hold his attention for very long. He didn't think he was going to have that problem now, and he had been blessed with a motherfucking bounty.

He ran his free hand over the hills and valleys that made up the plane of Arcas' chest, noting how warm and soft his skin was over all of those thick muscles. He danced his fingers over his mate's sides and pressed them into the thick muscles of his back, noting in passing that his Bear was not ticklish.

When he felt that, Arcas ran his fingers down his spine and gave his ass a good squeeze. He was so down with that. Marshal stuck his ass out further to see if Arcas would do it again, and he was rewarded by his confidence in that not only did Arcas squeeze again, he slid his fingers into Marshal's waistband

and... *rip*... there went his pants. Suddenly he was grateful for having kicked his shoes off by the door because a man standing and suckling on another man's nipple looked stupid if you were wearing shoes and socks. His socks were one hundred percent silk and therefore made his perfectly shaped legs look more manly and powerful... he told himself as he stepped out of the remains of a once very nice pair of Christian Dior dress pants.

He let go of Arcas' mouth-watering nipple when he realized his briefs were next. They matched the socks so no, he would not let them get torn off. Besides, he would have to borrow some clothing, and as he didn't believe trips to his apartment would be allowed later, he didn't want to wear someone's undies... or go commando in someone else's pants. That was just rude. And speaking of rude... "My dress clothes cost a lot of money."

"I'll buy you more."

That was an answer, he supposed, as his mate's arms wrapped around him under his very round cheeks, and lifted him, dragging his chest along that nice fluffy hair. Okay, the clothes could be forgiven.

"And I only brought so many changes of clothes with me..."

"You can borrow something of mine."

"Like I could fit in anything of yours without it looking like I was dressing up in daddy's clothing."

A low, bear-like growl rumbled from Arcas' chest. Oh, he liked that. Marshal wondered what he could do to make him rumble out that sound again.

He wrapped his legs around Arcas' waist -- not an ounce of fat for the cushioning, mind you -- and took a moment to revel in the strength of his Bear. This boded well for wall sex, and walking sex, and sex where Arcas moved him around on his cock like he was a fleshlight...

"You like that?"

"I like the idea of you smelling like me. I want you wearing my marks."

"And I was taught that the marks could scar up as a means of warning other creatures away from your property."

"You are not my property. You are my mate. But if I, from time to time, want to use you like a favorite sex toy, try to understand."

Marshal felt the rest of his blood leave his brain and slide right down to the smaller head. He even attempted to look down and see what rapid swelling looked like but all he could see was a muscled wall of red-furred flesh. This was a better sight, he decided. He had seen his own hard-on so many times that it wasn't even exciting anymore. But he could feel it, and yes, his damp silk boxer briefs offered up just enough friction for the sophisticated man to enjoy... and Marshal was that man. With glee, he began to hump the planes of his lover's stomach, closing his eyes and throwing back his head as pleasure began to tingle his limbs and dance up and down his spine.

"I thought we were fucking?" Arcas' growly voice made him look at and smile at what he saw. His lover's -- let's face it, at this point it was a done deal -- eyes glistened like the stars they were named for. "If you want to rub off on me, I'm down."

His Bear slowly licked his lips as he inhaled deeply, taking in the combined scents of the both of them. Mercy!

"You said you could have multiple orgasms..."

As he spoke, Arcas began walking toward his bed, his muscles shifting and sliding along his cock in his precum slick undies. Friction was a beautiful thing... which reminded him...

"Arcas?"

"Yes, my mate?"

He was being placed so tenderly in the center of the Bear's massive bed that he could cry. Finally he was the pretty, pretty princess... Well, maybe not, but his lover's actions, as sickeningly sweet romantic as they were, served to make him feel special.

His cock jerked inside his undies and reminded him of what he was about to tell his mate.

"I know we agreed to be mates..." Damn, this was hard.

"Yes."

"And in doing so, not be like our brothers..."

"That is true."

"Well, in the spirit of full disclosure, there are some things about my body that you may... no, that you will have to know..."

He let his words trail off as Arcas shimmied off the bed and popped the tie of his sweatpants. As Marshal watched, he eased them down over Norse godlike thighs -- wrong pantheon he knew, but he needed some meat to describe him -- and let them fall to the floor, leaving his pale lover in a pair of straining-to-stay-up-on-his-waist athletic briefs. They were shiny with Lycra though Marshal supposed it took that much elastic to hold that bulge in check, and in a shade of green that looked like his eyes. Goddess, he was perfect. His waist was not slim. In fact it was thick, but with the perfect amount of muscle. He could see where his red hair thinned as it sank below the waistband of those incredibly perfect set of underpants.

As Marshal watched, Arcas raked his fingers through his hair, sending it into a fall of wild waves that cascaded down his broad shoulders and massive chest.

"Full disclosure?" Arcas asked, placing his knees on the bed and, great Mother Bastet, he was crawling across the bed and hovering over him.

Marshal opened his mouth to speak, he really did, but somehow it was suddenly filled with a great red bear's tongue. So he did what any healthy young lad with a strong libido would do. He sucked it in, he nibbled on it, he opened his mouth wide and let that tongue explore all its owner wanted. Which only made him grateful for the shower and change of clothing he'd insisted on before making his way over to Arcas' floor.

All too soon, his lover was pulling back, placing slow, biting kisses on his lips and trailing down to his neck.

"You wanted to tell me something?" Arcas asked again, nibbling at a spot Marshal was sure his mate decided was the perfect place to mark him.

Marshal whimpered and closed his eyes, struggling to maintain what little control he had left. Really, it wasn't cool to be grinding up against your mate like you were in a raunchy music video... but it sure as hell felt good.

But he had a purpose in slowing down the festivities and it wasn't for kisses, no matter how great they were.

"Yeah." He moaned, throwing his head back and exposing his neck for more affection as Arcas settled some of his weigh on his smaller frame. "Um... dicks..."

"Yes," Arcas murmured, nipping him playfully with teeth that were a little too sharp to be human. "Dicks. Yours is pressing up against my stomach. It's what happens when two men who really, really like each other decide to mate."

"Smart ass," Marshal grumbled, easing his hips back to the sheets.

"Better than a dumb ass," Arcas solemnly informed him as he pressed more of his weight down on him before he rose up on his knees.

It was like looking up at a Greek statute come to life... and yes, he realized that was kind of what he had straddling his waist, with his huge hands sliding down his chest, plucking at his nipples, and generally making him forget his words... Something about Greek statues and irony...

"Dicks," he reminded himself... not that the subject matter was making it any easier for him to function, "Differences. Mine is a bit different."

"I know all about the circumcision thing, my Cat. And if you had it done I know about the ring of scarring that marks where you were cut."

"That would not be a problem here since I am uncut and I am assuming you are too."

"That would be correct."

"Besides very specific docking fantasies... *very* specific... the state of your foreskin isn't what's concerning me. What is, is the fact that even if they wanted to, they couldn't perform a circumcision on me even if my parents were so inclined."

"Are you trans? Is that a packer I'm feeling?"

"Glad you are knowledgeable about the appearance altering accessories some trans people use, but no, that one is all me. Kind of shocked that you know what a packer is."

"Marshal," Arcas pointed out to him in a calm voice, "I work in a BDSM club. I have been around for many centuries, and through no fault of my own, I have become a keen observer. Plus I like sex... just about any way I can get it. I like relationships where I can be monogamous with the person I am intimate with. I have had a few trans lovers, male and female, so I know what accessories are used to help them make their outsides match their insides. So if that is not what you are trying to tell me, maybe you want to get to that point? I want to make you come at least once before I climb on top of you and ride you like the sheriff and his posse are on my tail. So if you will --"

"Make me come one time?"

"Yes, then I can get a longer ride out of you. So what is it you want to tell me?"

"My cock comes in a sheath."

Arcas froze for a moment, blinked a few times as if some order in his head was being realigned, and then he nodded. "Okay."

"Okay?" Marshal was kind of confused, though you couldn't tell it from the condition of his cock... still hard and damp in his undies --

"Okay."

"Really?"

"My Cat, I work in a BDSM club... a magical BDSM club where sometimes magical creatures of every sort meet and --"

"You don't have to be an asshole about it," Marshal grumbled, feeling a little offended... no, not offended. Mightily intrigued. Marshal knew he was a voyeur at heart, and hearing good sex stories secondhand was almost as good as watching.

"You are not the first person of a magical persuasion I've taken to my bed, Marshal, though I intend on you being the last."

"I hear that." Marshal relaxed back in the bed, trying to wonder how he never realized he was so stressed about the matter. "And later, I'd really like to hear all about that."

"So, from your lineage, I am assuming I am dealing with some cat genetics somewhere."

"A few little things."

"Like how you leaped into the pit, dodged my blows, and reacted fast enough to shove your forearm into my mouth when I went for Caille?"

"Very observant."

"I spent a lot of time watching the world from up on high. My eyesight was perfect, as I was a hunter, my Cat. Is the penile sheath the only genetic thing I have to worry about?"

"Well, there is a spine."

"Glad you told me before I sank you into my ass."

"Arcas!"

"What? That might hurt in a way I am not prepared to deal with."

"It's a blunt spine," Marshal grumbled. "The only thing it can do is pound your prostate when I fuck you."

At his words, Arcas' eyes kind of flashed there, before despite his early warning, there was a rip and cool air surrounded the head of his unsheathed cock. So much for his silk undies and matching socks... and there went the socks.

"I need to see," his mate cooed as he bent down and gently gripped the triangular sheath where his cock usually rested. But instead of being slim and pink, Marshal's cock was thick, long, and ringed with swollen markings that made him kind of ribbed for his lover's pleasure.

Marshal let out a hiss as his lover gripped his shaft right below the rings that marked where the plump, heart-shaped head began.

"So uniquely beautiful," his lover praised and Marshal found himself blushing. "Oh, you like it when I praise you? Like a pretty little kitty --"

"I am not little."

"To me you are."

"To you, everyone is little." Marshal pouted, but that quickly turned into gasps of delight as Arcas pulled him deep into his mouth.

Oh, goddess the heat was unreal. It was like sinking his cock into a furnace, a soft, wet, silky furnace with an optional sucking feature.

Yes, Marshal Gray was getting his dick sucked by his most perfect redhaired mate and life was good.

The way Arcas pulled off for a second to arch a judging eyebrow at him informed him maybe he shouted that out loud.

No matter, he thought, reaching down to run his fingers gently though his mate's hair, got a good grip, and jerked his head back down where it belonged. If he choked him a little he would have to be forgiven because he had never had oral quite like this. He would make it up to His Bear, but his oral was too good to let his mouth off his cock for even a moment.

Arcas must have been okay with that because his whole body shuddered and he began to grind his own cock encased in those miracle drawers, against the sheets.

"Oh, fuck yeah, that's a beautiful picture... and I said that out loud again, didn't I?" Marshal stammered, and damned if his mate wasn't chuckling around his mouthful of cock.

"Oh yeah," he moaned as Arcas used his tongue to flick at the slit in the head of his cock while one of his hands massaged his sheath and the swelling balls underneath. "Fuck, just ignore me... God, baby, your mouth. Suck just a little bit harder..."

Some of his past lovers were not pleased to discover his talkativeness carried over into the bedroom but fuck them. From the way Arcas' ass... yeah, those were perfect mounds of man flesh straining against the Lycra in those majestic, ass cheek dividing undies he had on... uh... was working against the sheets, his lover didn't mind at all.

Marshal felt his toes curl as he drew his feet flat on the bed and thrust upwards.

Arcas moaned around his cock and started to move faster, tugging at his balls so Marshal gave him another thrust, and slowly began fucking his face. In for a penny, in for a pound, he decided as his grip on Arcas' red hair tightened.

"Gonna come," he panted, trying to warn Arcas, but that made him redouble his efforts. The man was trying to suck his brains out through his cock. And though he was Egyptian... related to a major goddess... he decided he liked his Bear's version of making him mindless rather than the ancient Egyptian sharpened stick up the nostrils. "Oh fuck... fuck fuck fuck..."

Marshal looked down and had to squeeze his eyes shut at the picture his mate made... his lips red with his efforts, his eyes narrowed and opened, staring straight into his soul, his jaws pulled in, highlighting his cheekbones as he sucked...

"Damn it, yes! Arcas!" *Houston, we have lift off.*

Marshal opened his mouth and moaned as he felt his balls draw up and his cock pulse.

He felt the pressure of his release shoot his spine up and out and, goddess mother, please help... his lover was suckling gently on it.

This sent his body into spasms of pleasure as a second orgasm raced through him on the heels of his first, leaving him shaking, sweating, unaware of the world around him and not really giving a shit.

He heard his mate swallowing and with his eyes still closed, he pulled at his hair until his Bear snaked his way up his body and sank his tongue inside of his panting mouth.

Marshal roared as the flavor of his own spend mixed in with his lover's taste flooded his mouth. He kissed Arcas hard, his tongue dancing with his Bear's as he tried to understand what his instincts were telling him... or maybe he was just relishing the flavor of his mark in his mate's mouth. Here was tangible proof his lover accepted him and everything about him, including how he accepted being marked in this intimate way.

All too soon the kisses trailed off as Arcas sat up and divested himself of those magnificent undies.

And okay, maybe the most magnificent thing about those undies was what they almost magically seemed to contain.

The undies came off and out flopped one of the biggest cocks he had ever had the good fortune to meet. Marshal Gray was a size queen. Sue him.

"That's... uh... some mighty big meat you're packing there..." Marshal let his words trail off as he examined his mate. Thick, check. Uncircumcised, check. One pale pink head emerging like a monster from the sea of his thick foreskin... double check. All his criteria were met. If he knew how to work that monster, Marshal decided he just may have the most perfect lover in the world.

"That's why you are fucking me first," Arcas pointed out as he gave his monster meat one hard stroke before reaching for the lube in his bedside table. Always, there was lube in the bedside table, like some cheap gay erotica book, Marshal thought... but really wasn't complaining. It was all about convenience.

But his mate had said something... "Huh?" he so intelligently asked.

"This is why you are fucking me first. You need to work up to taking me... or I need to work you up to take me," Arcas joked, a smile lifting those puffy, swollen, beautiful red lips.

"You are a daddy, not a dad. Stop it with the lame jokes."

And somehow that made Arcas smile even more.

"Shut up and get me ready," his Bear ordered, grabbing two of his fingers and lubing them up. It was an order Marshal was all too happy to obey.

He ran his dry hand over the heavy mounds of his mate's ass... goddess yes, runner's ass. It was round and high and had enough give to keep it from being too muscular...

"Are you going to just pet my ass all night or do you intend to actually get me ready to take your dick? You are not as large as me --"

"Not many are --"

"But," Arcas went on, talking over top of him, "I can't take you without prep. Get to petting."

"Can't I do both?" Marshal knew there was a whine in his voice, but he couldn't help it. He already had two orgasms and from the way his cock was trying to get hard, lucky number three was right around the corner. "Yeah, I'm doing both."

And if Marshal thought his Bear's mouth was heaven, his ass was a whole other plane of existence. It started out as kind of a struggle to get his fingers into the tight guardian muscles, but once he worked his way past that barrier it was smooth, silky, hot sailing.

"You feel like hot, slippery, velvet-lined silk," Marshal praised. "Do you know that?"

"Well," Arcas huffed, dropping to all fours above him. "I have stretched myself out before for a lover who couldn't due to various reasons and a few who wouldn't, which meant they only lasted until the fuck was over, no matter how good it was."

"You have standards," Marshal mused, fucking his fingers in and out of his mate's tight heat. When the muscles started to loosen he began to spread his fingers out too, slowly stretching his lover so as to not cause any more pain than necessary. "I like that in a man."

"Equality in the bedroom means I've been pegged a time or two... hundred," Arcas admitted with a wicked grin that made him look all kinds of porn star good, with his blood-red hair flowing about his shoulders, a light sheen of sweat beading up on his skin and looking like diamonds in his plentiful chest hair...

"Equal." Marshal nodded, curling his fingers until he hit --

"Fuck," Arcas shuddered. Yes, his whole huge, uber masculine body just trembled like a leaf as Marshal pegged his prostate dead on. "Yes, do that again," he purred. Did friggin' bears purr? Well, his did. "That is the best feeling..."

"It's an overwhelming shock of pleasure," Marshal agreed. "The next time you suck my dick, feel free to stick a few fingers up my ass and return the favor."

"Or I could get you a butt plug," Arcas spoke softly as Marshal targeted his P-spot dead on and began to stroke and caress it, feeling it out, checking out the size of it for anything unusual… okay. He took a deep breath and curbed the mother hen instincts. But really, Arcas was his good thing and he really didn't want anything happening to him.

His Bear closed his eyes and was slowly beginning to fuck back on his fingers. So, not really to be a dick but to tease him a bit more, he slid his fingers out and reached for the lube himself. More was better than less, so he lubed up again while his mate shot him the nastiest look.

Not wanting to see that pretty flushed face show any expression of displeasure, at least not in bed, Marshal quickly got back to opening him up and his lover began to play with his sheath.

"Your dick didn't go back in," his lovely Bear pointed out and he fought the urge to roll his eyes at him.

"I wasn't done with it yet, darling," he sing-songed in return.

"I thought it would slide back in and I would have to tease it out…" He was already doing a good job of teasing it to full hardness. Like a fascinated cub, his lover gently pawed at his cock, giving his sensitive sheath a few hard squeezes just to see him squirm. "Maybe next time."

"Next time," Marshal informed him, "you are splitting me open with that monster." So said, he reached out and grabbed that monster and watched as his lover shuddered again. It was the best thing ever… better than porn… better than masturbating for someone else… better than the sex he was imagining happening the next time.

So said, he dedicated himself to opening up his lover rapidly because, beside the fact he just had two orgasms, he was going to make his third one premature if he didn't hurry up. He at least wanted to work his way inside his mate before he blew like a teenaged geyser.

Now Arcas was riding back on his fingers hard, grunting at each thrust as Marshal remained a gentleman and gave his prostate lots of attention... and no, it had nothing to do with getting him ready to explode so he wouldn't look so bad when he went ten seconds after sliding inside of Arcas...

"Are you trying to fist me?" Arcas swept an arm through his hair, throwing the whole mass over his shoulders as he bounced so sweetly on Marshal's fingers, his whole body growing tighter and tighter as tension filled him. Marshal could see the delineation in all of his muscles as he began to moan softly. Arcas leaned forward and took his mouth in a steamy kiss, his tongue snaking along his until Marshal decided enough was enough.

"I know you want to bite me again, because a claiming mark on the arm, is so unsexy. But I want you to know as soon as I enter you, I am savaging your neck so any motherfucker bold enough to try and approach you will see and know your mate is one crazy bastard and not to be toyed with. Understand?"

"Fair," Arcas breathed, one hand gently running over the bandage that shielded his own shredded arm from view.

"Glad we've come to an accord. Now slide this beautiful ass over my cock and let's get this party started."

Letting out a short laugh, Arcas pulled free of his lover's fingers, his lover who was more than glad to grab the remains of his once awesome silk undies to clean off his fingers, and positioned Marshal's fully hard and throbbing cock... really, the rings were pulsing, under his hole.

Taking a deep breath, Arcas slid down, gasping as the stretch and sting caused him some small pain. Marshal gripped his hips, petting them, as Arcas slid down... sweet goddess that was perfect, and settled his cock fully within his ass.

Arcas shuddered, breathing slowly in through his nose and out through his mouth.

Marshal, on the other hand, was doing his best not to lose it there and then. Hot, silky, wet, and all his... It was almost too much. The Cat closed his eyes and tried to recall the lineup for the '81 Orioles. He pictured Manx naked... no, that was not helping... he pictured his lover shaving his beautiful mat of hair away and that almost made him weep. Even though Arcas obviously manscaped--the trim patch of blood-red hair that neatly surrounded his cock was proof enough of that -- he really didn't want the man to take any more off. He was a silky, sexy teddy bear of a man and he belonged to Marshal.

Another laugh from his lover made him think unkind thoughts about him for a second... sure, his cock wasn't Bear big but it was nothing to sneeze at either... when he realized he must have been speaking out loud again.

"Can we ignore my running mouth?" he asked as Arcas relaxed fully, though his Bear's hole's stranglehold on his cock never really relaxed.

"No, because I love to hear you babble."

Seriously, this was no way to have sexy times, Marshal thought. So to end the hilarity, he gripped Arcas' hips hard and thrust solidly upwards.

"Fuck yes," his Bear hissed as he began to ride Marshal like he was a damn cowboy. He rode him with the untamed raw joy of someone finally getting the dick they craved. He moaned loudly as he slid up until only the rings that marked the head of Marshal's cock were inside his body and then he plunged down hard.

Marshal may or may not have shouted his joy at that, but he wasn't going to ask and Arcas was too busy bouncing on his dick to tell.

His Bear's long, hard cock was slapping against his stomach, so hard it hit his skin with a meaty thump at each downward thrust. And his ass…

"I am not going to last long," Marshal admitted, panting as he arched his back, pressed his feet flat to the bed, and put his back into it. He not only was fucking back, he was making minute adjustments of his hips until he hit --

"There!" Arcas roared, leaning over Marshal and baring his suddenly not at all human teeth. Why was it such a fucking turn on? Was it the danger? It had to be because Marshal even thought that Hannibal Lecter was sexy in a refined depraved way… though this right here? This explosive sex with his mate, that was more than anything he'd ever dreamed.

So he did his best to do good by his lover by honing in on that spot and working it for all he was worth. He circled his hips, he thrust upward, he tried to move his Bear into the perfect position to give it to him good, and all the while he was praying he could hold out long enough to…

"Gonna come," Arcas was panting, riding high and proud as he pounded away, using Marshal for his pleasure until his whole body stiffened.

"Fuck," Marshal breathed as his lover froze, then lay his head back as a long, animalistic groan ripped from his throat. The walls of Arcas' ass began to spasm as his cock, untouched, began to paint Marshal's chest with his spend.

His lover seen to, he closed his eyes and let go, remembering to angle his cock so his cat-like spine shot out just so and…

"Marshal," Arcas cried, tears filling his eyes as his body began to jerk at the direct prostate stimulation.

It was then Marshal struck, leaning up to plunge his teeth into Arcas' neck, breaking the skin, filling his mouth with the rich taste of his mate.

Arcas screamed out as his body threw itself into another climax and that was it for The Cat.

Marshal groaned as his own release spurted from his cock, flooding his mate with his seed, as his body jerked in climax and his penile spine seemed to rub his lover the right way.

"Gonna die," Marshal moaned, as he felt his mate's body slowly drop down onto him as Arcas still worked his ass on his spine, wringing all the pleasure he could from the act before he carefully pulled himself off and collapsed at Marshal's side.

"We're a mess," Marshal had enough strength to complain. "And I find that I really don't care."

"Sleep now, shower later," Arcas agreed. "Gotta change the sheets anyway."

"Later is good," Marshal agreed, turning on his side to bask in the humid heat wafting from his mate's body… and the, you know, awesome chest hair. "Nap now."

"Nap, mate." Arcas' voice trailed off as the bond between them slowly slid into place, sending reassurances each partner was satisfied and now each needed rest.

"This bond, Arcas," Marshal felt compelled to comment on. "I think it's the best decision we made. Thomas was a fool to run from this."

"And you are no fool?"

"Damn straight, I'm not."

If his mate commented, he never knew as sleep pulled him down into a peaceful yet tastefully fuzzy dream.

Chapter Three

"Our god lives," their captive screamed, frothing at the mouth as if he was rabid, body glistening with sweat as he shook and trembled on the throne where he was manacled. "Soon he will revive and all of you unbelievers, traitors to our cause, all of you beasts will learn your place."

Unlike anyone would expect, the room was not dark and damp, deep beneath the earth, nor was it filled with the stench of old blood and new fear. Rather it smelled of lemon and verbena. And it was well-lit too; bright white lights scared away even the tiniest of shadows and showed the calm, almost placid look on the face of the torturer. It also gleamed on a small table set off the side, absolute covered in brilliantly clean metallic implements only the most skilled torturer would recognize.

Manx crossed their arms and tapped their bare foot lightly, the skin making a soft sound, waiting for their guest to get over this latest bit of shouting anything that wasn't the information they wanted. Manx was patient. They could wait.

"Our master is strong. Our master is bold. Our master will rise and rain unholy terror on you all! Dogs! Monsters! Heathens --"

"Right about now" -- Manx, finally showing some exasperation, cut off what the stalker wanted to say next --"I am wondering if I should have woken Kern up from his nap so he could enjoy this touching little scene."

"I'll tell you nothing!"

"How would you know that?" Manx inquired, raising one eyebrow. "I haven't even touched you yet, other than to place you on that seat."

That made their stalker snap his mouth closed so fast Manx wasn't sure if he had bitten his tongue or not, and from the wince that crossed his face, it was entirely possible. If he had, at least it would mean Manx might get some respite from the fear-filled tirade that flowed from the stalker's mouth.

"Good." Manx uncrossed their arms and padded softly to stand in front of the man, taking in his gray pallor and the fine trembling that shook his muscles. It looked like it wouldn't take much to make him crack. "Now maybe we can do this the easy way. I'll ask you some questions, one at a time, so you aren't rushed. And in return, all I want is truthful answers. And for every untruth you tell me, I take an appendage of my choice. How does that sound?"

"Not like it's easy," the man mumbled, a bit of blood showing on his bottom lip before he lapped it way.

"I didn't say it was going to be easy for you." A wave of their hand brought something that looked like the mutant bastard child of a pair of metal snips and a hand saw flying into their grasp. "And congratulations. You answered your first question honestly. You just saved your pinky. Keep this up and you might walk out of here with most of your body parts intact. Bully for you."

Manx stepped closer to the man in the throne and smiled. "Now, shall we begin?"

* * *

"Your people are annoyingly persistent."

Thomas spun around from where he was contemplating the sliver of daylight that flooded his cell -- well, more like staring at the dust motes that danced in that pale beam of light. He knew he was in someone's basement but underground was underground, and The Faunus, as a whole, didn't do underground well. That's why they stayed on islands and on mountain tops and danced in the sun.

He turned his head from where he was laying, his hands automatically going to protect the spark of life he could feel developing in his body. This voice was new so he slowly sat up on his little cot and paid attention.

"My people? You admit you took me from my people?"

"I admit I wanted us to have this meeting." The man stepped closer and Thomas squinted as he tried to make out his features in the dim light provided.

"And you couldn't have asked me for tea or come to audit one of my classes? I teach mythology, you know. And despite what mankind thinks, all mythology is based on fact. Maybe I could have helped you without all of the special treatment."

He waved a hand and gestured to his surroundings: the cell, the cot, the steel door someone had installed...

When he had stopped panicking and calmed enough to take a good look at his surroundings, he realized yes, he was in a basement and it seemed to have been made of honed rock and stone. He had never seen a structure quite like this one. The whole place carried the scent of neglect and decay. From the newer chips of bare stone that showed at their base, the bars seemed to have been placed there years after the structure went up. There was a steel door that looked like something someone could have ordered from a company specializing in security. This shit was manmade. He was in someone's basement, and from the shadows the dim light created, he could tell there were probably three more cells just like this one, all empty judging by the lack of sound coming from them.

"And help me you shall." The man stepped closer and Thomas inhaled, taking in the scent of decay from his surroundings and death from the man himself. "I think you are the key to bringing back our dear lord."

"You think?" A frisson of fear danced up Thomas' spine as the man drew even closer, close enough for Thomas to see his face. That alone scared him more than anything that had been done to him. A higher-up showing his face? History dictated that when people in power who wanted to remain anonymous did that, it generally meant death to the person they reveal themselves to.

"Oh, I know. I can feel the power flowing from you, young man." The man grinned and instead of the fangs Thomas would expect from someone who radiated so much evil, he had a perfect, toothpaste commercial smile.

His eyes were a pretty shade of brown and though his hairline was receding, he appeared to be an attractive and healthy man. How could someone at first look so normal when they radiated so much evil, Thomas hadn't a clue, but when the man moved fully into the light, Thomas had to force himself to remember he was caged and could not run away. As Faunus, one of his greatest natural powers was to determine when it was best to flee a situation he couldn't control. One part of him always resisted and forced him to stand and confront the thing that was chasing him but even that part was silent as he observed the man who was now close enough to grip the bars. He absently noted the damn things were not shifting or kicking up any dust when the man rested his weight on them and that was a damn shame. Loose bars meant he had a chance of breaking one or more of them away so he could do as his spirit wanted to do and fly to freedom. He was stronger than the average human, however not strong enough to be of service when fighting off high fanatics who wanted to toss people into vans like in a very bad mafia movie.

"The power?" He rested his hands protectively against his stomach and winced as he did so. He didn't want to draw attention to his pregnancy, and because Kern was the father, he knew his child would possess at least some of his god-like powers.

"The power, young man… or whatever you are. Your kind are so good at glamours sometimes it is hard to differentiate you from normal people."

"And you know I am wearing a glamour?"

"After all the time I've been doing this, I developed a feel for that sort of thing."

"And not knowing what I am, you still attempted to take me hostage?"

"Attempted and succeeded, though I feel we should have just put a bullet in the brain of the redhead and be done with it…" His voice trailed off as he tilted his head to the side and observed Thomas. "And now he has caused me no end of trouble."

"Has he, now? Well, in that case, don't you think it would be wise to just let me go before they find me?"

"Find you?" The man laughed and Thomas realized his hair wasn't blond like he'd imagined. Despite his middle-aged look, the man's hair was completely gray and not the fashionable gray young people were dyeing their hair now. His hair was the deep gray that came from age and time itself. It was unsettling to see but it looked like the only thing that was aging on the man was his hair. And now that he was closer, Thomas knew that he was looking at his executioner. The smell of death and rot wafting from his body was too strong. "I am counting on it, dear boy. But no matter what they do, it will be too late. And after all the trouble they brought to my doorstep, I want to have them here when I finally revive my god."

"Trouble? What did Arcas do, if you don't mind my asking?" Thomas stammered out, anything to stop this man from speaking of his imminent demise.

"I suppose it would do no harm in telling you." The man mused for a moment before he leaned in closer, his pale white skin glistening in that tiny ray of sun. "They brought attention to my operation. They brought destruction to my doorstep. They, your Bear and the ones who rescued him, almost single-handedly destroyed my organization's main source of income." He put his face right against the bars and Thomas was instantly reminded of Jack Nicholson in *The Shining*, sticking his face though the wood door he'd just chopped and spouting his iconic line, "Here's Johnny." But he wasn't a scared Shelly Duval trapped by a snowbound window with no place to flee. He was a pregnant Faunus trapped in the basement of a madman with no hope of fighting his way free.

"Your operation?" *Keep him talking*, he reminded himself. *Make him see your humanity.*

"My fights." He sighed sadly. "Your Bear ruined my whole operation with that nasty little trick. The cops confiscated all of my best champions, and in blood sport, the challenge is getting new champions to pit against one another for the discerning entertainment of those who can afford it."

"Blood sport?" Thomas' voice rose a little as he tried to comprehend even what that meant. "Like boxing?"

"No, like the gladiatorial games of ancient

Greece. You know about Greece, don't you, Professor?"

"I do, and the games were never as bloody as people made them out to be. Sure, criminals got torn apart by wild animals but there was a huge fine to pay if a gladiator killed one of his competitors."

"People won't pay to see warriors make nice with each other in the ring, Professor. People want to see blood, to see the struggle to survive, the urge to even tear and rend with your bare hands for the smallest chance to survive to fight another day. My clients didn't want to watch Romper Room, no. They paid to see the dawning realization in the eyes of the fighter that they will not make it out of that ring alive although they fight anyway. They pay to see the reality of humanity, small Professor. They pay to see the struggle, the spectre of death coming to claim its next victim. They pay to feel something, *anything*, and the excitement they gain while facing death from the safety of their own chairs. They want to see someone die. Almost always it's the animal that succeeds and lives to fight another day but sometimes, oh sometimes, there is a sliver of a chance the human will survive and they roar at the triumph of the human spirit overcoming impossible odds."

"Animals... you are feeding people to hungry lions --" Thomas broke off, appalled.

"Lions, and tigers, and the fucking Bear that didn't understand his purpose and refused to transform, refused to fight when he was supposed to."

"Refused to perform, you mean. He refused to perform for your amusement. And he embarrassed you?" Thomas allowed the man's words to help pull him from his shock and he again began to concentrate on pulling as much information from the man as possible. He would cheer for Arcas' success when the man was gone, holding on to that one gem of positivity that would help see him through another day trapped here. Now, he didn't want to piss the man off and instead wanted to keep him talking. "What? The other animals refused to go near him so he stood in your arena and pissed off your clientele?"

"He refused to fight and then, according to my people who managed to escape, he brought the police down upon our heads... him and that she-wolf."

"They tracked me?" He bit his lip to hold back a grin.

"I will figure out how they did it but they brought the local peacekeepers down upon our heads. Because of him and the people who rescued them I lost my lions and tigers and The Bear escaped, oh my, but I still have you."

"And what does that mean?"

"That means I'm going to have to move the timetable up on our little operation. Your help will be required."

"And locking me in a cage is how you request my help?"

"Demand, small Professor. We demand your help and we will have it whether you like it or not."

"So my cooperation is needed?"

"You need only make a choice. Usually this would be done under the light of a beautiful full moon but thanks to your Bear's stunt, we no longer have time to make that option. You are going to have to choose sooner than expected."

"And what illusion of choice are you giving me?"

"Illusion?" the madman chortled as he tilted his head and stared at Thomas, who in turn found himself struggling to stare back at the creature masquerading as a human being. "Funny coming from a being of such immense power who does nothing but pass off the old truths as new myths. Funny coming from a creature that by all rights should not exist, yet here you are, pretending to be something you are not and lecturing me about the use of illusions. If I didn't have proof of your intelligence, I would assume it was a dullard sitting there on that cot yapping at me about how I choose to live my life."

"And there you go, using words you know have no real meaning here," Thomas countered. "And there you go, a fanatic waving the word choice around when it only benefits you and your ilk --"

"My ilk?" the psycho interrupted.

"Your ilk. Fanatics that will see the world reshaped into their flawed image no matter who they hurt or destroy in the process."

"The sacrifices choose their fate."

"When put up against, what? Torture? Threats to their loved ones? All the abuse a magical creature can sustain until they break, and you know we can take a lot of damage. It's kind of like slavery in a way."

"There are no slaves here --"

"Just people who are forced against their will to agree to asinine bargains to make the hurting stop."

"They are not slaves --"

"And," Thomas spoke over the mad man, driving his point home, "Like slavery, I bet your institutions and your laws harbor and provide for all kinds of rapists, sadists, sociopaths, and psychos to do your dirty work all under the guise of belief in a god they no more believe in that I believe I am speaking to a sane man."

"My people believe," he countered, and for the first time, Thomas saw some cracks in his formidable mask of austerity.

"You people follow you so they can rape, maim, and kill with impunity. Your people do not believe the shit you are feeding them, they just see this as a means to drown themselves in blood and vice."

"You don't know of what you speak --"

At those words, Thomas rose to his feet and in a conscious decision, closed his eyes and let his glamour fall. The man stepped back, taken off guard by Thomas' actions. Pressing his advantage, no matter how meager it was, he stepped forward, a grin spreading across his lips as the man took another step back.

Thomas, for the first time since he left his family's safe island, flexed the full power of a Faunus. His horns exploded from his forehead and his eyes glowed an eerie red. The sound of rending cloth filled the air as the lower half of his pants split. His digitigrade legs flexed and fur flowed from the tears. The stitches in his shoes exploded as his hooves took the place of his human toes and feet. His nails began to elongate, and a slim goatee flowed from his chin.

His emerging tail ripped the rest of his pants, the material falling around his body as his fur thickened around his groin, hiding his most vulnerable parts from view. His nails continued to grow until they fully transformed into talons and his ears shifted and grew until they were delicate, pointed appendages that swiveled in the madman's direction. He maintained his shirt but it too began to fall apart as his shoulders broadened and his chest widened to help maintain his new mass. He was not the cute and cheerful creature that the Greeks had painted all over their walls and their pottery. He was a fierce thing, pureblooded and capable of surviving in forests filled with real and true predators who would gladly feast on his kind and not for the purpose of siphoning away their magic. He was a beast aware of his place in the circle of life, a creature of prey yet a dangerous one capable of using all of his gifts at his disposal to see to it he survived. And that tradition of survival was deeply entrenched within him, especially now he knew he was saving more than just his own life.

"Standing here in the dust and dried blood of your former victims," Thomas' voice took on a dangerous and deep tone, "being forced to stand where countless others have screamed and begged... I stand surrounded by the misery and despair sunk into the walls of this dying place, and lose myself in their sacrifice, and I tell you this."

Thomas closed his eyes, taking in the lingering aura of death and the decay that echoed in the very walls of his tiny basement, absorbing the energy of it and using it to fuel the true power of the Faunus... prophecy.

The future danced before him, unknown really, ever shifting, ever changing, paths of thought being destroyed and realized, being realigned and discarded as the factors he understood shifted and flowed around him.

When he opened his eyes, they glowed, shafts of amber and scarlet swirling as he for a moment stood outside of himself, his foreknowledge placing him as the fulcrum of the changes that were about to occur. Then he smiled, fangs elongating from his gums as the incomplete bond he possessed now came into play while aspects of his mate flowed through him.

The voice that emerged from his throat was no longer his own but that of his mate, who he could feel but not touch. The guilt and anger he felt at himself only added to the dark that now encompassed him, lending him both stealth and an anchor as he lifted his hand. He pointed one taloned finger at the pale man now backing up as he stared in both hunger and horror at the sight Thomas made.

"Death," he growled and abruptly the red faded from his eyes as his fangs withdrew up into his gums.

The smile that spread across his face was truly terrifying but now the madman reclaimed a step, his eyes wide as he stared at Thomas in his true form.

"Magnificent," he praised, though Thomas could feel the fear emanating off the man like the scent of rotting dead things. "You will be the perfect sacrifice."

"Death," Thomas repeated, then threw back his head and wailed as the glimpse of the future left him. The sound echoed throughout the building, shaking the very foundations of the place as dust motes rained down upon them and the steel door began to rattle.

The fanatic dropped to his knees, his hands over his head, as he began to laugh. As Thomas' wail trailed off, the madman's laughter increased until tears were running down his face and he scrambled to his feet, his heart racing as the acrid scent of urine filled the air.

"Magnificent," he praised. "Magnificent." He scurried backwards, leaving behind the scent of horror and delight as a look of madness settled on his face. "You will be the final one," he promised, ignoring the wet puddle he left behind as he gripped his arms in terror and delight, two conflicting emotions no sane man would experience at the same time. "Magnificent," he panted one last time before stumbling back into the shadows and what Thomas assumed was a door.

Some monsters came in human form.

Keeping to his true form, Thomas closed his eyes

and contemplated the bond, now physically represented in his mind as a band of red. Once he feared it and now he used it as comfort as he contemplated all that had happened. He absently placed one hand against his stomach and he smiled. Death was in the future... but he had something more important than his own life to protect now. It was up to his mate -- yes, that sounded perfect to him -- his mate to ensure the death he visited upon them would ensure the safety of him and his child.

* * *

In the innermost reaches of *The Wild Hunt*, a twisting, sweating, panting form lost in the throes of an unnatural sleep snapped open his eyes and sat up.

Chapter Four

"We have a lot to go over and precious little time to get through it."

The atmosphere in the room was tense and Manx wore an unusual frown upon their usually calm face. It didn't look like it belonged there and it was making the gathered people in their camp, especially the ones who knew them best, nervous.

"I have learned a great many things," they began calmly, looking at the people gathered, most sitting next to their partners. Here in their living room where so many happy family gatherings had taken place, their people were tense, hanging on to their every word. "Most of it disturbing on a cellular level, but the long and short of it is that Dagan the Fifteenth, after all these years, is about to be revived."

"As in now?" Marshal, The Cat, with his distinctive Egyptian spice and oil scent chimed in, sounding more than concerned... afraid. He sounded afraid as he leaned back into the arms of his mate.

The scent of the two of them was nearly overpowering but it read as being a healthy and complete bond. Manx didn't really know what had happened between the two of them but they approved wholeheartedly.

Caille, the Hunt's most beautiful Wolf, sat next to Bran, their Raven and newest ally on the huge sofa, nearly dwarfing it with the weight of their concern which seemed like another entity sitting next to them. Yet Caille leaned into Bran and he gently petted her wild blonde hair, the bandages she still wore, mostly for show, gleaming white in the soft light of the room as she quietly grieved for what had happened and what was about to come. Bran looked angry, his brow drawn down as his leg bounced in agitation, as if inactivity were driving him to find a way to release his pent-up energy.

Across from them and sharing a massive armchair, Marshal perched on Arcas' knee. Manx let their eyes linger on the new pairing for a moment, noting the very necessary bandages on The Cat's arm as one of Arcas' burly arms wrapped comfortably around his waist holding The Cat in place. Their huge, redhaired Bear had said little since he had recovered but his possessiveness when it came to his Cat was obvious. Clearly some things happened that Manx wasn't privy to know but they could feel the bond solid and tight between the two.

Manx let their eyes drift over their Raven and their Wolf, feeling the budding bond between them before absently comparing it to the robust and hearty bond shared between their Bear and their Cat and wondering what had suddenly happened between the couples that made them solidify their bonds in such a short time. Then they thought of Kern, trapped in his room while his mate remained missing, and their frown deepened.

"Are you going to keep us in suspense?" Marshal Gray spoke as he absently ran a thumb over the thick red hairs that peppered Arcas' arm. "Because after all that went down yesterday, I am feeling the need for some serious revenge."

"Just like a cat," Caille murmured, her eyes narrowed as she observed Marshal. "Feeling like your honor has been besmirched so you must seek revenge somehow."

"Honor?" their Cat hissed, sounding like his angry namesake. "My best friend and brother from another mother is missing, Wolf. Of course I want revenge. Who here doesn't?"

"I seek justice," Bran offered, tilting his head to the side as he examined Marshal carefully. It was very bird-like in action, and the thin tracery of tattoos around his neck glowed faintly. "I have never met your best friend but I know my best friend is now bereft, in an unnatural sleep while he awaits news of his mate, and that I can't abide."

"He is our brother," Arcas commented, the sadness reverberating in his voice even as he cuddled his mate. "He was the first of us and the one to bring us into the fold. What is happening to him is a travesty and none of us will rest until his Faunus is returned, but I have been around his captors." The bruises and bandages he still sported made that abundantly clear. "They have no care for our human emotions. All they see is a means to an end. They have tortured, murdered, made their hands red with the blood of innocents and their souls black with all the dead that lie at their feet. They are dangerous and connected and just because we gave them a black eye with our actions doesn't mean we can disregard common sense and go chasing in haphazardly."

"Not my intent," Marshal huffed. "I don't want to make things worse but damn it, I want Thomas back. He is innocent in all of this."

"So are the others who suffered at their hands. It's a fucking cult," Caille growled, leaning forward as she glared at The Cat. "They don't give a fuck about you or me or the man trapped in sleep so he won't destroy everything in his wrath because his mate is taken. They only care about what they most desire and that is death and destruction, the revival of their god and the power he can give them."

"He is awake," Manx interjected just then and all

eyes turned to them. "Last night, despite my spell, Kern has awakened because he felt his mate tug at their incomplete bond."

"Can we see him?" Caille nearly leapt from her seat but Bran held her back, shaking his head as she again settled at his side. "Manx?"

"He will join us soon," The Master of the Hunt consoled her with their words. "He is barely restraining himself as it is. Tonight, when we make our move, he will join us. I fear if he were to be released into the world right now the death toll would be unimaginable."

"He's that worked up?" Arcas asked in his quiet way.

"He is that and more." Manx sighed sadly, shaking their head. "He can barely retain his human form. He can feel his mate, but because of the incomplete bond he cannot travel to him. He can hear his pleas for help, feel his suffering, but is unable to reach for him. All he can do is send what energy he can through the incomplete bond to bolster his strength. And after last night, I fear we may need to move faster than I anticipated."

"What happened last night?" Bran asked as he leaned forward, his gaze unblinking as he stared at the Master of the Hunt.

"He drew upon the true power of the Faunus." Manx's voice grew deeper as a visible shudder racked their body.

"The true power --"

"Prophesy," Marshal cut off Caille, trying to rise to his feet but Arcas' grip on him held him in place. "The true power of the Faunus lies in their ability to become oracles if certain conditions are met. Don't you know your history, woman?"

"My history, yes," Caille snapped out. "The history surrounding my brothers, yes. But I have been a little more concerned with saving all manners of creatures fleeing from the Cult of Dagna the Fifteenth than researching every person we rescue and I don't contain encyclopedic knowledge of every mystical creature who crosses our path. And if you haven't noticed, Cat, we didn't actually have get-together kumbaya moments with the man who managed to turn my brother's life into a minor nightmare."

"So you are victim blaming?" Marshal all but roared, and it took some real energy for Arcas to hold him back.

"If he had completed the bond then none of this would have happened!" Caille screamed, her outrage obviously needing an outlet and finding one in her response to The Cat. "If he had completed the bond then the cult wouldn't have taken him and we wouldn't have been placed in a position to be savaged by wild fucking animals, and my brother would not be suffering. None of this would have happened if he'd just grown the fuck up and completed the bond he'd started."

"Children --" Manx tried to interject but The Cat spoke over them.

"He was afraid!" Marshal roared back at her. "He was scared and after his past he had every right to be. If your brother had explained himself and what was going on clearly then he wouldn't have felt the need to run and hide."

"Children --"

"So it's Kern's fault the little bastard bit him and then ran, leaving him vulnerable? It's Kern's fault Arcas was taken, beaten, drugged, and now has to dance to the tune of the humans who have no idea we actually exist?" Caille was faintly glowing, her outrage turning her eyes an odd amber color, wolf amber…

"Young ones --"

"Yes! Because if he was any kind of real mate --" Marshal's face was twisted in rage.

"*Shut the fuck up!*"

At Manx's roar the room dropped into a sudden, uncomfortable silence. The sound that emerged from Manx's throat had been inhuman, tri-toned, and terrifying.

The Master of the Hunt kicked their heavy coffee table out of the way and they all winced when it flew across the room and embedded itself in the wall. With their eyes narrowed, their brows low, and their hands fisted at their side, Manx radiated anger and danger in equal amounts. And what was more terrifying was that the Manx was not breathing. Their chest didn't rise and fall with a telltale need for oxygen the other beings in the room required for life.

Manx's eyes danced over each and every one of them and they all winced as they felt the tug and he pulled on the reins that held them all within their service. No one dared to move, lest they draw The Manx's ire.

"Now!"

Their voice still held on to that unearthly cadence.

"If we are done squabbling like children, I believe it is time to share what I know."

No one was stupid enough to object.

"They are in Daniels, an abandoned town in Ellicott City. It only cost our little stalker friend three toes before that information began to flow."

"So close…" Arcas murmured but quickly silenced himself when Manx's piercing eyes settled on him for a moment.

"The Cult of Dagna and I are diametrically opposed to one another, Arcas. I settled in this city because the strange and unexplainable happens here so much no one would notice or even show concern about a bondage club operating in the open in the middle of Baltimore. As long as I keep my liquor license current and there are no gun fights or drug busts happening, the people here really don't give a shit what I do. You know this."

"Master." Arcas lowered his eyes, a show of respect that pleased Manx and eased their ire a little.

"They are in Daniels, which is a nearly perfect place to hide a cult. It's a flooded out old mill town that went bust in the sixties... the nineteen sixties. That means there are buildings made of modern materials in which they can hide their base of operations, their only visitors are a few urban explorers and the usual kids sneaking out there to party, drink, do drugs, and all the other things their mommies and daddies would die of embarrassment to discover their little kiddies are doing."

"How do we access it?" Bran, ever the tactician, asked, leaning forward in his seat as he maintained his grip on Caille's hand.

"From the north." Manx allowed their voice to slowly sink back into human tones as they spoke, the need to discipline their wayward children and bring them back to task waning. "There are a few structures still standing though most are in ruin. There is a road we can take, Alberton Road, which is near Dogwood Road and a good five miles from the area we need targeted. Most people drive and then go on foot as Dogwood Road narrows into a footpath where they will undoubtedly have surveillance cameras set up and running."

"You think they will be expecting us?" Marshal asked, though The Cat still smelled of fear... no, not fear, caution where Manx was concerned. Good. The newest members needed to remember who was holding their reins.

"After the number you all did with their main source of income, undoubtedly. I assumed they would make their move quickly because of the police now holding onto any information they gathered from their animal fights. I am sure they wouldn't want some intrepid detective stumbling on their little cult activities, so the smart thing would be to carry out their plans as soon as possible to prevent them from being thwarted. And after the night Kern experienced along with his mate, I am not sure The Faunus will survive another day with them."

"So, no full moon," Caille murmured. "They must be desperate."

"Never have we ever needed to attack them directly before." Manx nodded, pleased their children were thinking once again about the issue at hand and not squabbling amongst themselves. They had to work together in order to pull this off.

"They never attacked us directly before," Arcas pointed out. "They broke the covenant."

"Bent it," Manx corrected, a low rumbling in their chest. "They can always fall back on the excuse they were bringing Thomas in to give him choices. Since the contract between them and us has always hinged on choice, they have used that little loophole to their advantage."

"But now they are pushing it." Bran nodded.

"Now they are pushing it too far. Probably because they can sense The Faunus is pure-blooded and filled with magic he rarely seems to use."

"Thomas hides," Marshal felt compelled to add. "He is afraid he is going to be discovered because he still doesn't fit in very well with human society."

"His fears are justified," Manx agreed. "But in this case, after the partial bond with Kern we all know he initiated, his façade began to crack and I am sure they just read power off him. I don't think they understand bonds the way we do. They probably just think Kern was sent to bring in a partially powerful practitioner or creature and they wanted that power for themselves."

"There's no way to be sure they don't know about the bond," Bran added, and Manx offered him an approving grin.

"That's very true, Raven. If they knew I am sure they would not have bothered to try and bring him in. They would know they would be under a direct attack from one of our most powerful Huntsmen. They seek to avoid direct confrontation because in a battle between theirs and ours, we would decimate them."

"So how do we get in?" Marshal was eager to stay on task and rescue his best friend. Loyalty. Manx approved.

"Bran, can you send your ravens to see if there is any activity in that ghost town?"

"I can." Bran closed his eyes and Manx felt a wave of energy emanate from him before he opened his eyes and nodded. "It is done. They will feed everything they know back to me."

"Great." Marshal shot The Raven a baleful glare. "That's awesome for you but the rest of us don't get a direct path into raven radio."

"Wireless earbuds." Caille waved away The Cat's complaints. "Bran can relay what he learns to us."

"And because there is surveillance, we are going to have to move into position carefully," Manx decided, stepping back to lean against a wall, a perfect place to observe all of their Huntsmen working together.

"Wolf or girl?" Caille looked toward Manx. "I can go as either. The surveillance cameras will not be fooled if I take on the guise of the maiden, but I can always dress down. Disguises don't always have to be magical."

"Take Bran with you," Manx decided. "Everyone who has seen his face has been detained by the police so that gives you some anonymity. You will be an urban couple exploring with your faithful dog." They nodded at Caille. "Your nose is more powerful in your wolf form. See if you can pick up any trails and lead us there. Take your time about it too; after all, you are explorers. And Bran, take a camera. We can link a digital camera to a signal so we can follow your steps. We need proper reconnaissance before we make a move."

"And after we have that information?" Marshal demanded. "What do we do then?"

"Well, I am sure everyone has seen Arcas' face." Manx offered The Bear a smile. "And I am sure a huge red bear tromping through the woods in Ellicott City would be sure to draw some attention, so I want you two to hang back in an SUV. I'll have Bran drive it there as part of his disguise and you two can keep an eye on them from a distance. As soon as he knows where Thomas is being held, we can send in the ravens for more detailed instructions so we may strike at sunset."

"We have to wait that long?" Marshal

complained. When Manx shot him a dark look, he buttoned his lips fast.

"We wait so we don't draw attention to ourselves, Cat. We wait so we won't go rushing in and cause them to prematurely sacrifice your friend. They have to wait until moonrise for them to perform the sacrifice so we have time."

"But they could be torturing him --"

"And he will have to endure!" Manx's roar brought silence into the room again and though they cursed their lack of control when it came to their temper, the cultists had pushed them to their limit. "He will endure because Kern is lending him strength. He will endure because he has to."

"And him using his true power... that oracle thing?" Marshal girded his loins enough to ask. "There has to be certain stipulations met before that even works. Do you think…"

"Do I think your Faunus murdered someone as a sacrifice to make it work?" Manx shook their head. "No. But I believe wherever they have taken him has enough residual sacrificial magic it allowed him to tap into his true powers and make a prophecy."

"But the prophecies aren't real, right?" Arcas asked, looking concerned. "If he truly has foresight then maybe he knows something they now know that will push them into harming him."

"No one can predict the future." Manx shook his head again. "Not truly. At most his power allows him to review lines of circumstance and predict the most probable outcome. Either way, if they saw this show of magic, they aren't going to want to let him go or harm him before they can force a choice on him. And from what I know after meeting with the young man, he will be too stubborn to give them what they want."

"So, torture?" Bran asked, and Marshal's scent suddenly turned fearful and dejected.

"Be prepared for it." Manx crossed their arms and signed deeply. "This is one of the reasons Kern will remain here with me as you soldier forth."

"He's not going to like that," Caille murmured, and the look Manx shot her caused her to look away fast.

"I don't care what Kern likes or dislikes about this plan right now," Manx snapped. "I am concerned about them reviving a pitiful excuse for a god who will do more harm than good to humanity as a whole because dead things shouldn't be brought back to life. If they succeed in murdering The Faunus they are that much closer to raining hell down on earth. You don't think the elder gods are going to happily let that one slide, do you? They will bring fire and destruction to humanity that allowed such things to happen and they won't care who is innocent or guilty as long as the danger is wiped out."

"So in order to save humanity they will kill humanity?" Marshal sounded incensed. "How is that even logical?"

"Logic doesn't come into play where the gods are concerned or this would not be an issue in the first place. Dagna the Fifteenth would have been smote the moment he got it in his head to bring back the powers his ancestors held for his benefit alone." Manx rose up from their slouch against the wall and turned to make their way out of the room. "You all have your orders. Why are you sitting here?"

Manx was on their way out to see what other information they could gather from their source when they suddenly paused.

"Congratulations on your bonding, Arcas and

Marshal," they called over their shoulder. "We will celebrate when this crisis is over and we have a lull until the next one."

Manx continued on their way but as they neared the private elevator that would take them to the basement, they overheard Marshal call out, "Hey, Bran? How is a raven like a writing desk?"

The amused groan from their Huntsmen pulled a small smile to their lips.

"'Cause they're both flat and produce a few notes." The Cat guffawed.

"And if you get hit by them they break bones," Bran growled back, and as they entered their elevator, Manx could hear the laughter from their children.

The Wild Hunt would be fine. This would work out for the best. But for now, it was time to get bloody again.

Chapter Five

"Time to eat... whoa." The man with a rather irritating high voice paused at the bars and just stared at Thomas.

Good, he thought. *Let them stare.*

The Faunus refused to retake his human shape, feeling his partial bond between his lover more this way. He could feel Kern sending him his strength through it, and he intuitively knew if the bond had been complete, he would be able to send so much more. But for now, Thomas was rested, content he had this small connection with his mate, which was epically important now because he could feel the new life growing beneath his heart. And partially channeling his mate did have some fringe benefits. His once dainty little horns had grown into a rather impressive ten-point rack, each point honed to a body-piercing degree while the fangs he now could drop and retract were kind of fun to play with.

Now, he turned and smiled at the men bringing to him what smelled like a meal, albeit the fast-food kind, and watched as they stumbled to a halt.

Slowly he rose to his feet, his hooves making a clopping sound as he stepped closer to the bars and inhaled deeply. They smelled of fear. Who could blame them? He looked down at his natural claws and noted they had become talons that even the fiercest monster would be wary of... let alone a pair of humans bearing a bag of greasy goodness.

He refocused on the humans and something about them tingled in his memory... just a bit.

"Have I seen you before?" Damn, his voice remained the same. Having a huge badassed monster voice would be so amusing right now, but probably not as funny as having his proper professor voice coming from his now decidedly monstrous body.

"Fuck…" one man breathed. "What the fuck?"

"Oh," Thomas' smile grew wider. "I remember you. You were the one who hit me on the head and tased my brother until he was still to let you to drug him." The man paled. "How's that working out for you?"

"Just give him the food," the second man stammered, eyes wide and his face pale.

"Please, just give me the food." Thomas' voice dropped deep into the tones of a disapproving academic as he stepped closer. "I hunger."

Only half of what he said was done to inject more fear into these men… and honestly for his own amusement because he was growing bored here. The other part of his statement was really true. He did hunger, hungered like he never had before. And not just for the processed crap in the bag. No, what he wouldn't mind right now was a huge bite of human flesh complete with the salty, thick splash of human blood tainted with fear.

This new hunger slightly disturbed him because it really wasn't coming from him. He was a Faunus; they didn't partake of human flesh. So the rational part of his mind could only come up with two reasons for his sudden craving for long pig. One, it was coming through his bond, which made the other legends about Cernunnos very true and very scary, or it was coming from the new life developing within his body. Either way, he was feeling more disturbed because he wasn't really upset about the cravings or about the changes flowing through his body courtesy of the bond. He just arched an eyebrow as the man went from pasty white to gray and Thomas wondered if he was going to pass out. If he did and his friend left him… and if he could reach through the bars to drag him closer --

"Just give him the fucking bag… and the water." The second man was now shoving the first man toward the steel door with its convenient food window cleverly disguised as a doggy door.

"I ain't getting no closer --"

Thomas cut off the first man. "But you did get closer, close enough to drag me off the streets and into this world of your creation. And there I was, minding my own business too. Come a bit closer and I'll show you how it feels when your chickens come home to nest. Please let me show you what you brought down upon your heads by bringing me here. Every action has consequences and repercussions. Please let me show you the folly of your ways."

The man abruptly dropped the bag and the bottle of water he had in his hand and bolted from the room, tracking through what was left of the drying puddle of urine left by their apparent boss before he too had fled.

Thomas eyed the remaining man and arched his eyebrow even higher, looking all scholarly and disapproving, until he retrieved the bag and bottle of water, sidling up to the doggie door.

"I had nothing to do with you being here," he began as he undid the latch and quickly slid the food inside before slamming the locks back in place.

"But you do have something to do with me being locked up now, like an animal."

"Look at you," the man countered, rising to his feet but not getting within arms' reach of the bars. Smart man. "You're not human!"

"I never claimed to be." Thomas snorted, resisting the urge to roll his eyes at the man's weak reasoning. "And are you human?"

"Of course I am." He sounded indignant.

"From where I stand, you are more of a monster than I. How many beings, how many people who were different did you help imprison here? How many were locked in here, tortured until they agreed death was better than staying alive one more moment at the tender mercy provided by your hands? How many people were given an impossible choice, forced into this by an insane creature in human guise because of his evil nature? How you must have smiled and cheered as the life left their eyes. How you and your ilk must have rejoiced as another soul was stripped from this world and force-fed into the dark, rotting maw of that thing that wanted mastery over those it felt more powerful." Thomas grew his fangs and licked at them, feeling the sharpness of them, envisioning how they could rip through human flesh and tissue. "We have a comparison for that, for people like you. You may call yourself human but those of us who can think logically call them Nazis... call *you* Nazis, and like those monsters in the guise of man, you too shall crash and burn."

The smile he offered the man caused him too to turn and exit the basement at a rapid clip, much to Thomas' continued amusement.

Ah, well, he thought as he retrieved the battered bag of food and the bottle of water. Since dinner decided to run away, it was time for him to consume something if only for the sake of his child.

Thomas placed his hands on his stomach and smiled. He would do everything in his power to protect this new life he had been gifted with until his Stag found him and he could complete the bond.

He hoped after that happened he could keep the horns and the fangs. They were badassed and he was enjoying them more than he thought possible. Not as much as he would have enjoyed taking a bite from one of those fools, but the burger would have to suffice.

So he ate the food, drank the water, and silently prayed his lover would come to him soon. He was growing tired of waiting.

Chapter Six

They fell on each other like animals, growling and tearing at their clothes. With everything going on, sex was the perfect escape and stress relief and they both were happy to indulge.

"God, you feel so good," Marshal babbled as he tore at Arcas' clothing.

Arcas said nothing as his mouth was occupied with nibbling and sucking on Marshal's throat. Marshal was, not oddly enough, down with that as he did his best to strip his Bear.

"You can help," Marshal finally spat, frustrated with the undressing portion of the action about to take place. His mate should just walk around nude.

"I can feel your frustration and it turns me on," Arcas pulled away enough to admit, blinking at him with big, innocent blue eyes.

"Feel my…"

"Through the bond." Arcas grinned showing some very sharp teeth. Those were pressing into his skin? Eh, wasn't worth complaining about when Marshal was honest enough with himself to admit he liked it.

"The bond?"

"You know, the thing we bit each other over --"

"I know that," Marshal snapped, realizing he was feeling his own frustration plus… amusement? That had to be from Arcas. "So… I guess the bond is really working now."

"The more we pay attention to it, feed it, the more effective it will be."

"You can't hear what I am thinking?"

"No, but I can feel your emotions, and you are a very angry, spitting little cat."

"I am not little. Everyone is little to your huge ass," Marshal snapped with no real bite, really concentrating on the bond. It was like a thing in the back of his mind but it was flowing with powerful emotions... Bears felt their feelings deeply. "And I swallow. I'm a good Cat even when I'm angry."

That said, Marshal thought now would be a good time to get some of that anger and aggression out... on his lover's pants.

"Damn me for not having claws," Marshal complained, but his mate, feeling his level of almost painful frustration, knew little Marshal was cramped and needed some room to stretch out, so he stepped back and easily divested himself of his clothing.

Marshal was stripped next, without loss of expensive clothing this time. His Bear was learning even before Marshal abused his credit limit by making him go shopping to replace what he had torn.

But once naked, he could stretch out without the binding of those not-silk briefs that had the club's logo across the crotch... really, Stag's horns? He recognized the placement of the horn points... and now he was really ready to play.

Almost like Marshal was magnetically drawn to it, his hands lashed out and gripped the thick hot length of his lover's cock.

"I want this... in me, in case you were wondering..."

"Never had a doubt," Arcas drawled back as they moved toward the bed. "As you reminded me earlier."

"So get the lube, get to stretching so I can have this inside of me... and by this I mean your cock... and I am babbling. Ignore me."

"I'd rather not." Arcas sent a wave of arousal

through the bond so thick and powerful it almost dropped Marshal to his knees. "I like it when you babble. I learn so much about you."

"Then learn all about my ass," Marshal responded with the most innocently sweet smile he could muster. "It makes me happy... the thought of your dick in my ass."

"I gathered." Arcas snorted before he pulled himself free of Marshal's grasp... no, Marshal didn't whine over it... okay he did, but come on. It was Arcas' dick and his ass, two prime pieces of real estate that were made to go together... like now.

"After I stretch you..." Arcas outright laughed this time and Marshal knew he was aroused and amused by his actions because of the feelings flowing through the bond. "Going to take my big thick fingers and stretch out that little hole of yours. Would you like that, kitty cat?"

"Oh fu-fuck," Marshal stammered as Arcas' hands lowered him to the bed, this time on his knees with his ass high up in the air and his head comfortably resting on some lush pillows.

It would have been an embarrassing position for a couple who were new at this whole sex together thing, but strangely enough, it made him feel sexy. Hell, it just felt right so he waggled his ass from side to side, hearing his mate inhale deeply as a sharp spike of desire raced through the bond.

"Yes," Arcas coaxed. "Show daddy where it aches."

"My hole, daddy," Marshal responded, unable to stay away from such arousing bedplay. He loved role playing, and letting Arcas be his daddy was the stuff of fantasies. Now if he could get the Bear into an apron and a jock strap...

"Greedy little hole," Arcas praised as Marshal heard the bedside table open and close, and the wet squelch of lube. "So tight and pink... Do you keep it tight for me, baby?"

"Yes, daddy," Marshal breathed, one hand snaking between his thighs to grip at his unseated cock. The rings were swollen and he could feel his balls tingle. He needed to be fucked right now. He sent his sense of urgency through the bond and Arcas just chuckled.

"So hungry..."

"So hungry, daddy."

"But good little boys listen to the rules. Do you want to hear the rules?"

"Yes, daddy."

"If I do anything you don't like, anything at all, you let me know."

"Can do."

"And if it's anything you want, you tell me and I'll do my best to give it to you."

"Your dick in my ass, daddy."

There was a chuckle and then Arcas was bending over to place small, biting kisses on his ass. The sharp sting felt delicious, and Marshal shuddered knowing just how dangerous those teeth could be. Adrenaline and arousal were a combination he just knew he would be experiencing all of the rest of his life.

"Gotta open you up, baby. Would you like daddy's tongue?"

Would he?! He liked the idea so much he reached back with both hands and spread his cheeks open, exposing himself fully.

He could hear Arcas growl right before he pounced.

Marshal squealed -- he was man enough to admit

it -- as Arcas buried his face in his ass, lapping at the sensitive hole and the guardian muscles that held him tight.

"Arcas," he trilled, ready to release his cheeks so he could grab his cock and start stroking when a sharp slap to one cheek had him changing his mind and pulling himself open wider.

"Fuck, yeah," Arcas growled, all pretense and playing done as he began to lick at his lover's hole, nibbling at the rim and sending fire shooting through Marshal's veins.

"So good," Marshal panting as his toes curled and his body began to sweat. "Eat me, daddy. Please."

And like a good daddy, Arcas complied, this time slipping two fingers inside his hole to pull him open.

Marshal whined at the familiar sting of being opened up so perfectly. The soft, wet licks by his mate did more to relax him than any stretching with his fingers could have done. And speaking of his fingers...

"Oh yes," he hissed, sounding very much like a cat as his lover slid two deep inside him.

It burned so beautifully, sending the desire to be penetrated throughout his body. Yes, it had been too long since he wanted anyone as much as he wanted his Bear and he couldn't hide it now. He knew he was broadcasting all kinds of need through the bond.

So his lover was stretching him open, filling him with his fingers and his glorious tongue, which danced in the inside of his walls like magic, and it was not enough.

"Please..." he begged, still torn between earning another slap to the ass if he let go and grabbed his cock or having more of this delicious torture heaped upon his body.

He didn't have long to ponder getting a delicious slap or more delicious oral because his lover pulled back and added another finger.

"Three, baby," he purred, leaning over Marshal's back to bite at the nape of his neck. Oh yeah, that was a good thing, Marshal thought as his lover nipped at his skin. He arched into the bite as he felt his mate's hairy chest press against his back. Now that was perfection, three thick fingers inside of him... four... four thick fingers stretching him open and his lover's body pressed on top of his. He felt dominated in a good way and again praised himself for shoving his forearm in his lover's mouth... and berated himself for not doing it sooner.

And then Arcas began to twist his fingers, stretching him open as he curled them and found...

"That's the spot," Marshal cried out, unable to control his muscles as they all turned to water and burned with fire at the same time. "Goddess, do that again..."

And Arcas did... again and again until Marshal was seeing bright colors parade in front of his eyes... and not those dull burgundies and browns... no. He was seeing a bright rainbow of electric jewel tones that made his head swim... Or maybe it was the stimulation to his sensitive prostate, but either way, if his mate didn't hurry up back there he was going to come without him.

Almost as if reading his mind -- no the bond did not lend itself to mind reading -- Arcas arched with his free hand and gripped Marshal's balls, giving them a sharp tug down.

Arcas' four fingers slipped free and Marshal let out a disappointed groan as his four fingers were rubbed up again and slid easily back into his ass. Then he gave out a groan of happiness because Marshal believed in complimenting good works, but how many fingers was his Bear going to stuff up his ass? He wasn't trying to get his whole hand up there because fisting was a thing Marshal shied away from, but maybe with his mate...

"No, I am not about to fist you." Arcas snorted, amused hunger pinging through the bond. "That takes days if not weeks of preparation and stretching. No, I just want you good and open and slick, hot for my dick in a way that won't cause you any pain."

"Appreciated," Marshal mumbled from where he was genuinely biting on his pillow. Yes, his lover had literally turned him into a pillow biter... "But I'm ready, baby."

"Just making sure," Arcas said before the delicious finger appetizer was withdrawn and his ass was ready for the main course... his mate's dick.

There was the sound of his lover lubing up and then he felt the fat head of his Bear's cock press against his rim. It was hot and wet and would feel so good going in if Arcas would allow it to...

"There," his Bear purred, rather not unlike a cat, and added some pressure and slowly, oh so slowly, inch by inch, Marshal's ass was being filled... by a telephone pole.

Okay, he thought wincing as the delicious feeling started turning into *maybe I bit off more than I could chew* feelings... Then his mate used one slick hand to grab his cock, first massaging his sheath before gripping the damp shaft.

He whimpered in pain... and then in pleasure as his lover sank deeper into his ass while his fingers teased at the swollen rings at the head of his cock.

"That's it," Arcas crooned to him. "Just open up

that tight little hole and let me in. Come on, baby. I know you can do it."

Arcas kept up the praise and a warm feeling settled in his brain. He wanted to do this for his Bear. He could do this... and despite the ache of being filled, he had never felt so close to another person before. His forays and flings meant nothing in the face of this ecstasy. Mentally and physically he was getting his needs seen to and it was enough to make him cry. Marshal could feel the truthfulness of his lover's words as he worked his way inside of him. And they had little to do with lust and more to do with the budding romantic feeling he could feel unfurling within him. His mate was totally invested in him, in his pleasure, in his happiness, and it was a feeling that made him want to weep with joy.

But first he had to conquer cock mountain and get his lover's oversized dong where it belonged, deep within his body.

Marshal arched his back further, thrusting a little into the hand that held him with just enough slack to tease him into thrusting harder, and pushing back onto the cock splitting him in two.

"Want me to pull out?" Arcas asked, concern flooding the bond.

"No," Marshal panted, trembling, sweating. "It's mine. I want it."

He pressed back further... really, how long was his dick anyway? And screamed as the fat head of his lover's cock pressed into his prostate.

"Oh fuck, oh fuck, oh fuck..." he chanted, because it wasn't a quick jab of pleasure. His mate was so big every movement of his cock applied direct pleasure to his P-spot.

"Yes, baby," Arcas was panting in his ear. "Take

it. Take it all. It's yours."

"It's mine," Marshal reiterated, just in case his mate didn't understand. "I want it all."

"You are taking it all," Arcas praised. "Yes, baby is swallowing me up good."

"Oh goddess," Marshal whimpered. His body was filled to bursting with pleasure. His ass was a constant barrage of feel-good sensations, and his cock was being stroked and teased just the way he liked it. He could feel his mate's hunger and pleasure as his body and his mind were swimming with endorphins. "This is the best fuck ever."

"Get used to it, my Cat," Arcas promised. "Every time we do this, it'll get easier to take, and soon you're going to be gaping open, your ass shafted around my dick to fit me perfectly. My bespoke little hole... feels so good, baby."

Marshal was writhing in pleasure. He was rubbing his sweating forehead into the pillow as it moved from side to side even as he pressed back further. One of Arcas' hands was on his hips, keeping him moving at a slow place no matter how much he tried to just press back and take it all.

He was lost in his own little world broadcasting lust and hunger and contentment and a little pain and all the pleasure through his bond. He was so lost in the reciprocating feelings that the press of his lover's soft hair against his stretched rim was almost a surprise.

"You took it all baby," his lover was praising him again. "How do you feel?"

"Full," Marshal managed while his ass muscles spasmed around the invader and his lover shuddered at the feel.

"Milking me so good, baby," Arcas moaned, biting the back of his neck harder before his shifted his hips, pulled out about an inch, and slid back in deep.

And then the joyous happy time came back. After three strokes his muscles relaxed and stopped firing, allowing his lover the freedom to pull back so just the head of his cock tugging at the inside of his rim before he slammed himself back in again.

"Sweet glorious mother!" Marshal wailed. He had been fucked before, several times no less because he was such a power bottom, but nothing had ever measured up to this.

His prostate was singing as every move stroked it, his body quivering, and he wanted to scream out his pleasure to the world... And since there was nothing stopping him... "Yes, fuck yes!" he shouted, slamming back despite Arcas' hold on his hip. "Please... oh goddess, fuck me!"

And always one to give him what he wanted -- he was spoiled like that -- Arcas pulled him up, sat him straight down on his dick, and told him to take what he wanted.

At first Marshal's breath was stolen as his lover sank deeper than he ever had been before... but the cushion of soft hair covered muscles comforted him almost as much as the thick, muscular arms that surrounded him. Bliss... it was sheer bliss and it could only get better if he...

Oh yeah. Marshal rose up and slammed himself back down. It didn't hurt and he finally had what was his due... mainly his lover's cock... right where he wanted it... deep in his ass.

Marshal threw his head back, and he began to swivel his hips, sliding up and slinking down like a snake. He was pole a dancer and the pole he was blessing was deep inside of him.

He gave light thrusts, heavy thrusts, he sat down

fully on it and just grinned, clenching his ass deliciously as every movement made his prostate feel mighty fine.

He bounced happily, an adult kid in adult playland before his lover gripped his thighs, hefted him up, and began to power thrust up deep inside of him.

"Oh shit, oh shit..." Marshal babbled as white-hot pleasure flooded his body. His nerves were on fire, his mind fading fast, his strength... holding out but waning. This was the real definition of getting buggered right proper.

He squirmed in his lover's hold but that only made Arcas growl harder and slam up into him faster than he thought was humanly possible, but then he wasn't thinking anything because his body tipped over into his first orgasm. He shuddered as his spend shot up out of his pulsing cock, shooting up to stripe his face and chest. His ass was going crazy over the hard, ungiving cock that pressed along his prostate even harder as his ass spasmed.

"Arcas," he panted, he cried, he screamed, and his lover kept on going. He had a worrying amount of staying power but Marshal would ponder that later. For right now, his oversensitive prostate was getting the beating of its long life, and he found himself tipping over again as he came a second time.

"That's what I wanted. Give it all up to me," his lover called out as his balls drew up and once again his cock shot his cum all over the place, his face, Arcas' face, the sheets... *laundry around here must be a new exercise in BDSM*. The stray thought floated thought his head as he felt himself become dizzy and a bit sore as his prostate was still being abraded by the world's largest cock.

Finally just as the feel-good sensation was starting to slide into the *a bit too much* range, Arcas cursed softly and stiffened. Marshal, coming down from his orgasmic high, felt his back channel flooded as his lover finally came. It was warm soothing feeling that almost threatened the return of his boner, but even his cock was too pooped to play any longer and merely jerked a little.

What was killer was the waves of release from his Bear he felt through the bond. It was like having a third orgasm without having to be fucked through the mattress first. Neat.

His lover shuddered against him and then very gently lowered him to his front.

Marshal sank flat to the mattress as he felt his lover gently pull himself out. It felt like it hadn't gone down at all and if it wasn't for the flood of cum that flowed from his ass, he would swear his Bear hadn't climaxed at all.

"Such a beautiful, dirty little gape." Arcas paused, sliding a finger easily into his ass and tugging at the rim. "It's perfect for me, my mate. Thank you for giving me this perfect little hole to play with."

"You're welcome, I guess," Marshal managed to mutter before he felt more than heard his lover laugh. He was fading fast and didn't know how much longer he could stay awake.

"Sore?" Arcas asked as he rose up from the bed. Marshal didn't really care where he was going so long as he was left to sleep... but he still better get his red hairy ass back here fast. Marshal wanted to cuddle too.

"Of course I am," he mumbled, before his lover come back with a cool damp cloth and cleaned him up. "You are big, you know."

"Good thing I have a bidet," Arcas teased. "You

can sit right on it and have a whore's bath."

"You calling me a whore?"

"Hell no." Arcas laughed. "Whores get paid. You are doing it for the love of sex and because you really, really like me."

"Was me begging you to plow me into next week your first clue?" Marshal asked, feeling a little, well, catty. He wanted to sleep. But he wanted to reassure his mate he really, really liked him. He sent his adoration for him through the bond.

"No, you walking into my bedroom and demanding we close the bond was my first clue."

"Arcas --"

"I observe a lot, little Cat. I observe how you tease people to ease tension and fear. I see how you would give everything of yourself to protect the ones you love and consider family. I see how brave you are, even though you hide it behind sarcasm and sass. And I see how you want to make things right for your best friend and brother. You are a fixer, my Cat. You want to fix the problems of the world. And now that I am here, I can help you so you won't get your beautiful self hurt."

"You think I'm beautiful?" Marshal asked after a few moments of silence where he absorbed the truthfulness of his mate's words.

"You are the most beautiful thing I have ever set my eyes on and I have observed and experienced the seven wonders of the old world. You, my Cat, are more beautiful than the hanging gardens of Babylon. More beautiful than the stars that twinkle in the night sky. Now that I have you, I don't know how my soul survived without you."

And Marshal didn't have words for that, but he had actions. He reared up and pulled Arcas down into a torrid kiss that had them both moaning and rubbing up against each other.

But that was as far as it went. Marshal was spent and they both needed to rest before the next phase in their plans.

Marshal closed his eyes and allowed himself to be enveloped in his lover's arms. Bear hugs were the best. He was blessed and knew it. Finally, he'd found one that made him feel special and his soul sing. His lover thought he was beautiful. How novel, the plain old cat beautiful.

He fell asleep with a bemused smile on his face covered by over two hundred pounds of happy, snoring, comfy bear.

* * *

"So... what do we do now?" Marshal was feeling on edge, nervous energy shooting through his body. Their interview with The Master had passed, giving him new insight on how a single being could be so powerful.

When Manx of no real gender got angry, the creature got scary. Feeling that power easily reach into his mind and jerk on the reins that held him in his thrall was scary as fuck. Marshal could see and feel how easily Manx could turn them into mindless zombies but the vow they willingly took with him, that oath they willingly created with The Master, largely went unused.

"We wait." Arcas placed a hand on the smaller male's back and guided him toward his floor. "Caille and Bran will handle communications. That falls clearly in her wheelhouse, and when she desires our attention she will let us know."

"Cell phone?" Marshal asked, curious as a cat as they exited the stairs they had taken in lieu of the elevator and entered Arcas' floor. They passed the large, sunken living room, with its central fireplace and round couches positively draped in furs of many different animals. Marshal was sure some of those breeds didn't exist any longer.

"She'll tug at the bond," he was informed as they entered a round room. At the edge of the stairs that contained four marble steps, he kicked off his shoes before he stepped down into some of the softest carpet he had ever felt beneath his feet. He looked back at Arcas to see the redhead had done the same, but had also removed his shirt before sinking into one of the couches that ringed the pit that the room was. Not that Marshal was complaining about getting another look at that magnificent body, draped and framed by the furs he knew Arcas had hunted.

"She can use the bond?" he asked as he followed suit and shook off the shirt he had borrowed from his mate -- how he liked the sound of that -- and threw himself down on the couch at his side.

"We all can," Arcas explained. "Let me show you how." He took Marshal in his arms again and The Cat willingly let himself be positioned to The Bear's liking.

Closing his eyes, he could feel the bond that held them to The Master and its golden hue shone brightly in his mind. The bond he held with Arcas was bright red...powerful, like the rays of the sun, and while touching it mentally he felt the strength of their bond as opposed to the overwhelming power of the one held by Manx.

"Really, what is Manx?" Marshal asked in his direct way. "To build bonds like this..."

"No one knows," Arcas admitted, his bright blue eyes looking off into his own thoughts. "Manx just is."

"We all have a beginning and an ending, Arcas.

And from what I can remember about the mythology of Manx, The Manx was a huge black dog that foretold death."

"Manx is whatever Manx wants to be. Manx was before any of us and probably will be around after. That black dog thing? If that's what it took to get a hunt done then Manx would do it."

"So what is Manx?" Marshal asked.

"Manx is a hunter. Manx is war and death incarnate, lover of the goddess The Morrigan, and the only creature not a god that has the power to hold a great multitude of people in thrall or to a bind."

"A demi-god maybe?" Marshal asked.

Arcas arched an eyebrow. "Manx is not a god, my mate, but the living embodiment of war and death. Since humans are almost constantly at war with each other, the power and strength they channel from that still grows. Hell, Marshal, it probably will never stop growing because of the nature of humanity. The power is such that Manx could easily control armies but they refuse to do such a thing. They don't even control us, though it is in their wheelhouse, so to speak."

"They don't, and I am so grateful they won't," Marshal admitted. "But why? Why all of this? Why is Manx so needed? Who is Them? I have a right to know since we are going to be together with Them for a really long time. Because Manx doesn't need to fight to channel the kind of power needed to unseat an imposter god who has the energy of thousands of souls sacrificed in his name."

Arcas took both of Marshal's hands as he began to explain. "Manx set up *The Wild Hunt* in direct opposition to Dagna and his ilk, but uses the club as a beacon to those in the magical community to seek asylum and protection. What goes on behind these walls and under this roof gives them a constant buzz of ready magic they can use without even tapping into their core. The controlled violence of sex, of dancing, of the acts that take place in the dungeons I know you have participated in a few times, all bolsters and enhances their power."

"You noticed me?" Marshal felt a little shyness coming on but decided to flirt with his lover instead. Anything to take Marshal's attention away from his blush. That was embarrassing after all he had done in his own sexual life...

"Sometimes." Arcas leered at him. "But you were always with someone else so I tried not to think about you. The night you came in with Thomas was the first time I saw you when you were not actively engaged with someone."

"I came on their passes," Marshal admitted with a laugh. "I couldn't afford a membership to this place, not on a college professor's salary. So... not upset I was getting laid so often with some very interesting characters?"

"Hmm, more upset I wasn't a part of it." Arcas licked his lips as he examined Marshal from head to toe. "I like to watch. It's in my nature after spending several hundred years in the stars."

That sobered Marshal real quick. Really, what did he know about his mate except he was pretty enough to walk a runway, when it came to his red hair the carpet matched the drapes, and he could turn into a great red bear--the kind he only saw in fiction and in anthropomorphic fantasy porn. He was also a soft-hearted man, still wracked with guilt over attacking him and Caille after drugs had been pumped into him. That was a lot but still it wasn't enough. He had to get to know his mate, as they would be together until the stars fell from the sky, so why not start now?

"So, you really are that Arcas? The one from the Greek myth?"

"I am."

"You are the son of a god."

"I am."

"And yet you are not as powerful at Manx?" That just didn't sound right. His mate was a real live demigod. And Thomas was going to have all kinds of kittens when he discovered who Arcas truly was.

"Who worships the stars?" His Bear's words pulled him out of his imaginings. "They are all myths and legends children learn in school. Astronomers do the most star gazing today, and even that is not a form of worship. That is a quest for knowledge that does nothing to lend me the power of a god."

"But you got out of the stars... you managed to escape alone, right?"

"I fell to earth, actually." Marshal chuckled. "Zeus started losing his power and control over the sky as worship of him began to fall out of favor. When cracks in the magic wards that held us began to form, at my mother's urging, I decided to fall to earth as to not be stuck in the heavens."

"As stars?"

"No, My Cat. The stars were a prison where I could look down on the land I once ruled. I watched as it fell apart, as my people died and slowly began to forget about me. I watched civilizations rise and fall, and the truth of me and my mother's captivity was forgotten."

"Your mother?"

"Tricked by Zeus and nearly killed by his sadistic asshole children."

"She could escape too?"

Arcas nodded.

"And she chose not to?"

"She was a simple woman and was still being visited by Zeus from time to time. Her conjugal visits if you will. I had no reason to like my father, let alone have any contact with him. I had a family of my own, a life of my own, and his actions stole them from me. It was a lonely existence and one that was slowly driving me mad, my mate. I didn't know how much more I could take when the cracks began to appear. When I escaped I dropped to the earth and hid near the ruins of the city that used to once be under my domain. Kern found me after some time and invited me to meet Manx. After several years struggling to understand humanity and their culture, I called upon Kern and curiosity drove me to accept his invitation to meet Manx."

"It seems Kern did that a lot, saving people and bringing them to Manx."

"He is The Traveler, amongst other things, and he really does care about those he brings to meet Manx. Out of all the time I've known our master, he's only ever had us three as Huntsmen, and that would be thousands of years, Marshal. Kern only selects people who he deems worthy to be part of his family to bring to Manx."

"So in his eyes, you are all special."

"He does seem to have a way to peer into your eyes and read the souls of people. Did you not feel that when you first met?"

"I thought he was hot and he was perfect for Thomas. That's what I limited myself to thinking about the man when I knew Thomas was getting serious about him."

"Very wise… and boring." Arcas laughed. "He

would not have minded if you wanted to share."

"Not when he's on a mating hunt... which I know nothing about because it seems I hunted you down instead."

"You slammed your arm into my mouth so I wouldn't harm Caille... You knew I couldn't really hurt her?"

"No," Marshal denied. "But if I knew that's what it took I may have tried to shove my hand in your mouth the first time I saw you."

"You say the sweetest things." Arcas threw back his head and laughed, and Marshal found himself charmed all over again.

"So how about you?" His Bear asked after his laugher had died down.

Me?"

"You are my mate too and as you say, I'm going to be spending a lot of time with you."

"First thing off the bat you should know I can't shapeshift into a cat."

Arcas nodded as if taking mental notes and Marshal began to break down the essential him. "I was granted my gifts from Mother Bastet. You know her?"

"Egyptian goddess of pregnancy, childbirth, and thieves?"

"Warrior goddess as well." Marshal smiled. "And as a direct descendent of hers I have inherited a few of her aspects."

"Like the ability to jump into a pit filled with wild animals and shove your arm in a roaring bearshifter's mouth?"

"I had to protect Caille," Marshal whined. "Besides, it was instinct. And I did think it was a stupid idea at the time but I felt like I was compelled by my nature to act so."

"You do know Caille could easily handle her own safety, that she was first a goddess in her own right?"

"Yes, but my instincts are powerful and not to be ignored. Like the instinct to create a bond with you."

As Arcas spoke, Marshal leaned in close, close enough to smell the soap he had showered with after their first round of very energetic sex.

"Weren't you afraid?"

"No," The Cat breathed. "I knew you wouldn't harm me. I didn't know about the mate bond forming because of the bite until I could feel your distress. Something inside me knew I had to go to you. The forming of the bond, a serious bond with you, was a shock but nothing I couldn't handle. Besides, I have seen what happens when you deny a bond. Look at Thomas and Kern. I didn't want either of us to suffer from what we both needed, our souls becoming complete. So I just went with it."

"Just that easy?" Arcas arched an eyebrow.

"Look at what happens when you don't pay attention and let fear control what you do. You get Kern and Thomas."

"This is more than the slow way Caille and Bran are moving. There is no way I could not take and grab on to what is mine with both hands. What they are doing… it's at odds with my nature."

"It's perfect for them but not for us." Marshal leaned into his mate before he began speaking again. "I know war is coming and I know I don't want to end up like Thomas, an incomplete bond putting me at danger." He reached up and turned his mate's face toward his and offered him his most heartfelt smile. "And I know my own mind, my mate. I wanted what I wanted and what I wanted most was you."

"And you don't care I've been topping subs for years in this place, even after I noticed you?"

"Do you care I've gotten around the magical community in a very intimate way and I wasn't true to my authentic self and ignored the attraction I felt for you from the moment I first laid eyes on you?"

"I felt your particular buzz of energy, my mate, but because you were always otherwise occupied, I never really paid attention. I was too busy facilitating bonds for Manx and fucking whoever I wanted to pay attention to a little tease like you."

"Tease implies I won't put out." Marshal laughed. "And I am really good at putting it in and out. Does that bother you?"

"Bottoming for you?"

"Yeah."

"Bottoming isn't a huge deal for me, Marshal. I used to do top and bottom at orgies held in my court when it came time to worship certain gods. I rarely have had an issue with my sex life, or anyone else's, over preconceived roles and stereotypes you find in the world today. I just do what feels good. This opening myself to my mate thing feels good. And opening my mate for... well, myself..." Arcas let his worlds trail off on a leer. "I can't wait to do it again."

"What now?" Marshal felt a sudden flash of desire and a tightening of his pants. Damn, his mate was sexy. "Now?"

"Why not? Got something better to do?"

They had the bones of a plan but Marshal knew trying to craft any plan too tightly tended to cause them to fall apart. Plans needed to be fluid to succeed. They could stay here and get to know one another better, to strengthen the bond through sex and conversation and... Damn it, he really wanted to fuck his mate again.

"Let's do this."

* * *

"There is lube in your couch cushions. How cliché can you get?" Marshal teased as he sank two fingers deep inside his lover. He was going to offer up his ass again. Let's face it, the sex has been transcendental, but he was still kind of sore. And by kind of he meant very. He did heal faster than the normal human being but still not as fast as the crew he was now attached to.

"You like it." Arcas, who was flat on his back in the soft furs, his feet flat on the couch, his knees spread wide so he could see Marshal open him up. "I can tell, I can feel it through the bond."

"Cheat," Marshal huffed. "It's going to be extra hard to tease you."

"You'll manage, I'm sure." Arcas arched his back and shuddered when Marshal's finger grazed his prostate. "Yes, keep doing that."

"I didn't know you were such a bottom."

"I am a dedicated switch who doesn't like labels," his mate corrected him.

"And that means?" Marshal asked, feeling the affection and something more budding in their bond.

"That means I expect equal dick time." He threw his head back in the furs as Marshal purposefully pressed his prostate hard. Arcas' arms went over his head and the beautiful muscles of his biceps popped as he strained. His bright red hair against a sea of white fur, his lips red from where he was biting at them as the pleasure grew... that was the most perfect thing ever. He could take photos and make a killing off selling this image but he would never do that. This perfect vision was his and his alone... and well, maybe he might let one of the Hunt watch, because he suspected they had all been lovers at one point and he was kind enough to shove their faces into what they couldn't experience again.

"You feel smug." Arcas opened his eyes to peer down at him as he hissed when a flash of lust ran through the bond.

"You have no idea what you look like, how beautiful you are. I could print a thousand pictures, photograph you a million times, and it won't do justice to the sight I have been blessed with today."

The blush that heated Arcas' face almost matched the deep red of his hair. Score one point for the cheesy shit that rolled out of his mouth whenever he had this beautiful vulnerable man just where he wanted him. God, he was feeling more than like for his mate and he couldn't hide that because of the bond.

But Arcas got his revenge. He sent a powerful wave of hunger through the bond and tightened the muscles of his ass at the same time. "I'm ready, my Cat," he purred. "Take me now."

Who would resist that? Marshal certainly couldn't, he thought, as he slid his fingers out of his ass and crawled up his lover's body, allowing his cock to drag along his soft hair covered stomach.

"Tease," Arcas swore and Marshal had to agree with him.

"That implies I won't put out," Marshal corrected, leaning down to take his mate's mouth in a slick, wet, biting kiss. Arcas' hand came up to tangle in his hair. Instead of pulling, he gently caressed, combing his fingers through his loose curls.

"I know you will, baby," Aracs answered honestly. "You love to see me happy."

"That, I do," Marshal agreed quietly. And to

prove it, he repositioned himself and pressed the hard head of his ringed cock to his lover's rim. "I always will give you want you need."

He slowly slid himself home, watching as his lover's eyes closed in the ecstasy of being taken. Marshal knew the delicious burn of it, craved it, but for now, it was all for his Bear.

"We'll look after each other," Arcas hissed, his whole body shuddering as Marshal bottomed out and held that position.

With tender hands, Marshal caressed his lover's face, his aquiline nose, his broad forehead, and high cheekbones. He looked into eyes that sparked like diamonds and glittered like stars, at the blood-red hair that framed that perfect face, the red, moist lips that begged for another kiss. He knew he was in trouble. He was falling in love with his mate. That niggling feeling budding in their bond, it had to be love. It was a warm, joyous expression of emotion he had never felt before. He was falling in love and he wasn't scared. In fact, he wanted to cultivate that emotion.

"I would do anything for you," Marshal promised. "If only to see and feel you happy."

"Then fuck me." Arcas closed his eyes and shuddered. "I am so full of you, my Cat. I can feel you in my soul, in my body..." He trailed off with a gasp as Marshal shifted his hips. "Make love to me and let my soul take flight."

That was so sappy, so romance novel, so... irresistible. Marshal pulled back until only the head of his cock rested within his lover and then he slid home hard.

Yes, home. Home was with this man. Home was within this man. Home was his mate in all ways.

"Yes." His breath was ragged as he pulled out

and thrust again. "Yes. Making love to you, my mate."

And he did. He bent low so his skin was abraded by his Bear's soft chest hair and then he began to work his hips, grinding him when he was deep inside and angling to hit Arcas' prostate with every thrust. He moved to the music singing in his soul, awash on the feeling of awe and love -- damn it, it was love that his mate was sending him and he absorbed it like the desert taking in the rains.

They moved together, Arcas' red hair wild on the furs, Marshal grabbing his cock and pumping it in time with the movements of his hips... everything was soft and perfect. He didn't want it to end but as he angled to slam into Arcas' prostate once more, his lover called out his name as his ass tightened around his cock and he began to tremble. One more thrust of his hips and pull of his hand sent his lover's seed spraying, turning into little pearls in his chest hair as he shuddered in orgasm.

The sight was enough to send Marshal over, his blunt spike nailing his lover's prostate as he flooded him with his seed.

"Oh goddess, baby," Marshal panted as his balls emptied themselves inside of his lover. "You are so perfect."

"Because of you," Arcas panted. "I feel you... your emotions, my Cat. I feel you. I know you. You belong to me."

"And you belong to me." Marshal smiled in agreement as he lowered himself onto his lover's body, feeling those hairy forearms lovingly encircle him.

Safe. For now they were safe and they were awash in each other's glowing love.

At this point, life was perfect. The furs were soft and warm, his lover was perfect and hot... so hot.

Marshal had never felt better in his life.

They slowly drifted off to sleep in each other's arms, until a few hours Caille popped into their little bubble of joy and brought reality with one sentence.

"It is time."

* * *

The drive to Ellicott City was mainly silent with Bran in the driver's seat and Caille in her blonde wolf form riding shotgun. In the back, Arcas sat with his Cat in his lap feeling the bond between them pulse with worry and fear.

"We will retrieve him," Arcas promised, tugging his lover over to him, pressing kisses to his face. "When the Huntsmen act as one, there is nothing that can keep us from our prey."

"Well I'm new to the whole Huntsman thing." Marshal turned his face up to receive more kisses from his larger lover. "Excuse me if I don't have the same faith as you do."

"It will come in time."

"And time is something we don't have." Marshal pulled back to examine his lover. Arcas was wearing all black, which made his pale skin all but glow and turned his hair into cascading rubies. He did good when picking this man and he was proud to know he would be forever his.

He looked down at his own gear, black and tactical, as Caille had pointed out before she all but threw the clothing at him. The weight of it all surprised him but then he realized it was all enforced with Kevlar and other things that would stop bullets from piercing his all too vulnerable body. "You do love me," he teased at the time and she snorted, before more carefully handing him the wireless earbud that connected him to the others.

"Only because Kern's mate considered you a brother."

"I took the oath," he pointed out. "I am legit as they come."

"A cat," Caille chided, but there was amusement breaking through the worry in her eyes. "Where are we going to put you on the high stage?"

"Worried I may take your place on the lounger with Manx?" He batted his eyelashes at her. "Most people don't allow dogs on the furniture --" Then he had to dodge as she came after him, leaping with canine grace that nearly countered his feline reactions. But those reflexes gifted to him through his direct connection with the goddess Bastet served him well. He was nimbly able to evade her charge, laughing all the while.

That had brought out the laughter in all of them and for a moment Marshal understood what it really meant to be a Huntsman. It was family, something sorely lacking in his and Thomas' life.

And now as he rode in the back of the huge black SUV to find his wayward brother, the connection was still there.

"We have time enough to share some real truths," Arcas informed him, taking his smaller hand into his larger one.

"Time for more sharing with the class?"

"Time for you to understand I will not allow anything to happen to you. You are the other half of my soul, Marshal. My soul is already dented and patched up, and held together with the bonds I share with my family. I would do anything for them, I would die for them, but for you... If something happened to you, I would live for you, My Cat, in hopes your soul would be reborn and find me once again. Do you understand?"

"Living is hard when everything you love is dead." Marshal nodded. "I understand."

"Then for saving me possible centuries of torment, you must not allow anything to happen to you." Arcas was serious, his blue-eyed gaze boring into his. "You are not built like us. You were not designed to go to war. We are. That is one of the reasons Kern found us and brought us together for Manx. We can heal ourselves preternaturally fast. We can recover from almost anything and it is not unknown for us to even regrow a limb or two. We are creatures made for the battlefield, made to take life with little to no remorse at all. Physically and psychologically we were bred for war. You were not."

"I can do it --"

"And if you were forced to kill someone, even in self-defense or in defense of one of us, it would torment you until you finally passed on to the next world and you know it."

"Arcas --"

"You may try and hide that soft exterior of yours, Marshal Gray, but I can feel the truth of you. I am bound to you in ways no other being can understand unless they are also bonded. I wanted you to stay at the Hunt --"

"That was not happening."

"This, I know." Arcas acknowledged that statement with a small kiss to his forehead that had Marshal melting like a snowball in the sun. What was it about forehead kisses that got to him? "This we all know. To that end, Caille has equipped you with the best body armor we could find. It is inscribed with runes of protection done by her own hand. That is why the blade you carry on your hip is one I have carried since before the Roman conquest of Europe. It is honed to perfection and able to slice the fine hair of your arm in half. The token sewn into your pocket is one given to me by Kern ages ago when he told me my mate would need to be protected to prevent me from running amok if I lost everyone I loved once again."

"And now he is in danger of that very thing." Marshal sighed.

"And if that happens, Manx would put him down."

"He is that powerful?" Marshal thought of the affable Black man who had an easy smile and such a friendly way about him. He thought of the romantic lunch he had packed for Thomas and how he doted on the man hand and foot, allowing him his own way even when The Stag knew what he wanted was dangerous. It was hard to see that man as anything other than a sap in love with his half-bonded mate.

"He is." Arcas nodded. "Only Manx can control him and often in times when he loses his temper, Manx has to struggle to do so."

"So... this is even more serious than we thought."

"And not just because of the revival of Dagna the Fifteenth. If in sacrificing Thomas the cult leader can bring back Dagna, then there will be a war on two fronts. One to stop that man who would be a god and another to kill Kern. There would be no other way to stop him taking his anger out on all of humanity."

"Because humans took his mate."

"And because humans allowed themselves to become what they are."

"And what is that?" Marshal was genuinely curious at this point. "What are humans?"

"Monsters in the skin of men, most of them, the

really powerful ones. And the ones who seek that power will do anything to their fellow man to achieve their goals."

"Not true of all humans," Marshal pointed out. "Some strive to do the correct thing, Arcas."

"And that is true, *agape mou*... my love." Arcas was running his thumb over the knuckles of the hand he still held and Marshal found himself leaning more into his lover. "And not all mosquitoes are ready to bite but if a swarm came at you and you were holding a can of bug spray, I am sure you would not try to single out the ones that would do you no harm."

And Marshal had nothing to say to that.

"So," Marshal changed the subject. "The plan? Let's go over it again."

"Okay. Bran and Caille will go forth with a camera that will send a feed back to us here in the SUV. He will be able to feed us information from his ravens and his observation as he moves. If anyone sees him, they will assume he's talking to his rather large, hairy dog."

The yip Caille sent toward them proved everyone was already listening in on their conversations and really, Marshal didn't care. There should be no secrets amongst family.

"People see what they want to see," Marshal called up to her. "And if they see you, all pretty and blonde and hairy, they are going to think you are a golden retriever mixed with something huge and give you wide berth."

"And while Bran is going walkies with Caille, we will monitor the situation from here. Manx will be on the wire and can feed us instructions as needed if we come across anything magical in nature, and seeing that these are the grounds where they perform sacrifices, I am sure we will run into a magical trap or two."

"Yay for magic." Marshal snorted. "And boo that my genetics prevent me from performing some."

"I don't know." Arcas winked at him. "You do a pretty good disappearing act with my dick so --"

"Really?" Bran sounded intrigued. "You do need to tell us more, my brother. Down his throat or up his ass?"

"Both," Arcas called out as if he were proud. and sharing these details was no big thing... while Marshal blushed. He could actually feel his face heat up with it and silently cursed them all for their oversharing nature.

"Can we watch?" Bran called back, reminding Marshal that voyeurism had been a long time honored tradition in some cultures.

"Really?" Marshal called out, his blush growing deeper. "We are going into a life and death struggle to stop the revival of a man who wants to be a god and you wanna talk about life porn?"

"Life, death, sex, it's all important, Cat," Caille called out, her voice sounding odd coming from a wolf's mouth. "Besides, I am curious to see if you can swallow it all down to the balls. I know how big he is and I am impressed you are walking straight because you don't have our healing factor."

"You talk like you would know..." Marshal eyeballed her and she let out a laugh mixed in with a canine yip.

"I have taken Arcas up the ass and in the va-jay-jay," she said almost proudly, and about as smug as a wolf with an oversized muzzle could look. "And a few times, I took on Kern and Arcas together. I had never felt so stuffed in my life."

"You get the butt plug next time we fuck," Bran snickered. "And later I want you to tell me how that went because I've seen Kern naked and I do hope for your sake he's a grower not a shower."

"It gets bigger," Arcas called up as Marshal's mouth dropped open in shock. "A lot bigger."

"So you've all fucked each other?" Marshal was sure he didn't squeak as he asked that question... and the visual that popped into his head... He quickly adjusted his pants where his burgeoning hard-on was making sitting a little uncomfortable.

"Not me," Bran called out. "I just got here and I really would love to watch you all orgy it up. They did hold orgies in your time, right, Arcas? They were largely ceremonial in my time, for the good of the harvest and the change of seasons..."

That's it. It was really time to change the subject, Marshal thought. "So, they are going walkies and reporting back to us."

"I will direct my ravens to find a power source if I can't find one and disable it myself," Bran spoke back to them. "It's all the better if I can take out their visual communications but best if the ravens can do it and make it look like an accident."

"If they can't, as soon as they discover where Thomas is being held, we will move in as covertly as possible, and we gather to infiltrate their holding pens."

"You think they have Thomas in a pen... like an animal?"

"They think we *are* animals, Marshal." Arcas turned to face his mate once more. "That's why they are so dangerous. You are either like them, made to be ruled, or you are an animal fit only for sacrifice. They have murdered so many..."

"So." Marshal shook his head, not willing to think of his gentle friend trapped in a cage like a wild beast. "Holding pen."

"Or sacrificial area." Arcas gave Marshal's hand a squeeze when his breath hitched on hearing that. "Manx pulled what information he could out of that stalker guy and he knew the cult would move fast now. They are in danger of being stopped and even thought it isn't a full moon, the sacrifice can still be carried out so long as the moon is visible. So they will move as fast as they can, which means tonight."

"If it's not tonight, we can get him out before it comes to that." Marshal didn't know if he was trying to reassure them or himself.

"If it's not the night, it's best we get Thomas back to Kern before he breaks free and kills every human he sees until he gets his mate back. Manx is so tired of all this bullshit they might just let him even if it means more arguing with The Morrigan."

"True words, my brother," Caille called back.

That was too terrifying to contemplate, Marshal thought. He remembered when Manx tugged on their bonds earlier. It was powerful and painful and if Kern was really let go then The Cat couldn't fathom what would happen to humanity.

"So we gather and get my brother."

"Caille can lead us right to him. There are bound to be cultists present and from what we saw at the animal pit, they will be well armed. So we hold nothing back."

"You are going to transform?" Marshal asked, looking excited again. "'Cause you are a huge sexy bear and the sight of you will send them running."

"And what am I?" Caille called back. "I'm scary."

"You are like Lassie. You look like a good ham

bone would distract you. Arcas is a bear… a really huge bear with really huge teeth and really huge claws…"

"And a really huge cock." Caille laughed and Marshal found himself nodding in agreement as he recalled the feel of his mate filling him to bursting.

"Yes, but that's not the point." That blush would never go away. "Visually, Arcas is more impressive than you, Caille, not to say you aren't fierce. But in a contest between the two of you, I think I would run faster if Arcas were after my ass than if you were trying to nip it."

"Transformations assuredly," Bran called out. "Makes me sad I can't transform into a raven myself."

"And peck their eyes out?" Marshal laughed. "Then again, if they saw Alfred Hitchcock's *The Birds*, they may piss their pants a little."

"And you, Cat?" Bran laughed. "What are you planning on doing?"

"Well, since I can't scratch their eyes out, as it were, I'll have to hang back and be safe behind you real preternatural creatures. I have a gun with a lot of clips and I can shoot them as they run past."

"And then we get Kern's mate and go home. It is official. They attacked us first so we are not breaking any rules set by the contract made by The Morrigan," Arcas added.

"And if we find the cult leader?"

"Unless he attacks us first, we can't kill him."

"Fuck," Marshal spat out before leaning back against his mate. "If he crossed the line of fire --"

"Plausible deniability!" Bran called out. "I hear that's a thing now. Say no more."

"Enough said," Marshal agreed, snuggling back into his lover and letting fantasies of bloody death dance through his head.

They were going to get his brother and then they were going to go home. It sounded like the perfect plan.

Chapter Seven

The sun was still relatively high in the sky when they pulled Thomas from his cell and marched him from the basement of an old abandoned building to the decaying remains of an old church. It was all done very covertly, a gun pointed at his head while another was aimed at his heart. They forced him to move under a canopy of heavily leafed trees with a backdrop of old, flooded out rusting cars to hide them all from view.

At first they tried to make him retake his human shape, but no, he wasn't going to do that. He didn't want to and he didn't have to. If they were intent on sacrificing magical creatures then they were going to get the whole magical creature, not just the parts that made them comfortable with their little game of torture and execution. Besides, wearing this form, enhanced by his mate's continued energy that leaked through the partial bond, just felt right. And if he managed to take a bite out of a person if they got too close, all the better. A pregnant person should always have their cravings offered up to them whenever possible.

It was rather too bad with all of his new accoutrements that came with sharing power with The Stag, height wasn't part of the deal. A few more inches would have pushed the horror into terror in the men who were escorting him. Of course, Van Man, as Thomas like to think of him, had not showed his face since he sent him fleeing from the basement with a few amusing words and gestures. His partner in crime was still there, though he looked a little... conflicted would probably be the best way to describe him, as he moved behind the Faunus with an electric cattle prod at his back. Since Thomas had no idea what electricity would do to a growing embryo, he felt it best just to play along… for now.

The golden sun came in splashes through the leaves as they silently moved toward the moss-covered stone ruins of the Saint Stanislaus Kostka Catholic Church. It was a place he had always wanted to come out and photograph because of how beautiful the remaining structures appeared on the few photographs he had seen. There was the usual graffiti and the tokens left behind by urban explorers but for now the place was oddly empty. Even the birds that hung out in the trees were silent observers to the quiet procession as it moved between the rusted out husks of old cars toward the cemetery, where a few headstones remained after the area was flooded out and abandoned.

They moved through the remaining stone arch and to the headstone of one Louise Cecilia, daughter of the Hickys, who only lived three months and sixteen days before she shuffled off this mortal coil. It was some dark irony that made him smile a bit as they pressed a complicated series of buttons on the base to that lone tombstone and then pushed it aside, exposing a set of steep steps.

"You fanatics have been busy," he commented as the psycho in the lead began his descent down the stairs. When no comment was forthcoming and the cattle prod began jamming into his lower spine, he flicked his tail in irritation and began to follow the stairs down. "Be that way," he griped as he was prodded again. "Not like I was expecting scintillating conversation from you cultists anyway."

"We are not a cult," someone, probably the one with the gun pointed at his head commented. "What we are doing isn't crazy."

"Well, let's look at the key points that prove you

are in a cult," Thomas said as he turned his head to the side to get his new horns down the shaft without hitting them. He remembered when he was a kid how he accidentally tore a horn nearly from its mooring on his head... and all the blood and crying that followed. Seeing that his horns were now bigger, the pain would probably be more intense. "Point one, you all oppose critical thinking."

"How so?" the Van Man's partner asked. Thomas couldn't turn around but he recognized his voice.

"Well, when I did put logic to you, you seemed to want to do nothing more than call me a monster, and that is not crafting an argument. That's just elementary name calling. Which brings me to my second point. You isolate your members and probably punish them if they try to leave."

"We are not isolated."

Thomas didn't even bother using his words to answer that one. He just waved a hand up at the woods and the trap door that hid the stairs he was tramping down now, and when silence reigned he knew he had made his point.

"Next, I am going to guess when I get down to the bottom of these stairs you are going to strap me on a table of some kind and extol the virtues of your false god while trying to convince me to willingly play a part in my own murder. Not sure how that works but I bet most of the poor people you had down here before probably agreed to the sacrifice just to get you all to shut up."

"Dagna the Fifteenth is real," one of the other guntoters commented. "And when he is revived we are going to have all the power."

"And why would he share?" Thomas asked as

the light from the sun began to diminish and he knew they were going very deep underground. "I mean, it took him years to convince his toadies to gather it for himself. And you think he's going to share? You are on the bottom of the totem pole so that probably means you are only going to get scraps, if anything at all. And before you try and tell me how important you are, you must know important people don't do menial chores like gathering the sacrifice for torture... or feeding them, or cleaning up the blood, and disposing of the body when they get what they want."

"We just feed them to the animals," the man snorted. "Not much work there, fun to watch, and it keeps the animals hungry for blood."

"If you had them. The head nut case already told me your exotic animal ring got busted so I guess that means you will have to find another means of disposal. And despite the fact we are in a cemetery you can't put any bodies here. From all the graffiti around I think the people who like to photograph this place would notice a fresh grave."

"Well, you look like a goat... we'll feed you to the dogs."

"I am a Faunus, thank you very much. I don't look like a goat. In fact, I probably look like I could steal your woman from you with little effort if she considered you hot... or your boyfriend," he added. "I don't mean to try and stereotype your sexuality."

The other men got a chuckle out of that and the gun man finally shut his trap after muttering, "You won't be so high and mighty after our leader gets done with you."

"Which brings up my next cult point." Thomas laughed. "Inappropriate loyalty to your leader."

"We admire him and his resolve," Van Man's

partner interjected. "He is a great man and we follow him eagerly."

"To the point where you commit cold-blooded murder to make him happy?" Thomas was now fully in the dark and carefully felt out the next step before taking it. He tilted his head as much as he dared and heard the man before him no longer stepping down so the floor must be in the next few steps. He carefully took another one down. "And I don't care how many people agreed to be a sacrificial lamb, I am quite sure that more than a few did it under duress and most probably were humans with a touch of something in their backgrounds. From the way your Grand Pooh-bah looked at me, I am probably one of the most powerful beings to fall into his trap. That means he missed out on the hundreds of those like me in this city and only managed to get a small fry, as it were."

"We do as he bids --" Gun Man began but Thomas cut him off.

"You murder in cold blood. No matter how you look at it, you take lives away and consign souls to some level of hell. And no matter what you tell yourself, the death of those beings is on your hands. That kind of killing stains your soul."

"What would you know of it?"

"I know the seething you are doing now would probably be a response to someone badmouthing your father... so..."

"My father has never done anything so great for me. Fuck him and those who always put me down."

"And that would be the dishonoring your family portion of the cult bullet point boards." Thomas snickered at Gun Man as he grumbled more before Van Man shushed him. "Crossing biblical boundaries and changing behaviors to those usually frowned on by your church are next... like I don't know... murdering people?" His next step put him on solid ground and he peered into the darkness, the shadows solidifying into shapes as he realized there had to be light coming in from somewhere. "The last point is separation from your church of choice... which I assume you've all done if you even were religious in the first place because, you know, worship of the weak weather god you are murdering people for... Oh wait. That would be weather god *adjunct,* because he's so far removed from the real deal I believe the only thing he could summon would be a light drizzle."

"Fuck you!" Gun Man shouted as the one holding the cattle prod gained the bottom floor along with Van Man's partner. "I can't wait to see you bleed --"

"And I rest my case." Thomas snorted, following along after the man who was in the lead. He inhaled deeply and smelled the scent of old blood, fear, and anger so much stronger than it was in the basement of the ruins he had been held in.

"And you are making friends."

Thomas groaned softly to himself. "If it ain't the Grand Pooh-bah. It's not been long enough between visits for me to deal with you again."

A few steps forward and suddenly the room exploded into light.

There were no torches for this modern-day pain dungeon. They had recessed lighting in the ceiling and it highlighted a wood table in the center of the room. Thomas felt a flash of fear run through his body and fought to hold it in check. This chamber... it smelled of death.

"We have time to work on that resolve," the leader of this cult stated, his eyes on the far wall where an unlit brazier stood. It was roughly the size of a coffee table and was surrounded by rust colored runes Thomas swore were written in blood. Still, what was worse was the smells... blood, bile, piss, shit, death... The longer he stood there the more distinct the smells were becoming. If he had to put a name to the pong permeated the room, he would have to call it evil.

A shove to the back by the man with the cattle prod had him stumbling toward the table where straps and buckles awaited him.

"Not so verbose now, are we?" the leader cackled -- from a safe distance, Thomas noted. "You are probably feeling the strength go to Lord Dagna --"

"Actually, I'm doing my best not to throw up." Thomas refused to show these brainwashed idiots a moment of fear from him. "If you come closer, I might even be compelled to vomit in your face. It's not like I even had a good last meal... fast food from a paper bag... Class. It's almost like something happened to freeze your assets. Plus, it's so empty in here I'd guess something happened to most of your minions. It's like they were arrested or something --"

"Silence!" the leader roared, his eyes narrowing and sparking green for a moment. "You speak of things you do not understand."

"Says the Grand Pooh-bah from across the room," Thomas hissed, feeling anger through the partial bond. He wasn't sure at first but now he understood. Because of its incomplete status, he could not send thoughts nor could Kern divine his location, but he could send and receive emotions. His lover had picked up on his fear and in return he was feeling furious rage he could not be there, he could not protect what was his. He understood now the fight Kern had with himself as he allowed Thomas to make his own decisions about the bond when everything in The Stag desired just to take him and give him the bite. His lover had gone against everything in his nature to give him a choice. If that wasn't love then it was damn close to it.

"I don't need to get any closer, monster," the leader said as Thomas was prodded onto the table.

Thomas allowed this because he was still fearful of something happening to his child, so he was laid flat and strapped down, hands above his head, hooves and thighs straight down, presumable so he couldn't kick. The spread open position was a bit worrisome but his thick fur had grown to cover his groin. It was a bit uncomfortable with his tail positioned beneath his butt, but at least it was safe from a quick snip because from the expression in Gun Man's face, he would start with everything that wasn't human when the real torture began... including his horns.

He hoped they didn't go for the horns first.

"Yes, great cult leader." Thomas snorted as his twisted his wrists to grab the nylon straps that held his wrists. Whatever his followers were, they were very proficient in strapping people down. They must have had a lot of practice -- and that thought didn't ease his worries any. "From across the room you are big and bad and bold but when faced with me and my true nature, you pissed your pants and ran away. Is this your first time beholding true power? Poor sod," Thomas taunted. "That must mean your god ain't shit."

He knew he was channeling Kern at the moment, feeding on his anger, but it was better he leaned into that emotion than burst out in tears. He wanted his mate. He wanted his safe apartment. He wanted to go home and pretend this had never happened. Most importantly, he wanted to find his Stag and let him complete the bond. He was a fool to run from his destiny, his fate. And look at him now... strapped down and trying his best not to show his fear. These assholes would feed on it and then they would feel safe enough to do all manner of vile things he saw swimming in their dead-looking eyes.

The cult leader snarled, stepping forward, brandishing his words like they were a holy weapon intent on stabbing Thomas in the brain and forcing him to his will.

"You will agree," he crooned, moving close enough to touch... almost but not quite close enough. "They all agree." He ran a shaking hand inches away from touching him, over his body, hovering as if he could feel the energy wafting off of Thomas.

Thomas closed his eyes, not wanting to see this mad creature violate him by placing his disgusting touch upon his skin when he felt another flash of anger -- but this wasn't from the bond.

Thomas' eyes popped open just as the leader's hand hovered over his heart. The rush of anger of protectiveness flowed up from his stomach right up to his mind and suddenly he knew where his streak of protectiveness was coming from. Kern was sending him his fierce anger through the bond but this protectiveness was coming from another source. His child was aware enough to know its mother, its vessel, was in danger, and it was unhappy.

Thomas lay back on the table and he began to laugh. He laughed so hard tears formed and fell from his eyes. This laughter was cold and cruel, not a hint of amusement to be found yet it was the laughter of the undefeated. It was the laughter born of frustration, of withheld need and desires. His baby wanted its bearer safe and it wanted to take a hefty bite out of the creature that snatched his hand back and now stood looking at Thomas as if *he* were the sick-o strapping people down and torturing them until they agreed to whatever he wanted just to face death and escape the pain.

"What is wrong with you?" he asked, stepping back, an unreadable look crossing his face. "What -- I have never --"

"Every creature has a choice, I believe, according to the pact your original leader made with the goddess The Morrigan."

"Any creature unaware or willing --"

"Which means they have a choice. The moment you bring them in here they are aware, are they not? They are aware and they have the right to choose. I bet you didn't tell them that, did you?"

"They agreed --"

"After you tortured them into it." Thomas snorted from where he lay on the table, his own eyes on the leader, daring him to say otherwise.

"They still said yes."

"And if you think I'm going to agree, no matter what you do to me, you have another think coming."

"They all agree... after suffering in my tender mercies."

"But you see, that's where you are wrong. You will not torture an agreement out of me and even if you did, you can't use me."

"And why is that, little Faunus? I have you strapped down on my table. My people are willing to do anything to serve my will including cutting the cute little horns from your head. I don't take trophies but I could easily start with you --"

"Because there is another person within me who

is very much aware by nature of his parenthood," Thomas crowed. "I am pregnant with the child of The Stag." His voice dropped into that deep growl once more as he spoke. "You have kidnapped and are about to torture the mate of the being known as Kern of *The Wild Hunt*... otherwise known as the god of travel and the keeper to the gates of hell. That's right. My mate is Cernunnos...the Celtic Devil... and his child thirsts for your blood."

Miles away in the sanctified bunker known as *The Wild Hunt*, Kern roared his anger and the wards on his room broke.

Transformed, the god went in search of his master. He would free him to find his mate or everyone in this world would perish in fire, screaming for mercy that would not be found. His mate needed him and nothing would stand between him and all he desired.

* * *

Bran noted a few other urban explorers vacationing nearby and gave them a nod. They moved in further and the trail got denser. Soon it felt like they were the only people left on earth. The sun was starting to go down, the heat of the summer day dissipating a bit as they moved. Then there was only space for them to move single file and they sped up a bit. It was still a ways off until moonrise but the sooner they could get to Thomas and get out, the better it would be for everyone.

The constant stream of information from his ravens assured him the site they needed was clear and that they had indeed moved Thomas earlier. They weren't sure how long had passed between then and now -- the ravens had a more abstract measurement of time, but the sun was past its zenith when they moved him, so sometime after noon.

"No one around, just us, girl," he called out to Caille, who streaked ahead a little further. He paused for a moment, leaning up against a tree where the ravens indicated there was a security camera and took a quick look around. There were the skeletons of old stone buildings and a few paths made by human feet, but nothing that would draw the attention.

Caille barked a bit, drawing his attention, and he moved on, noting several trees where his ravens had parked themselves, indicating where the cameras were hidden. "Looking for a power source now," he commented as he chased after Caille, who was sniffing around in a very canine way.

In the van Marshal was watching the feed from the camera that hung around Bran's neck, intent on the screen. Arcas was at his side, pointing out things he could see Bran might have missed.

"That huge tombstone to your left," The Bear muttered. "It looks newer than the others."

"Taking a break, Caille," Bran called out and a passing hiker paused, staring at the huge dog that bounded toward him.

"Beautiful animal," he called out as Caille began to sniff and scratch around the tombstone. "And so well trained."

"Thank you," Bran called back as the man moved closer.

"He could be in on it," Marshal spoke softly, knowing the mic he wore would pick up his words. "Be careful."

"You've been here before?" the man asked and Bran shook his head.

"Nope. First time. I'm here so late because I got a little lost."

"The trails can be treacherous if you don't know where you're going," the hiker cautioned. "If it's your first time, it's best you leave before it gets dark. That's what I'm going to do."

"Just here to take a few photos of the church." Bran indicated his camera on his chest. "Then I'll have something to blog about."

"You new to the area?"

"Nah." Bran shook his head, reaching into his pocket just to watch the man stiffen before he realized Bran was pulling out a pack of gum. "Just never made it out this far." He offered the gum to the man who took a piece, a smile on his face.

"Definitely in on it," Marshal said, and Bran nodded in agreement. "Be careful. He stiffened up when you went for the gum."

"So, which church?" the man asked, unwrapping the stick of gum and popping it into his mouth. Bran did the same with his.

"There are three, right?"

"Two." The man leaned on the tombstone and Caille left off sniffing to take a quick whiff of the man before Bran pulled her back. "Saint Stanislaus Kostka Catholic and Pentecostal Holiness. The best ruins are the Pentecostal one." The man grinned. "It has the most interesting graffiti."

"So, the Polish church?" Marshal laughed and Arcas agreed.

"He's trying too hard to get rid of you or re-direct you."

"I hope that gum is poisoned," Marshal added. "Poison won't kill you, right?"

Bran shook his head and spoke to the man. "Really? Then that's where me and my gal are headed."

Caille, who has resumed scratching around the tombstone, snapped at something before bounding off and making Bran hop to his feet. "Well, I gotta go get my dog." He laughed. "She's probably on the trail of a groundhog. Which way is the good church ruins?"

The man pointed and Bran nodded his thanks before chasing after Caille.

"So, not the power source but I have a feeling I know where it is. And Caille looks like she picked up the scent. Off we go."

"I didn't see anything," Marshal said and Arcas explained.

"See where the man was coming from?"

"Not really…"

"Then that is your first clue. People just don't appear out of thin air. So that is the direction we need to watch."

"Caille ran in that direction."

"So… is the gum poisoned?"

"More like drugged." Arcas laughed. "He'll be tripping balls in a few moments and we won't have to worry about him."

"So no on the power source?"

"Nope, but from the way Caille reacted, he had Thomas' scent on him."

"So ours would be in the direction the man came from."

"Logically." Arcas hugged Marshal and he found himself relaxing a little.

"And if it was blood, I think Caille would have gone after him, no matter what the plan."

"I knew I liked that woman." Marshal chuckled before returning his attention to the screen.

The man was gone, a raven taking off after him, and Bran had his camera out, snapping photos of the church the man had indicated.

"Going to look for the other church, baby," Bran called to Caille, who was sniffing around, and the two of them circled back to where the man had appeared.

It was there, near a tree that Caille started digging, and in a few seconds there was a *pop* and Caille sat back, looking as pleased as she could with a canine face.

Then the two of them were moving, Caille's nose to the ground as Bran followed, speaking softly.

"Ravens report the lights are out. Expect company."

As he spoke three men arrived in the area looking around, with suspicious bulges under their shirts.

"Got three on your six," Arcas called out as he made a move toward the door, Marshal on his heels.

"See them." Bran continued to communicate as Arcas and Marshal began to run down the path they took. "Playing stupid," he informed them as he took photos, talking to his dog.

"Excuse me. "A voice other than Bran's came through on his earbud and Marshal consciously picked up speed.

"Yes?" they heard Bran answer as they raced toward them, ignoring the branches slapping at their faces and arms.

"Have you seen a guy about my height wearing a black jacket come through here?" the voice asked and Bran sounded chipper as he spoke.

"Friends of his? Well, he gave me some sound advice about where to get some amazing shots."

"Did you see which way he went?"

"Sorry, no. Had to catch my dog."

By this time Arcas and Marshal were running

around the large tombstone, ignoring the body of the first cultist passed out along the trail, and moving rapidly toward Bran and Caille.

"Too bad," the man growled just was they both raced toward the church and had their fellow Huntsman in sight.

The ravens squawked and dived at the men just as Arcas roared and leaped toward them. The men were removing weapons from waist holsters when Arcas hit the men head on.

They went flying like bowling pins as Caille leapt for the throat of the man who was pointing his weapon at Bran. He screamed and threw his arms in front of his face as if to protect his throat. But he was guarding the wrong place. Caille pulled her jump short to land in front of the man and instead snapped her teeth around his balls.

The man, understandably, screamed as he fell back and into the man Arcas was mowing down. The redhead knocked all three men over as they swatted at the air and the ravens were dive bombing them.

Before Marshal's disbelieving eyes, Arcas lifted one man dead in the air -- his mate fucking bench pressed a cultist -- then broke his back over his knee before he cast him aside.

Well, Marshal thought. *At least he didn't tear him in half. Still sexy.*

At this point the third man, realizing he was in it deep after looking at one of his fellow cultists rolling in the dirt and clutching his nuts... and the second man who was looking like he was going to have to be catheterized for the rest of his life... turned tail and ran.

"So," Marshal hazarded a guess out loud, "More goons soon?"

"More goons soon," Arcas praised his mate's insight with a kiss.

"The entrance?"

"Behind us." Caille was gagging a bit, as if trying to clear a bad taste from her mouth -- Marshal was going to leave that one alone too... "I caught where the scent disappeared before they moved in behind us."

So all three of the men followed Caille, running to keep up until she stopped at a tombstone.

"Down there?"

"Yes." Caille moaned a little. "But I don't know how --"

"Keypad." Marshal snapped his finger. "Everyone, look for a keypad."

It took a few seconds before they finally found it, but it was a letdown for them.

"No electricity, no keypad," Arcas muttered.

"There has to be redundancies," Bran reminded them. "No one would build a system that would trap them in the event the power goes out.

They started searching the tombstone for a few moments before Arcas lost patience and began to shove it. It shifted.

"That's a whole lot of power in one body. He doesn't look big enough to do that," Bran noted as Arcas grunted and strained, pushing harder as his face turned red with his exertions.

"Wall sex." Marshal sighed and the others just stared. "What? I'm allowed. I mated him."

Nodding at his point, they watched as with a final grunt, Arcas succeeded in breaking the latch and snapping the hinges of the heavy stone that hid one very deep staircase.

"Not like this," Caille muttered before, with a twist and pull of the very air in front of them, she took her human guise, her shining blonde hair barely covering her bare breasts as she spun around to face them. "Did someone bring spare clothing?"

All the men were staring... and drooling a bit at her beauty.

"I sleep with that every night and I still can't believe how fortunate I am." Bran spoke to the two of them and Marshal had to resist the urge to pat him on his back. He was in a committed relationship with his Bear but that didn't mean he couldn't look. Besides, if that orgy thing paid off --

But his thoughts snapped back to the matter at hand as Bran tugged off the long tunic he wore and handed it to his woman. She slid it on without comment and then moved toward the stairs.

"I should go first," Arcas protested. Marshal had a feeling if Bran had voiced any objection, she probably would have bit his nuts too. "In my human guise I am more bulletproof than all of you right now."

"But a naked lady running toward them might distract them more." Then without a word she was gone, moving down the stairs.

"After me," Bran called as he swiftly moved down the stairs, two of his ravens sailing in and down as he disappeared from view.

"And you after me." Arcas stared at Marshal until he nodded. He really was more of a hindrance to them at this point with his mostly human body and he knew it. He checked to make sure his gun was properly set in its holster before he followed his mate.

It was dark and growing darker, and Marshal was pleased to use the one feature his ancestry gifted to him -- almost impeccable night vision. They moved swiftly down the stairs until a wail of pain drifted to their ears. Stealth and care for their personal bodies was forgotten and all four Huntsmen sped their way down the stairs. They followed the echo from the scream until they tumbled into a wide, circular room lit by several candles... and in the center on a table was strapped Thomas and the man who was murmuring softly, almost lovingly in his ear, standing up from pounding a nail through his wrist.

Chapter Eight

"What the fuck?"

Before he could even really think about what he was doing, Marshal was on the move, plans be damned. He had to get to his best friend and he had to get to him now.

Shoving the others out of the way, nimble as a cat, he raced forward, dodging the few people who were in his way, hissing and leaping, lashing out at anyone who tried to stop him.

His grace of movement was very poetic, and held the others in a trance for a moment. But when the first gun came out they were on the move. Bran ripped the softly glowing runes from his neck and cracked them like a whip, neatly severing the hand from the man who thought to draw on them while The Cat was making a direct line of chaos toward the man with the hammer.

His ravens were cawing, adding their raw voices to the havoc they were spreading, gouging eyes and even shitting in the enemies' faces. Their feathers flew as they tore at their victims, driven by their master's anger.

With a roar, the world twisted and bent around Arcas, who exploded into a mountain of red fur and anger. He was swatting at anything that came close to his mate, severing limbs and leaving small explosions of blood as he moved.

Caille shifted herself and was attacking the remaining men, creating more chaos and doing her best to try and keep her mate safe. She ran up the back of one man bent over screaming and holding onto the stump of where his arm used to be before it met the severe effect of Bran's whip. She used his back as a launch pad and went straight to the man who was holding the hammer as well.

In the screaming, fighting, bleeding mayhem that surrounded them, Marshal only had eyes for his friend and the one who did him harm.

They would pay. They would all pay.

Executing a neat flip over a fallen cultist, Marshal dove for his friend, who was whimpering on the table, his eyes glowing wildly in swirls of red and amber, his horns suddenly of an unusual size... and slammed into a barrier that damn near knocked him out.

"You can't get in," a man screamed, a man dressed in black robes who had both hands raised, staring at a huge brazier directly across from Thomas. "And every death just gives my lord more power."

This had to be the cult leader, he thought while trying to shake off the effects of the blow to the head he'd all but delivered to himself. He nearly missed the man diving for him and flinched back when he saw him, a knife in his hands and death in his eyes.

The timely swipe of a huge red paw saved his bacon as his mate lashed out and sent the man's head flying. Then, of course, he finally started paying attention to what was going on around him.

Pandemonium was a good way to describe what was happening in the large underground chamber. At one time, it had probably been a vault to protect whatever golden goodies the church had to display, but now it was a round chamber that housed about twenty people, all fighting for their lives. There was the barrier he was leaning against, the one that prevented him from getting to Thomas behind which a very bad man stood with arms upheld, looking for all the world like he was channeling black lightning from the forms of the dead and dying in the room.

"Fuck," Marshal breathed, taking in his mate standing before him like a furry red battering ram with teeth… massive teeth, and the others in the Hunt slaughtering people like it was going out of style. "I done goofed."

Through his bond he felt aggravation, protectiveness, a budding adoration that was the beginning of love. That was nice, something sweet in the middle of all the carnage. But now was not the time to dwell on that. People were dying, old gods were being revived. This shit had to stop.

"The barrier!" he called out and watched as the cult leader began to look a little frantic when all eyes turned to him and the man locked behind the barrier with Thomas. "I need… it needs…"

Spinning around, Arcas threw his full weight against it and nothing happened. In fact it seemed to use his force against him and threw Arcas back, but that was about it. The stressed look in the crazy man's eyes eased as a smirk spread across his face.

"Fuck," Arcas growled and Marshal found himself shuddering at the deep, dangerous bass tone that rolled from his mate's mouth. "There must be an anchor for this barrier inside with him."

Almost like a golden shadow, Caille slipped up beside them, and in a swirl of magic and air transformed back into her human self. Seeing a naked female did slow the momentum of the fights going on, but most of the fighting cultists were disarmed… literally. It seemed Bran didn't want anyone recovering enough to pick up a weapon so he did the expedient thing by removing most of the cultists' arms and hands. It was a bit gruesome, but what they had done to Thomas was much worse.

His friend, his brother, was staked to the table

like a sacrificial lamb. His new form was imposing and one Marshal had never seen before, but there, in those swirling, pain-filled eyes was his Faunus.

"Thomas," he whimpered, cursing the fact that he didn't have the power to just leap in and fix everything. His nature and his instincts were screaming at him to get in there and heal. He was a fucking helper. He was the man who could come up with solutions to problems when it came to his best friend. He was utterly useless in this bedlam they were trapped in. He wanted to cry.

A wave of heat, of understanding, and compassion suddenly flooded his mind. The anger and frustration eased, and he realized he was pulling some of this from his mate, experiencing his emotions as he observed a fellow magical creature being harmed and once again was powerless to do anything.

"We have to get in there." Caille was staring at Thomas and the smirking cult leader who gave his pet torturer a nod as he placed the hammer on the table and instead picked up a bone saw.

"You will agree," the cult leader growled to Thomas, who has shaking his head in denial. "You will agree for you and that demon seed you are carrying."

The torturer activated the small rotary saw and approached Thomas, gripping one of his horns.

"Fuck, no! No, please!" Thomas was wailing as Marshal felt the warmth of fur surrounding him, offering him some comfort because he couldn't look away. He wanted to, gods above how he wanted to, but to look away would dishonor his brother.

He began pounding on the glass as the blade touched the base of his right horn. Thomas' gze locked onto his. With tears pouring down his face and his whole body trembling, he stared at Marshal, fear in his eyes.

"No," Marshal whimpered, reaching up to run his own shaking hand over his face, when his hand hit the earbud. "The baby --"

He missed the frantic look that passed through the Huntsmen as his words were heard and understood. There was a baby... The Faunus was pregnant with Kern's -- with Cernunnos' child.

The Master of the Hunt... They needed them and they needed them now. "Manx!" he screamed with all his strength, feeling his throat burn as he bellowed for help. "Manx! We need you!"

* * *

An enraged Stag burst into Manx's rooms, nostrils flaring as he scented out his master. He had run all over *The Wild Hunt*, leaving behind broken furniture and scared men as he sought out the one who kept him trapped here. Manx would let him go or he would break his own vow and attack the one who had helped him survive for eons and gave him purpose.

"Manx," he roared, the floors shuddering under the weight of his contained magic with each step. He had dropped all pretense of humanity. His horns were massive twenty-point murder weapons that could slash and maim. His digitigrade legs were rippling with muscle under a thick layer of black fur. His hands were now tipped with long, thick black claws that clacked as he moved. His bare chest was covered in carved runes, announcing to all who could read them... and even to those who could only feel them, that death had arrived.

"Manx!" his dual-toned voice rolled out from his throat as he absently licked at the triple set of fangs that emerged from his upper gums. "I feel his pain. My child -- They will die."

Manx rose to their feet, their solid black eyes staring into Kern's scarlet ones and a smile pulled at their lips, exposing a quintuplet of fangs that would do any horror movie creation proud. Their hair had grown into a wild tangle of grasping tentacles as their body grew in size and weight. Black fur rolled over their skin as their face took on a more canine look. Their ears moved up to the top of their head as their fingers transformed into thick black claws that they retracted and exposed as they moved toward their Stag.

"They will fall at our feet."

A wave of his hand ended the spell that had *The Wild Hunt* on lockdown, and Manx reached out to gently caress Cernunnos' face. "They will die screaming, my Stag, and your child will be safe."

"Child -- He's --"

"I have their location." Manx pressed a gentle kiss to Cernunnos' lips before stepping back. "Feel the bond, Oh Traveler. Take us to them."

There was a flash of heat and light and then the pair just vanished.

* * *

"Thomas..." Marshal was whimpering now as he beat against the glass, watching with the light dying in his eyes as his best friend, his brother screamed as bits of bone and blood splattered the cult leader and his pet torturer.

"No! Never! I do not consent! Not me! Not my child! No!" Thomas wailed and screamed but he never gave him what they most desired. He refused to be a sacrifice.

His eyes locked on to each of the Huntsmen, and he struggled to smile in between screams, almost as if he could feel their helplessness at the situation and forgave them for not saving him.

Marshal felt his own frustration tripled by that of his mate, and the shared bond he held with his bothers. They all were in pain, desperate and tearing their own bodies apart by shoving them at the barrier.

Bran had changed his whip into a broadsword and was digging into the wall at the edge of the barrier, hoping to find a fragile point where he could tear into it.

Marshal's Bear hovered over him defensively even as he banged gigantic paws against the invisible barrier. Caille was muttering spells, trying anything in her wheelhouse to break the incantation that had created the barrier, and was growing angrier, her visage floating between old woman, young girl, and her usual human guise as she screamed at the barrier.

Just as Thomas' horn gave way with a loud *crack* and the torturer lifted it to show the smiling cult leader, there was sonic boom that knocked them all off their feet, and then Kern was there… no, not Kern, Cernunnos.

"You dare!" he bellowed, his voice shaking the rafters as he lowered his head and charged.

There was a static crack and the cult leader, now holding Thomas' horn suddenly didn't look so smug. He looked toward the brazier where the swirls of black energy floated around and above before turning horrified eyes to Cernunnos.

The man with bloody hands and a bone saw in his grasp stumbled back as Cernunnos backed up and charged again, his deadly horns, a larger match to the one he'd sawed off, sparked red and green, making the barrier visible for the first time.

It was almost pretty, Marshal thought. If only it wasn't the thing that was keeping them from saving his friend.

As Cernunnos stepped back for another pass, a large black paw of a hand reached out and gripped his shoulder. Cernunnos stepped back as The Manx took the field.

"Oh shit," Marshal screamed, hope filling him as he took in the shadowy dark figure that pulled Cernunnos back. "The Master is here and you are so fucked."

Chapter Nine

"*No, no, no!*" the cult leader was now screaming as he backed away, stolen horn in hand.

Manx stepped forward. Their visage was monstrous as they glared at the cult leader with dead, flat eyes as they approached and laid hands upon the now visible barrier.

Then they grinned, their mouth transforming into a gaping black maw that shook the leader to his core as all the color fled from his face and he had to stumble to the table that held Thomas to keep himself upright.

"Time to end this…" The voice that emerged from The Manx was unearthly, something few had heard and even fewer had survived. It carried with it the weight of old war and death, of eons and anger and rage. It was the trumpeting sound of monsters at the gates, of hounds baying out at their prey, of the most powerful magical being walking the earth being called to action.

With a wave of a huge, human-like paw, their thick black claws pierced the barrier and, with a swipe, tore it down. Before Marshal could blink, he watched as Cernunnos charged forth, his head lowered, smoke rolling from his nostrils, his bellow of anger now filling the room, a counterpart to the declaration of war issued by The Manx.

A blur of horns and fur swooped toward the man who still held the bone saw. He screamed as he threw it at the charging Celtic devil and screamed impossibly louder as there was a crunching sound, a thick, wet, tearing *pop*, and the man was hefted several feet into the air by the angered god. His screams became wails of agony, an accompaniment to the screams of denial by the cult leader as Cernunnos shook his massive head, sending blood and internal parts of the man's body flying around the room. The charnel smell of blood and death filled the room as the man struggled vainly against the horns that were shredding him with every move of Cernunnos' head.

Marshal himself blanched as Manx threw back their head and laughed, the tendrils of smoky energy that surrounded the brazier flowing instead to his hands as he tilted his massive head, hair reaching out and touching the remains of the barrier before they were snatched up and absorbed into his form.

The dying wails of the man impaled on Cernunnos' horns were now filling the air as Marshal saw his chance and darted toward Thomas just as the cult leader reversed the horn and slammed it down toward the Faunus' exposed belly.

Protect the child. That instinct, something passed down to him from his ancestor the goddess Bastet, went into overdrive as he bodily threw himself on top of Thomas.

"No!" he heard his mate wail and had enough consciousness to send a feeling of regret and apology to his mate before the sharp edge of the severed horn pierced his body.

Marshal groaned once as pain exploded in his mind and body, as he felt the sharp crack of his spine reaching, of his ribs cracking as the sharp tip of the horn slid deep. But it stopped inside of his body, sparing the life of his brother... and his unborn child.

Marshal lifted his head enough to meet Thomas' horrified eyes before he lost the strength to hold his head up. It dropped to the table with a groan as the cult leader began to chant.

* * *

"*No! Fuck no!*" Arcas shrieked as he raced forward, shedding his bear form as he moved so it was a huge naked redhead who reached his mate's side, his eyes flooding with tears, and he felt himself helpless once again, watching as the one he loved, the one he would live for, the perfect match to his soul shuddered and went still.

"Don't --" Manx called out but was ignored.

He threw back his head and roared his pain to the heavens, for at that moment, Arcas, The Bear, felt his soul split into two. He felt The Manx, his Master, moving toward him but he turned his eyes to the man who had murdered his mate, his eyes burning with hate, and acted.

He dove over the table, his hand transforming, as he swiped at the cult leader who stood there, a stunned look on his face as he watched his empire crumble around him. The leader stepped back, his eyes glowing softly before close to fifteen hundred pounds of angry red bear was upon him.

Arcas roared as he reached out, and with one paw pulled the leader into his arms. Still screaming his chant, the cult leader disappeared into the flowing red fur and Arcas pulled him to his chest, wrapped both arms around him and jerked.

Razor-sharp claws dug into the leader's body as blood poured down. Then with a wrench, the chanting cut off as, with a deep popping cracking sound, the man's body split in two, his head lolling to one side.

Arcas roared again and dropped him as the light faded from his eyes.

"This is going to be a problem." Manx's voice cut the silence as stillness filled the room.

Arcas turned to shout at his Master when the whole room began to tremble.

* * *

"He has absorbed enough sacrifice life energy over the years that this may --"

The brazier exploded into flame and cut off whatever Manx was about to say as they moved forward, both hands raised before them. The air grew cold as a dark shadow lifted from the cult leader's body and shot toward the brazier that erupted into black flames.

The moans of the dying grew louder as Manx moved forward, their eyes narrowed, their hair flowing around their body, snatching up tendrils of death that flowed from the body toward the dark flames that seemed to grow in intensity.

Manx threw up their hands, partially blocking their eyes as they moved onwards. "I refuse to bear witness to this atrocity," they shouted, their voice chilling the living to their core.

Another wave of their hand brought change as the dark flames lessened for a moment before they burst out stronger than before. Suddenly the flames themselves lashed out, encircling Manx's legs and arms, freezing them in place. The Huntsmen watched, terror in their eyes as their Master struggled with the weight of thousands of deaths that stretched out over the span of centuries.

This was no moral battle, no battle of right against wrong. This was a fight to keep the dark in its place, to keep balance as darkness fought to contain a portion of itself. They felt the pull of their bonds with The Master of the Hunt, felt their anger and frustration not at them, not at the situation, but at their lover, the goddess The Morrigan and her less than insightful means of dealing with this situation eons ago. And now Manx had to be the one to deal with his.

Fine. So be it.

With a flex of their power, Manx tore their hands free and gripped the flames that writhed and wiggled like a living thing.

"Dagna the Fifteenth, I presume," they growled as their claws pierced the flames, making them seemingly writhe in pain. "Pleased to meet you. Your people broke the contract between my lady goddess Morrigan and your ancestors, attempting to murder an unwilling sacrifice and even worse, his unborn child. Therefore, I face no repercussion from either nature, gods, nor man in doing this. Your legacy ends here in an abandoned church, under a graveyard. Here you will be forgotten, as the cultist behind your resurrection lies dead on the floor. Your supposed empire will fall, the fools that follow you dead, dying, or arrested and in the hands of human justice. You are finished."

That declared before witnesses, The Manx lifted their hands to their mouth and began to eat the flames. Suddenly wails spewed forth as their tentacle-like hair wrapped round the suddenly escaping flames, not allowing one tendril to leave. The Manx began to chew, the flames making a crunching sound as sparks shot out from Manx's toothy mouth as all the magic and energy of death was absorbed.

Manx began to glow softy, their face looking radiant and peaceful in a gory way as tendrils of flames sought to escape their chewing mouth, but to no avail. Soon their hair was lifting the lingering flames to their mouth to be consumed. With every bite Manx seemed to grow larger somehow, their presence filling up the room even more than before. The sheer majesty of them glowed as with a final slurp the flames were gone and Dagna the Fifteenth was no more.

The Manx turned to their Hunt, their face becoming more human even if the anthropomorphized hands his hair had become still remained. "Some things just don't know how to stay dead."

* * *

The silence that filled the chambers after that mayhem was broken by the low sobs coming from Arcas, who was once again in human form cradling the body of his mate.

Cernunnos tossed his head so the man who was stuck in his horns fell off, mostly in pieces. With blood dripping down to cover his face and body, he stomped over to his mate.

Thomas whimpered, and with a flex of his fingers, Manx pulled the nails from his hands and let them drop to the ground which, by now, was covered in sticky, coagulating blood. The smell of iron was almost as thick as the scent of human meat that filled the air.

Cernunnos rushed to his mate, his hands reaching for the Faunus as he weakly curled his arms protectively around his stomach.

"I -- I kept him safe..." he muttered before Cernunnos sobbed and pulled him up into his arms.

On the ground, Arcas sobbed again, wrenching the horn from his mate's body so he could pull him close to his. "How can I live without you?" he muttered into Marshal's hair as he slowly rocked his body back and forth, heedless of the blood that covered him almost from head to toe.

Caille threw back her head and howled, the sound odd coming from a human body but she didn't care as she dropped to her knees and crawled to Arcas, wrapping her arms around her brother. Bran was there too, bowing his head in honor of Marshal's sacrifice, his broadsword dropping from his hand to snap back around his neck, its glow fading with the sound of his lover's mournful cry.

"Marshal," Thomas gasped as Cernunnos pulled him into a seated position to better wrap his arms around his mate.

"He gave his life protecting you," Cernunnos whispered as the Manx drew near to their Hunt, to share in their mourning. "We will honor his bravery."

"Bravery, my ass," Thomas gasped through a voice that sounded rough with the pain that still racked his form. "Marshal. Wake the fuck up. Your nephew wants to meet you."

They all turned to stare at Thomas as if the ordeal he had just gone through had somehow damaged his mind.

"Baby..." Cernunnos began when Thomas threw back his head and bleated.

It was a strangled, sharp sound coming from the Faunus' throat but his bleat ended on a trill that had... Marshal's eyes jerking open.

"Oh fuck," he gasped as he drew in a deep breath and looked up at his mate. "I am never fucking doing that again."

"What the fuck?" Arcas almost dropped his bonded mate before he gathered control of himself and instead pulled him back into chest. "Marshal... gods, Marshal. How..."

Weakly Marshal lifted his arms and wrapped around his bonded Bear as he slowly began to breathe more evenly. "I'm a Cat," Marshal rasped. "I've got gifts from Mother Bastet... nine lives... well, seven now..."

Arcas' laugher filled the chamber as a sense of relief filled them all. Caille yipped before reaching around to touch Marshal's face. "Stupid Cat," she cackled as she caressed his tousled hair. "Don't ever do that to us again, nine lives or not…"

"Thank you." Cernunnos' deep voice reached them as he gently caressed his mate's stomach. "I don't know… I owe you so much…"

"Just bite the bitch so this will never happen again." Marshal strained his head back enough to stare at Cernunnos, for the first time getting a good look at the monstrous Stag his brother's mate had become. "And don't do it with those teeth. I don't think he would survive it."

"Yes," Thomas gasped, looking up at his mate. "Bite me."

"Thomas --"

"Kern," he insisted, his eyes losing their amusement as he caressed his belly. "I was coming to tell you to bite me. My stubbornness caused this, my fear. But after facing *that*, I don't think anything will scare me any longer."

"You need to rest, to heal…" Cernunnos ran his fingers gently over the spot where his lover's horn had been sheared from his body. "I don't think this will grow back, and your poor wrists…" Cernunnos lifted his mate's hand to his mouth, his long tongue lapping at the blood that sluggishly flowed from the circular wounds in his wrists. "I can wait --"

"For fuck's sack, bite him now!" Manx ordered, rubbing their belly as if in some pain. "It's what he wants, and if any element of Dagna's cult escaped death or incineration, we need assurance he is protected so we won't have to do this whole thing all over again."

"Are… you okay?" Caille hazarded the question as they all eyed the irritable creature that was more and more taking on the human form of Manx they all knew.

"I ate something that didn't really agree with me and I want to go sleep it off," Manx snapped. "Now, Cernunnos, bite your mate so we can go home. And you are responsible for fixing the mess you created. If any of the staff at *The Wild Hunt* quit because a deranged stag was running about the place tearing shit up, it's going to be up to you to find replacements. Just because it looks like the war is over it doesn't mean skirmishes won't occur. We still have to protect the innocent, those who are unsure of what they are and those who know but are in hiding. It is our job to hunt them down and protect them and if any stand in our way may the mercy of the goddess The Morrigan find them because in us they will find none."

"What they said," Thomas tried to joke though pain-filled eyes and he reached out to his mate. "Please, love. Do this for us."

Cernunnos looked around at his friend and family, at his Master who were all staring back and nodded. "Your will be done."

He lowered his head to Thomas' bared neck and sank his teeth in deep.

The snap of their bond popping into place was almost audible, and those observing felt the lash of magic as the bond opened up completely.

Thomas didn't magically heal and his horn would probably never grow back, but that was a reminder to himself not to behave so recklessly, to listen, and to not let his past poor judgment and wild behavior interfere with his new life.

Marshal, on the other hand, did magically heal. The gifts from Bastet didn't allow him to shapeshift like the others or to have any grand magical ability but he survived with seven lives to spare... though he would never tell how he lost the first one. Some secrets were to be kept no matter the cost.

Arcas got his mate. Arcas was no longer on the outside observing as the others lived their lives. His soul had repaired itself when his mate took his first deep breath and opened up his beautiful green eyes. He had the missing half of his soul and no one would ever take him away again... even from his own stupid actions... Not that saving Cernunnos' mate was stupid, but it just wasn't going to ever happen again. He would put a fucking bell on his Cat and keep him within eyesight at all times to ensure his safety... no matter what his feisty Cat thought about it.

Bran and Caille just snuggled closer together, content to let things slowly take their course. They watched the happiness that surrounded them and reveled in it, knowing someday they too would have those connections but were content to wait until the time was right.

Pulling his teeth free, Cernunnos lapped at the bite marks that proclaimed to the whole world Thomas belonged to him. They would scar and be a visible warning to all of those who would try him to leave his family alone. He watched as his Faunus' eyes widen as he felt the full force of the bond... and then tears filled his eyes as he felt his son respond, not an actualized manipulation of the parental bond that existed within him, but more of a quiet contentment and awareness he knew would grow as their child developed beneath his mother's... father's -- they would work out titles later -- heart.

"Let's go home." Cernunnos forced his gaze away from his mate and took in the rest of his family and smiled. He held his mate harder to his chest as he let his magical energy flow... and with a flash of heat and a flare of light, they all popped out of the chamber, landing safely back in their compound to clean up, recover, and prepare for another time when they would be called.

After all, there were innocents out there to be protected and monsters, some even in the guise of man, to bring low.

The End

Epilogue (After The End)

"Good evening, denizens of *The Wild Hunt*," a deep, smooth, feminine voice announced as the club stilled. "If I may direct your attention to the front of the stage, I would like to introduce your hosts for the evening. May I present to you, The Stag..." a spotlight flashed on the high, elevated platform shrouded by sheer black lace that cast intriguing shadows against the blood-red walls behind the people gathered there. The spotlight danced over what appeared to be three figures clustered around a large fainting couch before it settled on a large, muscular figure with the most amazing set of antlers attached to their head. As the stage lights brightened a little, the figure -- The Stag -- crossed arms over the most exquisite chest anyone had ever seen, and just before him on his knees sat a figure shrouded in black, one large horn protruding from the veil that shrouded their face and hair. The possessive hand on their shoulder proclaimed to any who looked his creature was taken. The rounded belly that showed even through the layers of sheer black material that covered them let everyone know The Stag was off the market... at least for now.

"The Wolf," the voice continued and the shadowed features of a woman with a set of very realistic wolf ears perched on her head, with a gorgeous animatronic tail that waved. She crawled over the fainting couch to lounge at the side of the figure who was beautifully reclined upon the massive thing but still cast in shadows. But this time, in her hand was a chain that led to a tall, dark haired man in loose black harem pants and a harness that the lights showed was crafted to look like feathers.

"The Raven," the voice said, and the man threw

back his head, his long hair flowing from his face before he perched against the back of the lounger, leaning over as The Wolf reached up to pet his hair.

"The Bear." And yes, that man highlighted was indeed a huge bear of a man. Taller and broader than The Stag, The Bear, near the bottom of the couch, crossed his arms as well and muscles popped.

And beside him stood a short man with wild, curly black hair and almost-glowing green eyes. On his head were a set of cat ears that twitched as the murmur of the crowd grew. From behind him, a long black tail lashed out before wrapping around the thigh of the red haired bear who lowered one hand to gently tug at that tail.

"And the beautiful, the charismatic, the dangerous owner of this fine establishment, ladies, gentlemen, those undecided, in between, or neutral, may I present to you... Master of The Hunt!"

The spotlights disappeared as the stage lights went up fully and everyone got their first real look at their hosts for the evening.

The Master of the Hunt was shrouded in black silk robes that hid their frame. Their face was covered in a lacy black veil that hid their face entirely. Their hair was a dark, wavy fall that was uncontained and allowed to fluff up wild and free, almost as if it had a mind of its own.

The Wolf was now lying at The Master's hip, her lightly tanned skin a startling contrast to the solid black of the fainting couch and the silk that surrounded The Master. Her light gray wolf's ears twitched as the painted black fingers of The Master gently stroked over them, and her matching tail thumped once in happiness. Her hair was a blending of perfect blondes that flowed over her shoulders and around a muscular body wrapped in bangles and chains of sparkling silver. She glanced over the crowd with disdain before stretching her long, tight frame and settling at The Master's side, contentment pouring off of her in waves Thomas could almost feel.

The Bear was a massive presence at the foot of the lounger, his long, startlingly red hair nearly the color of freshly spilled blood trailing over his massive chest. He was impressively large with a black leather harness that cut across a bare chest dotted with a liberal dusting of red hair and matching freckles. The smile that spread across his face was deadly, exposing some serious fang-type dentures and painted black gums that were sexy and scary at the same time. He had a rounded set of fuzzy red ears on the sides of his head, their attachments lost in the thick wavy hair he sported. He shifted, and his muscles on his arms again seemed to pop, the tattoos that covered his lower arms only adding to the look of overall strength he exuded like fine cologne.

The Hunt had gathered and together they radiated power and strength no one could match. The companions that appeared on the stage remained unnamed but they obviously knew their place as they confidently sat on that stage and preened, looking down at the gathered watchers as if they were mere peasants coming to bask in the greatness of their betters.

"I think it's time to get this party started." The Master of the Hunt's voice echoed out throughout the room, and as if by magic, golden sparkles began to rain down upon the party goers as the loud, pounding bass of the music kicked into high hear. "The Master commands it so."

Below *The Wild Hunt*, the masses danced and

partied, some braver souls sought out the sexual dungeons in the back rooms, others stood around the bar ordering drinks and celebrating what good fortune allowed them to enter the establishment this evening.

And for those in the know, the Hunt was a haven, a place of safety where they could come under the vows of protection by the strongest magical creatures who walked the earth.

Woe to those who would destroy that peace that existed in the unseen magical world that existed right along beside today's modern society... for the Hunt was always watching, always waiting, always ready to heed the call to arms and spring into action.

Stephanie Burke

Stephanie is a *USA Today* Best Selling, multi published, multi award-winning author, Master Costumer, handicapped, wife and mother of two.

From sex-shifting, shape-shifting dragons to undersea worlds, sexually confused elemental Fey and homo-erotic mysteries, all the way to pastel-challenged urban sprites, Stephanie has done it all, and hopes to do more.

Stephanie is an orator on her favorite subjects of writing and world-building, a sometime teacher when you feed her enough tea and donuts, an anime nut, a costumer, and a frequent guest of various sci-fi and writing cons where she can be found leading panel discussions or researching varied legends and theories to improve her writing skills.

Stephanie is known for her love of the outrageous, strong female characters, believable worlds, male characters filled with depth, and multi-cultural stories that make the reader sit up and take notice.

Stephanie at Changeling: changelingpress.com/stephanie-burke-a-30

Changeling Press E-Books

More Sci-Fi, Fantasy, Paranormal, and BDSM adventures available in e-book format for immediate download at ChangelingPress.com -- Werewolves, Vampires, Dragons, Shapeshifters and more -- Erotic Tales from the edge of your imagination.

What are E-Books?

E-books, or electronic books, are books designed to be read in digital format -- on your desktop or laptop computer, notebook, tablet, Smart Phone, or any electronic e-book reader.

Where can I get Changeling Press E-Books?

Changeling Press e-books are available at ChangelingPress.com, Amazon, Apple Books, Barnes & Noble, and Kobo/Walmart.

Changeling Press, LLC

ChangelingPress.com